WILMETTE PUBLIC LIBRARY

3 1239 00452 1735

THE
CONFORMIST

WITHDRAWN
Wilmette Public Library

D0913476

THE
CONFORMIST

A Novel

ALBERTO MORAVIA

TRANSLATED FROM THE ITALIAN BY TAMI CALLIOPE

STEERFORTH ITALIA

AN IMPRINT OF STEERFORTH PRESS · SOUTH ROYALTON, VERMONT

WILMETTE PUBLIC LIBRARY

Copyright © 1999 by R.C.S. Libri S.p.A. — Milan.
Copyright © 1951 by Valentino Bompiano & Co., S.A.

First published in 1951 by Farrar, Straus and Company.

ALL RIGHTS RESERVED

For information about permission to
reproduce selections from this book, write to:
Steerforth Press, P.O. Box 70,
South Royalton, Vermont 05068

Library of Congress Cataloging-in-Publication Data
Moravia, Alberto, 1907-
[Conformista. English]
The conformist: a novel / Alberto Moravia;
translated from the Italian by Tami Calliope.
p. cm.
ISBN 1-883642-65-5 (alk. paper)
I. Calliope, Tami. II. Title.
PQ4829.O62 C67813 1999
853'.912—dc21

99-047391

Manufactured in the United States of America

FIRST PRINTING

PROLOGUE

I

THROUGHOUT HIS CHILDHOOD, Marcello was as fascinated by objects as a magpie. Perhaps because at home his
parents, more from indifference than austerity, had never thought
to satisfy his desire to possess; or perhaps because other instincts,
deeper and as yet obscure, took on in him the mask of greed; he
was constantly assailed by furious desires for the most diverse objects. A pencil with an eraser at the tip, an illustrated book, a slingshot, a ruler, a portable rubber inkpot — any trifle could stir his
soul, first to an intense and unreasoning longing for the coveted
thing, then, once he possessed it, to an astonished, enchanted, un-
limited satisfaction. Marcello had a room all his own in the house,
where he slept and studied. Here, all the objects scattered on the
table or closed up in the drawers held for him the character of
things still sacred or lately deconsecrated, according to whether
their acquisition was recent or long-standing. They were not, that
is, similar to the other objects found in the house, but slivers of experience lived through or yet to come, bearing the whole weight

of passion and mystery. Marcello was aware, in his own way, of this singular character of his possessiveness and, while he obtained an ineffable enjoyment from it, at the same time he suffered, as if from a guilt that continually renewed itself and left him no time even to feel remorse.

Among all these objects, however, those that attracted him most, perhaps because they were forbidden him, were weapons. Not just the pretend weapons children play with — tin rifles, cap guns, wooden daggers — but real weapons, in which the idea of menace, danger, and death is not conveyed by the familiar shape alone, but is instead the whole reason for their existence. With a toy pistol one played at death without the slightest possibility of actually inflicting it, but with grown-up pistols death was not only possible but imminent, like a temptation held in check by prudence alone. Marcello had held these real weapons in his hands a few times, a rifle for hunting in the country, the old pistol that his father had shown him in a drawer one day, and each time he had experienced a thrill of connection, as if his hand had finally found a natural extension in the grip of the gun.

Marcello had many friends among the children of the neighborhood, and he soon realized that his taste for weapons had deeper and more obscure origins than their innocent military infatuations. When they played at soldiers they pretended to be pitiless and fierce, but in reality they pursued the game for love of playing, aping those cruel attitudes without any real participation. For him, instead, it was the opposite: it was cruelty and ferocity that sought an outlet in playing at soldiers and, when that was denied him, in other pastimes all attuned to his taste for destruction and death. At that time Marcello was cruel without remorse or shame, completely naturally, since cruelty provided him with the only pleasures he didn't consider insipid; and this cruelty was still childish enough so as not to awaken suspicions in himself or in others.

He happened, for example, to go down to the garden in the heat of the day, toward the beginning of summer. It was a small but lush garden in which plants and trees flourished in wild disorder, abandoned years ago to their natural luxuriance. Marcello

went down to the garden armed with a length of thin and flexible
rush that he had torn from an old carpet beater in the attic; and for
a while he wandered aimlessly through the playful shadows of the
trees and the blazing rays of the sun, along the graveled pathways,
observing the plants. He felt that his eyes were sparkling, that his
whole body was opening him to a sensation of well-being that
seemed to merge with the general vitality of the luxuriant, light-
filled garden, and he was happy. But it was a cruel and aggressive
happiness, almost yearning to measure itself in contrast to the unhappiness of others. When he saw, in the midst of a flower bed, a
beautiful patch of daisies crowded with white and yellow blossoms, or a tulip, its red corolla upright on a green stem, or then
again, a clump of lilies, with their tall, white, fleshy petals, Marcello would strike a single blow with his rush, making it whistle
through the air like a sword. The rush sliced neatly through the
flowers and leaves, which fell cleanly to earth beside the plant,
leaving the stems upright and headless. Doing this, he felt a burst
of vitality, the delicious satisfaction from venting an energy too
long suppressed, but at the same time a precise and inexplicable
sentiment of power and justice. As if those plants had been guilty
and he had punished them and had felt, too, that it was his right to
punish them. But he was not altogether ignorant of the forbidden
and blameworthy aspects of this pastime. Every once in a while,
almost despite himself, he would turn a furtive glance toward the
house, afraid that his mother from the living-room window, or the
cook from the window in the kitchen, might be observing him.
And he realized that what he feared was not so much a scolding as
the simple witness of acts that he himself perceived to be abnormal and mysteriously soaked in guilt.

The passage from flowers and plants to animals was impercep-
tible, as it is in nature. Marcello would not have been able to say
when he realized that the same pleasure he experienced when he
broke the plants and beheaded the flowers revealed itself to be even
more intense, more profound, when he inflicted the same violence
on animals. Perhaps it was only chance that thrust him on this
path, a blow from the rush that, instead of mangling a shrub, struck

a lizard across the back as it dozed on a branch; or perhaps it was a mix of boredom and satiety that prompted him to seek out new targets on which to exercise his as yet unconscious cruelty. In any case, one silent afternoon when everyone in the house was sleeping, Marcello suddenly found himself, struck as if by a thunderbolt of remorse and shame, standing over a massacre of lizards. There were five or six lizards that he had managed, in various ways, to flush out onto the branches of trees or the stones of the garden wall, striking them dead with a single blow of the rush just at the moment in which, suspicious of his looming presence, they sought to escape toward some refuge. Just how he had arrived at this point he would not have been able to say, or rather, he preferred not to remember, but by now it was all over and nothing remained except the sun, blazing and impure, on the bloody corpses, filthy with dust, of the dead lizards. He was standing on the cement walkway on which the lizards lay, the rush gripped in his fist, and he still felt on his face and throughout his body the excitement that had invaded him during the slaughter, no longer pleasurably passionate as it had been then, but already colored by remorse and by shame. He was also aware that this time a particular turmoil, new to him and inexplicably physical, had been added to his usual feeling of cruelty and power; and in the midst of his shame and remorse, he experienced a confused sense of terror. As if he had discovered within himself a completely abnormal character, of which he ought to be ashamed, which he must keep secret so as to feel ashamed only before himself and not before others, and that, in consequence, would separate him forever from the society of his peers. There was no doubt; he was different from other boys of his age who, whether together or alone, did not devote themselves to pastimes such as this. What was more, he was different in a definitive way. Because the lizards were dead, there was no doubt about that, and this death and the cruel, crazed things he had done to inflict it were irreparable. He actually was those actions, as in the past he had been other actions, entirely innocent and normal.

That day, to confirm this discovery, so new and painful, of his own abnormality, Marcello wanted a confrontation with a young

friend of his, Roberto, who lived in the house next door. Toward
dusk Roberto, having finished his studies, came down to the
garden; and until the dinner hour, by mutual consent of their families, the two boys played together, sometimes in one of their gardens, sometimes in the other. Marcello waited impatiently for that
moment throughout the long, silent afternoon, alone in his bedroom, stretched out on the bed. His parents had gone out and
there was no one in the house except the cook, whose voice he
heard at intervals as she sang softly to herself in the kitchen, on the
ground floor. Usually in the afternoon he played or studied by
himself in his room; but that day neither games nor studies attracted him; he felt incapable of doing the least thing and at the
same time furiously impatient in his idleness. Alarm over the discovery he seemed to have made and the hope that this alarm
would be dissipated by his imminent meeting with Roberto both
paralyzed and set him on edge. If Roberto would only tell him that
he, too, killed lizards and that he liked to kill them and saw no
harm in killing them, it seemed to Marcello that all sense of abnormality would disappear and he would be able to look with indifference on the slaughter of the lizards, as on an incident devoid
of meaning and without consequences. He could not have said
why he attributed such authority to Roberto. Dimly he thought
that if Roberto also did these things and in that way and with those
feelings, it would mean that everyone did them; and what
everyone did was not only normal but good. At the same time,
these reflections were not very clear in Marcello's mind and presented themselves more as feelings and profound impulses than as
precise thoughts. But it seemed to him that he could be sure of
one thing: his tranquillity of mind depended on Roberto's answer.

    In this hope and distress, he waited impatiently for the twilight
hour. He was just about to doze off when a long, warbling whistle
reached him from the garden: it was the agreed-upon signal with
which Roberto let him know he had arrived. Marcello got out of
bed and, without turning on any lights, in the penumbra of sunset,
walked out of his room, descended the stairs, and looked out onto
the garden.

In the dim light of the summer dusk the trees were motionless and gloomy; in the shadow of their branches it seemed already night. Floral exhalations, the odor of dust, and heat rising from the sun-warmed earth stagnated in the dense, still air. The gate that divided Marcello's garden from Roberto's had vanished completely beneath a gigantic ivy, so thick and deep that it resembled a wall of enveloping leaves. Marcello went straight to a corner at the bottom of the garden where the ivy and the shadows were thickest, scrambled up onto a large stone, and with a single deliberate gesture pushed aside a whole mass of the creeper. It was he who had invented that kind of doorway in the foliage of the ivy, to add a sense of secrecy and adventure to the game. Once the ivy was moved aside, the bars of the railing appeared and, between them, the thin, pale face and blond hair of his friend Roberto. Marcello stood on tiptoes on top of the stone and asked, "Has anyone seen us?"

This was the opening move of the game they shared, and Roberto replied as if reciting a lesson, "No, no one . . ." And after a moment: "Have you studied?"

He spoke in a whisper, another agreed-upon procedure. Whispering himself, Marcello replied, "No, today I didn't study . . . I didn't feel like it . . . I'll tell the teacher I was feeling sick."

"I wrote my Italian essay," murmured Roberto, "and I did one of the arithmetic problems, too . . . I still have another one to do . . . Why didn't you study?"

It was the question Marcello had been waiting for. "I didn't study," he answered, "because I was hunting lizards."

He hoped that Roberto would say, "Oh, really . . . sometimes I hunt lizards, too," or something of the kind. But Roberto's face expressed no complicity, not even curiosity. Marcello added with an effort, trying to hide his own embarrassment: "I killed them all."

Roberto asked cautiously, "How many?"

"Seven in all," replied Marcello. And then, forcing himself to a kind of technical and informative boast: "They were on the tree branches and on the stones . . . I waited till they moved and then I got them with just one blow of this rush . . . one blow each." He made a satisfied face and showed the rush to Roberto.

He saw the other boy look at him with curiosity, not unaccompanied by a kind of amazement: "Why did you kill them?"

"Just because." He hesitated; he was about to say, "Because I enjoyed it," but then, without even knowing why, he held back and answered, "Because they're harmful . . . don't you know that lizards are harmful?"

"No," said Roberto, "I didn't know that . . . harmful to what?"

"They eat the grapes," said Marcello. "About a year ago in the countryside they ate all the grapes off the arbor."

"But there aren't any grapes here."

"And then," he continued, without bothering to take notice of this objection, "they're bad . . . one, instead of running away when it saw me, came right toward me with its mouth wide open . . . If I hadn't stopped it in time, it would have jumped me." He was quiet for a moment and then added, more confidentially, "Haven't you ever killed any?"

Roberto shook his head and answered, "No, never." Then, lowering his eyes, he said contritely, "They say that you shouldn't hurt animals."

"Says who?"

"My mother."

"They say a lot of things," said Marcello, ever less sure of himself, "but try it, stupid . . . I promise you it's fun."

"No, I won't try it."

"And why not?"

"Because it's wicked."

So there was nothing to be done about it, thought Marcello with disappointment. He felt an impulse of anger toward his friend, who, without even realizing it, had nailed him, confirmed him in his abnormality. Still, he managed to control himself and proposed: "Look, tomorrow I'm going hunting for lizards again. If you come hunting with me, I'll give you that pack of Neapolitan cards."

He knew that this was a tempting offer for Roberto, who had expressed a desire to own those cards many times. And in fact Roberto, as if illumined by a sudden inspiration, replied, "I'll come hunting on one condition: that we take them alive and then shut them up in a little box and then set them free . . . and you give me the pack of cards."

"No way," said Marcello, "The very best part is hitting them with this rush . . . I bet you can't do it."

His friend said nothing. Marcello went on, "Come on, then, we agree on this . . . but you have to look for a rush, too."

"No," said Roberto obstinately, "I won't come."

"Why not? Those cards are new."

"No, it's no use," said Roberto, "I'm not killing any lizards, not even if . . ." He hesitated, trying to come up with an object of proportionate value, "not even if you give me your pistol."

Marcello understood that there was nothing to be done, and all of a sudden he surrendered to the anger that had been boiling for some minutes in his breast. "You don't want to because you're a coward," he said, "because you're afraid."

"Afraid of what? You make me laugh."

"You're afraid," repeated Marcello, enraged, "You're a rabbit . . . a real rabbit." Suddenly, he thrust a hand through the bars of the railing and grabbed his friend by the ear. Roberto had red ears that stuck out, and it was not the first time that Marcello had grabbed them; but never with so much anger and such a pointed desire to hurt him.

"Confess you're a rabbit."

"No, let go of me," the other boy began to whine, twisting and turning, "Ow . . . ow!"

"Confess you're a rabbit."

"No . . . let me go."

"Confess you're a rabbit."

In his hand Roberto's ear was burning, hot and sweaty; tears sprang up in the blue eyes of his victim. He stammered, "Yes, all right, I'm a rabbit," and Marcello let him go immediately. Roberto jumped down from the gate and as he was running away, he yelled: "I'm not a rabbit . . . when I said that I was thinking, 'I'm *not* a rabbit!' I tricked you." He disappeared, and his voice, tearful and mocking, was lost in the distance, beyond the groves of the garden next door.

This exchange left Marcello with a profound sense of distress. Roberto had refused him not only solidarity, but the absolution he sought and which seemed to him to be linked to that solidarity. So he was thrust back into abnormality, but not without having first shown Roberto how much it mattered to him to step out of it, to let himself go — he was perfectly aware of this — and yield to falsehood and violence. Now, added to his shame and remorse at having killed the lizards were the shame and remorse for having lied to Roberto about the motives that had driven him to ask for his complicity and for having revealed himself by that act of anger, when he had grabbed him by the ear. The first sin was joined by a second; and there was no way he could undo either of them.

Every so often, among these bitter reflections, he revisited in memory the massacre of the lizards, almost hoping to find it purified of all remorse, a simple fact like any other. But right away he realized that he wished the lizards had never died; and at the same time, vividly and perhaps not completely unpleasantly — but for this very reason, it was all the more repugnant — he was struck again by that sense of excitement and physical turmoil he had experienced while he was hunting; and this was so strong that it even made him doubt that he would be able to resist the temptation to repeat the slaughter in the days to come. This thought terrified him: so he was not only abnormal, but, besides being unable to suppress his abnormality, he could not even control it. At that moment he was in his room, sitting at the table in front of an open book, waiting for dinner. He rose impetuously, went to the bed, and throwing himself onto his knees on the bedside rug and joining his hands as he usually did when he recited his prayers, said aloud in a tone that seemed to him sincere: "I swear before God that I will never again touch the flowers, or the plants, or the lizards."

Nevertheless, the need for absolution that had driven him to seek Roberto's complicity lived on, changed now into its opposite: a need for condemnation. While Roberto could have saved him from remorse by falling in with him, he lacked the authority to confirm a sound base for that remorse and instill order in the

confusion of Marcello's mind with an irrevocable verdict. He was
a boy like himself, acceptable as an accomplice but inadequate as
a judge. But Roberto, in refusing his proposal, had invoked maternal authority to support his own repugnance. Marcello thought
that perhaps he, too, could appeal to his mother. Only she could
condemn or absolve him and, however it went, make some sort of
sense of what he had done. In reaching this decision Marcello,
who knew his mother, was reasoning in abstract, as if referring to
an ideal mother — what she should have been, not what she was.
In reality he doubted that there would be any good outcome of his
appeal. But there it was; she was the only mother he had, and besides, his impulse to turn to her was stronger than any doubt.

Marcello waited for the moment when his mother, once he
was in bed, would come into his room to tell him good-night. This
was one of the few times he could manage to see her alone, just
the two of them; most of the time, during meals or on the rare
walks he took with his parents, his father was always present. Although Marcello did not, instinctively, have much faith in his
mother, he loved her; and perhaps even more than loving her, he
admired her in a fond and perplexed manner, the way you might
admire an older sister of singular habits and capricious character.
Marcello's mother, who had married very young, had remained
morally and even physically a girl; besides which, though she was
not at all intimate with her son, to whom she paid very little attention due to her numerous social obligations, she had never separated her own life from his. Thus Marcello had grown up in a
continual tumult of rushed entrances and exits, of dresses tried on
and thrown down, of telephone conversations as interminable as
they were frivolous, of tantrums with tailors and salespeople, of
quarrels with the maid, of continuous mood swings for the
slightest reasons. Marcello could go into his mother's bedroom at
any moment, the curious and ignored spectator of an intimacy in
which he had no part. Sometimes his mother, as if rousing herself
from inertia because of some sudden remorse, would decide to devote herself to her son and would trail him behind her to a seamstress or milliner. On these occasions, constrained to sit on a stool

for long hours while his mother tried on hats and dresses, Marcello almost missed her usual whirling indifference.

That evening he understood right away that his mother was more rushed than usual; and in fact, before Marcello even had time to overcome his shyness, she turned her back on him and crossed the dark bedroom to the door, which had been left ajar. But Marcello did not intend to wait one more day for the judgment he needed. Pulling himself up to sit up in the bed, he called out in a loud voice: "Mamma."

He saw her turn round on the threshold, with an almost irritable gesture.

"What is it, Marcello?" she asked, approaching his bed again.

Now she was standing close to him, backlit, white and slender in her black, low-cut dress. Her pale, delicate face, crowned by black hair, was in shadow; still, Marcello could make out its hurried, irritable, and impatient expression. Nontheless, carried away by his impulse, he announced: "Mamma, I have to tell you something."

"Yes, Marcello, but make it quick . . . Mamma has to go . . . papà is waiting." Meanwhile she was fumbling with both hands at her neck, fiddling with the clasp of her necklace.

Marcello wanted to disclose the slaughter of the lizards to his mother and ask her if he had done something wrong. But her hurry made him change his mind — or rather, modify the statement he had mentally prepared. Lizards suddenly seemed to him animals too small and insignificant to catch the attention of such a distracted person. Right on the spot, without knowing why, he invented a lie that enlarged his own crime. He hoped, by the enormity of his guilt, to startle to life a maternal sensitivity that, in some obscure way, he knew to be obtuse and inert. He said with a sureness that amazed him: "Mamma, I killed the cat."

At that moment his mother finally managed to make the two parts of the clasp come together. Her hands joined on her neck, her chin tucked to her breast, she was looking down and every once in a while beating the heel of her shoe on the floor in impatience. "Oh, yes," she said in an uncomprehending tone, as if emptied of attention by the effort she was making. Marcello reaffirmed, feeling insecure: "I killed it with my slingshot."

He saw his mother shake her head in frustration and then take her hands from her neck, holding in one of them the necklace she had been unable to close. "This damned clasp," she said angrily. "Marcello . . . be a good boy . . . help me put on my necklace." She was sitting on the bed at a slant, her shoulders turned toward her son, and added impatiently, "But be sure to click the clasp shut . . . otherwise it will come undone again."

As she spoke, she displayed to him her thin shoulders, naked to the middle of her back, white as paper in the light spilling in through the door. Her long slim hands with their sharp, red nails held the necklace suspended on her delicate neck, shadowed by curled tendrils like down. Marcello thought to himself that once the necklace was clasped, she would listen to him with more patience; leaning forward, he took the two ends and joined them with a single click. But his mother rose to her feet immediately and said, bending over to brush his face with a kiss: "Thanks . . . now go to sleep . . . good-night." Before Marcello could even recall her with a gesture or a shout, she had vanished.

The following day was hot and overcast. Marcello, after eating in silence between his two silent parents, slid furtively out of his chair and went out into the garden through the French windows. As usual, digestion provoked in him a sort of dark unease mixed with a swollen, reflective sensuality. Walking slowly, almost on tiptoes on the crunching gravel under the shade of the trees buzzing with insects, he went to the gate and peered out. The road he knew so well appeared before him, sloping gently downward, flanked by two rows of pepper trees of a feathery, almost milky green. The road was deserted at that hour and strangely dark because of the low black clouds that blocked out the sky. Directly opposite, he glimpsed other gates, other gardens, other villas similar to his own. After observing the road attentively, Marcello detached himself from the gate, pulled the slingshot out of his pocket, and bent down to the ground. Mixed in among the minute chunks of gravel were a few larger white stones. Marcello chose one the size of a nut, inserted it in the leather pouch of the slingshot, and began to stroll along the wall that separated his garden from Roberto's. His idea, or rather his feeling, was that he was in a state of war with Roberto and must guard the ivy that covered the garden wall with the greatest attention and fire at the least movement — that is, let loose the stone he was holding so tightly in his slingshot. It was a game in which he expressed both his rancor at Roberto, who had not wanted to be his accomplice in the slaughter of the lizards, and the cruel and warlike instinct that had driven him to the slaughter to begin with. Naturally, Marcello knew very well that Roberto, who was usually asleep at that hour, was not spying on him from behind the foliage of the ivy; nonetheless, even knowing this, he acted with serious purposefulness, as if he were sure, instead, that Roberto was there. The ivy, old and gigantic, climbed all the way to the tips of the spikes of the railing, and its overlapping leaves, huge, dark, and dusty, like lace frills on the tranquil breast of a woman, were still and limp in the heavy, windless air. A couple of times it seemed to him that a very slight shudder made the foliage tremble; at least he pretended to himself that he had seen this shudder and immediately, with intense satisfaction, let fly his stone into the thick of the ivy.

Right after the hit, he bent down hurriedly, gathered another pebble, and repositioned himself for combat, his legs spread wide, his arms stretched out before him, his slingshot ready to fire. You never knew; Roberto could be behind the leaves aiming at him that very moment, with the advantage of being hidden while he, instead, was completely in the open. Finally, playing this game, he reached the bottom of the garden, where he had cut out the doorway in the ivy. Here he stopped, watching the garden wall with attention. In his fantasy, the house was a castle, the railings hidden by the creeper the fortified walls, and the opening a dangerous and easily crossed breach. Then, suddenly and this time without any possibility of doubt, he saw the leaves move from right to left, trembling and rocking. Yes, he was sure of it, the leaves were moving and someone must have made them move. All in the same moment he thought that Roberto was not there, that it was

only a game and that, since it was only a game, he could hurl the
stone; and at the same time, that Roberto was there and that he
should not hurl the stone unless he wanted to kill him. Then, with
instant and thoughtless decision, he pulled back the bands and let
fly the stone into the heart of the leaves. Not content with this, he
bent down, feverishly inserted another stone in the slingshot, shot
it, put in a third stone and shot that one, too. By now he had put
fears and scruples aside and no longer cared whether Roberto was
there or not; he felt only a sense of hilarious and bellicose excitement. Finally, panting, having torn the foliage to shreds, he let the
slingshot drop to earth and clambered up onto the garden wall. As
he had foreseen and hoped, Roberto was not there. But the bars of
the railing were very widely spaced, allowing him to stick his head
through into the adjacent garden. Stung by he knew not what curiosity, he did so and looked down.

On Roberto's side of the garden there was no creeper, only a
flower bed planted with iris that ran between the wall and the
graveled path. Then Marcello saw, right under his eyes between
the wall and the row of white and purple iris, lying on its side, a
large gray cat. An unreasoning terror took his breath away as he
noted the animal's unnatural position: lying sideways, with its
paws stretched out and relaxed, its muzzle abandoned to the soil.
Its fur, thick and bluish gray, appeared slightly ruffled and bristly
and at the same time lifeless, like the feathers of certain dead birds
he had observed awhile back on the marble table of the kitchen.
Now his terror increased. He jumped down, pulled out a pole supporting a rosebush, clambered back up and, stretching his arm
through the bars, managed to poke the flank of the cat with the
earthy tip of the pole. But the cat did not move. All of a sudden the
iris on their tall green stems, with their white and purple corollas
tilted forward, surrounding the motionless gray body, looked funereal, like so many flowers placed by a compassionate hand around
a cadaver. He threw the pole away and, without bothering to shove
the ivy back into position, leapt down to the ground.

He felt himself prey to various terrors and his first impulse was
to run and shut himself up in a closet, a shed, anywhere, actually,

where there was darkness and closure, to escape from himself. He was terrified, first of all, for having killed the cat, and then, maybe even more so, for having announced this killing to his mother the night before: an incontestable sign that he was, in some fatal and mysterious way, predestined to commit acts of cruelty and death. But the terror aroused in him by the death of the cat and the meaningful premonition attached to this death were as nothing compared to the terror inspired in him by one idea — that while killing the cat he had, in reality, intended to kill Roberto. It was only by chance that the cat had died in place of his friend. A not insignificant chance, however, since it was undeniable that there had been a progression from the flowers to the lizards, from the lizards to the cat, and from the cat to the murder of Roberto, thought about and desired and, although not executed, still possible and perhaps even inevitable. So he was abnormal, he couldn't help thinking, or rather feeling, with a vivid, physical awareness of this abnormality, an abnormal person marked by a solitary and threatening destiny, already launched on a bloody path on which no human force would be able to stop him. Full of these thoughts, he circled frantically in the small space between the house and the gate, lifting his gaze every once in a while to the windows, almost in hopes of seeing the figure of his frivolous and scatterbrained mother appear there. But by now there was nothing more she could do for him, even if she had been able to do anything to begin with. Then, with a flash of hope, he ran down to the bottom of the garden again, climbed up to the wall, and looked out through the bars of the railing. He had almost persuaded himself that he would find the place he had first seen the motionless cat empty. But the cat had not gone away, it was still there, gray and immobile within the funeral wreath of the white and purple iris. And its death was confirmed, with a macabre sense of rotting carrion, by a black file of ants that had turned aside from the pathway and marched up the flower bed, right up to the muzzle and even the eyes of the cat. He looked at it and all of a sudden, almost as if superimposed there, he seemed to see Roberto in place of the cat, he too stretched out among the iris, he too inanimate, with ants coming and going through his spent eyes and half-open mouth. With a thrill of horror, he tore himself away from this terrible contemplation and jumped down. But this time he was careful to pull the doorway of ivy back into place. For now, along with remorse and terror at his own self, he felt the fear of discovery and punishment blossom within him.

Still, as much as he feared it, he felt simultaneously that he *wanted* to be discovered and punished, if for no other reason than to be stopped in time on this slippery incline, at the end of which, inevitably it seemed, murder awaited him. But his parents had never punished him that he remembered; and this was not so much due — as he vaguely comprehended — to any educated concept excluding punishment as to indifference. Thus to the suffering incurred by suspecting himself to be the author of a crime and, above all, to be capable of committing other, even graver ones, was added that of not knowing whom to turn to to be punished, or even what that punishment might be. Marcello was dimly aware that the selfsame mechanism that had driven him to confide his guilt to Roberto in hopes of hearing him say it was not a crime but a common thing that everyone did, was now urging him to make the same revelation to his parents in the contrary hope: to see them exclaim with indignation that he had committed a horrible crime for which he must atone with appropriate pain. And it mattered little to him that in the first case Roberto's absolution would have encouraged him to repeat the action which, in the second case, would instead have exposed him to severe condemnation. In reality, as he himself understood, in both cases he longed to escape from the terrifying isolation of his abnormality at any cost and by any means.

Maybe he would have decided to confess the cat's murder to his parents if, that same evening at dinner, he had not had the sensation that they already knew all about it. In fact, when he sat down at the table, he noted with a mixture of dismay and uncertain relief that his father and mother seemed hostile and bad-tempered. His mother, her childish face assuming an expression of exaggerated dignity, sat very upright with her eyes lowered, in a clearly contemptuous silence. Opposite her, his father revealed, by different but no less speaking signs, analogous feelings of temper. His father, who was many years older than his wife, often gave Marcello the disconcerting sensation of being relegated, along with his mother, to a communal realm of infancy and submission, as if she were not his mother but his sister. He was thin, with a dry, wrinkled face, only rarely illuminated by brief bursts of joyless laughter, and in which two traits, undoubtedly linked to the same source, were especially notable: the inexpressive, almost mineral sheen of his bulbous eyes and the frequent flicker, under the drawn skin of his cheek, of who knew what frenetic nerve. Perhaps he had retained, from his many years in the army, a taste for precise gestures and controlled attitudes. But Marcello knew that when his father was angered, his control and precision became excessive, turning into their opposites — that is, into a strange, contained, and punctual violence whose purpose, it would seem, was to burden the simplest gestures with significance. Now, this evening, at the table, Marcello noticed right away that his father was strongly emphasizing, as if to call attention to them, habitual actions of no particular importance. He took up his glass, for example, drank a sip, and then returned it with a harsh bang to its place on the table; he reached for the saltcellar, took a pinch of salt from it, and then put it down with another loud bang; he grabbed the bread, broke it in half, and then put it back with a third bang. As if invaded by a sudden mania for symmetry, he began to square off — still banging everything around — the silverware surrounding his plate, so that the knife, fork, and spoon met each other at right angles around the circle of his bowl. If Marcello had been less preoccupied with his own guilt he would easily have recognized that these gestures, so dense with meaningful and pathetic energy, were not directed at him but at his mother, who, in fact, at each of these blows, withdrew into her own dignity with certain condescending sighs and certain long-suffering arcs of her eyebrows. But worry blinded him, so that he did not doubt that his parents knew all; surely Roberto, rabbit that he was, had told on him. He had wanted to be punished, but now,

seeing his parents so cross, he felt a sudden horror of the violence
he knew his father capable of in similar circumstances. Just as his
mother's demonstrations of affection were sporadic, casual, obviously dictated more by remorse than maternal love, so his father's
severities were sudden, unjustified, excessive — provoked, one
might say, more by a desire to catch up after long periods of distraction than by any instructive intent. All of a sudden, after some
complaint by his mother or the cook, his father would remember
that he had a son, would scream, throw a fit, and hit him. The
beatings frightened Marcello most of all, because his father wore
on his little finger a ring with a massive bezel that somehow,
during these scenes, was always turned in to the palm of his hand,
thus adding to the humiliating harshness of the slap a more pene-
trant pain. Marcello suspected that his father turned the bezel
around on purpose, but he wasn't sure.

Intimidated and afraid, he began to concoct a plausible lie in
furious haste: he had not killed the cat, Roberto had — and in
fact, the cat was lying in Roberto's garden, so how could he have
killed it through the ivy and the garden wall? But suddenly he remembered that the night before he had announced to his mother
the cat's murder, which had then actually happened the next day;
and he understood that any lie was out of the question. As distracted as she was, surely his mother would still have mentioned
his confession to his father and he, no less certainly, would have
established a connection between this confession and Roberto's
accusations; so there was no possibility of lying about it. At this
thought, passing from one extreme to the other, he felt a renewed
impulse of desire for punishment, as long as it came soon and was
decisive. What kind of punishment? He remembered that Roberto
had spoken one day about boarding schools, as places parents sent
their wayward sons for punishment, and to his surprise he found
that he longed vividly for this sort of penalty. It was an unconscious weariness of his disordered and loveless family life that expressed itself in this desire, not only causing him to yearn for what
his parents would have considered a chastisement, but also
leading him to trick himself and his need for it by reasoning al-

most slyly that he would, in this way, simultaneously pacify his own remorse and improve his condition. This thought immediately gave rise to images that should have been disheartening but were instead enticing: a severe, cold, gray building with large windows barred by gratings; icy dormitories bereft of decoration with rows of beds aligned beneath high white walls; dull schoolrooms full of desks, with the teacher's desk at the end; naked corridors, dark stairways, massive doors, unbreachable gates — everything, that is, as it might be in a prison, yet all preferable to the inconsistent, agonizing, unbearable freedom of his father's house. Even the thought of wearing a striped uniform and having his head shaved like the boarding-school boys he had sometimes run across as they filed down the street in columns — even this thought, humiliating and almost repugnant, seemed pleasant in his present desperate aspiration toward any kind of order and normality.

Lost in these daydreams, he was no longer looking at his father but at the tablecloth, dazzling with white light, onto which fell at intervals the nocturnal insects that had flown through the open window to collide against lampshade. Then he raised his eyes just in time to see, right behind his father on the windowsill, the profile of a cat. But before he could distinguish its color, the animal leapt down, crossed the dining room, and disappeared in the direction of the kitchen. Although he was not absolutely sure of it, nevertheless his heart swelled with joyous hope at the thought that it might be the cat that he had seen, a few hours before, stretched immobile among the iris in Roberto's garden. And he was happy in this hope, since it was a sign that, after all, he valued the life of the animal more than his own destiny.

"The cat!" he cried out, in a loud voice. Then throwing his napkin on the table and stretching a leg from his chair, he asked, "Papà, I'm done, can I get up?"

"You stay right there," said his father in a threatening tone. Marcello, intimidated, risked: "But the cat is alive . . ."

"I already told you to stay in your place," replied his father. Then, as if Marcello's words had broken the long silence for him, as well, he turned toward his wife, saying: "All right, say something, speak."

"I have nothing to say," she responded with a show of dignity, her eyelids lowered, her mouth twisted in contempt. She was dressed for evening, in a low-cut black dress; Marcello noticed that she was squeezing a small handkerchief between her thin fingers, dabbing her nose with it every so often. With her other hand she kept grabbing up a piece of bread and then letting it fall back onto the table — but not with her fingers, with the tips of her nails, like a bird.

"But say what you have to say . . . talk, damn it."

"I have nothing to say to you."

Marcello had just begun to understand that his killing the cat was not the reason for his parent's bad mood when suddenly everything seemed to fall apart. His father repeated one more time: "Talk, goddamnit," his mother shrugged her shoulders in answer; then his father grabbed a wineglass in front of his plate and, shouting loudly, "Are you going to talk or not?" he brought it down violently on the table. The glass broke, his father raised his wounded hand to his mouth with a curse, his frightened mother stood up from the table and rushed toward the door. His father was sucking the blood from his hand with an almost voluptuous pleasure, arching his eyebrows over it; but seeing his wife start to leave, he interrupted his sucking to shout at her: "I forbid you to go, do you hear me?" As an answer they heard the noise of the door being violently banged shut. His father got up, too, and sprang toward the door. Excited by the violence of the scene, Marcello followed him.

His father had already started up the stairs, one hand on the railing, without losing his composure or even, apparently, hurrying; but Marcello, coming behind him, saw that he was climbing the steps two by two, almost flying in silence toward the landing as if he were an ogre from a fairy tale clad in seven-league boots. And Marcello didn't doubt for a moment that this calculated and menacing ascent was provoked by his mother's wild haste as she escaped up the stairs just ahead of him, climbing them one by one, her legs hampered by her tight skirt. "Now he's going to kill her," thought Marcello, following his father. When she reached the landing, his mother made a little run for her bedroom, not so swiftly, however, as to keep her husband from slipping through the crack of the door behind her. Marcello saw all this while ascending the stairs on his short child's legs on which he could neither vault two stairs at a time like his father nor skip up them in a hurry like his mother. When he got to the landing he noticed that the din of the chase had now strangely given way to a sudden silence. The door to his mother's bedroom was still open. Marcello, somewhat hesitantly, walked to the threshold and looked in.

At first, in the half-light at the end of the bedroom, he saw only the two huge, filmy window curtains on either side of the wide, low bed, lifted up to the ceiling by some current of wind in the room so that they almost brushed the ceiling lamp. These silent, dazzlingly white curtains suspended in midair in the dark bedroom gave it a sense of being deserted, as if his parents in the heat of the chase had flown out of the wide-open windows into the summer night. Then in the strip of light from the hallway, which fell on the bed through the open door, he finally made out his parents. Or rather, he saw only his father, from the back, under whom his mother had vanished almost completely except for her hair, spread across the pillow, and one arm raised toward the headboard of the bed. This arm sought convulsively to grip the headboard with its hand, but to no avail; and meanwhile his father, crushing his wife's body under his own, was making gestures with his shoulders and hands as if he wanted to strangle her. "He's killing her," thought Marcello with conviction, standing still on the threshold. At that moment he felt an unusual sensation of cruel and aggressive excitement, and at the same time a strong desire to interfere in the struggle — whether to give a hand to his father or to defend his mother he didn't know. Simultaneously, he was almost encouraged by the hope of seeing his own crime canceled out by this, so much more serious one: what, in fact, was the murder of a cat compared to that of a woman? But just when he had overcome his hesitation and was moving across the threshold, fascinated and filled with violence, his mother's voice, not strangled at all — on the contrary, almost caressing — murmured softly, "Let me go," while, in contradiction to this plea, the arm she had till now kept raised to find the edge of the headboard, lowered itself to circle the neck of her husband. Astonished, almost disappointed, Marcello backed out into the hallway.

Very slowly, trying not to make any noise on the stairs, he went back down to the first floor and wandered toward the kitchen. Now he was stung once more by curiosity to know whether the cat that had jumped down from the windowsill in the dining room was the one he had feared he had killed. Pushing open the kitchen door, he found a tranquil, homey scene: the middle-aged cook and the young maid sitting down to eat at the marble table in the white kitchen, between the electric stove and the icebox. And on the floor beneath the window, the cat, absorbed in licking milk from a bowl with its rosy tongue. But, as he realized immediately with disappointment, it was not the gray cat but a completely different cat, with stripes.

Unsure how to justify his presence in the kitchen, he went over to the cat, squatted down, and caressed its back. Without bothering to stop licking the milk, the cat began to purr. The cook got up and went over to close the door. Then she opened the icebox, took out a slice of cake on a plate, put it on the table and, pulling up a chair, said to Marcello: "Do you want a little of last night's cake? I set it aside just for you."

Marcello, without saying a word, left the cat, sat down, and began to eat the cake. The maid said, "Well, I just don't understand certain things . . . they have so much time during the day, they have so much space in the house, and instead they have to quarrel right at the table in front of the child."

The cook replied sententiously, "If you don't want to take care of your children, it's better not to bring them into the world."

The maid observed, after a brief silence, "He could be her father at his age . . . it's obvious they don't get along . . ."

"If it was only a matter of that . . ." said the cook, casting a meaningful look in Marcello's direction.

"And what's more," continued the maid, "in my opinion that man's not normal . . ."

At this word Marcello pricked up his ears, though he continued slowly eating his cake.

"She thinks so, too, just like me," the maid went on, "Do you know what she said to me the other day when I was undressing her for bed? Giacomina, one day or another my husband will kill me. I said to her: But, Signora, why are you waiting around for him to do it? And she . . ."

"Ssshhh . . ." interrupted the cook, indicating Marcello. The maid understood and asked Marcello, "Where are Papà and Mamma?"

"Upstairs in the bedroom," replied Marcello. And then all of a sudden, as if driven by an irresistible impulse: "It's really true that Papà isn't normal. Do you know what he did?"

"No, what?"

"He killed a cat," said Marcello.

"A cat? How?"

"With my slingshot . . . I saw him in the garden, he was following a gray cat that was walking on the wall. . . . Then he picked up a stone and aimed at the cat and hit him in the eye. The cat fell into Robertino's garden and then I went to see and I saw it was dead."

As he went on talking he was carried away, without, however, abandoning the tone of an innocent, who with unconscious and candid naïveté recounts some crime he has witnessed.

"Just think," said the maid, clasping her hands, "a cat . . . a man of that age, a gentleman, taking his son's slingshot and murdering a cat . . . it stands to reason he's abnormal."

"Who's wicked to beasts is wicked to Christians, too," said the cook. "It starts with a cat and he ends up killing a man."

"Why?" asked Marcello suddenly, lifting his eyes from the plate.

"Well, that's what they say," replied the cook, giving him a caress. "Even though," she added, turning to the maid, "it's not always true . . . That man who murdered all those people in Pistoia . . . I read it in the newspaper . . . you know what he's doing now, in prison? He's raising a canary."

The cake was finished. Marcello got up and left the kitchen.

2

DURING THE SUMMER, at the seashore, the terror of that destiny so simply expressed by the cook, "It starts with a cat and he ends up killing a man," gradually vanished from Marcello's mind. He still thought often about that kind of inscrutable, pitiless mechanism with which his life had seemed enmeshed for a few days; but with ever less fear, taking it more as an alarm signal than the conviction without appeal that he had thought it to be for some time. The days passed happily, ablaze with sunshine, intoxicated by seasalt, filled with amusements and discoveries; and with every day that passed Marcello felt he was winning a victory, not so much over himself, as he had never felt guilty in any direct and voluntary way, as over the obscure, maleficent, astute, and extraneous force, colored completely with the dark shades of fatality and misfortune, that had carried him almost despite himself from the extermination of the flowers to the massacre of the lizards and from this to the attempt to murder Roberto. He felt this force as ever present and menacing though no longer impending; but as happens sometimes in nightmares when, terrified by the presence of a monster, we hope to fool it by pretending to sleep while in reality it is all a dream unfolding in sleep itself, he felt that, since he could not definitively distance the threat of that force, it was advisable to lull it asleep, so to speak, by pretending to a careless forgetfulness he was still far from achieving. That was one of the most unrestrained if not one of the happiest of Marcello's summers, and certainly the last in his life in which he was still a child without any disgust for his childishness and without any desire to escape it. In part this abandon was due to the natural inclinations of his age, but in part, too, it was due to his desire to extricate himself at all costs from that cursed circle of presentiments and fate. Marcello was not aware of it, but the impulse that drove him to throw himself into the sea ten times a morning, to compete boisterously with the most violent of his playfellows, to row for hours on the burning sea — to do everything, that is, that one does at the seashore with a kind of excessive zeal, was the selfsame impulse that had made him seek Roberto's complicity after the slaughter of the lizards and his parents' punishment after the death of the cat: a desire for normality; a longing to adapt to some recognized and general rule; a wish to be like everyone else, from the moment that being different meant being guilty. But the willed and artificial character of this behavior of his was betrayed every so often by a sudden, painful memory of the dead cat stretched out among the white and purple iris in Roberto's garden. That memory scared him the way the memory of his signature at the bottom of a document proving his debt scares a debtor. It seemed to him that with that death he had taken on an obscure and terrible responsibility that sooner or later he would no longer be able to avoid, even if he hid himself under the earth or crossed the oceans to wipe out his own tracks. At such moments he consoled himself by thinking that a month, two months, three months had gone by; that soon a year, two years, three years would have passed; and that, after all, the most important thing was not to wake the monster and to make the time go by. But these fits of dejection and fear were rare and toward the end of the summer they ceased altogether. By the time

Marcello returned to Rome, all that was left from the episode of the cat and those that had preceded it was a diaphanous, almost evanescent memory, as if of an experience that he had perhaps lived through but in another life, with which, at this point, he had no relationship except that of an irresponsible memory devoid of consequence.

Once he returned to the city, the excitement of going to school also contributed to his oblivion. Until now Marcello had studied at home, so this was his first year of public school. The novelties of his companions, professors, schoolrooms, and timetables — novelties through which shone, in a variety of aspects, an idea of order, discipline, and communal occupation — were extremely pleasing to Marcello after the disorder, lack of regulation, and solitude of his home. It was a little like the boarding school he had dreamed of that day at his table, but without constrictions or servitude, retaining only its pleasant aspects and devoid of the unpleasant things that would make it feel like a prison. Marcello soon realized that he enjoyed a profound aptitude for scholastic life. He liked to wake up to the alarm clock in the morning, wash and dress himself in a hurry, wrap up his package of books and notebooks neatly and tightly in oilcloth bound with rubber bands, and rush off through the streets to school. He liked to burst into the old *ginnasio* with a crowd of his companions, run up the dirty stairways and through the squalid and resonant halls, and then tone down the excitement of the race once he reached the classroom, with its desks aligned in front of the empty desk of the teacher. Above all he liked the ritual of the lessons: the professors's entrance; the roll call; the interrogations; the rivalry with his schoolmates to answer the questions; the victories and defeats of this rivalry; the teacher's placid, impersonal tone of voice; the very arrangement of the schoolroom, so eloquent — all of them in rows, united by the need to learn, in front of the professor who taught them. Marcello was, however, a mediocre scholar and even, in certain subjects, one of the slowest. What he loved about school was not so much studying but its whole new way of life, more in tune with his tastes than the one he had lived so far.

Again, it was *normality* that attracted him, and all the more so since it was neither fortuitous nor entrusted to the natural preferences and inclinations of the mind, but preestablished, impartial, indifferent to individual tastes, limited and supported by indisputable rules all directed toward a single end.

But his inexperience and candor made him awkward and uncertain when faced with those other rules, tacit yet extant, that governed relationships between the boys themselves, apart from school and its discipline. This, too, was an aspect of the new normality, but one more difficult to master. He experienced it the first time he was called to the teacher's desk to show him his written homework. After the professor had taken the notebook from his hand and, setting it in front of him on the desk, had begun to read it, Marcello, accustomed to the affectionate and familiar rapport he had enjoyed with the tutors who had, until now, instructed him at home, rather than standing to one side of the dais to wait for a response, very naturally put an arm around the teacher's shoulders and lowered his face so that they could read the homework together. The professor limited himself, without showing any surprise, to removing the hand Marcello had laid on his shoulder and freeing himself from the boy's arm; but the entire classroom burst into rowdy laughter in which Marcello seemed to perceive a disapproval different from the professor's, much less indulgent and understanding. With that naive gesture, he couldn't help reflecting later, as soon as he had managed to overcome the distress of his shame, he had failed to conform to two different norms — the scholastic one that demanded he be disciplined and respectful toward the professor, and the schoolboy one that required him to be spiteful and cagey in his affections. And what was even more singular, these two unspoken rules did not contradict each other; indeed, they complemented each other in some mysterious way.

But, as he understood right away, if it was easy enough to become an efficient scholar in a short span of time, it was much more difficult to become a shrewd and nonchalant schoolboy. This second transformation was hindered by his inexperience, his familiar habits, and even his physical aspect. Marcello had inherited from his mother a perfection of features that was almost precious in its regularity and sweetness. He had a round face with dark, delicate cheeks, a small nose, a sinuous mouth with a sulky, capricious expression, a prominent chin, and, under chestnut bangs that hid almost his entire forehead, eyes somewhere between gray and blue with a downcast, yet innocent and endearing expression. It was almost the face of a young girl; but the boys, uncouth as they were, would perhaps not have realized this had it not been confirmed by a few characteristics so very feminine as to make them wonder whether Marcello were not actually a girl dressed in boy's clothes: an unusual tendency to blush easily, an irresistible inclination to express his tenderness of spirit by caresses, a desire to please taken almost to servility and flirtatiousness. These traits were native and unconscious in Marcello. By the time he realized that they rendered him ridiculous in the other boys' eyes, it was already too late; even had he been able to control, if not to suppress them, his reputation as a sissy in long pants was already established.

They made fun of him almost automatically, as if his feminine character was by now beyond question. Sometimes they would ask him in make-believe earnest why in the world he didn't sit at a girl's desk and what idea had possessed him to exchange his skirt for pants; sometimes, how he spent his time at home, whether in embroidering or playing with dolls, sometimes, why he didn't have holes in his earlobes so that he could wear earrings. Once in a while they would sneak a small piece of cloth with a needle and spool of thread into his desk — a clear allusion to the type of work he should devote himself to; sometimes it was a compact for face powder; one morning it was even a pink brassiere that one of the boys had stolen from his older sister. And from the beginning, changing his name into a girl's nickname, they had called him Marcellina. When they teased him like this, he felt a mixture of anger and flattered satisfaction, as if a deep part of him were not altogether unhappy about it; however, he would not have been able to say if this satisfaction was due to the character of the teasing or just because, even though they were making fun, they were paying

attention to him. But one morning when they were whispering behind his back as usual: "Marcellina . . . Marcellina . . . is it true you
wear girl's underpants, *mutandine?*" he stood up and, raising his
hand for permission to speak, complained loudly in the sudden silence of the classroom that he was being called by a girl's nickname. The professor, a large, ugly, hirsute man, listened to him,
smiling through the gray hair of his beard, and then said, "So
they're calling you by a woman's name . . . and what is that?"

"Marcellina," said Marcello.

"And you don't like it?"

"No . . . because I'm a man."

"Come here," said the professor. Marcello obeyed and came
forward next to the platform. "Now," continued the professor
pleasantly, "show your muscles to the class."

Marcello obediently bent his arm, flexing his muscles. The
professor leaned over from his desk, touched his arm, shook his
head in sign of ironic approval, and then turned to the other
pupils and said "As you can see, Clerici is a strong boy, and he's
ready to demonstrate that he's a man and not a woman . . . who
wants to take him up on it?"

A long silence followed. The professor looked all around at the
class and concluded: "No one . . . well, that's a sign that you're
afraid of him, so stop calling him Marcellina."

The whole classroom burst into laughter. Red in the face, Marcello returned to his place. But that day, instead of ceasing, the
taunts redoubled, worsened perhaps by the fact that Marcello, as
the boys let him know, had told on them, thus betraying the unspoken law that united them: conspiracy of silence.

Marcello realized that to put a stop to the teasing he needed to
show his companions that he was not as effeminate as he seemed;
but he knew intuitively that flaunting the muscles in his arm,
as the professor suggested, would not be enough to pull it off.
He needed to do something more unusual, something that
would seize their imaginations and rouse admiration. What? He
wouldn't have known how to say it, precisely, but in a general
sense it would have to be an action or object that suggested ideas

of strength and manliness, maybe even of downright brutality. He
had noticed that his companions admired a certain Avanzini very
much, because he owned a pair of leather boxing gloves. Avanzini,
a skinny blond who was smaller and weaker than Marcello, didn't
even know how to use those gloves; all the same, they had con-
ferred a special status on him. Similar admiration was granted a
certain Pugliese because he knew, or at least pretended to know, a
Japanese wrestling move guaranteed, to hear him tell it, to put
your adversary on the ground. Put to the test, actually, Pugliese
had never known how to execute it, but this did not keep the boys
from respecting him the way they respected Avanzini. Marcello
understood that he had to either flaunt the possession of an object
like the gloves or think up some feat like Japanese wrestling. But
he also understood that he was not as shallow and amateur as his
schoolmates; that he belonged, whether he liked it or not, to the
race of those who take life and its responsibilities seriously; and
that, in Avanzini's place, he would have broken his adversary's
nose and that, in Pugliese's place, he would have broken his neck.
This incapacity of his for rhetoric and superficiality inspired in
him an obscure diffidence directed toward himself, so that, while
he wanted to provide his companions with the proof of strength
they seemed to require in exchange for their esteem, he was at the
same time dimly frightened.

One day he became aware that some of the boys, among them
his fiercest tormentors, were whispering together, and he understood from their glances that they were hatching some new plot
against him. Still, the lesson hour proceeded without incident:
only looks and whispers confirmed his suspicions. The bell rang
for dismissal and Marcello, without looking around him, began to
walk home. This was in the first days of November; the air was
stormy yet mild, and the last warmth and perfume of the summer,
already dead, seemed mixed together with the first, uncertain
rigors of autumn. Marcello felt vaguely excited by this atmosphere
of stripping bare and natural havoc, in which he perceived a
yearning for destruction and death very similar to that which,
months ago, had made him behead the flowers and murder the

lizards. Summer was a motionless, full, perfect season under the serene sky, trees laden with leaves and branches crowded with birds. Now he watched with delight as the autumn wind lacerated and destroyed that perfection, that fullness, that immobility, driving dark, torn clouds across the sky, ripping the leaves from the trees and whirling them to earth, chasing away the birds, which, in fact, could be glimpsed between the leaves and the clouds, migrating in black, orderly flocks. At a bend in the road Marcello became aware that a group of five boys was following him — there was no doubt that they were following him, since two of them lived in the opposite direction — but, immersed in his autumnal sensations, he paid them no heed. Now he was in a hurry to reach a broad avenue planted with plane trees from which, by way of a cross street, he could arrive at his own house. He knew that the dead leaves in that avenue were piled up in the thousands on the sidewalks, yellow and crackling, and he was looking forward to dragging his feet through the piles, kicking them around and making them rustle. Meanwhile, almost in fun, he was trying to shake off his followers, now slipping into a doorway, now losing himself in the crowd. But the five boys, as he soon realized after a moment of uncertainty, always found him again. By now the avenue was close, and Marcello was ashamed to be seen amusing himself with the dead leaves. So he decided to confront them; turning around suddenly, he asked: "Why are you following me?"

One of the five, the little blond with the sharp face and the shaved head, answered quickly, "We're not following you, the street belongs to everyone, doesn't it?"

Marcello said nothing and began to walk again.

Here was the avenue, between the two rows of bare, gigantic plane trees, with the houses full of windows lined up behind them; here were the dead leaves, as yellow as gold, scattered on the black asphalt and heaped up in the ditches. He could no longer see the five boys — maybe they had stopped following him and he was alone on the wide street and deserted sidewalks. Without haste he set his feet into the foliage scattered on the pavement and began to walk slowly forward, enjoying sinking his legs up to the knee in that light and mobile mass of sonorous leaves. But as he was leaning down to grab a handful of them, intending to throw them up in the air, he heard the taunting voices again: "Marcellina . . . Marcellina . . . show off your underpants, *mutandina*."

Then he was suddenly overtaken by an almost pleasureable desire to fight, which lit up his face with an aggressive excitement. He straightened back up and walked decisively over to his persecutors, saying, "Do you want to go away or not?"

Instead of responding, all five of them jumped on top of him. Marcello had thought that he would act a little like the Horatios and Curatios in the anecdotes of the history books: take them on one at a time, running here and there and striking each of them some great blow, so that they would be convinced to abandon their undertaking. But right away he realized that this plan was impossible: prudently, all five of them had closed in on him at once and now they held him, one by the arms, another by the legs, and two by the middle of his body. The fifth, he saw, had meanwhile hurriedly opened a bundle and was now approaching him warily, holding a little girl's skirt of dark blue cotton suspended from his hands. They all laughed now, still holding him firmly, and the one with the skirt said: "Come on, Marcellina . . . let us do this . . . we'll put the little skirt on you and then we'll let you go home to your mamma."

It was exactly the sort of joke Marcello had expected, suggested as usual by his insufficiently masculine mien. Red in the face, furious, he started to struggle with extreme violence; but the five were stronger than he was and, although he managed to scratch one on the face and punch another in the stomach, he felt that, gradually, his movements were being reduced. Finally, as he moaned, "Let go of me . . . idiots . . . let go of me," a cry of triumph issued from the mouths of his persecutors: the skirt had slipped over his head and by now his protests were lost as if in a sack. He struggled on, but in vain. The boys easily slid the skirt down to his waist, and he felt them tie it on him with a knot at the back. Then, while they were yelling, "Pull it . . . give it to him . . . tighter," he heard a tranquil voice ask, more in a tone of curiosity than of reproof: "Would you like to tell me what you're doing?"

The five boys let go of him immediately and ran away; he found himself alone, all disheveled and panting, the skirt tied around his waist. He raised his eyes and saw the man who had spoken standing before him. Dressed in a dark gray uniform, its collar tight under his throat, pale, gaunt, with deep-set eyes, a large, sad nose, scornful mouth, and crew-cut hair, he gave the impression at first of almost excessive austerity. But then, as Marcello noted after a second glance, some traits revealed themselves that were not at all austere, on the contrary: the anxious, ardent look in his eyes; something soft and almost overripe in his mouth; a general insecurity in his attitude. He bent down, gathered up the books that Marcello had let fall to the ground in his struggles, and said, holding them out to him: "But what did they want to do to you?"

His voice, too, was severe, like his face, but not without a strangled sweetness of its own.

Marcello answered irritably, "They're always playing jokes on me . . . they're really stupid." Meanwhile he was trying to untie the waistband of the skirt from the back.

"Wait," said the man, leaning down and undoing the knot. The skirt fell to the ground and Marcello stepped out of it, stamping on it and then kicking it away, onto a heap of dead leaves. The man asked, with a kind of timidity, "Weren't you, perhaps, on your way home?"

"Yes," answered Marcello, looking up at him.

"Well, then," said the man, "I'll take you there in my car," and he pointed out, not too far away, an automobile parked next to the curb. Marcello looked at it: it was a kind of car he didn't know, maybe foreign, long and black with an antiquated body. Strangely, it came to him that that motionless car, right there, only a few feet away from them, suggested a premeditation in the man's casual approaches. He hesitated before responding; the man insisted: "Come on, before bringing you home I'll take you for a nice ride . . . would you like that?"

Marcello would have liked to refuse, or rather, felt that he should. But he didn't have time: the man had already taken the bundle of books from his hand, saying, "I'll carry them for you," and was moving toward the automobile. He followed him, somewhat surprised by his own docility, but not unhappy. The man opened the car door, had Marcello climb into the seat next to his own, and threw the books onto the backseat. Then he got in behind the wheel, closed the door, drew on his gloves, and started up the car.

The automobile began to roll forward slowly, majestically, with a low rumble, along the tree-lined avenue. It really was an antique car, thought Marcello, but kept in perfect working order, lovingly polished, all its brasses and nickel platings gleaming. Now the man, keeping one hand on the steering wheel, had reached out with the other for a visored cap, which he adjusted on his head. The cap emphasized his severity of aspect and added to it an almost military air. Marcello asked, embarrassed, "Is this your car?"

"Call me *tu*," said the man, without turning, using his right hand to squeeze the bulb of a serious sounding horn as antiquated as the car. "It's not mine . . . it belongs to the person that pays me . . . I'm the chauffeur."

Marcello said nothing. The man, keeping his profile to him and continuing to drive the car with a detached and elegant precision, asked, "Does it bother you that it isn't mine? Are you ashamed?"

Marcello protested quickly, "No, why?"

The man smiled slightly with satisfaction and accelerated their pace. He said, "Now we'll be going up a hill for a while, up Monte Mario . . . all right?"

"I've never been there," replied Marcello.

The man said, "It's beautiful, you can see the whole city." He was quiet for a moment and then added, gently, "What's your name?"

"Marcello."

"Oh, right," said the man, as if speaking to himself, "They were calling you Marcellina, those friends of yours . . . My name is Pasquale."

Marcello scarcely had time to think that Pasquale was a ridiculous name before the man, almost as if he had intuited his thought, added, "But it's a ridiculous name . . . you can call me Lino."

Now the car was rolling down the broad and dirty streets of a run-down neighborhood, between squalid apartment buildings. Groups of breathless urchins playing in the middle of the street parted for them; disheveled women and ragged men watched their passage, so out of the ordinary, from the sidewalks. Marcello lowered his eyes, ashamed before their curiosity.

"It's the Trionfale," said the man, "but here's Monte Mario."

The car left the poor neighborhood and followed a tram up a broad, spiraling street between two rows of ascending houses.

"What time do you have to be home?"

"There's time," said Marcello. "We never eat before two."

"Who's waiting for you at home? Your papà and mamma?"

"Yes."

"Do you have brothers and sisters, too?"

"No."

"And what does your papà do?"

"He doesn't do anything," replied Marcello a little uncertainly.

At a bend in the road the car overtook the tram and the man, in order to take the turn as tightly as possible, leaned his arms on the steering wheel without moving his upper body, with an elegant dexterity. Then the car, still ascending, began to pass long, high, vine-covered walls, gates of villas, wooden fences. Every now and then an entranceway decorated with Venetian lanterns or an arch with a sign the color of oxblood revealed the presence of some restaurant or rustic inn. Lino asked suddenly: "Do your papà and mamma give you presents?"

"Yes," replied Marcello, somewhat vaguely, "sometimes."

"A lot or a few?"

Marcello did not want to confess that the presents were few and that, at times, the holidays passed without any presents at all. He limited himself to answering, "About medium."

"Do you like to get presents?" asked Lino, opening a little door under the dashboard, taking out a yellow cloth, and cleaning the windshield.

Marcello looked at him. The man was still in profile, sitting very erect, the cap's visor shadowing his eyes. He said without thinking, "Yes, I like it."

"And what present would you like to get, for example?"

This time the question was explicit and Marcello couldn't help thinking that the mysterious Lino, for some reason of his own, really intended to give him a gift. He suddenly recalled his attraction to weapons; and at the same time, almost with the sensation of making a discovery, he told himself that the possession of a real weapon would ensure the esteem and respect of his companions. A little nervously, aware of asking too much, he suggested, "For example, a pistol . . ."

"A pistol," repeated the man, without showing the least surprise. "What kind of pistol? A cap gun or a popgun?"

"No," said Marcello daringly, "a real pistol."

"And what would you do with a real pistol?"

Marcello preferred not to give the true reason. "I'd target shoot," he answered, "until I felt like I had perfect aim."

"Why does it matter to you so much to have perfect aim?"

It seemed to Marcello that the man kept asking questions more for the pleasure of hearing him talk than from any real curiosity. Nonetheless, he replied seriously, "With perfect aim you can defend yourself against anybody."

The man was quiet for a moment. Then he suggested: "Put your hand in that pocket there, in the door next to you."

Curious, Marcello obeyed him, and felt the chill of a metal object beneath his fingers. The man said, "Go ahead and take it out."

The automobile swerved swiftly to avoid a dog that was crossing the road. Marcello pulled out the metal object: it really was a pistol — an automatic, black and flat, heavy with destruction and death, its barrel extended before it as if ready to spit out bullets. Almost without wanting to, with fingers trembling from pleasure, he grasped the butt in his hand.

"A pistol like that one?" asked Lino.

"Yes," said Marcello.

"All right," said Lino, "if you really want it, I'll give it to you . . . not that one, though, that belongs to the car . . . another one just like it."

Marcello said nothing. It seemed to him that he had entered the magic atmosphere of a fairy tale, a world different from the ordinary one, in which unknown drivers invited you to climb into cars and gave you pistols. Everything seemed to have become extremely easy; but at the same time — even he was not quite sure why — it seemed that this ease, as enticing as it was, disclosed at second thought an unpleasant flavor, as if there were, linked to it and hidden by it, an as yet unknown but impending and soon-to-be-revealed danger. Probably, he thought coldly, there were two of them in that car with a purpose: his was to own a pistol, Lino's was to obtain in exchange for the pistol something as yet mysterious and perhaps unacceptable. Now it was just a question of seeing who of the two would get the best of the barter. He asked, "Where are we going?"

Lino replied, "We're going to the house where I live . . . to look for the pistol."

"And so where's the house?"

"Here, we're there now," the man answered, taking the pistol out of Marcello's hand and putting it in his own pocket.

Marcello looked: the car had stopped on a road that by now seemed just an ordinary country road, with trees, box-elder hedges, and, behind the hedges, fields and sky. But a little farther on you could see a gateway with an arch, two columns, and a gate painted green.

"Wait here," said Lino. He got out and went to the gateway. Marcello watched him as he shoved open the double doors of the gate and walked back to the car: he wasn't tall, although sitting down he had seemed so; he had short legs in proportion to his trunk and broad hips. Lino climbed back into the car and drove it through the gateway. A graveled driveway appeared, winding between two rows of small, stripped cypresses that were being tossed and tormented by the gusting wind. At the end of the driveway something shone blindingly in a fleeting ray of sun against the background of the stormy sky: the glass door of a veranda built into a house of just two floors.

"That's the villa," said Lino, "but there's nobody home."

"Whose the owner?" asked Marcello.

"A woman," said Lino, "an American . . . but she's out, she's gone to Florence."

The car came to a halt in front of the house. The villa, long and low, with rectangular sides of white cement and red brick, alternating here and there with the strips of mirrorlike glass of the windows, had a portico supported by squared pillars of rough stone. Lino opened the car door and jumped to the ground, saying, "All right, let's get out."

Marcello didn't know what Lino wanted from him and hadn't managed to guess it. But the diffidence of one who fears to be cheated was growing ever stronger in him. "And the pistol?" he asked, without moving.

"It's in there," replied Lino with some impatience, pointing to the windows of the villa, "now we're going to go get it."

"Will you give it to me?"

"Certainly, a lovely new pistol."

Without saying a word, Marcello got out of the car as well. He was instantly assailed by a great gust, hot and full of dust, of the intoxicating and funereal autumn wind. He didn't know why, but he felt at that gust a kind of presentiment and, still following Lino, he turned to look one last time at the graveled clearing surrounded by bushes and stunted oleanders. Lino was walking in front of him and Marcello noticed that something was bulging the side pocket of his tunic: the pistol that the man had taken from him in the car when they arrived. Suddenly he was sure that Lino had only that one pistol, and he asked himself why on earth he had lied and why he was now bringing him into the house. The suspicion of trickery grew in him, and with it a determination to keep his eyes open and not let himself be cheated. Meanwhile, they had entered a vast living room, scattered with groups of armchairs and sofas, with a fireplace with a red-brick hood at the back wall. Lino, still preceding Marcello, crossed the room and directed himself toward a door painted blue, in a corner. Marcello asked anxiously, "Where are we going?"

"We're going into my bedroom," replied Lino lightly, without turning around.

Marcello decided to put up some initial resistance, just in case, just so Lino would know that he had seen through his game. When Lino opened the blue door, he said, keeping himself at a distance: "Give me the pistol right now or I'm going away."

"But I don't have the pistol here," replied Lino, turning halfway around, "I have it in my bedroom."

"Yes, you do so have it," said Marcello, "You have it in the pocket of your jacket."

"But this one belongs to the car."

"You don't have any others."

Lino seemed to make a gesture of impatience, swiftly repressed. Marcello noticed again what a contrast there was between his dry, severe face and his soft mouth and anxious, pained, and pleading eyes.

"I'll give you this one," he said at last, "but come with me . . . what's it matter to you? Some farmer might see us here, with all these windows."

"So what if they see us?" Marcello would like to have asked; but he held back because he perceived dimly that, although he could not explain it, it really did matter. "All right," he said childishly, "but then will you give it to me?"

"Don't worry."

They entered a little white hallway and Lino shut the door. At the end of the hall there was another blue door. This time Lino did not precede Marcello, but came up beside him and put an arm lightly around his waist, asking, "Do you want your pistol so much?"

"Yes," said Marcello, incapable of speech because of the embarrassment that arm was causing him.

Lino removed his arm and led Marcello into the bedroom. It was a small, white room, long and narrow, with a window at the end. There was nothing in it except a bed, a bedside table, a wardrobe, and a couple of straight-backed chairs. All the furniture was painted a light green. Marcello noticed that a bronze crucifix of the most common kind was affixed to the wall above the bed. On the bedside table there was a thick book bound in black with red edging, which Marcello figured was a book of devotions. The room, empty of objects and clothes, seemed extremely clean; nonetheless there was a strong odor in the air, like soap made from eau du cologne. Where had he smelled it before? Maybe in the bathroom in the morning, right after his mother had washed.

Lino said to him carelessly, "Sit down on the bed, will you . . . it's more comfortable," and he obeyed in silence. Lino was now walking back and forth in the bedroom. He took off his cap and put it on the windowsill; he unbuttoned his collar and dried the sweat around his neck with a handkerchief. Then he opened the wardrobe, took out a big bottle of eau du cologne, wet the handkerchief with it, and rubbed it with relief over his face and forehead. "Do you want some, too?" he asked Marcello. "It's refreshing."

Marcello would like to have refused, for the bottle and handkerchief inspired in him an inexpressible disgust. But he let Lino run the palm of his hand in a cool caress over his face. Lino put the eau du cologne back in the wardrobe and came to sit on the bed in front of Marcello.

They looked at each other. Lino's face, dry and austere, had now assumed a new expression — consumed, caressing, supplicant. He contemplated Marcello and said nothing. Marcello, losing his patience, and also to put an end to that embarrassing contemplation, finally asked: "And the pistol?"

He saw Lino sigh and take the weapon, as if reluctantly, out of his pocket. Marcello held out his hand, but Lino's face hardened; he withdrew the gun and said hurriedly, "I'll give it to you . . . but you have to earn it."

Marcello felt almost a sense of relief at these words. So, just as he had thought, Lino wanted something in exchange for the pistol. Quickly, in a falsely ingenuous tone, as he did at school when he was bartering for pen nibs or marbles, he said: "You tell me what you want and we'll make a deal."

He saw Lino lower his eyes, hesitate, and then ask slowly, "What would you do to have this pistol?"

He noted that Lino had eluded his proposal: it wasn't a matter of exchanging some *thing* for the pistol but of something he must *do* to obtain it. Although he had no idea what that might be, he said, in the same falsely ingenuous tone: "I don't know, you tell me."

There was a moment of silence.

"Would you do anything?" Lino suddenly asked in an urgent voice, grabbing him by the hand.

The tone and gesture alarmed Marcello. He asked himself whether Lino were not a robber demanding that he join in. But a moment's thought told him he could throw out this guess. All the same he replied cautiously, "Well, what is it you want me to do? Why don't you tell me?"

Lino was playing with his hand now, looking at it, turning it over, squeezing and releasing it. Then, with an almost rude gesture, he let it go and said slowly, looking at Marcello, "I'm sure there are some things you wouldn't do."

"Just say it," insisted Marcello, with a kind of goodwill all mixed up with embarrassment.

"No, no," protested Lino. Marcello noticed that a peculiar, mottled blush was staining his pale face at the top of his cheeks. It seemed to him that Lino was tempted to speak but wanted to be sure that's what Marcello wanted. Then he made a gesture of deliberate yet innocent appeal; he leaned forward and held out his hand to grasp the hand of the man.

"Say it, come on, why don't you say it?"

A long silence followed. Lino looked first at Marcello's hand, then at his face, and seemed to hesitate. Finally he released the boy's hand again, but gently this time, rose, and took a few steps across the room. Then he came back to sit down and took Marcello's hand again in an affectionate way, a little like a father or mother taking the hand of their child. He said: "Marcello, do you know who I am?"

"No."

"I'm a defrocked priest," burst out Lino in a sorrowing, heartfelt, pathetic voice, "a defrocked priest, thrown out of the boarding school where I taught for indecent behavior . . . and you, in your innocence, don't realize what I could ask from you in exchange for this pistol you want so much . . . and I was tempted to abuse your ignorance, your innocence, your childish greed! That's who I am, Marcello."

He spoke in a tone of deep sincerity; then he turned toward the head of the bed and, in a wholly unexpected way, began to address the crucifix indignantly without raising his voice, as if complaining. "I've prayed to you so often . . . but you've abandoned me . . . and I always, always give in . . . why have you abandoned me?"

These words lost themselves in a kind of murmur, as if Lino were talking to himself. Then he rose from the bed, went to get the cap he had left on the sill, and said to Marcello, "Let's go. Come on, I'll take you back home."

Marcello said nothing. He felt stunned and unable, for the moment, to judge what had happened. He followed Lino down the hallway and then across the living room. Outside in the clearing the wind was still gusting around the big black car under an overcast, sunless sky. Lino got into the car and he sat beside him. The car began to move, rolled down the driveway, drove gently through the gateway onto the road. For a long time neither of them spoke. Lino drove as before, his upper body erect, the cap's visor pulled over his eyes, his gloved hands resting on the steering wheel. They had covered a good bit of road when he asked unexpectedly, without turning his head, "Are you sorry you don't have the pistol?"

At these words the avid hope of owning the object so greatly desired was rekindled in Marcello's heart. After all, he thought, maybe nothing was lost yet. He answered sincerely, "Sure, I'm sorry."

"So," asked Lino, "if I made an appointment with you for tomorrow at the same time as today, would you come?"

"Tomorrow is Sunday," Marcello replied judiciously, "but Monday's all right . . . We can meet on the avenue, the same place as today."

The man said nothing for a moment. Then, suddenly, in a loud and sorrowful voice, he shouted: "Don't talk to me anymore . . . don't look at me anymore . . . and if you see me on the avenue at noon on Monday, don't pay attention to me, don't say hello to me . . . understand?"

"What's the matter with him?" thought Marcello, rather annoyed. And he answered, "I don't care if I see you . . . it's you that made me come to your house today."

"Yes, but it must never happen again, never again," declared Lino. "I know myself and I know for certain that tonight all I'll do is think of you . . . and that Monday I'll be waiting for you on the avenue, even if today I decide not to do it . . . I know myself . . . but you must pay no attention to me."

Marcello said nothing. Lino went on, still with the same fury, "I'll think of you all night long, Marcello . . . and Monday I'll be on the avenue . . . with the pistol . . . but you should ignore me."

He kept circling the same phrase, repeating it: and Marcello, with his cold and innocent perspicacity, understood that, in reality, Lino wanted to make the appointment and that, on the pretext of warning him off, he was actually doing so.

After a moment of silence, Lino asked once more, "Did you hear me?"

"Yes."

"What did I say?"

"That Monday you'll be waiting for me on the avenue."

"That's not all I said to you," said the man sorrowfully.

"And that," finished Marcello, "I should ignore you."

"Right," confirmed Lino, "no matter what. Look, I'll call out to you, I'll plead with you, I'll follow you with the car . . . I'll promise you anything you want . . . but you have to keep on going and not listen to me."

Marcello replied impatiently, "All right, I understand."

"But you're just a child," said Lino, passing from fury to a kind of caressing sweetness, "and you won't be able to resist me . . . you'll come, there's no doubt . . . you're a child, Marcello."

Marcello was offended. "I'm not a child, I'm a boy. And besides, you don't know me."

Lino stopped the car very suddenly. They were still on the hill road, under a high garden wall. A little ahead you could glimpse the arch of a restaurant, adorned with Venetian lanterns. Lino turned toward Marcello. "Really," he asked, with a kind of painful anxiety, "Would you really refuse to come with me?"

"Aren't you," asked Marcello, who by now knew the rules of the game, "the one who's asking me to?"

"Yes, it's true," said Lino desperately, starting up the automobile again, "yes, it's true . . . you're right . . . it's me, madman that I am, who's asking you to . . . me."

After this exclamation, he said no more and there was silence. The car descended to the bottom of the road and traveled once more through the filthy streets of the poor neighborhood. Here was the broad avenue with its high plane trees, naked and white, the heaps of yellow leaves on the deserted sidewalks, the factories full of windows. Here was the neighborhood where Marcello lived.

Lino asked without turning, "Where is your house?"

"It's better if you stop here," said Marcello, aware of the pleasure he was giving the man by this token of complicity, "otherwise they might see me getting out of your car."

The automobile came to a halt. Marcello got out and Lino handed him his books through the window, saying decisively, "Monday, then, on the avenue, same place as today."

"But I," said Marcello, taking the books, "have to pretend I don't see you, right?"

He saw Lino hesitate and experienced a feeling of almost cruel satisfaction. Lino's eyes, burning intensely in their sunken sockets, smoldered at him with a look both imploring and anguish. Then he said passionately, "Do what you think . . . do what you want with me." His voice ended in a kind of sing-song, yearning lament.

"I warn you, I'm not even going to look at you," Marcello informed him for the last time.

He saw Lino make a gesture he didn't understand, but that seemed one of desperate assent. Then the car moved away, distancing itself slowly in the direction of the avenue.

3

EVERY MORNING MARCELLO was awakened at a fixed hour by the cook, who felt a particular affection for him. She would come into his bedroom in the dark carrying a breakfast tray, which she would place on the marble top of the chest of drawers. Then Marcello would watch as she hung onto the cord of the Persian blinds with both arms and pulled it up with two or three jerks of her robust body. She would put the breakfast tray on his knees and stand there to watch him eat, ready, as soon as he had finished, to throw back his covers and urge him to get dressed. She helped him with this, handing him his clothes, sometimes kneeling to put on his shoes. She was a lively, merry woman, full of good common sense; she had conserved the accent and affectionate habits of the province in which she was born.

That Monday Marcello woke up with a confused memory of having heard, while he was sleeping the night before, a burst of angry voices coming either from the first floor or from his parents' bedroom. He waited until he had consumed his breakfast and then casually asked the cook, "What happened last night?"

The woman gazed at him in pretended and exaggerated surprise. "What do I know, nothing."

Marcello understood that she had something to say: the false surprise, the mischievous sparkle of her eyes, her whole attitude denoted it.

He said, "I heard some yelling . . ."

"Oh, yelling," said the woman, "but that's normal. Don't you know that your papà and mamma yell at each other a lot?"

"Yes," said Marcello, "but they were yelling louder than usual."

She smiled and, leaning over with two hands on the headboard of the bed, said, "At least if they yell they may understand each other better, don't you think?"

This was one of her habits: to ask questions that required no answer, that were actually affirmations. Marcello asked, "But why were they yelling?"

The woman smiled again. "Why do people yell? Because they don't get along."

"Why don't they get along?"

"Them?" she cried, glad of the boy's question. "Oh, for a thousand reasons . . . One day it might be because your mamma wants to sleep with the window open and your papà doesn't . . . another day because he wants to go to bed early and your mother likes to go to bed late . . . There's never a shortage of reasons, is there?"

Marcello said suddenly, with gravity and conviction, as if expressing a long-held sentiment: "I don't want to stay here anymore."

"And what would you like to do?" cried the woman, even more gaily. "You're little, you can't just run away from home . . . you have to wait till you're big."

"I would prefer it," said Marcello, "if they put me in a boarding school."

The woman looked at him tenderly and then declared loudly, "You're right . . . in a boarding school at least you'd have someone who gave you a thought. Do you know why they were yelling so much last night, your papà and mamma?"

"No, why?"

"Wait, I'll let you see." She went to the door quickly and disappeared. Marcello heard her rush down the stairs and wondered once more what could have happened the night before. In a moment he heard the cook climbing back up the stairs; then she came into the bedroom with an air of gay mystery. She held in her hand an object Marcello recognized right away: a large photograph, taken when Marcello was scarcely more than two years old. You could see his mother, dressed in white, with her son, also in a little white gown, in her arms, a white bow in his long hair.

"Look at this photograph," cried the cook happily. "Your mamma came back from the theater last night and walked into the living room and the first thing she saw, on the piano, was this photograph . . . Poor thing, she almost fainted . . . just look at what your papà did to this photograph!"

Marcello looked at the photograph in astonishment. Someone, using the point of a pen knife or bodkin, had pierced holes in the eyes of both mother and son and then, with a red pencil, had drawn many small marks under both of their eyes, as if to indicate bloody tears spurting from the four holes. The thing was so strange and unexpected and so obscurely dismal that Marcello didn't know what to think for a moment.

"It's your papà that did this," cried the cook, "and your mamma was right to yell at him."

"But why did he do it?"

"It's a piece of witchcraft. Do you know what witchcraft is?"

"No."

"When you want to harm someone . . . you do what your papà did . . . sometimes instead of poking holes in the eyes, you poke holes in the chest . . . right around the heart . . . and then something happens."

"What happens?"

"The person dies, or some accident happens to him . . . it depends."

"But," stammered Marcello, "I've never done anything wrong to Papà."

"And what has your mamma done to him, then?" shouted the cook indignantly. "But do you know what your father is? Crazy! And you know where he'll end up? In Sant'Onofrio, in the madhouse! And now get up, get dressed, it's time you went to school . . . I'm going to put this picture back." She ran off, wholly happy, and Marcello was left alone.

Feeling blank, unable to explain the incident of the photograph in any way to himself, he started to get dressed again. He had never experienced any particular feeling for his father, so that his hostility, justified or not, did not grieve him; but the cook's words about the maleficent powers of witchcraft gave him something to think about. Not that he was superstitious and really believed that all it took to harm someone was to poke holes in the eyes of a photograph; but this madness of his father's reawoke in him an apprehension that he imagined he had definitively put to rest. It was the terrified and powerless sense of having entered into the orbit of a disastrous destiny, which had obsessed him all summer, and which now, as if answering the call of an evil attraction when faced with that photograph stained with bloody tears, was rekindled in his soul and stronger than ever.

What was disaster, he asked himself, what was it if not the black dot lost in the azure blue of the most serene skies that all of a sudden enlarges, becomes huge, becomes an awful, pitiless bird swooping down on its chosen one like a vulture on carrion? Or the trap that you have been warned against, that you can even see perfectly clearly, and in which, all the same, you can't help putting your foot? Or even a curse of clumsiness, imprudence, and blindness insinuated into your gestures, your senses, your blood? This last definition, he felt, was the most appropriate one, since it traced the source of disaster to a lack of grace, and the lack of grace to an intimate, obscure, native, inscrutable fate, to which his father's act, like a sign pointing to the entrance of a grim and fatal road, had recalled his attention. He knew that this fate required him to kill; but what frightened him most was not so much the thought of homicide as the sense of being predestined for it, whatever he might do. He was terrified, that is, by the idea that even his awareness was ignorance — but ignorance of so particular a kind that no one would deem it such, least of all himself.

But later, at school, with childish inconstancy, he suddenly forgot these premonitions. His deskmate happened to be one of his tormentors, a boy by the name of Turchi, the oldest and most ignorant student in the class. He was the only one who, having taken a few boxing lessons, knew how to fistfight professionally; his hard and angular face under crew-cut hair, with its snub nose and thin lips, sunk down into an athlete's sweatshirt, already seemed that of a professional boxer. Turchi understood nothing of Latin; but when the boys gathered in clusters on the streets outside of school, and he raised a gnarled hand to remove the last tiny vestige of a cigarette butt from his mouth and, wrinkling the many lines on his low forehead into a look of sufficient authority, declared: "What I say is, Colucci's going to win the championship," all the boys were struck dumb and full of respect. Turchi, who could on occasion demonstrate, by taking his nose between his fingers and dislocating it to one side, that he had a broken septum just like real boxers, was not only avid about boxing but also about football and any other popular and violent sport. He maintained a sarcastic attitude toward Marcello, almost sober in its brutality. It had been Turchi, in fact, who had held Marcello's arms two days ago while the others dressed him in the skirt; and Marcello, remembering this, believed he had finally found, this morning, a way to win his scornful and inaccessible respect.

Profiting from a moment when the geography professor had turned to indicate the map of Europe with his long pointer, he scribbled quickly in his notebook: "Today I'm getting a real pistol," and then shoved the notebook toward Turchi. Now, Turchi, his ignorance notwithstanding, was a model student as far as behavior. Always attentive, motionless, almost gloomy in his blank and and dull solemnity, his inability to come up with answers to the teacher's simplest questions, every time he was called on, astonished Marcello profoundly. He often wondered what in the world the boy was thinking about during lessons and why, if he didn't study, he was pretending to be so diligent. Now, when

Turchi saw the notebook he made an impatient gesture, almost as if to say: "Leave me alone . . . don't you see that I'm listening to the lesson?"

But Marcello insisted, nudging him with an elbow; and then Turchi, without moving his head, lowered his eyes to read the writing. Marcello saw him pick up a pencil and write in his turn: "I don't believe you."

Stung to the quick, he rushed to confirm it, in writing again: "Word of honor."

Turchi wrote back suspiciously: "What make is it?"

This question disconcerted Marcello; still, after a moment of hesitation, he replied: "A Wilson." He was mixing it up with Weston, a name he had heard dropped by Turchi himself some time ago.

Turchi wrote right away: "Never heard of it."

Marcello concluded: "I'll bring it to school tomorrow," and the dialogue suddenly ended because the professor turned around and called on Turchi, asking him to name the longest river in Germany. As usual, Turchi stood up and, after long reflection, confessed without embarrassment — almost with a kind of sporting honesty — that he didn't know. Right then the door opened and the janitor looked in to announce the end of lessons.

He must make sure at all costs that Lino kept his promise and gave him the pistol, thought Marcello later, hurrying through the streets toward the avenue of the plane trees. Marcello realized that Lino would give him the weapon only if he wanted to, and as he walked, he asked himself what attitude to take, what behavior to engage in to accomplish his purpose most surely. While he had not penetrated the true reason for Lino's yearning, with an instinctive, almost feminine coquetry he intuited that the quickest way to enter into possession of the pistol was the one suggested last Saturday by Lino himself: to pay no attention to him, to scorn his offers, to reject his supplications, to make himself precious, that is; finally, not to agree to get in the car until he was good and sure the pistol was his. But why Lino should feel so strongly about him and why he should be able to get away with this kind of blackmail,

Marcello couldn't have said. The same instinct that suggested he blackmail Lino allowed him to glimpse, behind his relationship with the chauffeur, the shadow of a strange affection, as embarrassing as it was mysterious. The pistol was foremost among his thoughts; but at the same time he could not have claimed that Lino's affection and the almost feminine part that was his to play were truly disagreeable to him. The only thing he would like to avoid, he thought, bursting out onto the avenue of the plane trees, all sweaty from his long run, was Lino putting his arm around him as he had done in the hallway of the villa the first time they saw each other.

As on Saturday, the day was stormy and overcast, buffeted by a hot wind rich with spoil it had snatched up here, there, and everywhere in its turbulent passage: dead leaves, pieces of paper, feathers, down, twigs, dust. On the avenue the wind had just that moment swept down on a pile of dead leaves, lifting great numbers of them high, high among the stripped branches of the plane trees. He amused himself by watching the leaves as they whirled through the air against the background of dark sky, like innumerable yellow hands with their fingers spread apart; and then, looking down, he saw through all those hands of gold twirling in the wind, the long, black, shining shape of the automobile, parked against the curb. His heart began to beat more swiftly, he would not have known how to say why; however, faithful to his plan, he did not hurry his steps, but walked forward until he was level with the car. He passed its window slowly, and right away, as if at a signal, the car door opened and Lino, without his cap on, stuck his head out, saying, "Marcello, do you want to get in?"

He couldn't help marveling at this very serious invitation after the vows of their first encounter. So Lino does know himself well, he thought, and it was even amusing to see him do something he had foreseen, despite all his determination to resist. Marcello walked on as if he hadn't heard and then realized, with obscure satisfaction, that the car was moving and following him. The wide sidewalk was deserted as far as the eye could see between the regularly spaced factories full of windows and the great, slanting trunks of the plane trees. The car was following him at his own pace, with a low rumble that almost caressed the ear; after about twenty meters, it passed him and stopped some distance ahead; then the car door opened again. He passed it without turning and heard once more the strained and urgent voice, pleading, "Marcello, get in . . . I beg you . . . forget what I told you the other day . . . Marcello, do you hear me?"

Marcello couldn't help telling himself that that voice was a little disgusting; why did Lino have to whine that way? It was lucky that no one else was going down the avenue, otherwise he would have felt ashamed. All the same, he didn't want to discourage the man completely, so this time as he passed the car, he turned around halfway to look behind him, as if to invite Lino to persevere. He realized he was launching an almost flattering, flirtatious glance in his direction, and all of a sudden he felt the same unmistakeable sensation of not unpleasant humiliation, of not unnatural pretence, that he had felt two days ago for a moment when his companions were tying the skirt around his waist. Almost as if, at heart, it wouldn't displease him — on the contrary, maybe he was made for it by nature — to act the part of a disdainful, flirtatious woman. Meanwhile the car had come up behind him again. Marcello queried himself as to whether it was yet time to surrender and decided, after reflection, that the moment had not yet come. The car passed him without stopping, only slowing down. He heard the man's voice calling to him: "Marcello . . ." and then, right afterward, the sudden roar of the car taking off. Now he worried that Lino had lost patience and left; he was invaded by a great fear of showing himself the next day at school with empty hands; and he started to run, shouting, "Lino! Lino, stop, Lino!"

But the wind carried his words away, scattering them through the air with the dead leaves in an anguished and resonant tumult. The car dwindled in the distance; evidently Lino had not heard him and was going away, and he wouldn't have the pistol; and Turchi would tease him one more time. Then he breathed again and began to walk at an almost normal pace, reassured: the car had pulled ahead, not to escape him, but to await him at a cross

street; in fact, now it was parked there, blocking the whole width
of the sidewalk.

He was assailed by anger with Lino for having provoked that
humiliating thumping of his heart; and in that same heart he decided, with a sudden impulse of cruelty, to make him pay for it
with calculated harshness. Meanwhile, without hurrying, he had
reached the cross street. The car was there, long, black, gleaming
with all its old brasses and antique body. Marcello started to go
around it, and right away the door opened and Lino looked out.

"Marcello," he said with desperate decision, "forget what I said
to you Saturday . . . You've gone beyond the call of duty . . . come
on, get in, Marcello."

Marcello had halted near the hood of the car. He took a step
backward and said coldly, without looking at the man, "I'm not
coming. But not because you told me not to come on Saturday . . .
It's just because I really don't want to."

"Why don't you want to?"

"Why should I? Why should I get in the car?"

"To give me pleasure . . ."

"But I don't want to give you pleasure."

"Why not? Do I disgust you?"

"Yes," said Marcello, lowering his eyes and playing with the
handle of the car door. He knew he was making a worried, hostile,
reluctant face and he no longer understood whether he was play-
acting or doing it in earnest. It was certainly a play, this thing he
was enacting with Lino; but if it was a play, why was he experiencing such a strong and complicated feeling, this mix of vanity,
loathing, humiliation, cruelty, and spite?

He heard Lino laugh softly and affectionately and then ask:
"Why do I disgust you?"

This time he raised his eyes and gazed in the man's face. It was
true, Lino did disgust him, he thought, but he had never asked
himself why. He looked at his face, almost ascetic in its thin
severity, and realized then why he didn't like Lino: it was because,
he thought, it was a double face, in which fraud had found an
exact physical expression. It seemed to him, looking at it, that he

recognized this fraud above all in the mouth: thin, dry, disdainful, chaste at first sight; but then, if a smile opened and turned out the lips, shining, in the exposed and inflamed inner membranes, with the mysterious saliva of desire. He hesitated, gazing at Lino, who was smiling, waiting for his answer, and then he said sincerely, "You disgust me because you have a wet mouth."

Lino's smile vanished, his face darkened. "What foolishness are you inventing now?" he asked, and then, regaining control immediately, he said with joking nonchalance, "Well, Signor Marcello, do you want to get into the car?"

"I'll get in," said Marcello, making up his mind at last, "on one condition."

"What condition?"

"That you really give me the pistol."

"That's understood . . . come on, get in."

"No, you have to give it to me now, right away," insisted Marcello obstinately.

"But I don't have it here, Marcello," the man said sincerely. "I left it in my bedroom on Saturday. Let's go to the house now and get it."

"Then I'm not coming," Marcello said decisively, in a way that surprised even him. "Good-bye."

He took a step forward as if to go, and this time Lino lost patience. "Come on, don't act like a child!" he exclaimed. Leaning out, he grabbed Marcello by one arm and dragged him onto the seat next to his own. "Now we're going straight to the house," he added, "and I promise you that you'll have the pistol."

Marcello, who was glad, actually, to be constrained by violence to enter the car, did not protest, but only assumed a childishly sulky expression. Lino, without wasting a motion, closed the door and turned on the engine, and the car set off.

For a long time neither of them spoke. Lino did not appear loquacious, perhaps, thought Marcello, because he was too happy to talk; for himself, he had nothing to say. Now Lino would give him the gun and then he would go back home and the next day he would take the pistol to school and show it to Turchi. His thoughts did not extend beyond these simple and pleasurable expectations. His only fear was that Lino might want to cheat him in some way. In that case, he thought, he would invent something spiteful to drive Lino to desperation and force him to keep his promise.

Sitting still with his bundle of books on his knees, he watched the great plane trees and buildings slide by until they reached the end of the avenue. When the car started up the hill, Lino asked, as if concluding a long reflection, "Who taught you to be such a coquette, Marcello?"

Marcello, who was not quite sure what the word meant, hesitated before answering. The man seemed to understand his innocent ignorance and added, "I mean, so sly."

"Why?" asked Marcello.

"Just to ask."

"You're the sly one," said Marcello, "since you promise me the gun and never give it to me."

Lino laughed; he slapped Marcello's bare knee with one hand and said in an exultant voice, "You know, Marcello, how happy I am that you've come today . . . when I think that the other day I begged you to ignore me, not to come, I realize how foolish we can be sometimes . . . really foolish . . . but luckily you had more sense than me, Marcello."

Marcello said nothing. He didn't understand what Lino was saying too well and besides, that hand resting on his knee was annoying him. He had tried to move his knee away a few times, but the hand had stayed put. Luckily, at a bend in the road they saw a car coming toward them. Marcello pretended to be frightened and exclaimed: "Watch out, that car's going to hit us," and this time Lino withdrew his hand to turn the wheel. Marcello let out his breath.

Here was the country road, between the garden walls and the hedges; here was the gateway with the gate painted green; here was the driveway, flanked by the sparse little cypresses and, here, at the end, was the twinkle of the veranda windows. Marcello noticed that, just as it had last time, the wind was tormenting the cypress trees under a dark, stormy sky. The car came to a halt, Lino leapt out and helped Marcello to descend, then set off with him toward the portico. This time Lino didn't precede him but held him by the arm, hard, almost as if he were afraid he would try to escape. Marcello would have liked to tell him to loosen his grip but he didn't have time. As if flying, holding him almost up off the ground by his arm, Lino made him cross the living room and then pushed him into the hallway. Here he unexpectedly grabbed him hard by the neck, saying, "Stupid boy that you are . . . stupid . . . why didn't you want to come?"

His voice was no longer playful but harsh and broken, although mechanically tender. Marcello, stunned, started to raise his eyes to look into Lino's face; but just then he was shoved violently backward. As one might hurl away a cat or a dog after grabbing it up by the collar, Lino had flung him into the bedroom. Then Marcello saw him turn the key in the lock, pocket it, and turn toward him with an expression in which joy was mixed with an angry triumph.

He shouted loudly, "That's enough now! You'll do what I want! That's enough, Marcello, tyrant, little swine, enough . . . behave, obey, not another word from you."

He uttered these words of command, disdain, and dominion with a savage joy, almost a voluptuous pleasure; and Marcello, as confused as he was, could not help but perceive that they were words without sense, more like the strophes of a triumphal song than the expressions of thought or of conscious will. Frightened, dumbfounded, he watched as Lino paced around the little room, taking long strides, ripping his cap off his head and flinging it onto the windowsill; balling up a shirt hung on one of the chairs and shoving it into a drawer; smoothing the rumpled bedcover; and performing all these practical actions with a fury full of obscure significance. Then he saw him, still yelling his incoherent declarations full of arrogance and power to the air, approach the wall above the bed, wrench free the crucifix, cross over to the wardrobe, and hurl it into the bottom of a drawer with ostentatious brutality; and he understood that in some way, by this gesture, Lino wanted to show him that he had set aside his last scruples. As

if to confirm him in this fear, Lino opened the drawer of the bedside table and took out the much-desired pistol; and showing it to
Marcello, he screamed: "See it? Well, you'll never get it! You'll
have to do what I want you to do without presents, without pistols
. . . for love or by force."

So it was true, thought Marcello, Lino wanted to cheat him,
just as he had feared. He felt himself go white in the face from
anger, and said, "Give me the gun or I'm going."

"Nothing, nothing . . . for love or by force!" Lino still bran-
dished the pistol in one hand; with the other he grabbed Marcello
by the arm and threw him onto the bed. Marcello fell to a sitting
position so violently that he hit his head against the wall. Immediately Lino, passing suddenly from violence to sweetness and from
command to supplication, fell to his knees before him. He circled
the boy's legs with one arm and placed his other hand, still grip-
ping the pistol, on the cover of the bed. He moaned and invoked
Marcello by name; then, still moaning, he embraced his knees
with both arms. The pistol was abandoned on the bed now, black
against the white coverlet. Marcello looked at Lino, down on his
knees, who was alternately raising his pleading face to him, wet
with tears and inflamed by desire, and lowering it to rub it against
his legs the way certain devoted dogs do with their muzzles. He
seized the pistol and, pushing himself up strongly, got to his feet.
Immediately Lino, perhaps thinking he wished to return his embrace, opened his arms and let him go. Marcello stepped forward
into the middle of the room and then turned.

Later, thinking about what had happened, Marcello had to remember that just the contact of the cold butt of the gun had
aroused in his soul a bloody and ruthless temptation; but in that
moment all he was aware of was a sharp pain in his head where he
had hit it against the wall and, at the same time, an irritation, an
acute repugnance for Lino. The man had remained on his knees
by the bed; but when he saw Marcello take a step backward and
point the pistol, he turned around completely without getting up
and, throwing his arms wide in a theatrical gesture, cried out histri-
onically: "Shoot, Marcello . . . kill me . . . yes, kill me like a dog!"

It seemed to Marcello that he had never hated him so much as at that moment, for his loathsome mixture of sensuality and austerity, repentance and lust; and, both terrified and self-aware, almost as if he must satisfy the man's request, he pulled the trigger.

The shot cracked out suddenly, echoing in the little room; and he saw Lino fall onto his side and then right himself, turning his back and clinging to the edge of the bed with both hands. Lino pulled himself up very slowly, fell onto his side on the bed, and remained motionless. Marcello approached him, placed the pistol on the bed, called out, "Lino," in a low voice, and then, without waiting for an answer, went to the door. But it was locked and Lino, he recalled, had taken the key from the keyhole and put it into his pocket. He hesitated, revolted by the idea of rummaging through the dead man's pockets; then his glance fell on the window and he remembered that he was on the ground floor. Climbing up onto the sill, he glanced around hurriedly, throwing a long, circumspect, fearful look at the clearing and the car sitting in front of the portico. He knew that if anyone came by at that moment, they would see him astride the windowsill; still, there was nothing else he could do. But no one was there and, beyond the sparse trees that surrounded the clearing, even the bare and hilly countryside appeared deserted as far as the eye could see. He clambered down from the sill, retrieved his bunch of books from the car seat, and began walking slowly toward the gate.

And all the time, as he was walking, an image was reflected in his consciousness as if in a mirror, the image of himself : a boy in short pants, his books under his arm, on the path flanked by cypresses, an incomprehensible figure filled with a stunned premonition of doom.

PART I

I

CARRYING HIS HAT IN one hand and using the other to pull the sunglasses off his nose and tuck them back into the breast pocket of his jacket, Marcello entered the lobby of the library and asked the usher where he might find the newspaper files. Then he headed unhurriedly toward the broad stairway, at the top of which the large window on the landing shone brilliantly in the strong May light. He felt light and almost vacant, aware of his perfect physical well-being and youthful vigor; and the new suit he was wearing, gray and simply cut, added the no less pleasant sensation of neat and serious elegance that was to his taste. On the second floor, after filling out a request slip, he made his way to the reading room, to a counter behind which an old usher and a girl were standing. He waited until it was his turn and then handed in his form, asking for the major daily newspaper's files for 1920. He waited patiently, leaning against the counter, gazing out at the reading room in front of him. Countless rows of writing desks, each with a lamp with a green lampshade, were lined up all the way to the end of the room. Marcello surveyed these desks, sparsely populated for the most part by students, and mentally selected his own, the last one in the room, on the right at the end. The girl reappeared, holding the large bound file of the newspapers he had asked for in her arms. Marcello took the file and went to the desk.

He placed the file on the slanted desktop and sat down, taking care to hike his pants a bit above the knee; then he calmly opened the file and began to flip through its pages. The headlines had lost their original clarity, their black had become almost green; the paper had yellowed; the photographs had no highlights and looked blurred and confused. He observed that the bigger and more extensive the headlines, the more they gave off a sense of futility and absurdity: announcements of events that had lost importance and significance the very evening of the day they had appeared and which now, clamorous and incomprehensible, defied not only memory but imagination. The most absurd headlines, he noticed, were those accompanied by a more or less tendentious comment; at once exaggerated and hollow, they reminded him of the extravagant ravings of a madman, which deafen but fail to move his listeners. Marcello compared his own feelings, faced with these headlines, to what he imagined he would feel when confronted with the headline that concerned him, and wondered whether even the news he was looking for would rouse the same sense of absurdity and emptiness in him. So this was the past, he thought, continuing to turn the pages, this uproar now silenced, this fury now spent, to which the very material of the newspaper, that yellowed paper that would soon crumble and fall into dust, lent a vulgar and contemptible character. The past was made up of mistakes, violence, deceits, foolishness, and lies, he thought again, reading the news items on the pages one after another; and these were the only things, day after day, that men considered worthy of publication and by which they wished to be remembered by generations to come. Normal life, with its depth, was absent from those pages; and yet, even as he was making these reflections — what else was he looking for if not the report of a crime?

He was in no hurry to find the report that involved him, though he knew the date with precision and could find it unerringly in a moment. Here was the twenty-second, the twenty-third, the twenty-fourth of October, 1920; he was getting ever closer, with every page he turned, to what he considered the most important fact of his life. But the newspaper made no preparations for the announcement; it ignored all the preliminaries. Among all those news items that had nothing to do with him the only one that concerned him would surface suddenly, without warning, as a fish rising to the bait will surface from the belly of the sea. He tried to joke with himself, thinking, "Instead of all these big headlines about political events, they should have printed: *Marcello meets Lino for the first time, Marcello asks him for the gun, Marcello agrees to get in the car.*" But then the joke died in his mind and a sudden anxiety took his breath away: he had reached the date he was looking for. He turned the page hurriedly and found the news in the crime reports, as he had expected, with a headline above one column that read: FATAL ACCIDENT.

Before reading it he looked around, almost as if he were afraid of being observed. Then he lowered his eyes to the newspaper. The report said:

> Yesterday the chauffeur Pasquale Seminara, residing at Number 33 Via della Camilluccia, accidently triggered off a few shots as he was cleaning a gun. Promptly treated, Seminara was taken by ambulance to the hospital of Santo Spirito, where doctors discovered a bullet wound in his chest near the heart and judged the case to be desperate. In fact, notwithstanding the medical attentions lavished upon him, Seminara died that evening.

The report could not have been more concise or conventional, he thought, rereading it. All the same, even the worn-out formulas of the most anonymous journalism revealed two important facts. The first was that Lino was really dead, something of which he had always been convinced but had never had the courage to confirm;

the second was that this had been attributed, evidently by suggestion of the dying man, to accident. So he was completely shielded,
safe from any consequence; Lino was dead, and his death could
never be pinned on Marcello.

But it was not to reassure himself that he had finally determined to look in the library for news of what had happened so
many years ago. His anxiety, never entirely soothed during those
years, had not focused on the practical consequences of his action.
Rather, he had crossed the library's threshold to discover how he
would feel when Lino's death had been confirmed. From this
feeling, he thought, he would be able to judge whether he was still
the boy he had once been, obsessed by his own fatal abnormality,
or the altogether normal man that he had afterward wished to be
and was convinced he was.

He felt an intense relief and, perhaps even more than relief,
surprise, when he realized that the news printed on the yellowed,
seventeen-year-old paper stirred no appreciable echo in his soul.
He was like, he thought, someone who has kept a bandage
wrapped over a deep wound for a long time, finally decides to remove it, and discovers with amazement that where he had expected to find at least a scar, the skin is smooth and seamless,
without any mark of any kind. Looking up the report in the newspaper had been like taking off the bandage, he thought again, and
discovering himself to be unmoved was like discovering that he
was healed. How this healing had come about, he couldn't say.
But without a doubt, it was not time alone that had produced such
a result. He owed a lot to himself, as well, to his conscious desire,
throughout all those years, to escape his abnormality and become
like other people.

Still, with a kind of scrupulousness, raising his eyes from the
newspaper and fixing them on the empty air, he willed himself to
think explicitly about Lino's death, something that until now he
had always instinctively avoided. The newspaper's report was
written in the conventional language used for news, and this
could also have contributed to his indifference and apathy; but
seeing it again could not fail to be vivid and tender, and, as such,

capable of reawakening the ancient terrors in his soul if they were
still there. So, following his memory, a pitiless and impartial guide
leading him backward in time, he walked down the same path he
had traveled as a young boy: the first encounter with Lino on the
avenue; his own desire to own a gun; Lino's promise; the visit to
the villa; the second meeting with Lino; the man's pederastic crav-
ings; himself, pointing the pistol; the man crying hystrionically
with open arms, kneeling next to the bed, "Kill me, Marcello . . .
Kill me like a dog." Marcello shooting almost as if he were
obeying him; the man collapsing against the bed, pulling himself
up, then falling still, tilted on his side. He realized immediately, as
he examined all these details one by one, that the indifference he
had noticed in himself when confronted with the news in the
paper was now confirmed, and had grown even stronger. In fact,
not only did he feel no remorse, but the emotions of compassion,
rancor, and repugnance for Lino, which had long seemed inseparable from that memory, did not even brush the motionless surface of his awareness. In other words, he felt nothing; and an
impotent man lying alongside the naked and desirable body of a
woman was not more inert than his mind confronted with that remote event in his life. He was glad of this indifference, a sure sign
that there was no longer any relationship — not even hidden, not
even indirect, not even suspended — between the boy he had
been and the young man he now was. He was truly another
person, he thought again, closing the file very slowly and raising
himself up from the desk, and although his memory was mechanically able to recall what had happened in that faraway October, in
reality his whole being, even down to its most secret fibers, had
forgotten it by now.

He walked slowly to the counter and gave the file back to the li-
brarian. Then, still with the measured and vigorous composure
that was his preferred attitude, he left the reading room and
headed down the large stairway toward the lobby. It was true, he
couldn't help thinking as he stepped over the threshold into the
strong light of the street, it was true — the news item and his deliberate recollection of Lino's death had aroused no echo in his

heart; but at the same time he did not feel quite as relieved as he had thought himself earlier. He recalled the feeling he had had as he leafed through the pages of the old newspaper: as if he were taking the bandages off a wound and finding to his surprise that it had healed perfectly. And he said to himself that maybe, under the unmarked skin, the old infection was still festering in the form of a closed and invisible abscess. He was confirmed in this suspicion not only by the fleeting quality of the relief he had felt for a moment when he discovered that Lino's death left him indifferent, but also by the faint melancholy that floated like a diaphanous funeral veil between his vision and reality. As if the memory of the fact of Lino, dissolved as it was by the powerful acids of time, had nonetheless cast an inexplicable shadow over all his thoughts and feelings.

As he walked slowly down the crowded, sunlit streets, he tried to establish a comparison between his self of seventeen years ago and his self of the present. He recalled that at thirteen he had been a shy boy, a bit feminine, impressionable, disordered, imaginative, impetuous, passionate. Now instead, at the age of thirty, he was not at all a shy man; on the contrary, he was perfectly sure of himself. He was altogether masculine in his tastes and attitudes, calm, orderly to an extreme, almost devoid of imagination, cold and controlled. He seemed to remember, too, that there had once been an obscure and tumultuous richness inside him. Now instead, everything in him was clear although perhaps a little dull, and the poverty and rigidity of a few ideas and convictions had taken the place of that generous and confused abundance. Finally, he had been inclined toward intimacy, expansive, at times positively exuberant. Now he was closed, always in the same even-tempered mood, lacking spark and, if not actually sad, at least silent. But the most distinctive trait of the radical change effected in those seventeen years was the disappearance of a kind of excess of vitality caused by the seething of unusual, perhaps even abnormal, instincts; these had now given way, it seemed, to a certain gray and restrained normality. Only chance, he thought again, had kept him from submitting to Lino's desires; and certainly a clouded,

unconscious, sensual inclination, combined with his childish
greed, had contributed to his behavior, so full of coquetry and
feminine despotism, with the chauffeur. But now he was really a
man, like so many others. He stopped in front of a store mirror and
looked at himself for a long time, observing himself with objective
detachment, without pleasure: yes, he was really a man like so
many others, with his gray suit, his sober tie, his tall and well-
proportioned figure, his dark, round face, his well-combed hair,
his dark sunglasses. At the university, he recalled, he had suddenly
discovered, with a kind of joy, that there were at least a thousand
young men of his own age that dressed, spoke, thought, and be-
haved as he did. Now that figure could probably be multiplied by
a million. He was a normal man, he thought with contemptuous
and bitter satisfaction, beyond the shadow of a doubt, even if he
couldn't say how it had happened.

Suddenly he remembered that he had finished his cigarettes
and turned in to a tobacconist's shop in the Piazza Colonna arcade. He went up to the counter and asked for his preferred brand
at the same time that three other people asked for the same cigarettes, and the tobacconist slid them rapidly across the marble of
the countertop toward the four hands holding out money — four
identical packs, which the four hands picked up with identical
gestures. Marcello noticed that he took the pack, squeezed it to
see if it was fresh enough, and then ripped off the seal the same
way the other three did. He even noticed that two of the three
tucked the pack back into a small inner pocket in their jackets, as
he did. Finally, one of the three stopped just outside the tobacconist's to light a cigarette with a silver lighter exactly like his own.
These observations stirred a satisfied, almost voluptuous pleasure
in him. Yes, he was the same as the others, the same as everyone.
The same as the men who bought the same brand of cigarettes,
with the same gestures, even the men who turned at the passage of
a woman dressed in red, himself among them, to eye the quiver of
her solid buttocks under the thin material of the dress. Even if, as
in this last gesture, the similarity was due more to willed imitation
in his case than to any real personal inclination.

A short, deformed newspaper seller came up to him, a bundle of papers in his arm, waving a copy and declaiming loudly, his face congested by the effort, some incomprehensible phrase in which the words VICTORY and SPAIN were still recognizable. Marcello bought the paper and attentively read the headline that covered the whole top of the page: once again, in the war in Spain, Franco's followers had won a victory. He was aware of reading this news with true satisfaction — one more demonstration, he thought, of his full and absolute normality. He had seen the birth of the war, from the first hypocritical headline, "What's Happening in Spain?" The war had spread, grown gigantic, become a dispute not only of arms but also of ideas. And gradually he became aware that he was following it with a singular emotion, completely divorced from any political and moral consideration (although such considerations came frequently to mind), very much like the feeling of a sports fan who roots for one football team against another. From the beginning he had wanted Franco to win, not fervently but with a sentiment both deep and tenacious, almost as if that victory would bring him confirmation of the goodness and rightness of his tastes and ideas, not only in the field of politics but also in all others. Perhaps he had desired and still desired Franco's victory for love of symmetry, like someone who is furnishing his house and takes care to collect furniture all of the same style and period. He seemed to read this symmetry in the events of the past few years, growing ever clearer and more important: first the advent of Fascism in Italy, then in Germany; then the war of Ethiopia, then the war in Spain. This progression pleased him, he wasn't sure why, maybe because it was easy to recognize a more-than-human logic in it, a recognition that gave him a sense of security and infallibility. On the other hand, he thought, folding the newspaper back up and putting it in his pocket, it couldn't be said that he was convinced of the justice of Franco's cause for reasons of politics or propaganda. This conviction had come to him out of nowhere, as it seems to come to ordinary, uneducated people: from the air, that is, as when someone says an idea is in the air. He sided with Franco the way countless other people did, common folk who knew little or nothing about Spain, uneducated people who barely read the headlines in the papers. For *simpatia*, he thought, giving a completely unconsidered, alogical, irrational sense to the Italian word. A *simpatia* that could be said only metaphorically to come from the air; there is flower pollen in the air, smoke from the houses, dust, light, not ideas. This *simpatia*, then, arose from deeper regions and demonstrated once more that his normality was neither superficial nor pieced together rationally and voluntarily with debatable motives and reasons, but linked to an instinctive and almost physiological condition, to a faith, that is, shared with millions of other people. He was one with the society he found himself living in, and with its people. He was not a loner, abnormal, crazy, but one of them: a brother, a citizen, a comrade; and this, after the long fear that Lino's murder would divide him from the rest of humanity, was highly consoling.

Franco or someone else, he thought; in the long run it mattered very little who, as long as there was a link, a bridge, a sign of connection and communion. But the fact that it was Franco and not someone else showed that, aside from being an indication of communion and solidarity, his emotional participation in the Spanish war was right, was real. What else could the truth be, in fact, if not that which was evident to everyone, believed by everyone, held irrefutable? Thus the chain was unbroken, all its links well soldered by his *simpatia*, felt before any reflection, to the knowledge that this feeling was shared by millions of other people in just the same way; from this knowledge to the conviction of being in the right; from the conviction of being in the right to action. Because, he thought, possession of the truth not only permitted action but demanded it. It was like a confirmation he must offer to himself and others of his own normality, which must be continually deepened, reaffirmed, and demonstrated lest it lose reality.

By this time he had arrived. The main entrance to the ministry yawned wide on the other side of the street, beyond a double row of moving cars and buses. He waited for a moment and then struck out in the wake of a big black automobile that was headed

right to the entrance. He went in behind the car, told the usher
the name of the official with whom he wished to speak, and then
sat down in the waiting room, almost glad to be waiting like the
others, among the others. He did not feel rushed or impatient or
intolerant of the order and etiquette of the ministry. On the contrary, its order and etiquette pleased him, seemed to him to be
signs of a vaster and more generalized order and etiquette to
which he gladly adapted. He felt entirely calm and cold; if anything — but this was not new to him, either — a little sad. It was a
mysterious sorrow, which by this time he considered inseparable
from his character. He had always been sad like this, or better,
lacking in gaiety, like certain lakes whose waters mirror a very high
mountain that blocks the light of the sun, making them black and
melancholy. One knows that if the mountain were removed, the
sun would make the waters sparkle; but the mountain is always
there and the lake is sad. He was sad like those lakes; but what the
mountain was, he couldn't have said.

The waiting room, a little room just beyond the porter's lodge
in the palazzo, was full of odd people, the very opposite of what
you would expect to find in the anteroom of a minister like that,
famous for his elegance and the worldliness of his officials. Three
individuals of a debauched and sinister cast, perhaps informers or
plainclothes agents, were smoking and chatting in low voices next
to a young woman with black hair and a white and red face, very
flashily dressed and made up, to all appearances the lowest kind of
prostitute. Then there was an old man, dressed neatly but poorly
in black, with a white beard and mustache, maybe a professor.
Then a thin little woman with gray hair and a breathless, anxious
expression, maybe the mother of a family. Then him.

He observed all these people from under his lashes with urgent
repugnance. It always happened like this: he thought he was
normal, like everyone else, when he imagined the crowd in abstract, a great, positive army united by the same feelings, the same
ideas, the same aims; and it was comforting to be part of this. But as
soon as individuals emerged out of that crowd, his illusion of normality shattered against the fact of diversity. He did not recognize

himself at all in them and felt both disgust and detachment. What did he have in common with those three sinister, vulgar individuals, that streetwalker, that white-haired old man, that breathless and humble mother? Nothing except this disgust, this pity.

"Clerici," yelled the voice of the usher. He started and rose to his feet. "The first stairway to the right." Without turning, he headed toward the place the man had pointed out.

He climbed up a long, very wide staircase with a red carpet snaking up its center and found himself, after the second flight, on a vast landing with three big double doors. He went to the one in the middle, opened it, and stepped into the half-light of a large room. There was a long, massive table in it and in the middle of the table was a globe of the world. Marcello wandered around this room for a few moments; it was probably not in use, judging by the locked shutters on the windows and the dustcovers draped over the couches lined up against the walls. Then he opened one of its many doors and looked out into a dark, narrow corridor between two rows of glass shelves. At the end of the corridor he could see a door that had been left ajar, through which a little light was filtering. Marcello approached it, hesitated, and then very slowly and gently pushed on it. It was not curiosity but the desire to find an usher who could point out the room he wanted that led him to do it. Putting his eye to the crack, he realized that his suspicion of being in the wrong place was not unfounded. Before him stretched a long, narrow room, blandly illuminated by a window curtained in yellow. In front of the window was a table and sitting at the table in profile, his back to the window, was a young man with a broad, heavy face and corpulent body. Standing up against the table with her back to Marcello was a woman clothed in a light dress of big black flowers on a white background, a wide, black lace hat with a veil on her head. She was very tall and very slender in the waist, but broad at the shoulders and hips, with long legs and thin ankles. She was leaning over the table and speaking softly to the man, who was listening to her and sitting still, in profile, looking not at her but at his own hand fiddling with a pencil on the table. Then she came around to the side of the armchair close to the man and began talking to him in a more intimate way, her back toward the table and her face to the window; but the black hat tilted over one eye kept Marcello from seeing her face. She hesitated, then leaned awkwardly to the side with her leg in the air, like someone bending down to a fountain to receive the gush of water in her mouth, and pressed her lips to the lips of the man, who let himself be kissed without moving or giving any sign that the kiss pleased him. She turned, hiding both their faces behind the broad brim of her hat, then swayed and would have lost her balance if the man had not held her up by putting an arm around her waist. Now she was standing up, her body hiding the man in the chair; maybe she was stroking his head. Then his arm, which was still wound around her waist, seemed to relax its hold; his thick, coarse hand slid over the woman's buttock as if pulled down by its own weight and stayed there, wide open, fingers spread like a crab or a spider resting on a smooth, spherical surface that rejects its grip. Marcello closed the door.

He turned back down the hallway to the room with the globe. What he had just witnessed confirmed the minister's fame as a libertine — the man he had watched in the other room was the minister himself; Marcello had recognized him right away. But strangely, considering his tendency to moralize, what he had seen did not shake the foundation of his convictions at all. Marcello felt no *simpatia* whatsoever for the worldly, womanizing minister; on the contrary, he disliked him; and he felt that this intrusion of his erotic life into his official one was highly improper. But none of this affected Marcello's political faith even minimally. It was the same when people he trusted told him about other important public figures — that they were stealing, or incompetent, or using their political influence for personal ends. He registered this sort of news with an almost gloomy indifference, as if these kinds of things had ceased to concern him from the moment he had made his choice, once and for all; and he didn't intend to change it. Besides, such things no longer surprised him, since in a certain sense he had taken them for granted for as long as he could remember, with his precocious awareness of the less amicable aspects of man.

But above all, he perceived that there could be no relationship between his loyalty to the regime and the extremely rigid morality
that informed his own conduct. The reasons for that loyalty had
origins deeper than any moral standard, and they were not about
to be shaken by a hand feeling up a woman's bottom in a state office, or by a theft, or by any other crime or error. He couldn't have
said, precisely, what these origins were; the dull, opaque veil of his
stubborn melancholy came between them and his thoughts.

Impassive and calm yet impatient, he opened another door in
the big room, peered down another corridor, withdrew, tried a
third door, and finally found himself in the waiting room he was
looking for. People were sitting on the couches all around the
walls; ushers in braided uniforms stood near the thresholds.
Speaking in a low voice, he communicated the name of the official he wanted to see to an usher and then went to sit down on one
of the couches. He reopened his paper to pass the time. News of
the victory in Spain filled every column and he realized that this
tasteless excess annoyed him. He reread the dispatch in bold type
announcing the victory and then passed on to a long comment in
italics, which he quit reading almost immediately because the
forced and unconvincing martial stance of the special correspon-
dent irritated him. He stopped reading for a moment to wonder
how he, himself, would have written the article, and he surprised
himself by thinking that if it had been up to him, not only the article from Spain but also all other aspects of the regime, from the
least important to the most prominent, would be completely different. Actually, he thought, there was almost nothing about the
regime that he didn't dislike deeply; all the same, this was his path
and he had to remain faithful to it. He reopened the paper and
skimmed over a few of the other items, carefully avoiding the patriotic articles and the propaganda. At last he raised his eyes from
the paper and looked around.

At that moment there was no one left in the waiting room except one old white-haired man with a round head and a lively
face, whose expression was a mixture of impudence, cunning, and
greed. Dressed in light-colored clothes, a sporty, youthful jacket

ripped down the back, big rubber-soled shoes on his feet and a
flashy tie on his chest, he gave the impression of being at home in
the ministry, walking up and down the room and carelessly con-
sulting the obsequious ushers posted at the threshold of the doors
with an air of playful impatience. Then one of the doors opened
and a middle-aged man emerged: bald, thin except for a prominent belly, with an empty yellow face, eyes lost at the bottom of
large, dark sockets, and a ready, sceptical, spirited expression on
his sharp features. The old man went straight up to him with an
exclamation of playful protest; the other saluted him ceremoni-
ously and deferentially; and then the old man, with an intimate
gesture, took the man with the yellow face not by an arm but right
by the waist, as if he were a woman. Walking across the room beside him, he began speaking to him, whispering urgently in a very
low voice. Marcello, who had been following the scene with an indifferent eye, suddenly realized to his astonishment that he was
feeling an insane hatred for the old man and he didn't even know
why. Marcello was not unaware that at any moment and for the
most diverse reasons one of these excesses of hatred could burst
through the deadened surface of his usual apathy; but each time it
happened he was amazed, as if faced with an unknown aspect of
his own character that gave the lie to all the other known, secure
ones. That old man, for example: he felt that he could easily kill
him or have him killed; more, that he actually wanted to kill him.
Why? Maybe, he thought, it was because scepticism, the fault he
hated most, was so clearly painted on that ruddy face of his. Or because his jacket had a tear in the back and the old man, who was
keeping his hand in his pocket, was lifting one of the flaps, ex-
posing the back of his pants, which were too big and floppy and
made him look disgustingly like a tailor's dummy. Anyway, he
hated him with such great and unbearable intensity that at last he
preferred to lower his eyes to his newspaper again. When he raised
them once more, after some time, the old man and his companion were gone and the room was deserted.

One of the ushers came over to murmur that he could go in,
and Marcello rose and followed him. The usher opened one of

the doors, standing back to let him pass through. Marcello found himself in a vast room with frescoed ceiling and walls, at the end of which was a table scattered with papers. Behind the table sat the man with the yellow face whom he had glimpsed already in the waiting room; to one side sat another man, whom Marcello knew well, his immediate superior in the Secret Service. At Marcello's appearance the man with the yellow face, who was one of the ministry secretaries, rose to his feet; the other man stayed in his chair and greeted him with a nod. This last, a thin old man with a military aspect, a stiff scarlet face, and a mustache as black and bristling as a false mustache on a mask, made, he thought, a complete contrast with the secretary. He was, in fact and as he knew, a loyal, rigid, honest man, accustomed to serving without protest, putting what he considered to be his duty above everything else, even his conscience. While the secretary, as far as he remembered, was a more recent and altogether different sort of man: ambitious and sceptical, worldly, with a taste for intrigue pushed to the point of brutality, beyond any professional obligation and every boundary of conscience. All of Marcello's goodwill was directed toward the old man, naturally, and also because he seemed to recognize in that red and ruined face the same obscure melancholy that so often oppressed him. Maybe, like him, Colonel Baudino was feeling the contrast between an unshakeable, almost spellbound loyalty that had nothing rational in it and the too-often deplorable character of daily reality. But maybe, he thought, looking at the old man again, it was just an illusion and he — as can happen — was lending his own feelings to his superior because he liked him, almost in the hope that he was not alone in feeling them.

The colonel said dryly, without looking at Marcello or the secretary, "This is the Dottor Clerici I spoke to you about some time ago," and the secretary, with ceremonial and almost ironic eagerness, leaned over the table, extended his hand, and invited him to sit down. Marcello took a seat. The secretary seated himself as well, took up a box of cigarettes, and offered them first to the colonel, who refused, and then to Marcello, who accepted.

Then, after lighting a cigarette for himself, he said, "Clerici, I'm very pleased to meet you. The colonel here does nothing but sing your praises . . . It would appear that you are, as they say, an ace." He underlined "as they say" with a smile and went on, "The minister and I have examined your plan and found it excellent, absolutely . . . Do you know Quadri well?"

"Yes," said Marcello. "He was my professor at the university."

"And you're sure Quadri doesn't know you're an agent?"

"As sure as I can be."

"Your idea of faking a political conversion to inspire their trust, infiltrating their organization, and maybe even being given a mission to carry out in Italy," proceeded the secretary, lowering his eyes toward some point on the table in front of him, "is a good one . . . The minister agrees with me that something of the kind must be attempted without delay. When were you thinking of going, Clerici?"

"As soon as necessary."

"Very good," said the secretary, somewhat surprised even so, as if he had been expecting a different answer, "excellent. All the same, there's a point we should clear up . . . You are proposing to carry out a mission that is, let us say, somewhat delicate and dangerous. The colonel here and I were saying that in order not to be too obvious you should find, think up, invent some plausible pretext for your presence in Paris. I'm not saying that they know who you are or that they'll be able to figure it out . . . but, well, you can't ever be too careful . . . all the more so since Quadri, as you tell us in your report, was not unaware at the time of your feelings of loyalty toward the regime . . ."

"If it hadn't been for those feelings," said Marcello dryly, "there could hardly be a conversion."

"Right, absolutely right . . . but you don't go to Paris just to present yourself to Quadri and tell him: I'm here. You have to give the impression, instead, that you find yourself in Paris for private, not political reasons, in other words, and are taking advantage of the occasion to reveal your spiritual crisis to Quadri. You need," concluded the secretary abruptly, lifting his eyes to look at Marcello, "to combine the mission with something personal, something unofficial." The secretary turned toward the colonel and added, "Don't you think so, Colonel?"

"That's my opinion, as well," said the colonel, without raising his eyes. And he added after a moment, "But only Dottor Clerici can find the pretext that suits him."

Marcello bowed his head and thought of nothing. It seemed to him that there was nothing to respond at the moment, since an excuse of this kind had to be thought about deliberately and calmly. He was just going to reply, "Give me two or three days' time and I'll think about it," when, suddenly, his tongue seemed to move for him, almost against his will: "I'm getting married in a week . . . I could combine the mission with my honeymoon trip."

This time the secretary's surprise, although he covered it up with an eager enthusiasm, was evident and profound. The colonel, instead, remained completely impassive, as if Marcello had not spoken.

"Very good . . . excellent," exclaimed the secretary with a disconcerted air, "you're getting married . . . You couldn't find a better excuse . . . the classic honeymoon in Paris."

"Yes," said Marcello, without smiling, "the classic honeymoon in Paris."

The secretary was afraid he had offended him. "What I meant to say is that Paris is just the place for a honeymoon trip. Unfortunately, I'm not married . . . but if I did get married, I think I'd go to Paris, too . . ."

This time Marcello said nothing. He often responded this way to people he disliked: with complete silence.

The secretary turned toward the colonel for reassurance: "You're right, Colonel . . . Only Dottor Clerici could have come up with this sort of pretext. Even if we had thought of it, we couldn't have suggested it."

This statement, uttered in an ambiguous, half-serious tone of voice, cut both ways, Marcello thought. It could be real, if somewhat ironic, praise: "God, what fanaticism!" or it could be the expression instead of a stupid contempt: "What servility — he doesn't even respect his own honeymoon." Probably, he thought, it was both, since it was clear that for the secretary the boundary between fanaticism and servility was not very precise; both were means he used — now one, now the other — but always to reach the same ends. Marcello noticed with satisfaction that the colonel also refused to smile, a response the secretary seemed to be inviting with his two-way statement.

A moment of silence followed. Marcello stared straight into the secretary's eyes with a motionless composure that he knew and wished to be disconcerting. In fact, the secretary could not stand up to it and suddenly, supporting himself with both hands on the tabletop, he rose to his feet.

"All right, then . . . You, Colonel, can come to an agreement with Dottor Clerici about the instructions for the mission. You," he went on, turning to Marcello, "ought to know, moreover, that you have the minister's full support, and mine. Actually," he added with affected carelessness, "the minister has expressed the desire to meet you personally."

Marcello replied nothing to this, either, limiting himself to standing up and making a slight, deferential bow. The secretary, who had probably expected some words of gratitude, gave another start of surprise which he immediately suppressed.

"Stay here, Clerici," he said. "The minister ordered me to bring you directly to him."

The colonel stood up and said, "Clerici, you know where to find me." He held out his hand to the secretary, but the man — attentive, obsequious, ceremonious — was determined to accompany him to the door at all costs. Marcello watched them shake hands; then the colonel disappeared and the secretary turned to him.

"Come with me, Clerici. The minister is extremely busy — nonetheless, he's absolutely determined to see you and let you know how pleased he is . . . This is the first time, isn't it, that you're being introduced to the minister?"

As he was saying this, they were passing through a small waiting room adjacent to the secretary's office. Now he went up to a door, opened it, nodded to Marcello to wait and disappeared, only to reappear almost immediately and beckon him to follow.

Marcello entered the same long, narrow room he had observed a while ago through the crack of the door; but now it presented itself from the other side, with the table in front of him. Behind it sat the man with the broad, heavy face and overweight body he had spied letting himself be kissed by the woman in the big black hat. He noticed that the table was cleared and polished like a mirror. There were no papers on it, only a large bronze inkwell and a closed briefcase of dark leather.

"*Eccellenza*, this is Dottor Clerici," said the secretary.

The minister stood up and held out his hand to Marcello with an attentive cordiality even more marked than the secretary's, but completely devoid of pleasantry — on the contrary, decidedly authoritarian.

"How are you, Clerici?" he asked, pronouncing his words carefully, slowly, and imperiously, as if they were full of particular significance. "You've been praised very highly to me . . . The regime needs men like you."

Then he sat back down and, pulling a handkerchief out of his pocket, blew his nose as he examined some papers the secretary was showing him. Marcello retired discreetly to the farthest corner of the room. The minister looked at the papers while the secretary whispered in his ear, and then he looked at his handkerchief. Marcello saw that the white linen was smeared with red and recalled that when he had come in, the minister's mouth had seemed redder than was natural: the lipstick of the woman in the black hat. Still continuing to examine the papers the secretary was showing him, without losing his composure or worrying about being observed, the minister started rubbing his mouth hard with the handkerchief, looking at it every once in a while to see if the lipstick was still coming off. At last the examination of the papers and of the handkerchief ended together, and the minister stood up and held out his hand to Marcello once more.

"Good-bye, Clerici. As my secretary will have told you, the mission you're setting out on has my complete, unconditional support."

Marcello bowed, shook the thick, blunt hand, and followed the secretary out of the room. They returned to the secretary's office, where he put the papers the minister had examined on his table and then accompanied Marcello to the door.

"Well, Clerici, best of luck," he said with a smile, "and congratulations on your wedding."

Marcello thanked him with a nod of the head, a bow, and a murmured word. The secretary shook his hand with a final smile. Then the door closed.

2

*B*Y NOW IT WAS LATE; as soon as he was out of the ministry, Marcello quickened his gait. He got in line at the bus stop with the rest of the hungry, restless midday crowd, and patiently waited his turn to climb into the already crowded bus. He spent part of the ride hanging on outside on the footboard; then, with a great effort, he managed to insinuate himself onto the platform, where he remained, jostled on every side by other passengers as the bus, jerking and rumbling, wound its way out of the city center and climbed up the streets toward the periphery. These discomforts, however, did not irritate him; on the contrary, they felt useful inasmuch as they were shared with so many others, contributing in some small measure to his similarity to everyone else. Besides, he liked these contacts with the crowd, unpleasant and uncomfortable as they were, and preferred them to contact with individuals; from a crowd, he thought, as he stood on tiptoes on the platform to breathe more freely, he got the comforting sensation of multiple communion, whether it involved being crushed inside a bus or the patriotic enthusiasm of a political rally. But individuals only caused him to doubt himself and others, like this morning during his visit to the ministry.

Why, for example, he thought again, right after he had offered to combine his honeymoon trip with the mission, had he felt the painful sensation of having committed an act of unasked-for servility or obtuse fanaticism? Because, he told himself, his offer had been made to that sceptical, scheming, corrupt man, that unworthy and hateful secretary. It was he, just by his presence, who had inspired shame in Marcello for an act so deeply spontaneous and selfless. And now, as the bus rolled from one stop to the next, he reassured himself that he would have felt no shame if he had not found himself in front of a man like that, for whom neither loyalty nor dedication nor sacrifice existed, only calculation, prudence, and his own interests. In fact, Marcello's offer had not been the result of any mental speculation but had emerged from the obscure depths of his nature, which surely proved that his posture of social and political normality was authentic. Someone else, the secretary for example, would have made such an offer only after long and sly reflection, whereas he had simply improvised. As for the impropriety of combining his honeymoon with his political mission, it wasn't worth wasting the time to examine it. He was what he was and everything he did was right if it conformed to what he was.

Lost in these thoughts, he got down from the bus and headed toward a street in the white-collar district; pink and white oleanders were planted beside the sidewalk. The massive, shabby palazzi of the state employees opened their huge entranceways onto the street, and he caught glimpses of vast and squalid courtyards behind them. Alternating with the entranceways were modest shops, which Marcello knew well by now: the tobacconist's, the baker's, the greengrocer's, the butcher's, the grocery store. It was noon, and even among those anonymous buildings the tenuous, ephemeral joy characteristic of the suspension of work and the reunion with family revealed itself in many ways: kitchen smells wafting out of the half-open windows on the ground floors; badly dressed men in such a hurry they practically ran through their front doors; bits of radio voices, fragments of sound from record players. From an enclosed garden in a recess of one of the palaces, the espalier of climbing roses on the railing greeted his passage with a wave of sharp, dusty fragrance. Marcello quickened his pace, turned into entranceway number nineteen along with two or three other employees — imitating their haste with satisfaction — and headed up the stairs.

He started to climb slowly up the broad flights, in which squalid shadow alternated with brilliant light from the large windows on the landings. But on the second floor he recalled that he had forgotten something: the flowers that he never failed to bring his fiancée, every time he was invited to lunch at her house. Happy to have remembered in time, he ran back downstairs and into the street and went directly to the corner of the palazzo, where a woman huddled up on a stool displayed seasonal flowers in jars. He hastily chose a half-dozen roses, the most beautiful the florist had, long and straight-stemmed, a dark red. Holding them to his nose and breathing in their perfume, he re-entered the palazzo and climbed the stairs, this time to the top floor. Here only one door opened onto the landing; a very short flight of steps led to a rustic porch, beneath which the strong light of the terrace was shining.

He rang the bell, thinking, "Let's hope her mother doesn't come to the door."

His future mother-in-law, in fact, displayed an almost yearning love for him that embarrassed him deeply. In a moment the door opened, and in the twilight of the entrance hall Marcello made out, to his relief, the figure of the maid — who was almost a child — bundled up in a white apron too big for her, her pale face crowned by a double twist of black braids. She shut the door behind them, not without poking her head out a moment to look curiously around the landing; and Marcello, flaring his nostrils to breathe in the strong cooking smells that filled the air, passed on into the living room.

The living-room window was half-shut to keep the heat and light from coming in, but it was not too dark for him to distinguish the dark faux-Renaissance-style furniture cluttering the room among the thin shadows. They were heavy, severe, densely carved pieces, and formed a strange contrast with the room's knick-knacks, all shoddily made and common in taste, that were scattered over the shelves and on the table: a small nude woman kneeling on the edge of an ashtray, a blue majolica sailor playing a harmonica, a group of black-and-white dogs, two or three lamps shaped like blossoms or flowers. There were a lot of metal and porcelain ashtrays that had originally contained, as he knew, the *confetti*, or sugared wedding almonds, that friends and relatives of his fiancée had given them. The walls were papered with fake red damask, and landscapes and still lifes painted in bright colors and framed in black were hanging from them. Marcello sat down on the couch, already sporting its summer slipcover, and looked around with satisfaction. It was truly a bourgeois apartment, he reflected once again, product of the most conventional and modest middle class, similar in every way to the other apartments of that same palazzo and that same district. And this was the most pleasant aspect of it for him: the sensation of viewing something very common, even cheap, and yet perfectly reassuring. He realized that he felt, at that thought, an almost abject sense of pleasure at the ugliness of the place. He had grown up in a beautiful, tasteful home and knew very well that everything that surrounded him was ugly beyond remedy; but it was exactly what he needed, this anonymous ugliness — one more thing he would have in common with his peers. He recalled that for lack of money, at least in the first years, Giulia and he would live in that house once they were married, and he almost blessed his poverty. Acting by himself, following the dictates of his own taste, he could never have put together a house this ordinary and ugly. Soon this would be his living room; as the Liberty-style bedroom in which his future mother-in-law and her deceased husband had slept for thirty years would be his bedroom; and the mahogany dining room in which Giulia and her parents had consumed their meals twice a day their whole lives long would be his dining room. Giulia's father had been an important official in some min-

istry, and this apartment, assembled according to the fashion of
the times when he was young, was a kind of temple pathetically
erected in honor of the twin divinities, respectability and normality. Soon, he thought again with an almost greedy, wanton joy
that was also sad, he would insert himself by right into this normality and respectability.

The door opened and Giulia came in impetuously, still talking
to someone in the hallway, maybe the maid. When she had finished speaking, she shut the door and came quickly toward her fiancé. At twenty, Giulia was as full-bodied as a woman of thirty,
with a coarse, almost common shapeliness that was still fresh and
solid, revealing both her youth and some unknown, carnal illusion and joy. She had an extremely white complexion and large
eyes, limpid, dark, and languid; thick, beautifully wavy chestnut
hair; blooming red lips. Watching her come toward him, dressed
in a light outfit with a masculine cut from which the curves of
her exuberant body seemed to explode, Marcello couldn't help
thinking with renewed pleasure that he was marrying a totally
normal, completely ordinary girl, very like the living room that
had given him such solace a moment before.

A similar solace, almost a relief, came over him again when he
heard her drawling, good-natured, Roman vernacular saying,
"What beautiful roses . . . But why? I already told you you
shouldn't bother. It's not as if it's the first time you've come to
lunch with us." Meanwhile she went over to a blue vase perched
on a column of yellow marble in a corner of the room, and put the
roses in it.

"I like bringing you flowers," said Marcello.

Giulia heaved a sigh of satisfaction and let herself fall full-
length on the couch next to him. Marcello looked at her and saw
that a sudden embarrassment had taken the place of the willful
nonchalance of the moment before, an unmistakable sign that she
was about to be aroused. All of a sudden she turned to him and
threw her arms around his neck, murmuring, "Kiss me."

Marcello put his arm around her waist and kissed her on
the mouth. Giulia was sensual and during these kisses, almost

invariably requested by her from a reluctant Marcello, there was always a moment when her sensuality insinuated itself aggressively into the kiss, transforming the chaste and proper character of their relationship as fiancés. This time again, just as their lips were about to separate, she suddenly shuddered with desire, and encircling Marcello's neck with one arm, glued her mouth back firmly to his. He felt her tongue thrust between his lips and begin to move rapidly, twisting and rolling in his mouth. Meanwhile, Giulia had grabbed one of his hands and guided it up to squeeze her left breast. She was blowing through her nostrils and sighing heavily, with an innocent, hungry, animal sound.

Marcello was not in love with his fiancée, but he liked Giulia, and these sensual embraces never failed to excite him. All the same, he didn't feel inclined to return her rapturous caresses: he wanted his relations with his fiancée to remain within the traditional bounds. It almost seemed to him that greater intimacy might bring back into his life the disorder and abnormality he had been trying so hard to shake off. So after a while he removed his hand from her breast and gently, slowly pulled it away.

"Uh, how cold you are," said Giulia, drawing back and looking at him with a smile, "really, there are times I could think you didn't love me."

Marcello said, "You know I love you."

Changing subject rapidly, as she often did, she said, "I'm so happy . . . I've never been this happy. By the way, did you know this morning Mamma insisted again that we take her bedroom . . . she'll move into that little room at the end of the hallway. What do you think? Should we accept?"

"I think," said Marcello, "she'd be hurt if we refused."

"That's what I think, too. Imagine, when I was a little girl I dreamed of sleeping in a bedroom like that one someday. Now I don't know if I like it that much anymore . . . do you like it?" she asked in a tone both doubtful and pleased, but afraid to hear his opinion of her taste, but hoping for approval.

Marcello was quick to reply, "I like it very much. It's really beautiful." And he saw that these words gave Giulia visible satisfaction.

Filled with joy, she planted a kiss on his cheek and then continued, "I met Signora Persico this morning and I invited her to
the reception. Can you believe she didn't know I was getting married? She asked me so many questions . . . When I told her who
you were, she said she knew your mother, she'd met her at the
seashore a few years ago."

Marcello said nothing. Talking about his mother, with whom
he had not lived for years and whom he rarely saw, was always very
unpleasant for him. Luckily Giulia, unaware of his discomfort,
changed the subject again.

"Speaking of the reception, we've made the guest list. Do you
want to see it?"

"Yes, show it to me."

She pulled a piece of paper out of her pocket and handed it to
him. Marcello took it and looked at it. It was a long list of people,
grouped by families: fathers, mothers, daughters, sons. The men
were indicated not only by name and last name but also by their
professional titles: doctors, lawyers, engineers, teachers; and when
they had them, by honorifics: *commendatori*, high-ranking offi-
cers, knights. Next to each family Giulia, to be on the safe side,
had written down the number of people in the family: three, five,
two, four. Almost all the names were unknown to Marcello, yet he
seemed to have known them always: all members of the middle
and lower middle class, professionals and state employees; all
people who undoubtedly lived in apartments like this, with living
rooms like this and furniture like this; and who had daughters very
much like Giulia to marry off, and who married them off to young
men with degrees and jobs very much (he hoped) like himself. He
examined the long list, dwelling on certain of the more common,
typical names with a deep satisfaction tinged, nonetheless, with
his usual cold and motionless melancholy.

"Who is Arcangeli, for example?" he asked at random. "*Com-
mendatore* Giuseppe Arcangeli with his wife Iole, daughters Sil-
vana and Beatrice, doctor-son Gino?"

"No one, you don't know them. Arcangeli was a friend of poor
Papà's, at the ministry."

"Where does he live?"

"Just a minute away, in Via Porpora."

"What's his living room like?"

"Do you know how funny you are, with your questions?" she exclaimed, laughing. "What do you think it's like? It's a living room, like this, like a lot of others . . . why does it interest you that much to know what Arcangeli's living room is like?"

"Are his daughters engaged?"

"Yes, Beatrice is . . . But why?"

"What's her fiancé like?"

"*Uffa* . . . the fiancé, too . . . All right, her fiancé has a strange name. Schirinzi, and he works in a notary public's office."

Marcello noted that there was no way to infer anything about her guests from Giulia's responses. Probably they had no more character in her mind than they had on the page: names of respectable, indistinguishable, normal people. He skimmed the list again and stopped randomly at another name.

"Who's Dottor Cesare Spadoni, with his wife Livia and lawyer-brother Tullio?"

"He's a pediatrician. His wife was one of my friends at school, maybe you've met her: really pretty, dark, small, pale . . . Her brother's a handsome young man . . . They're twins."

"And Cavaliere Luigi Pace with his wife Teresa and four sons Maurizio, Giovanni, Vittorio, Riccardo?"

"Another of poor Papà's friends. The sons are all students . . . Riccardo's still going to the *liceo*."

Marcello realized that it was useless to keep asking for details about the people written down on the list. Giulia could not tell him much more than what was on the list itself. And even if she informed him in every particular about the characters and lives of those people, he thought, her information could hardly exceed the extremely narrow confines of her judgment and intelligence. But he was aware of being happy — almost voluptuously though joylessly so — to enter and form part of this ordinary society, thanks to his marriage. A question was still on the tip of his tongue, however, and after a moment of hesitation, he decided to ask it.

"Tell me, do I resemble your guests?"

"You mean . . . physically?"

"No. I wanted to know if, according to you, I have any points in common with them . . . in the way I look and act, in appearance . . . I mean, if I resemble them."

"You're better than any of them to me," she answered impetuously, "but as far as the rest goes, yes, you're a person like them. You're serious, educated, well-mannered, cultured . . . I mean, you can see that you're a decent, respectable person, like them. But why do you ask?"

"Just thinking."

"How strange you are," she said, gazing at him almost curiously. "Most people want to be different from everyone else, but it seems that you want to be just *like* everyone else."

Marcello said nothing and handed her the list, observing mildly, "Anyway, I don't know a single one of them."

"What do you think, that I know them all?" asked Giulia gayly. "Only Mamma knows who a lot of them are. Besides, the reception will be over quickly . . . an hour or so and then you'll never see them again."

"I don't mind seeing them," said Marcello.

"I was just talking . . . Now, listen to the menu from the hotel and tell me if you like it." Giulia pulled another piece of paper from her pocket and read aloud:

> Cold consommé
> Filets of sole alla mugnaia
> Young turkey hen with rice and supreme sauce
> Seasonal salad
> Assorted cheeses
> Ice-cream and cake
> Fruit
> Coffee and liqueurs

"What do you think?" she asked, in the same doubtful yet satisfied tone with which she had spoken of her mother's bedroom a little earlier. "Does it sound good to you? Do you think we're giving them enough to eat?"

"It sounds very good and generous to me," said Marcello.

Giulia continued, "As far as champagne, we've chosen Italian champagne. It's not as good as the French but it's good enough to make toasts with." She was silent a moment and then added with characteristic unpredictability, "Do you know what Don Lattanzi told me? That if you want to get married you have to take communion and if you want to take communion you have to go to confession . . . otherwise, he won't marry us."

For a moment Marcello, caught by surprise, didn't know what to say. He was not a believer and it had been perhaps ten years since he had entered a church for any religious purpose. Besides, he had always been convinced that he nurtured a distinct dislike of all things ecclesiastical. Now instead, he realized to his astonishment, this idea of confession and communion, far from annoying him, actually pleased and attracted him, somewhat in the same way the wedding reception, those guests he didn't know, his marriage to Giulia, and Giulia herself — so ordinary, so similar to all the other girls — pleased and attracted him. It was one more link, he thought, in the chain of normality with which he sought to anchor himself in the treacherous sands of life. And what was more, this link was made of a nobler and more enduring metal than the others: religion. He was almost surprised not to have thought of it earlier and attributed this forgetfulness to the obvious and pacific nature of the religion into which he had been born and to which he had always felt he belonged, even without practicing it. He said, however, curious to hear what Giulia would respond, "But I'm not a believer."

"So who is," she replied calmly. "Ninety percent of the people who go to church — do you think they believe? And the priests themselves?"

"But do you believe?"

Giulia made a gesture with her hand in the air. "Sort of, up to a certain point . . . Every once in a while I say to Don Lattanzi: 'You don't fool me with all your stories, you priests' . . . I believe and I don't believe. Or rather," she added scrupulously, "let's say that I have a religion all my own . . . different from the priests."

"What does it mean to have your own religion?" thought Marcello. But knowing by experience that Giulia often spoke without knowing too well what she was talking about, he didn't insist. Instead he said, "My case is more radical. I don't believe at all, and I have no religion."

Giulia made a gay, indifferent gesture with her hand. "So what does it cost you? Go all the same . . . It matters so much to them, and it does you no harm."

"Yes, but I'll be forced to lie."

"Words . . . and anyway, it would be lying for a good end. You know what Don Lattanzi says? That you have to do certain things as if you believed, even if you don't . . . faith comes afterward."

Marcello was silent a moment and then said, "All right, then I'll confess and take communion." And as he said this, he felt once more that shiver of dark delight that the guest list had inspired in him earlier. "So," he added, "I'll go confess to Don Lattanzi."

"You don't really have to go to him," said Giulia. "You can go to any confessor, in any church."

"And for holy communion?"

"Don Lattanzi will do that the day we get married . . . We'll take it together. How long has it been since you went to confession?"

"Well . . . I don't think I've confessed since I made my first communion, when I was eight," said Marcello with some embarrassment. "Then I never did again."

"Just think!" she exclaimed joyfully. "Who knows how many sins you have to tell!"

"And if they don't give me absolution?"

"They'll give you absolution for sure," she replied affectionately, caressing his face with one hand. "Besides, what sins could you have? You're good, you have a gentle heart, you've never done any harm to anyone. They'll absolve you right away."

"It's complicated to get married," said Marcello.

"Yes, but for me all these complications and preparations are so enjoyable . . . After all, we're going to be united for the rest of our lives, aren't we? And by the way, what are we deciding about the honeymoon?"

For the first time Marcello felt, along with his usual indulgent and lucid affection, a sense of pity for Giulia. He knew that there was still time for him to backtrack, to go somewhere else for their honeymoon instead of tó Paris, where he was to carry out his mission. He could tell the minister he declined the task. But at the same time he realized that this was impossible. The mission was perhaps the firmest, most compromising and decisive step on his way to absolute normality. His marriage to Giulia, the wedding reception, the religious ceremonies, confession and communion were steps in the same direction, but less important ones.

He stopped only a moment to analyze this reflection, whose dark and almost sinister depths did not escape him, and said quickly, "Well, I thought we might go to Paris."

Giulia clapped her hands for joy. "Oh, good, Paris! My dream!" She threw her arms around his neck and kissed him feverishly. "If you knew how happy I am . . . I didn't want to tell you how much I wanted to go to Paris . . . I was afraid it would cost too much."

"It will cost about the same as any other place, more or less," said Marcello, "but don't you worry about the money. For this once we'll come up with it."

Giulia was ravished. "How happy I am," she repeated. She pressed herself passionately against Marcello and murmured, "Do you love me? Why don't you kiss me?"

And so once more Marcello had his fiancée's arm around his neck and her mouth on his. This time the ardor of her kiss seemed redoubled by gratitude. Giulia sighed; her whole body wriggled; she took Marcello's hand and crushed it against her breast, rapidly and spasmodically moving her tongue in his mouth.

Aroused, Marcello thought, "If I wanted to I could take her now, right here, on this couch," and it seemed to him that he perceived, one more time, the fragility of what he called normality.

At last they separated and Marcello said, smiling, "It's lucky we're getting married soon. Otherwise I'm afraid we'd become lovers one of these days."

Giulia, her face still all flushed from the kiss, shrugged her shoulders and answered with her own kind of exalted and innocent impudence, "I love you so much, I couldn't ask for anything better."

"Really?" asked Marcello.

"Even right away," she said passionately, "even here, now . . ."

She had taken one of Marcello's hands and was kissing it slowly, looking up at him with shining eyes full of feeling. Then the door opened and Giulia pulled back as her mother came into the room.

She too, thought Marcello as he watched her approach, was one of the many people brought into his life by his quest for a redemptive normality. He had nothing in common with this senti mental woman, who was always overflowing with a consuming, yearning tenderness — nothing but his desire to bind himself deeply and enduringly to a solid, established human society. Giulia's mother, Signora Delia Ginami, was a corpulent woman in whom the breakdowns of advancing age seemed to manifest themselves in a kind of decay both of body and spirit, the first afflicted by a trembling, boneless obesity, the second by a tendency to mawkish, physiological outbursts of sentimentality. With every step she took it seemed that entire parts of her swollen body listed and shifted on their own under her shapeless clothes; and at the least trifle, a wracking emotion seemed to overwhelm her faculties of self-control, filling her watery blue eyes with tears as she joined her hands together in a gesture of ecstasy. Lately the imminence of her only daughter's wedding had plunged Signora Delia into a condition of perpetual emotionality: she did nothing but cry — for joy, she explained — and she felt a constant need to hug Giulia or her future son-in-law of whom, she declared, she was already as fond as if he were her son. Marcello, whom these effusions filled with embarrassment, understood nonetheless that they were simply one more aspect of the reality in which he wished to insert himself; and as such, he endured and even appreciated them, with the same slightly melancholy satisfaction that the ugly furniture in the house, Giulia's monologues, the wedding celebrations, and Don Lattanzi's religious demands inspired in him.

This time, however, Signora Delia was not tender but indignant. She was waving a piece of paper in her hand and after she had greeted Marcello, who had risen to his feet, she said, "An anonymous letter . . . But first of all let's go eat, it's ready."

"An anonymous letter?" cried Giulia, rushing after her mother.

"Yes, an anonymous letter. How disgusting people are, really."

Marcello followed them into the dining room, trying to hide his face with his handkerchief. This news of an anonymous letter had deeply shaken him and it was important to him not to let the two women see it. Hearing Giulia's mother exclaim, "An anonymous letter," and immediately thinking, "Someone wrote about what happened with Lino" had been one and the same thing for him. At this thought the blood rushed from his face, he couldn't breathe; he was assaulted by feelings of dismay, shame, and fear — inexplicable, unexpected, lightning-swift — that he had never experienced since the first years of his adolescence, when the memory of Lino had still been fresh. It was stronger than he was; and all his powers of self-control had been swept away in one moment, the way a thin cordon of policemen is swept away by the panicked crowd it was supposed to contain. He bit his lips till the blood came as he approached the table. So he had been mistaken, in the library, when he had looked up the news of the crime and been convinced that the ancient wound was completely healed: not only was the wound not healed, but it was also much deeper than he had suspected. Luckily his place at the table was against the light, with his back to the window. Silently, rigidly, he sat down at the head of the table, with Giulia on his right and Signora Ginami on his left.

The anonymous letter now lay on the tablecloth, next to Giulia's mother's plate. Meanwhile, the child-maid had come in, holding in both hands a platter heaped with spaghetti. Marcello sank the serving fork into the red, oily skein of spaghetti, lifted out a small amount, and deposited it on his plate.

Immediately the two women protested, "Too little . . . what, are you fasting . . . take some more." Signora Ginami added, "You're a working man, you need to eat."

Giulia impulsively forked up some more spaghetti from the platter and put it on her fiancé's plate.

"I'm not hungry," said Marcello, in a voice that seemed to him absolutely anguished and spent.

"Appetite comes with eating," replied Giulia emphatically as she served herself.

The little maid left, taking away the almost empty platter, and the mother said immediately, "I didn't want to show it to you . . . I didn't think it was worth it. What a world we live in, though . . ."

Marcello said nothing, but bent his head over his plate and filled his mouth with spaghetti. He was still afraid that the letter had to do with Lino, although his mind told him that this was impossible. It was an irresistible fear, stronger than any reflection.

Giulia asked, "Well, for goodness' sake, will you tell us what's written in it?"

Her mother answered, "First of all, though, I want to tell Marcello that even if they had written things a thousand times worse, he could still be sure that my affection for him would stay the same . . . Marcello, you're a son to me, and you know that a mother's love for her son is stronger than any insinuation." Her eyes suddenly filled with tears and she repeated, "A real son." Then, grabbing Marcello's hand and bringing it to her heart, she said, "Dear Marcello."

Not knowing what to do or say, Marcello remained still and said nothing, waiting for the effusion to be over.

Signora Ginami gazed at him with soft eyes and added, "You have to forgive an old woman like me, Marcello."

"Mamma, that's ridiculous, you're not old," said Giulia, too used to these maternal outbursts to give them any weight or even be surprised by them.

"Yes, I'm old, and I don't have many years left to live," replied Signora Delia. This imminent death was one of her favorite subjects, perhaps because she thought it had the power to move others as much as it moved her. "I'll die soon and that's why I'm so happy to be leaving my daughter with a man as good as you, Marcello."

Marcello, whose hand Signora Delia was pressing against her heart, and who found himself in an uncomfortable position over his spaghetti, could not repress a very slight movement of impatience, which did not escape the old woman. However, she took it as a protest of her excessive praise.

"Yes," she said emphatically, "you're good . . . so good. Sometimes I say to Giulia: You're lucky to have found such a good young man. I know very well, Marcello, that in these days goodness is no longer fashionable, but let someone tell you who's a lot older than you are: nothing matters in this world but goodness . . . and luckily you are so, so, so good."

Marcello frowned and said nothing.

"Let him eat, poor thing," exclaimed Giulia. "Don't you see that you're getting sauce on his sleeve?"

Signora Ginami let go of Marcello's hand and, picking up the letter, said, "It's written on a typewriter . . . with a Roman postmark. I wouldn't be surprised, Marcello, if one of your office colleagues had written it."

"Oh, Mamma, would you just tell us what's written in it?"

"Here it is," said her mother, handing the letter to Giulia. "Read it . . . but don't read it aloud. They're ugly things that I don't like to hear . . . Then when you've read it, give it to Marcello."

Not without anxiety, Marcello watched his fiancée read the letter. Then, twisting her mouth in contempt, Giulia said, "How disgusting." And she handed it to him.

The letter, written on onion skin, contained only a few lines typed out on a faded ribbon:

"Signora, in allowing your daughter to marry Dottor Clerici, you are doing something worse than making a mistake, you are committing a crime. Dottor Clerici's father has been shut away in an insane asylum for years, being afflicted with a madness that is syphilitic in origin, and, as you know, this illness is hereditary. You still have time: stop the marriage. A friend."

"So that's all it is," thought Marcello, almost disappointed. He understood, then, that his disappointment was even greater than his relief; he had almost hoped that someone else would learn of his childhood tragedy and free him, at least in part, from his burden of knowledge. He was struck, all the same, by the phrase: "As you know, this illness is hereditary." He knew very well that the source of his father's madness was not syphilitic, and that there was no danger that he would go mad someday like his father. Still, it seemed to him that that sentence, so menacing and malignant, alluded to another sort of madness, which actually could be hereditary. This idea, immediately rejected, did no more than lightly brush his mind. Then he gave the letter back to Giulia's mother, saying mildly, "There's no truth to that."

"Well, I know there's no truth to it," she replied, almost offended. After a moment she added, "I only know that my daughter is marrying a good, intelligent, honest, serious man . . . and a handsome boy," she concluded, somewhat flirtatiously.

"Above all a handsome boy, you can say it loud and clear," confirmed Giulia, "and that's why whoever wrote that letter is insinuating that he'll go crazy like his father. Seeing him so handsome, they can't believe he doesn't have a screw loose . . . idiots."

"Who knows what they'd say," Marcello couldn't help thinking, "if they knew that when I was thirteen I almost had sexual intercourse with a man and that I killed him." He realized, now that the fear roused by the letter had passed, that his usual melancholy, speculative apathy had returned. "Probably," he thought, looking at his fiancée and Signora Ginami, "they wouldn't even care . . . Normal people have thick skins." And he understood that he envied the two women, once again, their "thick skins."

Suddenly he said, "Actually, I have to go visit my father today."

"Are you going with your mother?"

"Yes."

The pasta was finished; the young maid came back in, changed the plates, and set a platter full of meat and vegetables on the table. As soon as she had left, the mother picked up the letter again and examined it, saying, "I really would like to know who wrote this letter."

"Mamma," said Giulia suddenly, instantly and excessively serious, "hand that letter over to me."

She took up the envelope, looked at it attentively, then took out the piece of paper and scrutinized it, frowning. Finally she exclaimed in a high, indignant voice, "I know very well who wrote this letter, there's no doubt about it . . . oh, wicked!"

"So who is it?"

"A bad man," replied Giulia, lowering her eyes to the table.

Marcello didn't say anything. Giulia worked as a secretary in a lawyer's office; probably, he thought, the letter had been written by one of the many assistants.

Her mother said, "Someone who's jealous, for sure . . . Marcello has a position at thirty that a lot of older men would like to have."

Although he wasn't really curious, Marcello asked his fiancée, pro forma, "If you know the name of whoever wrote the letter, why don't you say it?"

"I can't," she answered, by now more thoughtful than indignant, "but I told you: he's a bad man."

She gave the letter back to her mother and served herself from the platter the maid was holding out for her. For a moment none of the three said a thing. Then Signora Ginami began again, in a tone of sincere incredulity, "But I just can't believe that there's someone so evil that he'd write this sort of letter about a man like Marcello."

"Well, not everyone loves him like we do, Mamma," said Giulia.

"But who?" asked her mother emphatically. "Who couldn't love our Marcello?"

"You know what Mamma says about you?" asked Giulia, who now seemed restored to her usual gaiety and volubility. "That you're not a man, but an angel. So that one of these days, you never know, instead of coming into our apartment through the door . . . you'll come in through the window, flying." She suppressed a laugh and and added, "That should please the priest when you go to confess, finding out you're an angel. That's not something he does every day, I bet, listening to the confession of an angel."

"Now she's making fun of me, as usual," said her mother, "but I'm not exaggerating at all. For me Marcello *is* an angel." She

gazed at Marcello with intense, saccharine tenderness and immediately her eyes filled visibly with tears. After a moment she added,
"I've only known one man in my life who was as good as Marcello
. . . and that was your father, Giulia."

This time Giulia became serious, as was suitable to the subject, and lowered her eyes to her plate. Meanwhile, her mother's
face was undergoing a gradual transformation: her eyes were overflowing with tears, while a pathetic grimace was twisting her soft,
swollen face under her tufts of disheveled hair, so that colors and
features seemed to merge and waver, as if seen through a glass
pane submerged in deep waters.

She rummaged around hastily for her handkerchief and stammered, bringing it up to her eyes, "A truly good man . . . a real
angel . . . and we were so happy together, the three of us . . . and
now he's dead and gone . . . Marcello reminds me of your father
because of his goodness, and that's why I love him so much . . .
When I think that that good, good man is dead, it just breaks my
heart." Her final words were lost in the handkerchief.

Giulia said tranquilly, "Eat, Mamma."

"No, no, I'm not hungry," sobbed her mother. "You two must
excuse me . . . You're happy and happiness shouldn't be troubled
by the sorrow of an old woman." She rose abruptly and went out
the door.

"Just think, it's been six years," said Giulia, looking after her,
"and it's as if it were always the first day."

Marcello said nothing. He had lit a cigarette and was smoking
with his head lowered. Giulia reached out and took one of his
hands in hers. "What are you thinking about?" she asked almost
pleadingly.

Giulia often asked him what he was thinking; the serious and
closed expression on his face roused her curiosity and sometimes
even alarmed her.

Marcello answered, "I was thinking about your mother. Her
compliments embarrass me. She doesn't know me well enough to
say I'm good."

Giulia squeezed his hand and said, "She's not just doing it to flatter you. Even when you're not here, she often says to me, 'How good Marcello is.'"

"But how can she know that?"

"You can just tell these things." Giulia got up and came to stand next to him, pressing her round hip against his shoulder and passing a hand through his hair. "Why? Don't you want people to think you're good?"

"That's not what I'm saying," answered Marcello. "I'm saying that maybe it isn't true."

She shook her head. "Your trouble is that you're too modest. Look: I'm not like Mamma, who wants to think everyone's good . . . For me, there are good people and bad people. Well then, as far as I'm concerned, you're one of the best people I've ever met in my life. And I'm not just saying that because we're engaged and I love you . . . I'm saying it because it's true."

"But what does this goodness consist of?"

"I told you, you can just see some things. Why do you say a woman is beautiful? Because you can see that she's beautiful . . . the same way one can see that you're good."

"That may be," said Marcello, lowering his head. The two women's conviction that he was good was not new to him, but it always disconcerted him deeply. What *did* this goodness consist of? And *was* he really good? Or was the quality Giulia and her mother called goodness actually his abnormality, that is, his detachment, his distance from ordinary life? Normal men weren't good, he thought, because normality must always be paid for at a high price, whether consciously or not, by various but always negative complicities, by insensitivity, stupidity, cowardice, even criminality.

He was roused from these reflections by Giulia's voice saying, "By the way, you know the dress has arrived. I want to show it to you . . . wait for me here."

She rushed out impetuously and Marcello rose from the table, went to the window, and opened it wide. The window looked onto the street, or rather, since it was the top-floor apartment, onto a ledge of the palazzo that jutted so far out that you could see nothing below it. But on the other side of the void, the top floor of the palazzo opposite was visible: a row of windows with their shutters flung open, through which you could see the inside of the rooms. It was an apartment very similar to Giulia's: a bedroom with what looked like unmade beds; a "good" living room with the usual fake, dark furniture; a dining room with a table around which three people were currently sitting, two men and a woman. These rooms opposite him were very close because the street was narrow, and in fact Marcello could distinctly see the three people eating together in the dining room: a stocky older man with a great white mane of hair; a younger man, thin and dark; and a mature, blond, rather opulent woman. They were eating tranquilly at a table like the one at which he himself had sat a few minutes ago, under a chandelier not much different than the one in the room he was in now. Nonetheless, even though he could see them so clearly he almost had the illusion he could hear the things they were discussing, yet they seemed incredibly distant and remote, perhaps because of the sense of abyss created by the projecting ledge. He couldn't help thinking that those rooms represented normality, were normality. He could see them; by raising his voice just a little he could even have spoken to the three people eating, yet he remained outside, in a moral as well as a physical sense. Yet for Giulia that distance and extremity did not exist; they were purely physical facts, and she was inside those rooms, had always been inside them. If he had asked her to, she would have furnished with complete indifference all the information she possessed on the people who lived there, just as she had done shortly before with the guest list for the wedding reception. It was an indifference that denoted not only familiarity, but careless familiarity. In truth she had no name for normality, since she was in it up to her eyes, the way we believe that animals, if they talked, would give no name to nature, being an integral and undivided part of it. But he remained outside, and for him normality was called normality precisely because he was excluded from it and because he felt it to be in such contrast to his own abnormality. To be like Giulia, you had to be born that way, or . . .

The door behind him opened and he turned around. Giulia stood before him in a wedding dress of white silk, holding the full veil falling from her head in both hands so that he could admire it.

She said exultantly, "Isn't it beautiful? Look!" And still holding the veil out with both hands, she turned in a circle in the space between the window and the table, so that her fiancé could admire the wedding dress from every side. It was, thought Marcello, similar in every way to any other bride's dress; but he was glad that Giulia was happy with something so common, in just the same way that millions and millions of other women had been happy before her. Her body's strikingly round and exuberant curves strained awkwardly against the shining white silk.

Suddenly she came close to Marcello and said to him, letting go of her veil and offering up her face, "Now give me a kiss. But don't touch me or the dress will get wrinkled."

At that moment Giulia turned her back to the window so that Marcello could see it. As he bent to brush her lips with his own, he saw the diner with the white hair get up and leave the room of the apartment opposite them; and immediately the other two, the thin, dark young man and the blond woman, rose almost automatically from the table and began to kiss each other. The sight pleased him; after all, he was acting like those two, from whom he had felt divided by such an unbridgeable distance shortly before.

Right then Giulia exclaimed impatiently, "To hell with the dress," and without detaching herself from Marcello, closed the shutters with one hand. Then, thrusting her whole body hard against his, she threw her arms around his neck. They kissed in the dark, hampered by the veil; and as his fiancée pressed and writhed against him, sighing and kissing him, Marcello thought once more how innocently she was acting, without perceiving the slightest contradiction between this embrace and the wedding dress she was wearing: one more proof that normal people were entitled to take the greatest liberties with normality itself.

At last they separated breathlessly and Giulia murmured, "We musn't be impatient . . . Another day or two and you can even kiss me in the street."

"I have to go," he said, wiping his mouth with his handkerchief. "I'll see you out."

They left the dining room in the dark and passed into the hall.

"We'll see each other tonight after dinner," said Giulia.

Tender and softened, she leaned against the doorjamb and watched him from the threshold. The veil on her head had been mussed by their kiss and now hung crookedly to one side. Marcello went up to her and put it back in place, saying, "That's better."

At the same time they heard the sound of voices on the landing of the floor below. Giulia drew back in embarrassment, flung him a kiss with the tips of her fingers, and hurriedly closed the door.

3

*T*HE IDEA OF CONFESSION worried Marcello. He was not
religious in practice and did not participate in any formal
rites; nor was he sure that he had any natural religious inclinations. Nonetheless, he would have considered Don Lattanzi's
request for confession quite willingly, as one of the many conventional acts he must undertake in order to anchor himself definitively in normality, if such a confession had not involved the
revelation of two things that, for different reasons, he felt himself
unable to confess: the tragedy of his childhood and the mission in
Paris. He intuited dimly that a subtle link united these two things,
though it would have been hard for him to say clearly what made
up this link. He also realized that among the many available
norms, he had not chosen the Christian one, which forbids
killing, but another completely different, political, and recent
one, which did not shrink from bloodshed. He did not trust the
power of the Church, with its hundreds of popes, its innumerable
churches, its saints and martyrs, to restore him to that communion

with humankind from which the matter of Lino had barred him; he attributed that power instead to the fat minister whose mouth was smeared with lipstick, to his cynical secretary, to his superiors in the Secret Service. Marcello intuited all this obscurely rather than thinking about it; and his melancholy increased, as in someone who sees only one way out, all the others being closed, and who does not like the way left open to him.

But he needed to make a decision, he thought, as he climbed on the trolley car going to Santa Maria Maggiore; he needed to choose whether to make a complete confession, according to the rules of the Church, or to limit himself to a partial confession just to please Giulia. Although he neither practiced nor believed, he was drawn to the first alternative, almost hoping that through confession he might not change his own destiny, but at least conform to it more fully. As the trolley rolled forward, he wrestled with this problem in his usual pedantic and rather dully serious manner. As far as Lino was concerned, he felt more or less tranquil: he would be able to tell it all as it had actually happened and the priest, after the customary examination and advice, could not refuse to absolve him. But the mission, which, as he knew, involved the deceit, betrayal, and ultimately perhaps even the death of a man, was a completely different matter. With the mission, it was not just a question of obtaining approval, but of talking about it at all. He was not at all sure he could do it, since talking about it would mean abandoning one standard for another, submitting to Christian judgment something he had till now considered completely independent of it. He would be betraying an implicit promise of silence and secrecy, putting the whole laborious edifice of his insertion into normality at risk. But it was still worth trying, he thought, if only to convince himself one more time, by means of a definitive test, of the solidity of that edifice.

Yet he was aware of considering these alternatives without much emotion, with the cold and passive mind, almost, of a spectator; as if in reality he had already made his choice and foreseen everything that was to happen in the future, though he knew not how or when. He was so far from harboring any doubt that as he entered the vast church, its cool, shadowy silence truly consoling after the light, noise, and heat of the street, he actually forgot about the confession and began to wander around the deserted stone floor from one nave to another, just like any idle tourist. He had always liked churches; they were points of security in a fluctuating world. In other times these structures, built with such specific intent, had given massive, splendid expression to what he was seeking: an order, a standard, a rule. The truth is, he often found himself wandering into one of the many churches in Rome and sitting down in a pew without praying, to contemplate something he thought he might have done if only conditions had been different. What seduced him in the churches were not the solutions they offered, which he could not possibly accept, so much as a result he could not help but admire and appreciate. He liked all churches, but the more imposing and magnificent, that is, the more profane they were, the better he liked them. In these kinds of churches, in which religion had evaporated into a majestic and ordered worldliness, he seemed almost to be able to see the transition point between a naive religious faith and a society that had grown into adulthood, but which still owed its very existence to that ancient faith.

At that hour the church was deserted. Marcello approached the altar and then, standing near one of the columns in the right-hand nave, looked down the whole length of the floor, trying to abolish the sense of height and gaze, as it were, from ground level. How vast the floor was, seen from that perspective, the way an ant might see it, almost like a great plain; it made him dizzy. Then he raised his eyes, and his gaze, following the faint gleam that the dim light cast on the convex surfaces of the enormous marble shafts, traveling from column to column until it reached the front door. At that moment someone came in, lifting the heavy quilt in the doorway in a splinter of crude white light: how small the figure of the believer was, standing there at the threshold down at the bottom of the church. Marcello walked behind the altar and looked at the mosaics in the apse. The figure of the Christ between four saints caught his attention: whoever had depicted him that way, thought Marcello, had certainly nurtured no doubt about what was normal and what was abnormal. He lowered his head, starting off slowly in the direction of the confessional in the right-hand nave. He was thinking, now, that it was useless to regret not having been born in other times and under other conditions; he was what he was precisely because his times and conditions were no longer those that had encouraged the building of that church, and it was in the awareness of this reality that his entire task lay.

He approached the confessional, made of dark, carved wood and enormous in proportion to the basilica, and was in time to glimpse the priest seated inside it close the curtain and sequester himself; but he was unable see his face.

Before kneeling, he hitched his pants up over the knees so they wouldn't wrinkle, a habitual gesture; then he said in a low voice, "I would like to confess."

From the other side the voice of the priest, low-pitched but frank and brusque, replied that he could do so and said no more. It was the deep, large, sing-song voice of a mature man with a strong accent of southern Italy. In spite of himself, Marcello conjured up the figure of a monk with a black beard, thick eyebrows, a massive nose, and ears and nostrils full of hair. A man, he thought, made of the same dense, heavy material as the confessional, without suspicions and without subtleties. The priest, as he had expected, asked him how long it had been since he had last confessed, and he replied that he had never confessed except as a child and that he was doing so now because he was about to get married.

The priest's voice, after a moment of silence, said from the other side of the grate somewhat indifferently, "You've done something very wrong, my son. How old are you?"

"Thirty," said Marcello.

"You've lived in sin for thirty years," said the priest, in the tone of an accountant announcing a debit on the balance sheet. He continued after a moment, "Thirty years you've lived like a beast and not like a human being."

Marcello bit his lips. Now he realized that the confessor's authority, expressed by his brusque and familiar way of judging the case even before knowing its details, was unacceptable and irritating to him. Not that he disliked the priest, probably a good man who carried out his office conscientiously, nor that he disliked the place or the rite; but as opposed to government offices, where he disliked everything but where the authority seemed to him obvious and incontestable, here he felt an instinctive desire to rebel.

However, he said with an effort, "I've committed all the sins . . . even the gravest."

"All of them?"

He thought, "Now I'll tell him I've killed and I want to see how it affects me to say it." He hesitated and then by pushing himself slightly to do so, managed to say in a clear, firm voice, "Yes, I've even killed a man."

Right away the priest exclaimed keenly, but without any indignation or surprise, "You've killed a man and you haven't felt the need to confess."

Marcello thought that that was precisely what the priest should have said: no horror, no amazement, only an official displeasure for not having confessed such a serious sin sooner. And he was grateful to the priest, as he would be grateful to a captain of police faced with this same confession, who arrested him swiftly without wasting his time in comments. Everyone, he thought, had to play their part and only in this way could the world endure. Meanwhile, however, he realized once more that he felt no particular emotion at revealing his tragedy; and he marveled at his own indifference, in such contrast to the profoundly disturbed reaction he had experienced when Giulia's mother announced that she had received the anonymous letter.

He said in a calm voice, "I killed when I was thirteen years old . . . and to defend myself and almost without wanting to . . ."

"Tell me how it was."

He shifted position a little on his stiffening knees and began: "One morning when I got out of school, a man approached me on some pretext. At that time I wanted very badly to own a pistol . . .

not a toy one but a real gun. By promising me that he would give me the pistol, he managed to get me to climb into his car . . . He was some foreign woman's chauffeur and he had the car for his own use all day because the owner had gone off on a trip. At that time I was totally ignorant and when he made certain proposals to me, I didn't even understand what he was talking about."

"What kind of proposals?"

"Sexual proposals," said Marcello soberly. "I didn't know what physical love was, either normal or abnormal . . . so I got in, and he took me to his employer's villa."

"And what happened there?"

"Nothing or almost nothing. First he tried something, but then he regretted it and made me promise not to pay any attention to him anymore, even if he invited me to get into his car again."

"What do you mean by 'almost nothing'? Did he kiss you?"

"No," said Marcello, a little surprised. "He just put his arm around my waist for a minute, in the hallway."

"Go ahead."

"He knew ahead of time, though, that he wouldn't be able to forget me. And in fact, the next day he was waiting again outside the school. This time, too, he said he would give me the gun, and since I wanted it so badly, first I made him beg me a little and then I accepted and got in the car."

"And where did you go?"

"The same place as the other time, to the villa, in his bedroom . . ."

"And this time how did he act?"

"He was completely changed," said Marcello. "He seemed to be out of his mind . . . He told me he wouldn't give me the gun and that for better or worse I was going to have to do what he wanted. While he was saying these things he was holding the gun in his hand . . . Then he grabbed me by the arm and threw me on the bed, making me hit my head against the wall. Meanwhile, the gun had fallen onto the bed and he was kneeling in front of me hugging my legs . . . I picked up the pistol, got up from the bed, and took a few steps backward, and then he threw out his arms and shouted, 'Kill me, kill me like a dog . . .' So I . . . it was almost like I was obeying him . . . I shot him and he fell down on the bed. This all happened many years ago. Recently I went to look up the newspapers of the time and found out that the man died the same night, at the hospital."

Marcello had not rushed through his story; he had chosen his words with care and uttered them with precision. As he talked he was aware that he felt nothing, as always; nothing but that sense of cold, distant sorrow that he always felt, whatever he did or said.

The priest asked immediately, without commenting on the story in any way, "Are you sure you told the whole truth?"

"Yes, of course," replied Marcello, surprised.

"You know," continued the priest, suddenly agitated, "that by hiding or bending the truth or even a part of it, you render your confession invalid and commit a grave sacrilege besides. What really happened between you and that man, the second time?"

"But . . . what I told you."

"There was no carnal relationship between you? He didn't use you with violence?"

So, Marcello couldn't help thinking, the murder was less important than the sin of sodomy. He confirmed, "No, there was nothing more than what I told you."

"One might think," continued the priest inflexibly, "that you killed the man to revenge yourself for something he had done to you."

"He did absolutely nothing to me."

There was a brief silence, full of what Marcello perceived as poorly dissimulated incredulity.

"And so," asked the priest suddenly in a wholly unexpected manner, "have you ever had sexual relationships with men after that?"

"No, my sexual life has been and still is perfectly normal."

"What do you mean by a normal sexual life?"

"That as far as that goes, I'm a man like all the others . . . I knew a woman for the first time in a whorehouse when I was seventeen, and after that I've only had sex with women."

"And you call that a normal sexual life?"

"Yes, why?"

"Because that's abnormal, too," said the priest triumphantly, "that's a sin, too . . . Hasn't anyone ever told you, poor boy? What's normal is to get married and have sexual intercourse with your own wife in order to bring children into the world."

"That's what I'm about to do," said Marcello.

"Good, but it's not enough. You can't approach the altar with blood on your hands."

"Finally," Marcello couldn't help thinking. For a moment he had almost believed that the priest had forgotten the principal object of the confession. He said as humbly as he could, "Tell me what I should do."

"You must repent," said the priest. "Only by sincere and profound repentance can you expiate the wrong you've done."

"I have repented," said Marcello thoughtfully. "If repentance means wishing with all my heart I had never done certain things, I've repented for sure." He would like to have added, "But this repentance was not enough . . . It couldn't have been enough," but he held himself back.

The priest said hastily, "My duty is to warn you that if what you're saying now isn't true, my absolution is worthless. Do you know what awaits you if you're deceiving me?"

"What?"

"Damnation."

The priest uttered this word with particular satisfaction. Marcello searched his imagination for what the word conjured up and found nothing, not even the ancient image of the flames of hell. But at the same time he felt that the word meant more than the priest had intended by it. He shivered painfully, almost as if he understood that damnation existed, whether he repented or not, and that it was not within the priest's power to free him from it.

"I have truly repented," he repeated bitterly.

"And you have nothing else to tell me?"

Marcello remained silent for an instant before responding. Now, he realized, the moment had come for him to speak of his mission, which, as he knew, involved actions not only open to condemnation but condemned already by Christian law. He had foreseen this moment and had rightly attributed the maximum importance to his own ability to reveal the mission. Then, with a calm, sad sense of preordained discovery, he realized as soon as he opened his mouth to speak that something would not let him go forward. It was neither moral disgust, nor shame, nor any other manifestation of guilt, but something very different that had nothing to do with guilt. It was an absolute inhibition, dictated by a profound complicity and loyalty. He was not to speak of the mission, that was all; the same conscience that had remained mute and passive when he had announced to the priest, "I have killed," now imposed this silence on him with great authority. Not yet completely convinced, he tried to speak once more, but felt that resistance bind his tongue and block his words again, as automatically as a lock clicks in when the key turns. So once again — and this time with much more evidence — the strength of the authority represented at the ministry by the despicable official and his no less contemptible secretary was confirmed beyond doubt. It was, like all authorities, mysterious, and seemed to plunge its roots into the very depths of his soul, while the Church, apparently so much more powerful, only reached its surface.

He said, lying for the first time, "Do I have to reveal what I told you today to my fiancée before we get married?"

"You've never told her anything about it?"

"No, it would be the first time."

"I don't see the necessity," said the priest. "You'd disturb her for no reason . . . and you'd endanger the peace of your family."

"You're right," said Marcello.

A new silence followed. Then the priest said in a conclusive tone, as if asking the final and definitive question, "And tell me, son . . . Are you now, or have you ever been, part of any subversive group or sect?"

Marcello, who had not expected this question, was struck dumb for a moment in amazement. Evidently, he thought, the priest was asking that question by orders from higher up, for the purpose of checking the political tendencies of the congregation. Still, it was significant that he had asked it. He was asking Marcello, who had formally approached the rites of the Church, as external ceremonies of a society he wished to join, not to set himself against that society. This, rather than that he not set himself against himself.

He would have liked to reply, "No, I'm part of an organization that hunts down subversives." But he repressed this malicious temptation and said simply, "To tell the truth, I'm an employee of the state."

This response must have pleased the priest, because after a brief pause, he went on placidly, "Now you must promise me that you'll pray. But you musn't just pray for a few days or a few months or a few years, but all your life. You'll pray for your soul and for the soul of that man . . . and you'll make your wife pray, and your children if you have them . . . Only prayer can attract the attention of God to you and bring down His mercy on you . . . do you understand? And now collect yourself and pray with me."

Marcello lowered his face mechanically and heard, from the other side of the grate, the low, hurried voice of the priest reciting a prayer in Latin. Then in a louder voice but still in Latin, the priest pronounced the formula of absolution; and Marcello rose up from the confessional.

But as he was passing in front of it, the curtain opened and the priest motioned him to stop. Marcello was amazed to see that he was similar in every way to how he had imagined him: heavy, bald, with a large, round forehead, thick eyebrows, round brown eyes, serious but not intelligent, a thick, fleshy mouth. A country priest, he thought, a begging friar. Meanwhile, the priest was silently handing him a thin booklet with a colored image on the cover: the life of Saint Ignatius of Loyola, for the use of Catholic youth.

"Thank you," said Marcello, examining the booklet.

The priest made another gesture as if to say, "It was nothing," and drew the curtain shut. Marcello headed toward the entrance.

But as he was on the point of leaving, his glance embraced the entire church with its rows of columns, its paneled ceiling, its deserted floors and altar; and it seemed to him that he was saying farewell forever to the ancient and outlived image of a world he desired but now knew was no longer accessible. A kind of reverse mirage erected in an unrecoverable past, from which his own footsteps carried him steadily further away.

Then he lifted the quilt and walked out into the strong light of the cloudless sky, into the piazza echoing with the loud clanging of trolleys, against the vulgar background of anonymous palazzi and commercial shops.

4

WHEN MARCELLO GOT OFF the bus in his mother's neighborhood, he realized almost immediately that a man was following him at a slight distance. As he walked unhurriedly beside the garden walls, down the deserted street, he glanced at him out of the corner of his eye. He was a man of middle stature, a little heavyset, with a square face whose expression, although honest and good-natured, was not without a certain sly craftiness, as is often true of country people. He was wearing a light suit of a faded color somewhere between brown and purple and a light gray hat pulled down well on his head, but with the brim pushed up in front in the peasant style. If he had seen him in the piazza of a village on market day, Marcello would have taken him for a farmer. The man had been on the same bus as Marcello, had gotten off at the same stop, and was now following him along the opposite sidewalk without bothering much to hide it, adjusting his pace to Marcello's and never taking his eyes off him. But the man's fixed gaze was uncertain, as if he were not entirely sure of Marcello's identity and wished to study him in person before approaching him.

So they walked up the sloping street together like this, in the silence and heat of the early afternoon hours. Behind the bars of the closed gates there was no one to be seen in the gardens, just as there was no one to be seen for the entire length of the street, under the green tunnel formed by the clustered crowns of the pepper trees. This solitude and silence, such favorable conditions for a surprise attack, finally made Marcello suspicious; they might not have been chosen by chance by his pursuer. Abruptly, with instant decision, he stepped down from the sidewalk and crossed the street, moving toward the man.

"Were you looking for me?" he asked, when they found themselves a few steps away from each other.

The man had also stopped; at Marcello's question he looked almost frightened and said in a low voice, "Excuse me, but I only followed you because we might both be going to the same place . . . otherwise I would never have dreamed of it. Excuse me, aren't you Dottore Clerici?"

"Yes, I am," said Marcello. "And who are you?"

"Secret Service agent Orlando," said the man, giving a little, quasi-military salute, "Colonel Baudino sent me. He gave me both your addresses . . . of the *pensione* where you live and this one. Since I didn't find you at the *pensione*, I came to look for you here, and by a coincidence you were on the same bus . . . It's an urgent matter we're dealing with."

"Please come with me," said Marcello, heading without another word toward the gate of his mother's house. He dug the key out of his pocket, opened the gate, and invited the man to enter. The agent obeyed, removing his hat respectfully and uncovering a completely round head with sparse black hairs and, in the center of them, a circular white bald patch that resembled a tonsure. Marcello preceded him up the pathway and headed toward the end of the garden, where he knew there were two iron chairs and a table set under the pergola. As he walked in front of the agent he couldn't help but notice the wild, neglected character of the garden once again. The clean white gravel he had loved to run up and down on as a child had vanished years ago, ground under or dispersed; the pathway, which had been taken over by weeds, was revealed mostly by the two small myrtle hedges, misshapen and broken in places but still recognizable. On the two sides of the hedges, the flower beds were also covered with rampant field weeds; the rosebushes and other flowering plants had given way to prickly shrubs and hopelessly tangled brambles. Here and there in the shade of the trees, you could see piles of trash, broken-down packing crates, smashed bottles, and other similarly unappealing objects usually confined to the attic. Disgusted, he averted his gaze from the mess, asking himself yet one more time in sincere astonishment, "Why don't they clean it up? Why don't they put it back in order? It would take so little! Why?"

Farther on, the path ran between the wall of the villa and the wall of the garden — that same wall covered with ivy across which he used to talk with his neighbor Roberto when he was a child. He preceded the agent under the pergola and sat down in one of the iron chairs, inviting his guest to sit also. But the agent continued to stand respectfully.

"Signor Dottore," he said hurriedly, "It's a small thing we're talking about — I'm charged to tell you on behalf of the colonel that on the way to Paris you're to stop at S.," and the agent named a city not far from the border, "and look for Signor Gabrio, at Number 3, Via dei Glicini."

"A change of program," thought Marcello. It was characteristic of the Secret Service, as he knew, to change its instructions at the last moment on purpose, the better to disperse responsibility and cover its tracks.

"So, what's in Via dei Glicini?" he couldn't help asking, "a private apartment?"

"Actually not, Dottore," said the agent with a broad, half-embarrassed, half-sly smile. "There's a whorehouse there. The madame's name is Enrichetta Parodi, but ask for Signor Gabrio. The house, like all those houses, is open till midnight — but it would be better, Dottore, if you went early in the morning . . . when no one's around . . . I'll be there, too." The agent fell silent for a moment and then, unable to interpret Marcello's completely inexpressive face, added in embarrassment, "It's to be more secure, Dottore."

Marcello, without saying a word, raised his eyes toward the agent and considered him for a moment. It was time to take his leave of him, but he wanted — he couldn't have said why, maybe because of the honest, familiar expression of the broad, square face — to add some unofficial sentence or two, as a show of friendly feeling on his part. Finally he asked, at random, "How long have you been in the service, Orlando?"

"Since 1925, Dottore."

"Always in Italy?"

"Better say almost never, Dottore," answered the agent with a sigh, obviously eager to be on familiar terms. "Eh, Dottore, if I told you what my life has been and what I've gone through . . . always on the go — Turkey, France, Germany, Kenya, Tunisia . . . never a moment's rest." He fell silent for a moment and stared at Marcello fixedly; then, with rhetorical yet absolutely sincere emphasis, added, "Anything for the family and homeland, Dottore."

Marcello raised his eyes and looked again at the agent, who was standing very straight, hat in hand, almost at attention. Then, with a gesture of dismissal, he said, "All right, then, Orlando. Go ahead and tell the colonel that I'll stop at S., as he wishes."

"Yes, Signor Dottore." The agent saluted him and walked away, alongside the wall of the villa.

Left alone, Marcello stared into the empty air in front of him. It was hot under the pergola and the sun, filtering through the leaves and branches of the creeper, spangled his face with medallions of dazzling light. The little table of enameled iron, once spotless, was now a dirty white, stained black in many places and peeling in rusty strips. Beyond the pergola, he could see the tract of wall where the door in the ivy used to be, the opening through which he used to communicate with Roberto. The ivy was still there, and perhaps it would still be possible to look into the adjacent garden, but Roberto's family no longer lived in the villa; there was a dentist there now who used it as his office. A lizard suddenly

scampered down from the trunk of the creeper and walked fearlessly onto the table. It was a big lizard of the most common kind,
with a green back and a white belly that throbbed against the yellowed enamel of the table. It approached Marcello rapidly with
little, darting steps and then halted, its sharp head lifted toward
him, its tiny black eyes staring. Marcello looked at it with affection
and remained still for fear of frightening it. He remembered
when, as a boy, he had killed the lizards and then, to free himself
from remorse, had searched in vain for complicity and solidarity
from timid Roberto. But at the time he had not been able to find
anyone who could lighten the burden of his guilt. He had been
left alone to face the death of the lizards, and in this solitude he
had recognized the clue to the crime. But now, he thought, he
was not and would never again be alone. Even if he committed a
crime — as long as he committed it for certain ends — the state;
the political, social, and military organizations that depended on
the state; great masses of people that thought as he did; and, outside of Italy, other states and other millions of people would stand
behind him. What he was about to do, he reflected, was certainly
much worse than killing a few lizards; just the same, so many
people were with him — to begin with, agent Orlando, a good
man, married, father of five.

"For the family and homeland": this phrase, innocent despite
the emphasis, similar to a beautiful banner of bright colors un-
furling on a sunny day in a playful breeze while the fanfare re-
sounds and the soldiers pass by, this phrase echoed in his ear,
stirring and melancholy, a mixture of hope and sorrow. "For the
family and homeland," he thought, "is enough for Orlando . . .
why shouldn't it be enough for me?"

He heard the sound of an engine in the garden near the entrance and rose immediately, with an abrupt movement that made
the lizard run off. Without hurrying, he left the pergola and began
to walk toward the entrance. An old black automobile was parked
in the driveway, not far from the still-open gate. The driver,
dressed in white livery with blue braiding, was just closing it, but
when he saw Marcello he stopped and took off his cap.

"Alberi," said Marcello in his quietest voice, "today we're going to the clinic, don't bother to put the car back in the garage."

"Yes, Signor Marcello," replied the chauffeur. Marcello looked at him askance. Alberi was a young man with an olive complexion and eyes as black as coal, their whites the shining white of porcelain. He had very regular features, clenched white teeth, and black, carefully pomaded hair. Although not tall, he gave one a sense of great proportion, perhaps because of his very small hands and feet. He was Marcello's age but appeared older, due, perhaps, to the Oriental languor expressed in his every feature, a languor destined, it seemed, to turn to fat with the passage of time. Marcello looked at him again, as he closed the gate, with profound aversion; then he set off toward the villa.

He opened the French doors and walked into the living room, which was almost in darkness. He was immediately assailed by the stench that fouled the air, still faint in comparison to the other rooms in which his mother's ten Pekinese dogs wandered freely, but all the more noticeable here where they were rarely allowed. Opening the window, he saw for a moment, in the pale light he had let in, the furniture draped in its gray dustcovers, the carpets rolled and perched upright in the corners, the piano muffled in sheets held in place by pins. He crossed the living room and dining room, passed through the hallway, and started up the stairs. Halfway up on a marble step (the threadbare carpet had disappeared some time ago and had never been replaced) there was a mound of dog turds and he circled around it so as not to step in it.

When he reached the landing, he went to the door of his mother's bedroom and opened it. Before he had even had time to open it completely all ten Pekinese, like a long-contained flood suddenly spilling over, launched themselves between his legs and scattered in a flurry of barking throughout the hallway and down the stairs. Uncertain and annoyed, he watched them run away, graceful creatures with their plumed tails and sullen, almost cat-like faces. Then, from the bedroom immersed in shadow, he heard the voice of his mother.

"Is that you, Marcello?"

"Yes, Mamma, it's me . . . but these dogs?"

"Let them go, poor saints . . . they've been shut in all morning . . . let them go where they want."

Marcello frowned to signal his displeasure and went in. At once he felt that he could not breathe the air in that bedroom. The closed windows had contained the mingled odors of the night — the different smells of sleep, dogs, and perfume — and the heat of the sun burning behind the shutters seemed already to have fermented and soured the air. Rigid, wary, almost as if he feared by moving to dirty himself or be contaminated by those smells, he went to the bed and sat down on its edge, his hands on his knees.

Now, slowly, as his eyes adjusted to the half-light, he could see the whole bedroom. Beneath the window, in the diffuse light coming from the long, stained, yellowed curtains, which seemed to be made of the same limp material as the many pieces of underwear strewn around the room, a number of aluminum plates full of dog food were lined up in a row. The floor was littered with shoes and stockings; in a dark corner near the bathroom door he caught sight of a pink bathrobe, draped over a chair where it had been thrown the night before, half on the floor, its sleeve hanging empty. His cold glance, full of disgust, turned from the room to the bed where his mother lay. As usual, she had not thought to cover herself at his entrance and was partly naked. Stretched out, her arms raised and her hands joined behind her head against the backboard quilted in worn, soiled blue silk, she stared at him in silence. Under her mass of hair, spread out in two great dark wings, her face appeared thin and pinched, almost triangular, devoured by eyes enlarged and darkened by shadow so as to appear almost deathlike. She was wearing a transparent, light green slip that barely covered the top of her thighs; and again, this made him think, not of the mature woman she was, but of an aged and withered little girl. Her scrawny upper chest showed like a rack of small, sharp bones; behind their veil, her flattened breasts were revealed by two dark, round stains on an absolutely flat surface. But her thighs, above all, roused both repugnance and pity in Marcello: skinny and meager, they were those of a child of twelve who has not yet grown into her woman's curves. His mother's age showed in certain softened stretchmarks on her skin and in her coloring: a chilly, nervous white stained by mysterious bruises, some of them bluish, others livid.

"Blows," he thought, "or bites, from Alberi."

But beneath the knee her legs appeared perfect, with tiny feet and straight, narrow toes.

Marcello would have preferred not to let his mother see his displeasure, but once more he could not hold himself back. "How many times have I told you not to receive me like this, half-naked," he said in annoyance, without looking at her.

She replied, impatiently but without rancor, "Oh, what an austere son I have," pulling an edge of the cover up over her body. Her voice was hoarse, and this, too, was unpleasant to Marcello. He remembered hearing it, in his childhood, as sweet and pure as a song; the hoarseness was the effect of alcohol and abuse.

He said, after a moment, "So, today we go to the clinic."

"Let's go, then," said his mother, pulling herself up and looking for something behind the headboard of the bed, "though I don't feel well and our visit will mean absolutely nothing to him, poor thing."

"He's still your husband and my father," said Marcello, taking his head in his hands and looking at the floor.

"Yes, he surely is," she said. Now she had found the light switch and turned it on. On the bedside table the lamp, which seemed to Marcello to be enveloped in a woman's blouse, gave out a faint illumination.

"But even so," she continued, sitting up in bed and putting her feet on the floor, "I'll tell you the truth, sometimes I wish he would die . . . especially since he wouldn't even be aware of it. And I wouldn't have to spend anymore money on the clinic . . . I have so little. Just think," she added, in sudden complaint, "just *think*, I may have to give up the car."

"So, what's wrong with that?"

"A lot," she said, with childish resentment and impudence. "The way things are, with the car, I have an excuse to hire Alberi and see him whenever I want. Afterward, I won't have the excuse anymore."

"Mamma, don't talk to me about your lovers," said Marcello calmly, digging the nails of one hand into the palm of the other.

"My lovers . . . he's the only one I have. If you're going to talk to me about that hen of a fiancée, surely I have the right to talk about him, poor dear, who's so much nicer and more intelligent than she is."

Strangely, these insults to his fiancée, spoken by his mother who could not abide Giulia, did not offend Marcello. "Yes, it's true," he thought, "it may even be that she resembles a hen — but I like her the way she is." He said, in a gentler tone, "All right, will you get dressed? If we want to go to the clinic, it's time to get moving."

"Of course, right away." Light, almost a shadow, she crossed the room on tiptoes, grabbed the pink robe from the chair in passing and, throwing it around her shoulders, opened the bathroom door and disappeared.

Immediately, as soon as his mother had gone, Marcello went to the window and threw it open. Outside the air was hot and still, but he still felt an acute relief, as if he were looking out, not onto the stifled garden, but onto an iceberg. At the same time, it almost seemed to him that he could feel the movement of the inside air in back of him, heavy with perfumes gone sour and the stink of animals, as it flowed gradually and slowly out through the window, dissolved into space — as if the air itself were vomiting forth from the jaws of the fouled house. For a long moment he stayed there, his eyes lowered to gaze at the thick foliage of the wisteria whose branches circled the window; then he turned back toward the room. Once again he was struck by its disorder and sloppy shabbiness; this time, however, he was inspired more by sorrow than disgust. He seemed suddenly to remember his mother as she had been in her youth, and experienced a vivid, heartfelt sensation of dismayed rebellion against the decadence and corruption that had changed her from the young girl she had been to the woman she was. Something incomprehensible, something irreparable was surely at the source of this transformation: not age or passion or financial ruin or lack of intelligence, and not any other precise reason — something he felt without being able to explain it and that seemed to him to be all of a piece with that life; indeed, something that had been, at one time, her best quality and which had later become, by some mysterious transmutation, her fatal flaw. He withdrew from the window and approached the chest of drawers, on which, perched among the many knickknacks, there was a photograph of his mother as a young woman. Looking at that delicate face, those innocent eyes, that sweet mouth, he asked himself with horror why she was not still as she had been. With this question, his disgust for every form of corruption and decadence resurfaced, rendered even more unbearable by a bitter feeling of remorse and filial sorrow: maybe it was his fault that his mother was reduced to such a state, maybe if he had loved her more or in a different way, she would not have fallen into such squalid and irremediable abandon. He noted that at this thought his eyes had filled with tears, so that the photo now appeared all cloudy, and he shook his head hard. At the same moment, the door to the bathroom opened and his mother, in her robe, appeared on the threshold. Immediately she threw up her arm to cover her eyes, exclaiming, "Shut it! Shut that window! How can you stand all this light?"

Marcello went over swiftly to lower the shutter; then he approached his mother and, taking her by the arm, made her sit next to him on the edge of the bed and asked her gently, "And you, Mamma, how can you stand all this mess?"

She looked at him, unsure and embarrassed. "I don't know how it happens . . . I know everytime I use something I should put it back in its place . . . but somehow I never manage to remember."

"Mamma," said Marcello suddenly, "every age has its way of being decorous . . . Mamma, why have you let yourself go this way?"

He was holding one of her hands; in the other hand she was holding a cane up in the air, from which a dress was hanging. For a moment he seemed to glimpse in those enormous and childishly miserable eyes a sentiment of almost self-aware sorrow; his mother's lips, in fact, began to tremble slightly.

Then, suddenly, a spiteful expression drove out all other emotion and she exclaimed, "You don't like anything I am or anything I do, I know . . . You can't stand my dogs, my clothes, my habits . . . but I'm still young, my dear, and I want to enjoy life in my own way. Now leave me alone," she concluded, withdrawing her hand abruptly, "or I'll never get dressed."

Marcello said nothing. His mother went to a corner of the bedroom, shrugged her robe off onto the floor, then opened the closet and pulled on a dress in front of the closet-door mirror. Clothed, the excessive thinness of her sharp hips, hollow shoulders, and nonexistent breasts revealed itself even more clearly. She looked at herself for a moment in the mirror, smoothing her hair with one hand; then, hopping a little, she slipped on two of the many shoes scattered all over the floor.

"Now let's go," she said, taking her purse from the bureau and heading toward the door.

"Aren't you going to put a hat on?"

"Why? There's no need to."

They started down the stairs.

His mother said, "You haven't talked to me about your wedding."

"I'm getting married the day after tomorrow."

"And where are you going for your honeymoon?"

"To Paris."

"The traditional honeymoon trip," said his mother. When they had reached the vestibule, she went to the kitchen door and warned the cook, "Matilde, don't forget now . . . Let the dogs back in the house before dark."

They went out into the garden. The car was there, black and opaque, parked in the driveway behind the trees.

His mother said, "So it's decided, you don't want to come stay here with me. Even though I don't like your wife, I would have made the sacrifice . . . and then I have so much room."

"No, Mamma," replied Marcello.

"You prefer to live with your mother-in-law," she said lightly, "in that horrible apartment: four rooms and a kitchen."

She bent down to pick up a blade of grass, but swayed and

would have fallen if Marcello, ever ready, had not supported her, taking her by the arm. Under his fingers he felt the meager, soft flesh of her arm, which seemed to move around the bone like a rag tied around a stick, and once again he felt compassion for her. They got into the car; Alberi held the door open, with his cap in his hand. Then Alberi climbed into his own place behind the wheel and drove the car out of the gate.

Marcello took advantage of the moment when Alberi got out again to shut the gate behind them to say to his mother, "I'd come stay with you gladly, if you fired Alberi and put a little bit of order in your life . . . and if you quit those injections."

She looked at him askance with uncomprehending eyes. But a shiver ran from her pointed nose down to her little, withered mouth, where it turned into a faint, distraught smile.

"You know what the doctor says? That one of these days I could die from them."

"Then why don't you quit?"

"You tell me why I should quit."

Alberi got back into the car, adjusting his sunglasses on his nose. Marcello's mother leaned forward and put a hand on the chauffeur's shoulder. It was a thin, transparent hand, with the skin stretched over the tendons and stained with red and bluish splotches, and scarlet nails so dark they were almost black. Marcello would have preferred not to look, but couldn't help himself. He saw the hand move across the man's shoulder to tickle his ear with a light caress.

His mother said, "Now we're going to the clinic."

"Very good, Signora," said Alberi, without turning around.

She closed the dividing glass and threw herself back on the cushions while the car rolled gently forward. As she fell back on the seat, she looked askance at her son and said, to Marcello's surprise, since he had not expected such intuition from her, "You're angry because I caressed Alberi, aren't you?"

As she said it, she looked at him with her childish, desperate, and slightly feverish smile. Marcello couldn't manage to modify the expression of disgust on his face.

"I'm not angry," he answered. "I would have preferred not to see it."

She said, without looking at him, "You can't understand what it means to a woman not to be young anymore . . . It's worse than death."

Marcello said nothing. Now the car was rolling silently under the pepper trees, whose feathery branches brushed against the window glass.

His mother added after a moment, "Sometimes I wish I were already old. I'd be a thin, clean old woman." She smiled happily, already distracted by this fantasy. "I'd be like a dried flower pressed between the pages of a book." She put a hand on Marcello's arm and asked, "Wouldn't you prefer to have an old woman like that for a mother, well-seasoned, well-preserved, as if she were in mothballs?"

Marcello stared at her and answered in embarrassment, "Someday you'll be like that."

She became serious and said, looking up at him under her lashes and smiling miserably, "Do you really believe that? I don't. I'm convinced that one of these mornings you'll find me dead in that room you detest so much."

"Why, Mamma?" asked Marcello; but he realized that his mother was speaking seriously and that she might even be right. "You're young and you have to live."

"That doesn't mean I won't die soon — I know, they read it to me in my horoscope." Suddenly she stuck her hand out in front of his eyes and added, without any transition, "Do you like this ring?"

It was a big ring with an elaborately worked bezel and a hard stone of a milky color.

"Yes," said Marcello, barely glancing at it, "it's pretty."

"You know," said his mother, changing the subject again, "sometimes I think you got everything from your father. When he could still reason, he didn't like anything, either . . . Beautiful things didn't mean a thing to him. All he thought about was politics, like you."

This time, he wasn't sure why, Marcello couldn't repress his vivid irritation.

"It seems to me," he said, "that there's nothing in common between my father and me. I am a perfectly reasonable, normal person . . . He, on the other hand, even before he was in the clinic — as far as I recall, and you've always confirmed it — was always . . . how shall I put it? A little overexcitable."

"Yes, but you do share something in common. Neither of you enjoy life and you don't want anyone else to enjoy it, either . . ." She looked out the window a moment and then added suddenly, "I'm not coming to your wedding. You shouldn't feel offended, you know I don't go anywhere. But since you're my son, after all, I think I should give you a present . . . what would you like?"

"Nothing, Mamma," answered Marcello indifferently.

"What a shame," said his mother coyly. "If I'd known you didn't want anything, I wouldn't have spent the money. But now I've already bought it . . . take it." She rummaged around in her purse and dragged out a small white box tied with a rubberband. "It's a cigarette case . . . I've noticed you put the pack in your pocket."

She opened the box and drew out a flat, heavily lined silver case and clicked it open, offering it to her son. It was filled with Oriental cigarettes and she took the opportunity to take one of them and ask Marcello to light it.

A little embarrassed, he looked at the open cigarette case on his mother's knees without touching it and said, "It's very beautiful, I don't know how to thank you, Mamma . . . it may be too beautiful for me."

"*Uffa*," she said, "how boring you are."

She closed the case and stuck it with a graceful, willful gesture into Marcello's jacket pocket. The car turned a corner awkwardly, and she fell onto him, taking advantage of the moment to put both her hands on his shoulders and say, pulling back a little to look at him, "Give me a kiss for the present, will you?"

Marcello leaned over and brushed his lips against his mother's cheek.

She threw herself back on her seat and said with a sigh,

bringing one hand to her breast, "What heat . . . When you were little, I wouldn't have had to ask you for that kiss. You were such an affectionate child."

"Mamma," said Marcello suddenly, "do you remember the winter Babbo got sick?"

"Do I," said his mother easily. "It was a terrible winter . . . He wanted to leave me and take you away with him. He was already crazy . . . Luckily, I say luckily for you, he went mad altogether and then they could see I was right to want to keep you with me. Why?"

"Well, Mamma," said Marcello, careful to avoid looking at her, "that winter my dream was not to live with you, you and Babbo, anymore, and to be sent off to a boarding school. It didn't keep me from loving you, but . . . you see, when you say I've changed since then, you're saying something wrong. I was the same way then as I am now, and then as now I couldn't stand all the chaos and disorder . . . that's all."

He had spoken dryly and almost harshly, but regretted it almost immediately when he saw the hurt expression that darkened his mother's face. All the same, he didn't want to say anything that would sound like a retraction; he had told the truth, and unfortunately, could tell nothing but the truth. But at the same time he felt the oppression of his usual melancholy return stronger than ever, reawakened by his unpleasant awareness of having failed in filial pity.

His mother said, in a resigned tone, "Maybe you're right." The car came to a halt.

They got out and walked toward the clinic gate. The street was in a peaceful neighborhood, on the edges of an ancient ducal villa. It was a short street: on one side five or six small, old palazzi were lined up in a row, partially hidden by the trees; on the other ran the railing of the clinic grounds. At the end, the old gray wall and thick vegetation of the ducal park cut off any further vista.

Marcello had visited his father at least once a month for many years; all the same, he was not yet accustomed to these visits and felt, every time, a sense of dismay mixed with dejection. It was almost the same sensation, but even stronger, than the one inspired in him by his visits to his mother, in the villa where he had spent his childhood and adolescence: his mother's disorder and corruption seemed still reparable, but there were no remedies for his father's madness, which seemed to suggest a more general and entirely irremediable disorder and decay. He felt it this time, too, as he entered the clinic at his mother's side: a hateful uneasiness that oppressed his heart and made his legs fold at the knee. He knew he had turned pale and for a moment, just as he was glimpsing the black lances of the clinic's railing, he experienced a hysterical desire to renounce the visit and go off on some excuse. His mother, who was unaware of his turmoil, stopped in front of a small black gate, pressed the porcelain button of a doorbell, and said, "Do you know what his latest fixation is?"

"What?"

"He thinks he's one of Mussolini's ministers . . . it started up about a month ago . . . maybe because they let him read the papers."

Marcello frowned but said nothing. The gate opened and a young attendant in a white shirt appeared: heavy, tall, blond, with a shaved head and a white, rather puffy face.

"Hello, Franz," said his mother graciously. "How are things going?"

"Today we're feeling better than yesterday," said the attendant, with his own particular, harsh German accent. "Yesterday we were doing very badly."

"Very badly?"

"We had to wear the straightjacket," explained the attendant, continuing to make use of the plural, like a simpering governess when she speaks of children.

"The straightjacket . . . what a horror."

Meanwhile they had entered and were walking along the narrow path between the garden wall and the clinic wall.

"The straightjacket, you should see it . . . it's not really a shirt but more like two sleeves that hold his arms still . . . before I saw it, I thought it was a real, true nightshirt like the ones with the fret at the bottom . . . it's so sad to see him tied up that way with his arms so tight to his sides." His mother continued to talk lightly, almost gaily.

They circled around the clinic and emerged in a clearing in front of the main facade. The clinic, a white, three-story villa, looked like a normal house except for the bars that obscured the windows.

Hurriedly climbing the steps that led to the porch, the attendant said, "The professor is waiting for you, Signora Clerici." He preceded the two visitors into a bare, dark entranceway, and went to knock on a closed door above which, on an enameled nameplate, one could read: ADMINISTRATION.

The door opened right away and the director of the clinic, Professor Ermini, exploded out of it, precipitating himself, with all the impetuousness of his massive and towering bulk, toward the visitors.

"Signora, my respects . . . Dottore Clerici, good-day." His booming voice resounded like a bronze gong in the frozen silence of the clinic, between those bare walls. Marcello's mother held out a hand that the professor, bending his huge body wrapped in its white coat with visible effort, tried gallantly to kiss; Marcello, on the contrary, limited himself to a sober greeting. The professor's face very strongly resembled a barn owl's: big round eyes, great curved nose like a beak, red mustache drooping over the wide, clamorous mouth. But its expression was unlike the melancholy nightbird's; far from it, it was jovial — even if the joviality was studied and shot through with veins of cold cunning. He preceded Marcello and his mother up the stairs.

When they were halfway up the flight, a metal object hurled with great force from the landing sailed, ricocheting, down the stairs. At the same time, a piercingly sharp scream rang out, followed by scornful laughter. The professor bent down to pick up the object, an aluminum plate.

"Donegalli," he said, turning to the two visitors, "no fear . . . we're just dealing with an old woman who's usually as peaceful as she can be, except that now and then she decides to throw whatever she finds at hand . . . hah hah . . . she'd be a *bocce* champion, if we'd let her." He continued to chat as they went down a long corridor, between two rows of closed doors. "And how is it, Signora, that you're still in Rome? I thought you'd already be in the mountains or at the seaside."

"I'm leaving in a month," said his mother. "But I don't know where I'll go . . . I'd like to avoid Venice for once."

"A word of advice, Signora," said the professor, turning the corner of the corridor, "go to Ischia. I was there the other day on an outing . . . it's a marvel. We went into a certain Carminiello's restaurant and ate a fish soup that was simply a poem." The professor turned halfway and made a vulgar but expressive gesture with two fingers at the corner of his mouth. "A poem, I tell you: *tocchi* of fish this big . . . and then, a little of everything — *polpetto, scorfanello, palombetto, ostricuccia tanto buona, totanuccio,* and all with a *sughillo alla marinara* . . . garlic, oil, tomato, peperoncino . . . Signora, I say no more."

Having adopted a false, jocular Neapolitan accent to describe the fish soup, the professor now fell back into his native Roman dialect, adding, "Do you know what I said to my wife? What do you bet we get a little cottage in Ischia before the year's out?"

Marcello's mother said, "I prefer Capri."

"But that's a place for intelligentsia and homosexuals," said the professor, with a kind of distracted brutality. At that moment a heart-stopping scream reached them from one of the cells. The professor approached the door, slid open the spy-hole, looked in for a minute, closed the spy-hole again, and then, turning around, concluded, "Ischia, dear woman . . . Ischia's the place: fish soup, sea, sun, life in the open air . . . nothing beats Ischia."

The attendant Franz, who had preceded them by a few paces, was waiting for them now, standing motionless by one of the doors, his massive figure outlined in the pale light from the window at the end of the hall.

"Has he taken the medicine?" the professor asked in a low voice.

The attendant nodded in the affirmative. The professor opened the door and entered, followed by Marcello and his mother.

It was a little bare room, with a bed attached to the wall and a small table of white wood in front of the window, which was barred with the usual grating. With a thrill of revulsion, Marcello saw — seated at the table, his back to the door, intent on writing — his father. A fury of white hair stuck out from his head, above a slender neck lost in the wide collar of a stiff, striped jacket. He was sitting a little crookedly, his feet thrust into enormous felt slippers, his elbows and knees turned out, his head leaning to one side. He was just like a puppet with broken strings, thought Marcello. He did not turn around at the entrance of his three visitors; on the contrary, he seemed to redouble his zealous attention to writing.

The professor went to put himself between the window and the table and said, with false joviality, "Major, how's it going today, eh? How's it going?"

The madman did not answer but limited himself to raising a hand as if to say, "One moment, don't you see that I'm busy?"

The professor launched a glance of complicity at Marcello's mother and said, "Still those memoranda, eh, Major? But won't they be too long? Il Duce doesn't have time to read things that are too long . . . he's always brief and concise . . . brevity, concision, Major."

The madman repeated his gesture of acknowledgment, raising and agitating his bony hand; then, with the strange fury particular to him, he flung a piece of paper through the air over his inclined head. It fell down in the middle of the room and Marcello leaned over to pick it up. It contained only a few incomprehensible words written in a calligraphy full of flourishes and underlines. Maybe they weren't even words. While he was examining the piece of paper, the madman began hurling away others, always with the same, furiously busy gesture. The pieces of paper flew over his white head and scattered around the room. Gradually, as he continued to launch the paper, the madman's gestures became ever more violent until the whole room was now filled with pieces of graph paper.

Marcello's mother said, "Poor dear . . . he always did love writing."

The professor leaned a little toward the madman. "Major, here are your wife and your son. Don't you want to see them?"

At last, this time, the madman spoke, in a low, stumbling, hurried, hostile voice, just like someone who has been disturbed while doing an important job. "They should come by again tomorrow . . . that is, if they have no concrete proposals to make . . .

don't you see that I have a waiting room full of people I can't find time to see?"

"He thinks he's a minister," Marcello's mother whispered.

"Minister of Foreign Affairs," confirmed the professor.

"The Hungarian affair," said the madman suddenly in a swift, low, labored voice, continuing to write, "the Hungarian affair . . . that government chief in Prague . . . what are they doing in London? And why don't the French understand? Why don't they understand? Why? Why? Why?"

Each "why" was uttered by the madman in an ever louder voice, until, at the final "why," offered up almost in a shout, the madman leapt from the chair and turned to face his visitors. Marcello raised his eyes and looked at him. Beneath his bristling white hair, the thin, ruined face, dark and deeply scored by vertical wrinkles, appeared to assume an expression of contrite and solemn gravity, an expression almost anguished from the effort to adapt to an imaginary occasion calling for both rhetoric and ceremony. He held one of his papers at eye level, and without further comment, in a strange and breathless haste, began to read it:

"Duce, chief of heroes, king of the earth and of the sea and of the sky, prince, pope, emperor, commander, and soldier" — here the madman made a gesture of impatience, tempered however by a certain amount of formality, as if to signify, "etcetera, etcetera" — "Duce, in this place that" — the madman made a new gesture, as if to say, "I'll skip over this, these things are superfluous," then continued, "In this place I have written my memoranda, which I beg you to read from the first" — the madman stopped and stared at his visitors — "to the last line. Here are the memoranda."

After this debut, the madman threw the piece of paper into the air, turned to the desk, took up another one, and began to read the memoranda. But this time Marcello could not grasp a single word. The madman read in a clear, very loud voice, it's true, but a singular haste made him slide one word into another, as if the entire discourse were no more than one continuous word of a length never seen before. The words, thought Marcello, must melt on his tongue before he could even pronounce them; it was almost as if the devouring fire of madness had dissolved their shapes like wax, amalgamating them into one single soft, elusive, indistinct oratorical material. Gradually, as he read, the words seemed to penetrate more deeply one into the other, shortening and shrinking, and the madman himself began to seem overwhelmed by the verbal avalanche. With growing urgency he began to throw away the papers after reading just the first lines; then, all of a sudden, he ceased to read entirely, leapt with surprising agility onto the bed, and there, withdrawing into a corner and standing upright against the wall, began — or so it appeared — to deliver a speech.

Marcello gathered that he was addressing a crowd more by his gestures than by his words, which were as disconnected and senseless as ever. Exactly like an orator standing on an imaginary balcony, the madman would raise both arms to the ceiling, lean down to thrust out a hand as if to imply some subtlety, threaten them with his closed fist, lift both open palms to the level of his face. At a certain point, the imaginary crowd to whom the madman was speaking must certainly have broken out into applause, since he, with the characteristic gesture of the downturned palm, seemed to be calling for silence. But clearly the applause not only did not cease, but grew in intensity, since the madman, after requesting silence once more with his supplicatory gesture, jumped down from the bed, ran to the professor, grabbed him by the sleeve, and asked, in a tearful voice, "Will you make them shut up . . . what does applause matter to me . . . a declaration of war . . . how can you make a declaration of war, if they keep you from speaking by clapping?"

"We'll make the declaration of war tomorrow, Major," said the professor, looking down at the madman from his towering height.

"Tomorrow, tomorrow, tomorrow," yelled the madman, giving way to an instantaneous rage in which anger and desperation were all mixed up, "always tomorrow . . . the declaration of war has to be made right away."

"And why is that, Major? What's it matter to us? In this heat? Those poor soldiers — do you want them to make war in this heat?" The professor shrugged his shoulders slyly.

The madman stared at him, perplexed; evidently the objection disconcerted him. Then he shouted, "The soldiers will eat ice cream! We eat ice cream in the summer, don't we?"

"Yes," said the professor, "we eat ice cream in the summer."

"Right, then," said the madman with a triumphant air, "ice cream, lots of ice cream, ice cream for everyone."

Muttering to himself, he went over to the table and, standing up, grabbed the pencil, wrote a few hurried words on one last piece of paper, then came back to hand it to the doctor.

"Here is the declaration of war. I can't deal with it anymore. . . you take it to whoever will . . . these bells, oh, oh, these bells!" He gave the paper to the doctor and went over to huddle on the floor in the corner near the bed like a terrified beast, squeezing his head between his hands and repeating in anguish, "These bells . . . can't these bells stop a minute?"

The doctor glanced at the piece of paper and then handed it to Marcello. At the top of the page was written: "Slaughter and gloom," and underneath, "The war is declared," all in the usual large handwriting full of flourishes. The doctor said, "Slaughter and gloom is his motto. You'll find it written on all those papers. He's fixated on those two words."

"The bells," moaned the madman.

"But does he really hear them?" asked Marcello's mother, perplexed.

"Probably so. They're aural hallucinations, like the applause earlier. Mentally ill people can hear different kinds of sounds . . . even voices saying words . . . or animal cries, or engine noises, a motorcycle, for example."

"The bells!" screamed the madman in a terrible voice.

Marcello's mother backed up toward the door, murmuring, "But it must be so frightening. Poor dear, who knows how much he suffers . . . if I find myself under a belltower when the bells are ringing, I feel like I'm going mad."

"Does he suffer?" asked Marcello.

"Wouldn't you suffer if for hours and hours you heard huge bronze bells ringing as loud as they could right next to your ear?"

The professor turned toward the sick man and added, "Now we're going to make the bells stop ringing . . . we're going to send the bellringer off to sleep. We'll give you something to drink and you won't hear them anymore."

He nodded to the attendant, who left immediately; then, turning to Marcello, he said, "These are fairly serious sorts of anguish . . . The afflicted person passes from a frenetic euphoria to a profound depression. A little while ago when he was reading, he was exalted, now he's depressed. Would you like to say something to him?"

Marcello stared at his father, who continued to moan piteously, his head between his hands, and said in a cold voice, "No, I have nothing to say to him, and besides, what would be the use? He wouldn't understand me anyway."

"Sometimes they understand," said the professor. "They understand more than you think; they recognize people, they trick even us doctors . . . eh, eh, it's not so simple."

Marcello's mother approached her husband and said affably, "Antonio, do you recognize me? This is Marcello, your son. He's getting married the day after tomorrow . . . do you understand? He's getting married."

The madman looked up at his wife almost hopefully, as a wounded dog looks at his master, who is leaning over him and asking him in human words what's wrong.

The doctor turned toward Marcello, exclaiming, "Wedding, wedding . . . Dear Dottore, I knew nothing about this. My most heartfelt congratulations . . . very sincere best wishes."

"Thank you," said Marcello dryly.

His mother said ingenuously as she headed for the door, "Poor dear, he doesn't understand. If he understood, he'd be unhappy, the same way I'm unhappy."

"Please, Mamma," said Marcello briefly.

"It doesn't matter, your wife has to please you and nobody else," answered his mother conciliatorily. Then she turned toward the madman and said, "Good-bye, Antonio."

"The bells," whimpered the madman.

They went out into the hallway and crossed paths with Franz, who was coming in with a glass of sedative in his hand.

The professor closed the door and said, "It's curious, Dottore, how the insane keep themselves informed and up-to-date, how sensitive they are to everything that touches the collective. Now there's Fascism, there's Il Duce, and so you'll find a lot of them that fixate, like your father, on Fascism and Il Duce. During the war you couldn't even count the insane that thought they were generals and wanted to stand in for Cadorna or Diaz . . . and more recently, when Nobile flew to the North Pole, I had at least three patients who knew for certain where the famous red tent could be found, and they had invented a special gadget to rescue the survivors. Crazy people are always up-to-date. Actually, despite their madness, they don't stop participating in public life, and it's precisely their madness they use to participate in it — good, up-standing, crazy citizens that they are, of course."

The doctor laughed coldly, very much satisfied by his own humor. Then he turned to Marcello's mother (but with the clear intention of flattering Marcello) and said, "But as far as Il Duce is concerned, we're all as crazy as your husband, isn't that right, Signora? All crazy as loons, we should be treated with the cold shower and the straightjacket . . . All Italy is just one big insane asylum, eh, eh, eh."

"As far as that goes, my son is crazy for sure," said his mother, innocently seconding the doctor's adulation. "In fact, on our way here I said to Marcello that there were points of similarity between him and his father."

Marcello slowed his pace so as not to hear them. He saw them walk toward the end of the hall and then turn and disappear, still chatting. He stopped. He was still holding the scrap of paper on which his father had written his declaration of war. He hesitated, then pulled his wallet out of his pocket and put the piece of paper in it. Then he hurried forward and reached the doctor and his mother on the ground floor.

"Well . . . good-bye, Professor," said his mother, "but that poor dear . . . is there really no way to cure him?"

"For now science can do nothing," replied the doctor without any solemnity, as if repeating a dull, mechanical formula.

"Good-bye, Professor," said Marcello.

"Good-bye, Dottore, and again — sincere and heartfelt congratulations."

They walked down the graveled pathway, came out onto the street, and headed for the car. Alberi was there, next to the open door with his cap in his hand. They got in without saying anything and the car started up.

Marcello was silent for a moment and then said, "Mamma, I'd like to ask you a question. I think I can speak to you frankly, can't I?"

"What question?" asked his mother distractedly, looking into the mirror of her compact and touching up her face.

"The man I call father, the man we just visited — is he really my father?"

His mother started to laugh. "Really, sometimes you are *so* strange. Why shouldn't he be your father?"

"Mamma, at that time you already had," Marcello hesitated and then finished, "lovers. Could it be . . . ?"

"Oh, it couldn't be anything, absolutely nothing," said his mother, with calm cynicism. "The first time I decided to cheat on your father, you were already two years old. The really curious thing is," she added, "that it was with just exactly this idea, that you were someone else's son, that your father's madness began . . . He was obsessed with the idea that you weren't his son. And you know what he did one day? He took a photograph, of me and of you when you were a baby . . ."

"And he poked holes in both our eyes," finished Marcello.

"Oh, you already knew," said his mother, a little surprised. "Well, then, that was the real beginning of his madness. He was obsessed by the idea that you were the son of someone I was seeing back then, from time to time . . . useless to tell him it was his own imagination . . . You're his son, all right, it's enough to look at you."

"Actually, I resemble you more than him," Marcello couldn't help saying.

"Both of us," said his mother. She put the compact back in her purse and added, "I already told you: if nothing else, you both have this fixation on politics — he as a madman and you, thank God, as a sane person . . ."

Marcello said nothing and turned his face to the window. The idea of resembling his father inspired intense disgust in him. Familiar relationships based on flesh and blood had always repulsed him. But the resemblance his mother was alluding to not only repulsed, but obscurely frightened him. What link was there between his father's madness and his own most secret being? He recalled the phrase he had read on the scrap of paper, "Slaughter and gloom," and shivered painfully. As far as gloom went, he wore it like a second skin, more sensitive than his real skin; and as to slaughter . . .

Now the car was traveling through the downtown streets of the city in the false blue light of dusk.

Marcello said to his mother, "I'm getting out here," and leaned forward to tap on the glass to let Alberi know.

His mother said, "Then I'll see you when you get back," implying that she would not be coming to the wedding. And he was grateful to her for her reticence; lightness and cynicism were good for that much, at least.

He got out, closed the door hard, and walked away, losing himself in the crowd.

PART II

I

*A*S SOON AS THE TRAIN started moving, Marcello left the window at which he had been standing to converse with — or rather, to listen to — his mother-in-law and went back inside the compartment. But Giulia remained at the window; from the compartment he could see her in the corridor as she hung out the window, waving a handkerchief so anxiously that her otherwise very ordinary gesture was filled with pathos. Doubtless, he thought, she would remain there to flutter her handkerchief until she could no longer see the figure of her mother on the platform; and losing sight of her would be, for Giulia, the clearest sign of her definitive farewell to life as a girl. He knew she both feared and desired this farewell, which, as she departed on the train, leaving her mother behind, assumed a painfully concrete character. Marcello gazed for another moment at his wife as she hung out the window, clothed in a light dress that rode up and wrinkled over the full curves of her body as she raised her arm, and then he let himself fall back against the cushions, closing his eyes. When he opened them after a few minutes, his wife was no longer in the corridor and the train was already rolling through open countryside, an arid, treeless plain wrapped in the shadows of twilight beneath a green sky. Every once in a while the terrain broke out into barren hills; to his amazement, the deep valleys that lay between them were deserted, without houses or human figures. Occasional brick ruins on the hilltops reinforced this sensation of solitude. It was a restful landscape, thought Marcello, conducive to reflection and imagination. In the meantime, the moon had risen over the horizon beyond the plain: a full moon as red as blood, with a shining white star to its right.

His wife had vanished, and Marcello hoped that she would not come back for a minute or two; he wanted to think and to feel himself alone for the last time. He went over the things he had done in the past few days in his memory and was aware as he did so of feeling a deep and sincere satisfaction. This, he thought, was the only way to change oneself and one's life: to act, to move through time and space. As usual, the things he liked most were those that affirmed his connection to a normal, predictable world.

The morning of the wedding: Giulia in her bridal dress, running happily from one room to another in a rustle of silk; he himself, entering the elevator with a bouquet of lilies of the valley in one gloved hand; his mother-in-law throwing herself into his arms, sobbing, as soon as he walked in the door; Giulia pulling him behind the closet door to kiss him at her leisure; the arrival of the witnesses — two friends of Giulia's, a doctor and a lawyer, and two friends of his from the ministry; leaving the house for the church, while people watched from the windows and sidewalks, in three cars — the first for him and Giulia, the second for the witnesses, and the third for his mother-in-law and her friends.

On the way to the church, there was a strange little incident. The car had stopped at a traffic light, when suddenly someone appeared at the window: a red, bearded face with a high, bald forehead and prominent nose. A beggar. But instead of asking for money, the man had asked, in a hoarse voice, "Will you give me a *confetto*, newlyweds?" and at the same time had thrust his hand into the car.

The sudden apparition of the face at the window and that rude hand reaching toward Giulia had irritated Marcello, who had answered, perhaps with excessive severity, "Go on, get out of here, no *confetti* for you."

At this the man, who was probably drunk, had shouted with what voice he had, "A curse upon you!" and had disappeared.

Giulia, who had squeezed up against Marcello in alarm, murmured, "He'll bring us bad luck!"

And he had replied, shrugging his shoulders, "It's nothing . . . a drunk." Then the car moved forward and he forgot the incident almost immediately.

In the church everything had been normal, that is, peacefully solemn, ritualistic, ceremonial. A small crowd of relatives and friends had gathered in the first few pews in front of the main altar, the men dressed in dark suits, the women in spring pastels. The church, very rich and ornate, was dedicated to a saint of the Counter-Reformation. Behind the main altar, under a canopy of gilded bronze, there was a statue of this saint in gray marble, larger than life, kneeling with his eyes turned toward heaven and his palms open. Behind the statue you could see the apse, completely covered with baroque-style frescoes, vividly painted and full of scrolls and flourishes. Giulia and he were kneeling in front of the marble balustrade on a red velvet cushion. The witnesses were standing behind them, two by two. The service was long; it had been important to Giulia's family to give it the utmost solemnity. From the very beginning an organ in the balcony over the entrance had been playing uninterruptedly, sometimes in a low rumble, sometimes in loud, triumphant notes that spread and echoed under the high vaults. The priest had been very slow; so that Marcello, after noting with satisfaction all the details of the ceremony — which was exactly as he had imagined and wanted it to be — and having convinced himself that he was doing precisely what millions of grooms had done for hundreds of years before him, became distracted and began to observe the church. It was not a beautiful church, but it was vast, conceived and constructed with an intention of theatrical solemnity, like all the Jesuit churches. The

enormous statue of the saint, kneeling under his canopy in an ec-
static attitude, loomed over an altar painted to resemble marble and
crowded with silver candelabras, vases full of flowers, small decorative statues, and hanging bronze lamps. Behind the canopy curved
the apse, frescoed by a painter of the epoch: fluffy clouds that might
have been painted on a theater curtain at the opera floated in an
azure sky streaked with rays of light from a hidden sun; and seated
above the clouds were various sacred figures, boldly painted with
more of a decorative than a religious spirit. Standing out from the
others, towering over them all, was the figure of the Eternal Father;
and suddenly Marcello, despite himself, saw in that bearded head
adorned with its triangular halo the face of the beggar, who shortly
before had stuck his head in at the car window to ask for *confetti* and
then had cursed him. Right then the organ began to play more
loudly, with an almost menacing severity that seemed to leave no
room for any sweetness; and at that, the resemblance, which in
other circumstances would have made him smile (the Eternal Father disguised as a beggar sticks his head in the window of a taxi to
ask for sugared almonds) had recalled to mind, he was not sure why,
the biblical verses concerning Cain. A few years after Lino's death
he had happened to open a Bible by chance to these words:

> What hast thou done? The voice of thy brother's blood
> crieth unto me from the ground. And now art thou cursed
> from the earth, which hath opened her mouth to receive
> thy brother's blood from thy hand. When thou tillest the
> ground, it shall not henceforth yield to thee her strength; a
> fugitive and a vagabond thou shalt be in the earth.
>
> And Cain said unto the Lord: My punishment is greater
> than I can bear. Behold, Thou hast driven me out this day
> from the face of the earth; and from Thy face shall I be
> hid; and I shall be a fugitive and a vagabond in the earth;
> and it shall come to pass, that every one that findeth me
> shall slay me.
>
> But the Lord said unto him: No, it shall not be so. For
> whosoever slayeth Cain, vengeance shall be taken upon

him sevenfold. And the Lord set a mark upon Cain, lest any finding him should kill him.

That day those verses had seemed written just for him, cursed for his involuntary crime, and at the same time rendered sacred and untouchable by the curse itself. And that morning in the church, as he was looking at the figure in the fresco, they had returned to mind; and once again they seemed to him perfectly adapted to his case. Coldly, but not without a dark conviction of sinking the tool of his reflection into soil fertile with analogies and significance, he had speculated on this point as the service continued: if there was truly a curse, why had it been hurled at *him?* At this question, his continual stubborn melancholy returned to oppress him. He was like someone who has lost himself and knows that he can do no other but lose himself; and he knew, if not consciously, then at least by instinct, that he was cursed. But not because he had killed Lino; but because he had sought and was still seeking to free himself from the burden of repentance, corruption, and abnormality of that long-ago crime outside of religion and its rites. But what could he do, he thought; that was how he was and it was not in his power to change himself. Really, there was no intentional evil in him, only an honest acceptance of the conditions into which he had been born and of the world in which he found himself living. Conditions very far from religion, a world that seemed to have replaced religion with other things. Certainly he would have preferred to entrust his life to the ancient and affectionate persons of Christian religion: to the Father, so just; to the Virgin, so maternal; to the Christ, so merciful. But at the very moment he felt this desire, he realized that this life did not belong to him and that he could not entrust it to whomever he wished; that he stood outside religion and could not reenter it, even to purify himself and become normal. Normality, he thought, lay somewhere else by now; or perhaps it was yet to come and must be reconstructed with enormous effort, with doubt, with blood.

At that moment, almost as if to confirm these thoughts, he had looked at the woman beside him who would, in a matter of minutes, be his wife. Giulia was kneeling, her hands joined in prayer, her face and eyes turned toward the altar; she seemed almost rapt, in a happy, hopeful ecstasy of her own. All the same, at his glance — as if she had felt it on her body like the touch of a hand — she had immediately turned and smiled at him with both her eyes and mouth: a tender, humble, grateful smile of almost animal innocence. He had returned the smile, a little less openly; and then, as if it had been born from that smile, he had felt — perhaps for the first time since he had known her — a surge, if not of love, at least of deep affection, all mixed up with compassion and tenderness.

Then for one strange moment, he seemed to undress her with his glance, to strip the wedding dress and even her most intimate underclothes from her body, and to see her — full-breasted, round-bellied, young and glowing with health — kneeling completely naked on the red velvet cushion beside him, with her hands clasped in prayer. And he was as naked as she was; and outside of every ritual consecration, they were about to join themselves together in truth, to mate like the beasts in the woods; and this union, whether or not he believed in the rite in which they were participating, would really happen, and from it, as he hoped, children would be born. At this thought it seemed to him that he was setting his feet on solid ground for the first time, and he reflected, "In a little while she'll be my wife . . . and I'll take her . . . and once I've taken her, she'll conceive children. And for now, in the absence of anything better, this will be the departure point for normality . . ."

But right then he had seen Giulia move her lips in prayer, and at that fervent motion of her mouth her nudity had been instantly reclothed, as if by magic, in the wedding dress; and he had understood that Giulia, unlike him, firmly believed in the ritual consecration of their union. He had not been displeased but relieved at this discovery. For Giulia, normality was not, as it was for him, something to seek or reconstruct; it simply *was*; and she was immersed in it, and whatever happened, she would never step outside it.

So the ceremony had concluded with enough emotion and affection on his part; an emotion and affection of which he had al-

ways before believed himself incapable and which had been inspired by profound reasons of his own, not suggested by the place
and by the rite. In the end it had all worked out according to the
traditional norms, in such a way as to satisfy not only those who believed in them, but also himself, who did not believe but wished to
act as if he did.

Coming out of the church with his wife on his arm, he had
halted for a moment under the portal above the church steps and
had heard Giulia's mother behind him, saying to a friend, "He's
so, so good . . . You saw how moved he was. He loves her so much
. . . Giulia really couldn't have found a better husband."

He had been glad to have been able to inspire such an illusion.

Now, having brought his thoughts to a conclusion, he felt an
ardent, almost biting desire to take up his role of husband again,
right at the point he had left off, after the wedding ceremony. He
turned his eyes from the window, which, with the advent of night,
had filled with a black, faintly sparkling darkness, and peered into
the corridor looking for Giulia. He was aware of feeling a slight irritation at her absence; this pleased him, since it seemed an indication of how naturally he played his part by now. At this point he
wondered whether he should take Giulia in the uncomfortable
bunk of the sleeping car or wait until they reached S., where they
were stopping after the first stage of their journey; and at the very
thought he felt a surge of strong desire and decided he would take
her in the train. That's what must happen on honeymoons, he
thought, and besides, that's what he felt like doing, prompted not
only by sexual hunger but by a kind of satisfied loyalty to his part as
the groom. But Giulia was a virgin, as he knew for sure, and it
would not be easy to possess her. He thought he might like it if,
after trying in vain to break through this virginity, he was constrained to wait for the hotel at S. and the comfort of a double bed.
These things happened to newlyweds; they might be ridiculous
but they were normal. And he wanted to act like the most normal
of all normal people, even at the risk of seeming impotent.

He was about to look out into the corridor when the door
opened and Giulia came in. She was only wearing a skirt and

blouse; she had taken off her jacket and was carrying it over her arm. Her ample breasts thrust exuberantly against the white linen of the blouse, informing it with the faint rose color of her flesh; her face was lit up with happy satisfaction. Only her eyes, larger, more languid and melting than usual, revealed both trepidation and desire, an almost frightened excitement. Marcello noticed all this with satisfaction: Giulia was truly a bride, on the verge of giving herself up for the first time. She turned a little awkwardly (she always moved awkwardly, he thought, but hers was a lovable clumsiness, as if she were a healthy, innocent animal) to shut the door and close the curtain; then, standing in front of him, she started to hang up her jacket on one of the hooks of the luggage rack. But the train was going very fast; it switched tracks abruptly, and the whole car seemed to tilt. Giulia fell on top of him. She righted herself mischievously, by sitting down on his knees and throwing her arms around his neck. Marcello felt the whole weight of her body on his thin knees and put an arm mechanically around her waist.

She said softly, "Do you love me?" and lowered her face, searching his mouth with her own.

They kissed for a long time, as the train continued to roll forward with complicit speed, so that at every jolt their teeth bumped together and Giulia's nose seemed to want to penetrate his face. At last they separated and Giulia, without getting off of his knees, conscientiously took a handkerchief from her purse and wiped his mouth, saying, "You have at least a ton of lipstick on your lips."

Marcello, whose knees were growing numb, took advantage of another jolt of the train to slide her heavy body off onto the seat.

"You bad boy, don't you want me?" she said.

"They haven't come in to make up the bunks yet," he said, a little embarrassed.

"Just think," she said without transition, "this is the first time I've ever been in a sleeping car."

Marcello couldn't help smiling at the innocence in her voice and asked, "Do you like it?"

"Yes, I like it a lot." She looked around again. "When are they coming to make up the beds?"

"Soon."

They fell silent. Marcello looked at his wife and realized that she was looking back at him with a new expression, shy and apprehensive, which overlay but did not erase the happy radiance of a moment before. She saw that he was staring at her and smiled at him apologetically; without saying a word, she took one of his hands in hers and squeezed it. Then two tears sprang up in her tender, liquid eyes and slid down her cheeks, followed by two more. Giulia wept even as she kept gazing at him and trying pitifully to smile between the tears. Finally she lowered her head with a sudden impulse and began to kiss his hand furiously. Marcello felt disoriented by these tears; Giulia was generally gay and unsentimental, and he had never seen her cry before.

However, she left him no time for supposition, since she stood up and said hurriedly, "Excuse me for crying . . . but I was thinking how much better you are than me and how unworthy I am of you."

"Now you're talking like your mother," said Marcello with a smile.

He watched her blow her nose and then answer calmly, "No, Mamma says these things without knowing why. But I have a real reason."

"What reason?"

She looked at him for a long moment and then explained, "I have to tell you something and after I do maybe you won't love me anymore . . . but I have to tell you."

"What?"

She replied slowly, gazing at him attentively, as if she wanted to discover the expression of contempt she feared at the first moment of its appearance, "I'm not what you think I am."

"Meaning?"

"I'm not . . . I mean, I'm not a virgin."

Marcello looked at her and suddenly understood that the normal character he had until now attributed to his wife did not, in reality, exist. He did not know what was hidden beneath that initial confession, but he now knew for certain that Giulia was not, according to her own statement, what he had believed her to be. He was struck by a sense of satiety already at the thought of what he was about to hear and felt a desire, almost, to refuse the confidence. But above all, he needed to reassure her; and this would be easy, since in truth he cared nothing at all about her famous virginity, whether or not it was intact. He replied in an affectionate tone, "Don't worry about it . . . I married you because I love you, not because you were a virgin."

Giulia said, shaking her head, "I knew it, I knew you had a modern mentality . . . that it wouldn't be that important to you . . . but I had to tell you all the same."

"A modern mentality," Marcello couldn't help thinking, almost amused. The phrase was so like Giulia; it made up for her missing virginity. It was an innocent phrase, though of an innocence different than what he had supposed. He said, taking her hand, "Come on, let's not think about it anymore." And he smiled at her.

Giulia smiled back. But as she smiled, tears filled her eyes again and ran down her cheeks.

Marcello protested: "Come on, what's wrong now? When I told you it doesn't matter?"

Giulia made a strange gesture. She threw her arms around his neck but hid her face against his chest, bending her head so that Marcello could not see it.

"I have to tell you everything."

"Everything what?"

"Everything that happened to me."

"But it doesn't matter."

"I beg of you . . . maybe it's a weakness . . . but if I don't tell you, I'll feel like I'm hiding something."

"But, why?" asked Marcello, caressing her hair. "So you've had a lover . . . someone you thought you loved . . . or someone you really loved . . . why should I know about it?"

"No, I didn't love him," she replied immediately, almost spitefully, "and I never thought I loved him. We were lovers, you could say, right up to the day you proposed to me. But he wasn't young like you . . . he was an old man of sixty, disgusting, harsh, demanding, bad . . . a family friend, you know him."

"Who is he?"

"The lawyer Fenizio," she said briefly.

Marcello started. "But he was one of the witnesses . . ."

"Right, he insisted. I didn't want him there, but I couldn't refuse. It was already a lot that he let me get married . . ."

Marcello recalled that he had never liked the lawyer, Fenizio, whom he had often encountered at Giulia's house: a little, bald, blondish man with gold glasses, a sharp nose that wrinkled when he laughed, a mouth without lips. A very calm and cold man, he remembered, but even in that calm coldness, aggressive and petulant in his own unpleasant way. And strong: one day when it was hot he had taken off his jacket and rolled up his shirtsleeves, revealing large white arms swollen with muscles.

"But what did you see in him?" he couldn't help exclaiming.

"He saw something in me . . . and very early . . . I wasn't just his lover for a month or a year, it was six years."

Marcello made a rapid mental calculation: Giulia was twenty-one now, or anyway, just a little over that. Stunned, he repeated, "Six years."

"Yes, six years. I was fifteen when . . . do you understand what I'm saying?"

Giulia, he observed, although speaking of things that to all appearances still grieved her, talked in her usual drawling, good-natured tone of voice as if relaying the most irrelevant gossip. "You might say he began abusing me the same day poor Papà died . . . if it wasn't that same day, at least it was that same week. Well, actually, I can tell you the exact date: just eight days after my father's funeral . . . my father, mind you, whose intimate and trusted friend he was . . ."

She fell silent for a moment, as if to underline by her silence the impiety of the man; then she went on: "Mamma did nothing but cry, and naturally, she was in church a lot . . . He came by one evening when I was alone in the house; Mamma had gone out and the maid was in the kitchen. I was in my bedroom sitting at

my desk, concentrating on writing my homework for school . . . I
was in the fifth form at the *ginnasio* and was getting ready to earn
my diploma . . . He came in on tiptoes, walked up in back of me,
bent over my homework, and asked me what I was doing. I told
him, without turning around — I wasn't suspicious at all, first of
all because I was as innocent, and you can believe this, as a two-
year-old baby, and then because he was almost like a relative to
me . . . I called him "uncle," just imagine . . . so I told him that I
was working on my Latin essay and he — do you know what he
did? He grabbed me by the hair, with just one hand, but hard . . .
he did that often, as a joke, because I had magnificent hair, long
and wavy, and he used to say that it tempted his fingers. Well,
feeling him pull on it, I thought it was a joke this time, too, and I
said to him, 'Stop it, you're hurting me,' but instead of letting me
go, he forced me to get up and, holding me at arm's length, he
guided me toward the bed, which was where it is now, in the
corner near the door. Just think, I was so innocent I still didn't understand, and I said to him, I remember, 'Let me go . . . I have to
do my homework.' Right then he let go of my hair . . . but no, I
can't tell it to you . . ."

Marcello was about to ask her to go on, thinking that she was
ashamed; but Giulia, who had only stopped to increase the effect
of her story, continued: "Although I wasn't yet fifteen, I was already very developed, like a woman . . . well, I didn't want to tell
you because just to talk about it still hurts me . . . He let go of my
hair and grabbed my breasts, so hard that I couldn't even scream
and I almost passed out . . . maybe I really did faint . . . then, after
he grabbed me, I don't know what happened. I was stretched out
on the bed and he was on top of me and I understood everything
and all my strength had left me and I was like an object in his
hands, passive, lifeless, without any will of my own. So he had his
way with me. . . Later I cried, and then, to console me, he told me
he loved me, that he was crazy about me, you know, the usual
things. But he also told me, in case I wasn't convinced, that I
shouldn't talk about it to my mother unless I wanted to ruin him.
It seems that Papà, at the end, made some business mistakes and

that now our living conditions depended completely on him, Fenizio . . . He came back other times after that day, but not with any consistency, always when I didn't expect him. He would come into my bedroom on tiptoe, lean over me, and ask me in a severe voice, 'Have you done your homework? No? Then come do it with me . . .' and then usually he would grab me by the hair and lead me at arm's length to the bed. I'm telling you, he had a real thing about taking me by the hair." She laughed almost affectionately at this memory, this habit of her old lover's, as one might laugh at some characteristic and lovable trait. "We went on that way for almost a year. He kept swearing that he loved me and that if he didn't have a wife and children he'd marry me . . . and I'm not saying he wasn't sincere . . . but if he really loved me the way he said he did, there was only one way to show it: leave me alone. After a year, I'd had enough . . . I was desperate, I made an attempt to free myself. I told him I didn't love him and that I would never love him, that I couldn't keep going on this way, that I couldn't manage to do anything anymore, that I was struggling, that I hadn't gotten my diploma, and that, if he didn't leave me alone, I would have to give up my studies . . . And then he — do you know what he did? He went and told Mamma that he understood my temperament and was convinced I wasn't cut out for studying and that since I was sixteen already, it would be better for me to go to work. Right off he offered me the position of secretary in his office . . . understand? Naturally, I resisted as hard as I could, but Mamma, poor thing, told me I was an ingrate, that he had done and continued to do so much for us, that I shouldn't let a chance like that slip out of my fingers, and finally, I was forced to accept . . . Once I was in the studio with him all day long, as you can imagine, there was no way to quit. So I started up again and finally I just got into the habit of him and stopped rebelling, you know how it is. I thought there was no more hope for me, I had become a fatalist. But a year ago, when you told me you loved me, I went straight to him and told him that this time it was over for good. But he's vile, he's a coward; he protested, threatening to go and tell you everything . . . do you know what I did then? I grabbed a sharp paperknife that he had on the desk and I put the point to his throat and I said, 'If you do, I'll kill you,' and then I said, 'He'll find out about our relationship . . . that's only right . . . but I'll be the one to tell him, not you . . . from today on, as far as I'm concerned, you don't even exist. And if you just try to put yourself between him and me, I'll kill you, I may go to jail but I'll kill you,' and I said it in a certain tone so that he knew I meant it. And from then on he didn't breathe a word, except to avenge himself by writing that anonymous letter where he talked about your father . . ."

"Ah, that was him," Marcello couldn't help exclaiming.

"Of course. I recognized the paper and the typewriter right away."

She was quiet for a moment; then, immediately anxious, she took Marcello's hand and added, "Now I've told you everything and I think I feel better . . . but maybe I shouldn't have told you, maybe now you won't be able to stand me, maybe you'll hate me."

Marcello did not answer her; he remained silent for a long time. Giulia's story had roused neither hatred in him toward the man who had abused her, nor pity for her whom he had abused. The apathetic and reasonable way in which she had told it, even as she was expressing disgust and contempt, excluded feelings as clear as anger and pity. As if by contagion, he even felt inclined to a viewpoint much like hers, a mixture of indulgence and resignation. What he did feel was an overwhelmingly physical sense of astonishment, disconnected from any judgment whatsoever, as if he had fallen into an unforeseen pit. And on the rebound, his habitual melancholy deepened, confronted with this unexpected confirmation of a norm of decadence to which he had hoped that Giulia would prove an exception. But strangely, his conviction of Giulia's profoundly normal character remained unshaken. Normality, as he suddenly understood, did not consist in staying away from certain experiences, but in the way these experiences were evaluated. Destiny had dictated that both he and Giulia would have something to hide, and consequently to confess, in their lives. But while he felt entirely unable to speak of Lino, Giulia had not hesitated to disclose her relationship with the lawyer to him; and she had chosen the most suitable moment to do so, according to her own ideas: the moment of matrimony, which, in her mind, abolished the past and opened the door to a whole new way of life. This thought pleased him because, despite everything, it confirmed Giulia's normality, which consisted precisely in her capacity for redemption through the customary, ancient means of religion and love. Distracted by these thoughts, he turned his eyes to the window without realizing that his silence was frightening his wife.

Then he felt her try to hug him and heard her voice asking him, "Aren't you going to say something? Then it's true . . . I disgust you . . . Tell the truth: you can't stand me anymore and I disgust you."

Marcello would have liked to reassure her, and moved to turn around and hug her. But a jolt of the train led his gesture astray so that, without wanting to, he poked her in the face with his elbow. Giulia interpreted this involuntary blow as a gesture of rejection and stood up immediately. At that moment the train entered a tunnel, with a long, melancholy whistle and a thickening of shadows against the glass of the little windows. In the midst of the roar and rumble, doubled by vaults' answering echo, he thought he heard a wailing cry emerge from Giulia as, holding her arms stretched out in front of her, swaying and stumbling, she moved toward the door of their compartment.

Surprised, he called without getting up, "Giulia!"

As answer he saw her, still in that sorrowful, stumbling way, open the door and disappear into the corridor.

For a moment he stayed where he was, then, suddenly alarmed, he rose and went out, as well. Their compartment was in the middle of the car; right away he saw his wife moving hurriedly down the deserted corridor toward the end where the exit door was. Watching her flee down the broad, soft carpet between the mahogany walls, the threat she had made to her old lover came back to him: "If you talk, I'll kill you," and he thought that he had perhaps ignored, till now, an aspect of her character, mistaking her easygoing good nature for a passive cowardice. In the selfsame moment he saw her lean down and jerk at the handles of the door. In one leap he reached her and grabbed her by the arms, forcing her to stand back up.

"What are you doing, Giulia?" he asked in a low voice, despite the rumbling of the train. "What did you think? It was the train . . . I wanted to turn around and instead I hurt you."

She was rigid between his arms, as if preparing for a struggle. But at the sound of his voice, so tranquil and so sincerely surprised, she seemed to calm down immediately. She said after a moment, bowing her head, "Forgive me, maybe I was mistaken, but I had the impression you hated me and so I wanted to end it all . . . It wasn't an act, if you hadn't come I would really have done it."

"But why? What were you thinking of?"

He saw her shrug her shoulders. "Just because, just to stop struggling so hard . . . For me, getting married was a lot more important than you thought. When I seemed to . . . when I thought you couldn't stand me anymore, I felt, I just can't go on anymore . . . ." She shrugged her shoulders again and added, lifting her face at last toward his and smiling, "Think, you would have become a widower the day you were married."

Marcello gazed at her for a moment without speaking. Clearly, he thought, Giulia was sincere; she had truly attached much more importance to getting married than he could imagine. Then, with a sense of astonishment, he understood that this humble statement demonstrated a complex participation in the wedding ritual, which was for Giulia — unlike himself — truly what it should and must be, neither more nor less. Thus it was hardly surprising that after such passionate devotion, she should think of killing herself at the first disappointment. He told himself that this was almost a kind of blackmail on Giulia's part: either you forgive me or I kill myself; and once more he experienced relief, at finding her to be so completely what he had wanted. Giulia had turned around again and seemed now to be looking out the little window. He put his arms around her waist and murmured in her ear, "You know I love you."

She turned immediately and kissed him with a passion so violent that Marcello was almost frightened. This is the way, he thought, that certain devotees kiss the feet of the statues, the crosses, the reliquaries in churches. Meanwhile, the noise of the tunnel gave way to the usual swift beat of the wheels running in open air; and they separated. Still, they remained standing one against the other, hand in hand in front of the window, contemplating the darkness of the night.

"Look," said Giulia finally, in a normal tone of voice, "look down there . . . what can it be? A fire?"

And in fact a fire now shone in the center of the dark glass like a red flower.

Marcello said, "Who knows?" and lowered the window.

The mirrorlike gleam of glass disappeared from the night, a cold wind blew in their faces, but the red flower remained — whether far or near, high or low was hard to tell — mysteriously suspended in the dark. After looking for a long time at those four or five petals of flame, which seemed to shift and throb, he turned his gaze toward the escarpment of the railroad track along which the faint lights of the train were sliding, as were his and Giulia's shadows, and was suddenly seized with an acute sense of bewilderment.

Why was he on that train? And who was the woman standing by his side? And where was he going? And who was he, exactly? And where did he come from? This bewilderment caused him no suffering; on the contrary, it pleased him, being an emotion with which he was familiar and which constituted, perhaps, the very foundation of his most intimate being.

"Yes," he thought coldly, "I'm like that fire, down there in the night . . . I'll flare up and then I'll go out, without reason, without sequel . . . a bit of destruction suspended in the dark."

He was roused by the sound of Giulia's voice saying, "Look, they must have made up the beds already," and understood that, while he had been lost in contemplation of that faraway fire, she had never ceased thinking about their love or, to put it more precisely, the imminent union of their two bodies — what she was doing in the moment, in other words, and nothing else. She was already headed, with a kind of contained impatience, toward their compartment; Marcello followed her at a little distance.

He delayed on the threshold to let the conductor pass through into the corridor, and then he went in. Giulia was standing in front of the mirror, seeming not to care that the door was still open; she was taking off her blouse, unbuttoning it from the bottom up.

She said without turning, "You take the top bunk. I'll take the bottom one."

Marcello closed the door, climbed up onto the bunk, and began to undress right away, putting his clothes onto the luggage rack as he took them off. Then he sat on top of the covers holding his knees in his arms, naked and waiting. He heard Giulia moving around, heard a glass tinkle against a metal bracket, a shoe fall onto the rug on the floor, and other small sounds. Then with a dry click, the brightest of the lights went out, yielding to the violet glow of the nightlight; and Giulia's voice said, "Do you want to come here?"

Marcello stuck out his legs, turned around, put one foot onto the bunk below, and crouched down to one side to get in. As he did so, he saw Giulia naked and supine, one arm thrown over her eyes, her legs outstretched and spread wide. In the false, low light, her body was the cold white of mother-of-pearl, stained with black at the groin and armpits and with dark pink at the tips of her breasts. She looked inanimate, not only because of this deathlike pallor, but also because of her perfect, abandoned immobility.

But when Marcello got on top of her she came to life all of a sudden, with the violence of a trap springing shut, drawing him to her and throwing her arms around his neck, opening her legs and locking her feet at his back. Later she pushed him away harshly and huddled against the wall, curled up on herself with her forehead pressed to her knees. And Marcello, lying by her side, understood that what she had taken from him with such fury and then closed up around and cherished with such jealousy in her own womb, no longer belonged to him; it would grow inside her. And he had done this, he thought, to be able to say at least once: "I have been a man like all other men . . . I have loved, I have joined myself to a woman and generated another man."

2

*A*S SOON AS HE THOUGHT Giulia was asleep, Marcello got up from the bed, put his feet on the floor, and began to get dressed. The room was immersed in a cool, transparent half-light that hinted at the beautiful June sun flooding both sky and sea. It was a real Riviera hotel room, high and white, decorated with blue stucco flowers, stems, and leaves. The furniture was all light wood in the same floral style as the stucco-work, and a large green palm stood in a corner. When he was dressed, he tiptoed to the shutters and pushed them aside to look out. Right away he saw the shining expanse of the sea, made even vaster by the perfect clarity of the horizon. It was a limpid, almost violent blue, and every wave seemed afire, beneath the gentle breeze, with a tiny sparkling flower of sunlight. Marcello lowered his eyes from the sea to the promenade. It was deserted: no one was sitting on the benches that faced out to sea in the shade of the palms; no one was walking on the clean gray asphalt.

He stared out at this vista for a long time, then closed the shutters again and turned to look at Giulia stretched out on the bed. She was naked and sleeping. She was lying on one side, and the position of her body thrust up a round, pale, full hip, from which her torso seemed to hang limp and lifeless, like the stem of a wilted flower in a vase. Her back and hips, as Marcello knew, were the only tight, solid parts of that body; on the other side, invisible but present to his memory, was the softness of her belly, falling into soft folds on the bed, and of her breasts, pulled down by their weight, one on top of the other. He could not see his wife's head, since it was hidden by her shoulder; and remembering how he had possessed her only a few minutes before, he suddenly had the sensation of looking not at a person but at a machine made of flesh, lovely and lovable but brutal, made for love and love alone.

As if awakened by his merciless gaze, she suddenly moved and sighed deeply, then said in a clear voice, "Marcello."

He went to her quickly and said with affection, "I'm here."

He watched her turn over, heavily shifting her weight of feminine flesh from one side to the other; then she raised her arms blindly and wrapped them around his hips. Then, with her hair falling over her face, she nuzzled him slowly and persistently with her nose and mouth, searching out his sex. She kissed it with a kind of humble and passionate fetishism, remained motionless for a moment with her arms still around him, and then fell back onto the bed, conquered by sleep, her face wrapped in her hair. She had fallen asleep again in the same position as before, except that she had changed sides and now lay on her right side instead of her left. Marcello slipped his jacket from a hanger, tiptoed to the door, and went out into the hall.

He walked down the broad, echoing staircase, crossed the threshold of the hotel, and stepped out onto the promenade. The sun, reflected from the sea in blades of sparkling light, dazzled him for a moment; he closed his eyes, and, as if called up from the darkness, the sharp odor of horse urine assailed his nostrils. He found the carriages behind the hotel in a strip of shade, three or

four in a row with their drivers asleep on their boxes and the passenger seats draped in white covers. Marcello went up to the first
carriage and climbed in, calling out the address, "Via dei Glicini."
He saw the coachman launch a brief, meaningful look at him and
then crack his whip over the horse without saying a word.

The carriage rolled along the seashore for a good while and
then entered a short street full of villas and gardens. At the end of
the street the Ligurian hill rose skyward, luminous, covered in
vineyards and dotted with silver olive trees, an occasional tall red
house with green windows standing upright on its slopes. The
street they were on led straight toward the foot of the hill; at a certain point the sidewalks and asphalt stopped, yielding to a kind of
grassy path. The carriage came to a halt and Marcello raised his
eyes: at the end of a garden he could see a gray, three-story house
with a black roof of slate tiles and mansard windows.

The driver said dryly, "It's here," took the money, and turned
the horse around quickly. Marcello thought that he had been offended, perhaps, at having to bring him to this place; but maybe,
he reflected as he pushed on the gate, he was simply attributing to
the coachman the revulsion he felt himself.

He walked down a path between two hedges whose glossy
leaves and small white flowers were dulled with dust. He had always hated these houses and had been to one only two or three
times, as an adolescent, bringing back with him each time a sense
of revulsion and repentance as of something unworthy of him,
which he shouldn't have done. Sick at heart, he climbed the two
or three steps and pushed on the glass-paned door, setting off a
gossipy alarm, then found himself in a Pompeian entrance hall in
front of a stairway with a wooden railing. He recognized the sickly-
sweet stench of face powder, sweat, and male semen; the house
was immersed in the silence and torpor of the summer afternoon.
While he was looking around, a kind of maid emerged from who
knows where, dressed in black, with a white apron tied at the
waist, small, slim, with the sharp face of a ferret enlivened by two
brilliant eyes; she appeared before him with a shrill "good
morning" uttered in a cheerful voice.

"I have to speak to the *padrona*," he said, taking off his hat with perhaps excessive urbanity.

"All right, handsome, you can talk to her," answered the woman in dialect, "but in the meantime go into the salon . . . The *padrona* will come . . . go in there."

Marcello, offended by her familiarity and by the misunderstanding, nonetheless let himself be pushed toward a half-open door. The salon appeared in the dim half-light, long and rectangular, deserted, with little sofas covered in red material lined up all around the walls. The floor was as dusty as the waiting room of a train station; even the cloth of the couches, filthy and threadbare, confirmed the squalor of this public place within the intimacy and secrecy of the house. Marcello, unsure of himself, sat down on one of the sofas. At the same time, like a belly whose bowels, after long immobility, suddenly discharge their burden, there came from all over the house a disintegration, a clatter, a ruinous rush of feet down the wooden stairs. And then what he had feared would happen happened. The door opened and the petulant voice of the maid announced: "Here are the young ladies . . . all for *you*."

The women who came in were listless and indifferent. Some of them were partly naked, others more fully dressed. There were two with dark hair and three blonds, three of medium build, one decidedly small, and one who was enormous. This last woman came to sit next to Marcello, letting herself fall full-length on the sofa with a sigh of weary satisfaction. At first he averted his face; then, fascinated, he turned it a little and looked at her. She was really enormous, pyramidal in shape, with hips broader than her waist, waist broader than her shoulders, and shoulders wider than her head, which was tiny, with a flat, snub face and a black braid wound around her forehead. A yellow silk brassiere bound her swollen, low-hung breasts; beneath her navel a red skirt opened widely, like a theater curtain, onto the spectacle of the black pubis and massive white thighs. Seeing that she was observed, she smiled conspiratorially at one of her companions who was seated against the front wall, heaved a sigh, and then slid one hand between her legs as if to open them and cool off. Marcello, irritated by this passive shamelessness, would have liked to pull away the hand with which she was stroking herself beneath her belly; but he didn't have the strength to move.

What struck him most about this female livestock was the irreparable character of their fall, the same character that made him shiver with horror before his mother's naked body and his father's madness, the origin of his almost hysterical love for order, calm, neatness, and composure.

Finally the woman turned toward him and said, in a benevolent, playful tone, "Well, don't you like your harem? Are you going to decide?" and immediately, on an impulse of frantic disgust, he rose and ran out of the salon to the accompaniment, or so he thought, of laughter and some obscene fragments of dialect. Furious, he headed toward the stairs, meaning to go up to the next floor and look for the madame, but at that moment the doorbell rang behind him again, and when he turned, he saw the astonished and — to his eyes, in those circumstances, almost paternal — agent Orlando.

"Dottore, hello . . . but where are you going, Dottore?" exclaimed the agent immediately. "It's not up there that you're supposed to go."

"Really," said Marcello, suddenly stopping and calming down, "I think they took me for a client . . ."

"Stupid women," said the agent, shaking his head. "Come with me, Dottore, I'll take you there myself. They're waiting for you, Dottore."

He preceded Marcello through the glass-paned door and into the garden. Walking single file, they followed the driveway by the hedge and circled behind the villa. The sun was burning this part of the garden, with a dry heat made bitter by dust and vegetation run wild. Marcello noticed that all the shutters of the villa were closed, as if it were uninhabited; the garden, too, was full of weeds and seemed abandoned. The agent was now heading toward a low white building that occupied the entire end of the garden. Marcello remembered observing housing like this at the end of similar gardens and in the back of similar villas in seaside towns; in the summer the proprietors rented their villas, restricting themselves, for love of money, to a couple of rooms.

The agent, without knocking, opened the door and looked in, announcing: "Here is Dottor Clerici."

Marcello stepped forward and found himself in a little room furnished minimally as an office. The air was thick with smoke. At the table sat a man, his hands joined and his face turned toward Marcello. The man was albino; his face had the shining, rosy transparence of alabaster, scattered with yellow freckles; his eyes were a burning blue, almost red, with white lashes, like those of certain savage beasts that live in the polar snows. Used to the disconcerting contrast between the dull bureaucratic style and often ferocious duties of many of his collegues in the Secret Service, Marcello couldn't help admitting that this man, at least, was perfectly in his place. There was more than cruelty in that spectral face, there was a kind of ruthless fury, but contained within the conventional rigidity of a military attitude. After a moment of embarrassing immobility, the man stood up brusquely, revealing his small stature, and said, "Gabrio."

Then he sat down immediately and continued, in an ironic tone, "Well, here you are, finally, Dottor Clerici." He had an unpleasant, metallic voice.

Without waiting for him to offer one, Marcello took a seat in his turn and said, "I arrived this morning."

"And in fact I expected you this morning."

Marcello hesitated: should he tell him that he was on his honeymoon? He decided not to and finished peaceably, "It wasn't possible for me to be here any sooner."

"So I see," said the man. He pushed the box of cigarettes toward Marcello with a "do you smoke?"devoid of pleasantry; then he lowered his head over a piece of paper lying on the table and began to read it.

"They leave me here, in this perhaps hospitable but certainly not secret house, without information, without directions, almost without money . . . here." He read a moment longer and then added, lifting his face, "In Rome you were told to come find me, right?"

"Yes, the agent who brought me in came to notify me that I would have to interrupt the trip and introduce myself to you."

"Just so." Gabrio took the cigarette out of his mouth and placed it carefully on the lip of the ashtray. "At the last minute, it seems, they changed their minds. The plan is altered."

Marcello didn't bat a lash; but he felt a wave of relief and hope, whose source was mysterious to him, wash over him and swell his heart. Maybe he would be allowed to keep his trip separate, reduce it to its apparent motive: a honeymoon in Paris. He said, however, in a clear voice, "Meaning?"

"Meaning, the plan has changed and, in consequence, your mission," continued Gabrio. "The aforesaid Quadri was to be kept under surveillance, you were to establish a relationship with him, inspire his trust, maybe even get him to give you some task or other . . . Now instead, in this last message from Rome, Quadri is designated as an undesireable to be eliminated."

Gabrio picked up his cigarette again, breathed in a mouthful of smoke, and set it back on the ashtray. "In substance," he explained in a more conversational tone, "your mission is reduced to almost nothing. You will limit yourself to contacting Quadri, making use of the fact that you already know him, and pointing him out to agent Orlando, who is also going to Paris. You could, perhaps, invite him to some public place where Orlando will be waiting — a café, a restaurant . . . Just so Orlando can see him and verify his identity. This is all that's being asked of you; then you can devote yourself to your honeymoon in whatever way you wish."

So, even Gabrio knew about his honeymoon, thought Marcello, stunned. But this first thought, he realized immediately, was no more than an affected mask beneath which his mind sought to hide its own turmoil from itself. In reality, Gabrio had revealed something more important than his knowledge of Marcello's honeymoon: the decision to eliminate Quadri. With a violent effort, he forced himself to examine this extraordinary and ominous piece of news objectively. And he concluded something fundamental right away: his presence and participation in Paris were not at all necessary for the elimination of Quadri; agent Orlando could find and identify his victim very well by himself. In reality, he thought, they only wanted to involve him, even if it wasn't really necessary, compromising him completely once and forever. As far as the change in plan was concerned, he did not doubt that it was only apparent. Surely, at the time of his visit to the minister, the plan just now disclosed by Gabrio had already been decided on and defined in all its details; and the apparent change was due to their characteristic method of dividing and confusing responsibilities. Neither he nor, probably, Gabrio had received written orders; in this way, if things went wrong, the minister would be able to declare his own innocence, and the blame for the assassination would fall on him, on Gabrio, on Orlando, and on the others who actually executed the orders.

He hesitated and then, to gain time, objected, "I don't see that Orlando needs me to find Quadri . . . I think he's even in the telephone book."

"Those are the orders," said Gabrio, answering almost too quickly, too readily, as if he had foreseen the objection.

Marcello lowered his head. He understood that he had been lured into a kind of a trap; and that having offered a finger, he was now being manipulated into giving a whole arm; but strangely, once he had gotten over his first surprise, he realized that he felt no rebellion at the change of plan, only a sense of dull and melancholy resignation, as if confronting an ever more thankless, yet unalterable and inevitable duty. Agent Orlando was probably not aware of the hidden mechanics of this duty, while he, Marcello, was; but it was only in this way that they differed. Neither he nor Orlando could disobey what Gabrio called "the orders," but which were actually personal circumstances, by now fixed, outside of which there was nothing for either of them but chaos and lawlessness.

At last he said, raising his head, "All right. Where will I find Orlando, in Paris?"

Gabrio replied, glancing at the same piece of paper on the table, "You give him your address there . . . Orlando will find you."

So, Marcello couldn't help thinking, they didn't altogether trust him; at any rate, they didn't choose to disclose the agent's address in Paris to him. He named the hotel where he would be staying, and Gabrio noted it at the foot of the page.

Then he added, in a more affable tone, as if to indicate that the official part of the visit was over, "Have you ever been to Paris?"

"No, it's the first time."

"I was there for two years before I ended up in this hole," said Gabrio, with a kind of bureaucratic bitterness. "Once you've been to Paris, even Rome seems like a dump . . . and as for a place like this, well, you can imagine." He lit a cigarette from the stub of his last one and added, boasting dryly, "In Paris I had it made . . . apartment, automobile, friends, affairs with lots of women . . . you know, as far as *that* goes, Paris is ideal."

Although he was repulsed, Marcello felt that he must make some response to Gabrio's affability, so he said, "But with the whorehouse right here around you, you must not get too bored."

Gabrio shook his head. "Pah, how the hell can you have fun with that recruited mass of flesh they sell for so much a pound? No," he went on, "the only real resource here is the casino. Do you play?"

"No, never."

"Still, it's interesting," said Gabrio, settling back into his chair as if to signify that their conversation was over. "Fortune can smile on anyone, on me or on you . . . They don't call her a woman for nothing. It's all a matter of grabbing her in time."

He rose, went to the door, and threw it open. He was truly small, observed Marcello, with short legs and a rigid chest stuffed into a green jacket cut in the military style. He stood still for a moment in a ray of sun that seemed to accentuate the transparency of his clear, pinkish skin and said, staring at Marcello, "I don't suppose we'll see each other again. You're returning directly to Rome after Paris."

"Yes, almost certainly."

"Do you need anything?" asked Gabrio suddenly, with reluctance. "Have they provided you with enough funds? I don't have much here with me . . . but if you need something . . ."

"No thanks, I don't need anything."

"Well, good luck, then — break a leg."

They shook hands and Gabrio closed the door in a hurry. Marcello headed toward the gate.

But when he was back on the path between the dusty hedges, he realized that in his furious escape from the salon, he had forgotten his hat there. He hesitated; it disgusted him to think of going back into that big room that stank of old shoes, face powder, and sweat, and he also feared the flattery and bawdy witticisms of the women. Then he decided; he turned back and pushed open the door, setting off the same doorbell.

This time no one appeared, neither the maid with the face of a ferret, nor any of the girls. But the loud, well-known, good-natured voice of agent Orlando reached him from the salon through the open door; and, encouraged, he peered in from the threshold.

The room was empty. The agent was sitting in a corner next to a woman Marcello didn't remember having noticed when the girls had presented themselves at his first entrance. The agent had put his arm around her waist in an awkward, intimate gesture and didn't bother to remove it when he saw Marcello. Embarrassed and vaguely irritated, Marcello averted his eyes from Orlando and looked at the woman.

She was sitting up rigidly, almost as if she wished in some way to drive off or at least distance her companion. She was a brunette with a high, white forehead, clear eyes, a long, thin face, and a large mouth, enlivened by dark lipstick and an expression of what looked like contempt. She was dressed almost normally, in a white, sleeveless, low-cut dress. The only whorish thing about her was the split in her skirt, which opened just below the waist to reveal her belly and groin, and her long, dry, elegant, crossed legs, as chastely beautiful as the legs of a dancer. She was holding a lit cigarette between two fingers, but she was not smoking; her hand lay on the armrest of the sofa and the smoke spiraled up in the air. Her other hand lay abandoned on the agent's knee as if, thought Marcello, on the faithful head of a big dog. But what struck him most was her forehead, not so much white as *illuminated* in some mysterious way by the intense expression of her eyes, with a purity of light that made him think of one of those diamond tiaras that women crowned themselves with long ago at gala balls. Marcello stared at her, astounded, for a long time; and as he looked, he realized he was feeling an incomprehensibly painful regret and irritation. Meanwhile, Orlando had risen to his feet, intimidated by Marcello's insistent stare.

"My hat," said Marcello.

The woman remained seated and was now looking at him, in her turn, without curiosity. The agent crossed the room quickly to retrieve the hat from a distant divan. Suddenly, then, Marcello understood why the sight of the woman had inspired that painful sense of regret in him: actually, he realized, he didn't want her to do the agent's bidding, and seeing her submit to his embrace had made Marcello suffer as if confronted with an intolerable profanity. Surely she knew nothing about the light radiating from her forehead, which did not belong to her anyway, as beauty does not generally belong to the beautiful. Just the same, he felt it was almost his duty to keep her from lowering that luminous forehead to satisfy Orlando's erotic whims. For a moment he thought of using his authority to take her out of the room; they could talk awhile and then, as soon as he was sure the agent had chosen another woman, he would go. Crazily, he even thought about rescuing her from the whorehouse and getting her started on another sort of life. But even as he was thinking these things, he knew that they were fantasies; she could not help resembling her companions, like them irreparably and almost innocently ruined and lost. Then he felt a touch on his arm: Orlando was holding out his hat. He took it mechanically.

But the agent had had time to consider Marcello's long, strange look. He took a step forward and proposed, pointing to the woman the way someone might offer a drink or something to eat to an honored guest, "Dottore, if you wish, if this one pleases you . . . I can always wait."

At first Marcello didn't understand. Then he saw Orlando's smile, at once respectful and malicious, and felt himself blush right up to the ears. So Orlando was not renouncing her, only adapting, from friendly courtesy and bureaucratic discipline, to the situation, letting Marcello go first — just as if they were at the counter of a bar or the table of a buffet.

Marcello said quickly, "No, you're crazy, Orlando . . . do what you want, I have to go."

"In that case, Dottore," said the agent with a smile. Marcello saw him recall the woman with a nod and then, to his sorrow, he saw her — tall and straight, with her diadem of light on her forehead — rise immediately and obediently at that nod and move toward the agent without hesitation or protest, with professional simplicity.

Orlando said, "Dottore, we'll see each other soon," and stood aside to let the woman pass. Marcello drew back as well, almost despite himself; and she walked unhurriedly between the two of them, her cigarette between her fingers.

But when she was in front of Marcello, she stopped for an instant and said, "If you want me, my name is Luisa."

Her voice, as he had feared, was loud, hoarse, and indelicate; and feeling she should add some enticing gesture to her words, she stuck out her tongue and licked her upper lip. This gesture, combined with her words, rescued Marcello in part from the regret he was feeling for not having kept her from going with Orlando.

Meanwhile Luisa, who was preceding the agent, had reached the stairway. She threw her lit cigarette on the ground, crushed it out with her foot, lifted up her skirt with both hands, and started climbing the stairs in a hurry, followed one step behind by Orlando. Finally they disappeared behind a corner of the landing. Now someone else, probably one of the girls and her client, was coming downstairs, talking. Marcello rushed out of the house.

3

*A*FTER CHARGING THE HOTEL porter to call Quadri's number, Marcello went to sit down in a corner of the lobby. It was a big hotel and the lobby was vast, with columns supporting the vaults, groups of armchairs, writing desks and coffee tables, and glass cases displaying luxury items; a lot of people were coming and going from the entrance to the elevator cage, from the porter's counter to the management's counter, and from the restaurant to the lounges that opened up beyond the columns. Marcello would have liked to distract himself by watching the spectacle in this gay and crowded lobby while he was waiting, but despite himself his thoughts, as if dragged down toward the depths of memory by his present anguish, turned to the first and only visit he had ever made to Quadri, many years ago.

Marcello was a student then and Quadri was his professor; he had gone to Quadri's home in an old red palazzo near the station, to consult him about his thesis. As soon as he had entered he had been struck by the enormous number of books accumulated in every corner of the apartment. Even in the entrance hall he had noticed some old curtains that appeared to be drawn over doorways; but pushing them aside, he had discovered rows and rows of books lined up in the recesses of the walls. The maid had proceded him down an extremely long and tortuous hallway that seemed to wind all around the courtyard of the palazzo, and it, too, was cluttered with shelves full of books and papers on both sides. Finally they had reached Quadri's study, and Marcello had found himself between four walls densely packed with books, reaching from the floor to the ceiling. More books were on the desk, placed one on top of another in two orderly stacks between which, as if through a crack, the bearded face of the professor could be seen. Marcello noticed right away that Quadri had a curiously flat and asymmetrical face, like a papier-mâché mask with the eyes rimmed in red and a triangular nose, to which, lower down, a beard and false mustache had been carelessly glued. Even on his forehead, his wet, too-black hair resembled a badly applied toupé. Between his toothbrush mustache and mutton-chop beard, both suspiciously black, you could glimpse a very red mouth with shapeless lips; and Marcello couldn't help wondering whether all that badly distributed hair was hiding some kind of deformity — for instance, a total lack of chin or a frightening scar. All in all, it was a face in which he could see nothing true or secure; everything in it was false, just like a mask.

The professor had risen to welcome Marcello, and with this gesture had revealed his small stature and the hump, or rather, the deformity of his left shoulder, which added a sorrowful air to the excessive, affectionate sweetness of his manner. Shaking hands across his books, Quadri had gazed at his visitor near-sightedly, peering over his thick glasses, so that for a moment Marcello had had the sensation of being scrutinized not by two eyes, but by four. He had also noticed Quadri's old-fashioned style of dressing: a jacket a financier might wear, black with silk lapels; striped black trousers; a white shirt with starched cuffs and collar; a gold chain draped over his vest. Marcello did not particularly like Quadri; he knew him to be anti-Fascist; and in Marcello's mind Quadri's po-

litical stance, his cowardly, unwarlike character, his unhealthiness
and ugliness, his erudition and books — everything about him, in
fact — seemed to represent to perfection the conventional image
of the negative and impotent intellectual, which the party's propaganda was continually holding up to scorn. And Quadri's extraordinary sweetness repulsed Marcello, as well; it had to be phony; it
seemed impossible to him that a man could be so gentle and kind
without deceit and hidden agendas.

Quadri had welcomed Marcello with his usual expressions of
almost saccharine affection. He had asked him a number of questions, frequently interjecting them with words like "dear boy,"
"my son," and "dear son," and waving his little white hands over
the top of his books. First he had asked him about his family and
then about him personally. When he had heard that Marcello's
father had spent years in a clinic for the mentally ill, he had exclaimed, "Oh, poor boy, I didn't know, what a misfortune, what a
terrible catastrophe . . . and science can do nothing to lead him
back to reason?"

But he had not listened to Marcello's response and had passed
on immediately to another subject. He had a throaty voice, modu-
lated and pleasant, extremely sweet and full of apprehensive
solicitude. But curiously, within this declarative and mawkish solicitude, Marcello had seemed to glimpse, like a watermark on
paper, the most complete indifference: it was possible that Quadri,
far from being truly interested in him, didn't even see him. Marcello had also been struck by the entire absence of nuance and in-
flection in Quadri's voice; he always spoke in the same uniformly
affectionate and sentimental way, whether the subject merited
such a tone or not. At the conclusion of his numerous questions,
Quadri had finally asked whether Marcello were Fascist. Re-
ceiving an affirmative answer, he had explained almost casually,
without changing tone or appearing to have any reaction, how difficult it was for him, whose anti-Fascist sentiments were well
known, to continue teaching subjects like philosophy and history
under the Fascist regime. At this point Marcello, embarrassed, had
tried to bring the conversation back to the reason for his visit.

But Quadri had interrupted him immediately. "Perhaps you're asking yourself why in the world I'm telling you all these things . . . dear boy, I'm not saying them idly or to unburden myself to you . . . I wouldn't dream of wasting your time, which you must devote to your studies. I'm telling you this to somehow justify the fact that I'll be unable to give you or your thesis any attention. I'm leaving teaching."

"You're leaving teaching," Marcello repeated, caught by surprise.

"Yes," said Quadri, stroking his mouth and mustache with one hand in a habitual gesture. "Although I do so with sorrow, with real sorrow, since up until now I've devoted my whole life to you students. But I really feel I must leave the school." After a moment the professor had added, with a sigh but without emphasis, "Eh, yes, I've decided to pass from thought to action . . . The phrase may not be new to you, but it mirrors my situation faithfully."

Right then Marcello had almost smiled. In fact, it had seemed funny to him that this professor, this little man in a banker's suit, hunchbacked, near-sighted, and bearded, sitting in an armchair between his stacks of books, was declaring that he had decided to pass from thought to action. What he meant by the phrase was perfectly clear: Quadri, after years of opposing the regime passively, cloistered in his thoughts and his profession, had decided to become politically active, perhaps even to engage in conspiracy.

Marcello, with an instant surge of hostility, had not been able to keep himself from warning the professor, in a cold and threatening tone, "You do yourself a disservice, telling this to me. I'm a Fascist and I could denounce you."

But Quadri had replied with extreme gentleness, switching from the more formal *Lei* he had been using to the informality of *tu*, "I know that you're a good, dear boy, an honest and upright boy, and I know that you would never do anything of the kind."

"He can go to hell," Marcello had thought in annoyance. And he had answered sincerely, "Yet I *could* denounce you. Honesty, for us Fascists, consists precisely in the denunciation of people like you, and in removing them from positions where they can do harm."

The professor had shaken his head. "My dear son, you know even as you speak that what you're saying isn't true. You know it, or your heart knows it . . . and in fact, honest youth that you are, you wanted to warn me. Do you know what someone else would have done, a real informer? He would have pretended to approve of me and then, once I was compromised by some really indiscreet statement, he would have denounced me. But you warned me."

"I warned you," Marcello had answered harshly, "only because I don't believe you're capable of what you call action. Why aren't you satisfied just being a professor? What kind of action are you talking about?"

"Action . . . it's not important to say what it is," Quadri had replied, staring at him fixedly. At these words, Marcello had not been able to keep from raising his eyes toward the walls and their shelves full of books.

Quadri had intercepted his glance and had added, still with the utmost sweetness, "It seems strange to you, doesn't it, to hear me talk about action? Surrounded by all these books? Right now you're thinking, 'What action is he prattling on about, this little humpbacked, crooked, near-sighted, bearded man?' Tell the truth, that's what you're thinking . . . Your party's pamphlets have described the man who can't act, doesn't even know how to act, the *intellectual*, so many times for you, that now you smile compassionately, recognizing me in that image . . . isn't that right?"

Surprised by such acumen, Marcello had exclaimed, "How did you know that?"

"Oh, my dear boy," Quadri had answered as he stood up, "my dear boy, I knew it right away. But it's not written anywhere that you have to have a golden eagle on your beret or braid on your sleeve to take action. Good-bye, at any rate, good-bye, good-bye and good luck . . . good-bye."

And so saying, he had gently, inexorably pushed Marcello out the door.

Now Marcello, thinking back to that encounter, realized that a lot of youthful impatience and inexperience had contributed to his rash disdain for Quadri, bearded, hunchbacked, and pedantic as he may have been. Quadri himself, by his subsequent deeds, had been the one to show Marcello his error: he had escaped to Paris shortly after their conversation, and once he was there, had swiftly become one of the leaders of anti-Fascism — perhaps the most able, prepared, and aggressive of them all. His specialty, it seemed, was recruitment. Profiting from his experience as a teacher and his knowledge of the workings of young men's minds, he was often successful at converting those who had been indifferent or even opposed to his stance, and then pushing them into enterprises that were daring, dangerous, and almost always disastrous — if not for him, their inspiration, at least for the actual executors. He did not seem to feel, as he cast his disciples into the conspiratorial struggle, any of those humanitarian concerns that one would have been tempted to attribute to him, given his character. On the contrary, he sacrificed his disciples with nonchalance in desperate actions that could only be justified by extremely long-range plans requiring a cruel indifference to human life. Quadri, in other words, had some of the rare qualities of a true politician, or at least a certain category of them: he was at once astute and enthusiastic, intellectual and active, open and cynical, thoughtful and daring. In the course of his work, Marcello had had frequent occasions to study Quadri, whom the police defined as "a very dangerous element," and he had always been struck by the man's ability to accommodate so many contrasting qualities in one profound and ambiguous character. In this way, slowly but surely, because of what he had managed to learn at a distance from information that was by no means always precise, Marcello's initial contempt had turned into an irritable respect. His original dislike had held firm, however, because he was convinced that courage was not to be counted among Quadri's many qualities. He based this assumption on the fact that, although the professor thrust his followers into mortal danger, he never exposed himself personally.

He was roused from these thoughts by the voice of one of the hotel staff, who was rapidly crossing the lobby, calling out his name. For a minute he almost thought it was someone else's name, and was aided in his illusion by the man's French pronunciation. But this "Monsieur Clarisi" was him, all right; as he realized with a kind of queasiness while pretending to himself that he really believed it was someone else and trying to imagine what he would be like: him, with his face, his figure, his clothes. Meanwhile, the hotel employee was walking away in the direction of the writing room, still calling him. Marcello got up and went directly to the telephone booth.

He picked up the receiver, which had been placed on the shelf, and brought it to his ear. A limpid, feminine, somewhat lilting voice asked in French who was there.

Marcello replied, in the same language, "I'm Italian . . . Clerici, Marcello Clerici . . . and I'd like to speak to Professor Quadri."

"He's very busy . . . I don't know if he can come to the phone . . . did you say your name was Clerici?"

"Yes, Clerici."

"Wait a moment."

He heard the sound of the receiver being set on a table, then footsteps walking off, and finally silence. He waited a long time, expecting the sound of footsteps to announce either the woman's return or the arrival of the professor. Instead, all of a sudden, Quadri's voice was booming in his ear, shattering the deep silence without warning.

"*Pronto*, Quadri here . . . who's speaking?"

Marcello explained in a rush, "My name is Marcello Clerici . . . I was one of your students when you were teaching in Rome . . . I'd like to see you."

"Clerici," repeated Quadri doubtfully. Then, after a moment, he said decisively, "Clerici. Don't know him."

"But you do, professor," insisted Marcello. "I came to find you a few days before you quit teaching . . . I wanted you to look at my thesis project."

"One moment, Clerici," said Quadri. "I don't remember your name at all. But that doesn't mean you're not right . . . and you want to see me?"

"Yes."

"Why?"

"No particular reason," answered Marcello. "Since I was one of your pupils and I've heard a lot of talk about you lately . . . I wanted to see you, that's all."

"All right," said Quadri in a yielding tone. "Come see me at my house."

"When?"

"Today if you like . . . this afternoon . . . after lunch, come and have coffee . . . around three o'clock."

"I should tell you," said Marcello, "that I'm on my honeymoon. May I bring my wife?"

"But of course, naturally. I'll see you later."

Marcello heard the phone being put down, and after a moment's thought he did the same. But before he had time to leave the booth, the same man that had called out his name in the lobby shortly before stuck his head in and said, "They want you on the telephone."

"I already talked to them," said Marcello, trying to pass by.

"No, someone else wants you."

Mechanically, he went back into the booth and picked up the receiver again.

Immediately a loud, jolly, friendly voice yelled into his ear, "Is that you, Dottore Clerici?"

Marcello recognized agent Orlando's voice and answered calmly, "Yes, it's me."

"Did you have a good trip, Dottore?"

"Yes, excellent."

"Your wife is well?"

"Very well."

"And what do you think about Paris?"

"I haven't left the hotel yet," answered Marcello, a little put out by this familiarity.

"You'll see . . . Paris is Paris . . . So Dottore, shall we meet?"

"Certainly, Orlando. You tell me where."

"You don't know Paris, Dottore, so I'll make the appointment for somewhere easy to find . . . the café on the corner of a piazza called della Maddalena . . . you can't go wrong, it's on the left coming from Rue Royale . . . it has a lot of little tables outside. But I'll be waiting for you inside . . . There won't be anyone else there."

"All right, what time?"

"I'm already at the café. But I'll wait for as long as you want . . ."

"Half an hour, then."

"Perfect, Dottore. Half an hour."

Marcello emerged from the booth and headed toward the elevator. Just as he was getting in, he heard the same employee call out his name for a third time; and this time he was really astonished. He almost hoped it was some superhuman intervention, an oracle using the black Bakelight receiver of the telephone to speak a word and tell him something decisive about his life. In a kind of suspension he retraced his steps and entered the booth for the third time.

"Is that you, Marcello?" asked the caressing, languid voice of his wife.

"Oh, it's you," he couldn't help exclaiming, whether with disappointment or relief he couldn't say.

"Yes, of course. Who did you think it was?"

"Nothing . . . it's just that I was expecting a phone call . . ."

"What are you doing?" she asked, in yearning, tender tones.

"Nothing . . . I was just about to come up to tell you I was going out and I'd be back in an hour."

"No, don't come up, I'm about to get in the bath. I'll be waiting for you in an hour, in the hotel lobby."

"It could be an hour and a half."

"All right, an hour and a half . . . but please don't be late."

"I said that so you won't have to wait. But you'll see, I'll only be an hour."

She said quickly, as if she were afraid that Marcello was going, "Do you love me?"

"Well, of course, why are you asking me?"

"Just because . . . If you were here with me right now, would you give me a kiss?"

"Of course . . . do you want me to come up?"

"No, no, don't come up . . . but tell me . . ."

"What?"

"Tell me, did I please you tonight?"

"What questions, Giulia!" he exclaimed, a little embarrassed.

She said immediately, "Forgive me . . . even I don't know what I'm saying . . . so you love me?"

"I already told you I did."

"Forgive me . . . all right, it's agreed, I'll be waiting for you in an hour and a half . . . good-bye, love."

This time, he thought as he hung up the receiver, he really couldn't expect another phone call. He went to the door, pushed on the panel of crystal and mahogany and went out into the street.

The hotel looked out on the embankments of the Seine. As he stepped across the threshold, he stopped a moment and stood still, surprised by the thriving spectacle of the city and by the beautiful, sunny day. Alongside the river for as far as the eye could see, huge, leafy trees rose up from the sidewalks, crowned with shining spring foliage. They were trees he didn't know: maybe horse chestnuts. The brilliant sun shone on every leaf and was transformed into a glad, clear, luminous green. Lined up on the parapets, the stalls of old book dealers offered rows of used books and stacks of printed matter of all kinds; people strolled slowly beside the stalls beneath the trees in the shifting play of light and shadows; it all had the soothing atmosphere of a tranquil Sunday outing. Marcello crossed the street and went to look over the parapet between one stall and another. Beyond the river he could see gray palaces with mansard roofs on the other shore; beyond that, the two towers of Notre Dame; even farther away the spires of other churches, profiles of huge apartment buildings, roofs and chimneys. He noticed that the sky was paler and vaster than in Italy, as if resonant with the invisible, teeming presence of the immense city lying beneath its vault. He lowered his eyes to the river: flowing between massive, crooked stone walls, flanked by clean footpaths, it seemed no more than a canal at that point; the oily, thick, cloudy green water swirled around the white piers of the nearest bridge in whirlpools that sparkled like jewels. A black and yellow barge slid rapidly downriver, creating no wake on the dense water; its funnel spewed out smoke in jerky puffs; he could see two men talking on the prow, one in a light blue shirt and the other in a white undershirt. A fat, familiar sparrow came to rest on the parapet next to Marcello's arm, twittered vivaciously as if telling him something, and then flew off again in the direction of the bridge. A skinny, badly dressed young man with a beret on his head and a book under his arm, probably a student, attracted his attention; he was walking slowly in the direction of Notre Dame, stopping every once in a while to look at the books and printed material. As he was watching him, Marcello was struck by a sense of his own liberty, despite all the duties that oppressed him. Why, *he* could be that young man, and then the river Seine, the sky, the trees, all of Paris would have a completely different meaning for him. At the same time he saw a taxi rolling slowly forward on the asphalt and hailed it with a gesture that almost surprised him; he hadn't thought of it a moment before. He climbed in and gave the address of the café where Orlando was waiting for him.

Facing backward on the cushions, he gazed out at the streets of Paris as the taxi maneuvered through it. He noted the cheerfulness of the city, lovely and gay despite its grayness and age, and filled with a kind of intelligent sweetness that seemed to come in through the windows in gusts along with the wind of their journey. He liked the guards standing upright at the crossroads, he wasn't sure why; they seemed so elegant, with their hard, round *kèpi*, their short capes, their slender legs. One of them looked in at the window to say something to the driver: a pale, energetic little blond, his whistle clamped between his teeth, his arm holding a white stick stretched out behind him to stop the traffic. He liked the big horse chestnuts lifting their branches toward the shining windows of the old gray facades; he liked the antiquated signs hanging over the shop doors, with their white writing full of flourishes on brown or wine-colored backgrounds; he even liked the unesthetic shape of the taxis and buses, with their hoods that looked like the lowered muzzles of dogs sniffing along the ground. After a brief stop, the taxi passed in front of the neoclassical temple of the Chambre des Députés, turned onto the bridge, and speeded toward the obelisk of the Place du Concorde. So, he thought, staring at the immense military square, closed at the end by porticos lined up like regiments of soldiers on parade, so, this was the capital of France, which must be destroyed. It seemed to him now that he had loved this city stretched out before his eyes for a long time, from way before this day, his first day here. Yet this admiration for the majestic, cultured, cheerful beauty of the city only emphasized his unhappiness at the duty he was about to carry out. Perhaps if Paris had been less lovely, he pondered, he would have been able to elude that duty, escape, free himself from his fate. But the city's beauty reconfirmed the hostile, negative part he had to play, as did the many repulsive aspects of the cause he served. As he was thinking these things, he became aware that he was trying to explain the absurdity of his position to himself. And he understood that he was explaining it this way because there was no other way to explain it and so to accept it consciously and freely.

The taxi came to a halt and Marcello got out in front of the café designated by Orlando. The tables set out on the sidewalk were packed with people, as the agent had said they would be; but as soon as he entered the café, he saw that it was deserted. Orlando was sitting at a table set into the recess of a window. As soon as he saw Marcello, he rose to his feet and gestured him to come over.

Marcello approached the agent unhurriedly and sat down opposite him. Through the window glass he could see the backs of the people sitting outside in the shade of the trees and, in the distance, part of the colonnade and triangular pediment of the church of the Magdalen. Marcello ordered a coffee.

Orlando waited until the waiter had left and then said, "Maybe you think, Dottore, that they're going to make you an espresso like they do in Italy, but you'll be disappointed. Good coffee like ours doesn't exist in Paris . . . you'll see, Dottore, what kind of dishwater they'll bring you." He was speaking in his usual respectful, calm, good-natured tone of voice.

"An honest face," thought Marcello, casting a sidelong glance at the agent as he poured out a little of the despised coffee with a sigh, "the face of a farmer, a sharecropper, a small rural land-owner." He waited for Orlando to drink his coffee and then asked, "Where do you come from, Orlando?"

"Me? From the province of Palermo, Dottore."

Marcello, for no particular reason, had always thought that Or-lando was native to central Italy, Umbria perhaps, or the Marche. Now, looking at him more closely, he understood that he had been led into this error by the agent's rural, level-headed aspect. But his face bore not a trace of Umbrian mildness or the placidity of the Marche. Yes, it was a friendly, honest face, but the black, somewhat weary eyes were informed with a feminine, almost Oriental gravity never seen in central Italy. The smile on the wide, lipless mouth beneath his small, crudely shaped nose was not meek or placid, either.

Marcello murmured, "I never would have thought it . . ."

"Where did you think I was from?" asked Orlando, showing some spirit.

"From central Italy."

Orlando seemed to reflect for a moment; then he said, respect-fully but frankly, "Even you, Dottore — I bet even you participate in the general prejudice."

"What prejudice?"

"The prejudice of the north against southern Italy, and in par-ticular against Sicily . . . You don't want to admit it, Dottore, but it's true." Orlando shook his head in sorrow.

Marcello protested, "Really, I wasn't thinking about that at all . . . I thought you were from central Italy because of how you look."

But Orlando was no longer listening to him. "I'll tell you, it's a steady stream of abuse, *uno stillicidio*," he replied emphatically, ob-viously satisfied by the unusual word he had used. "On the street, at home, everywhere, even in the Secret Service . . . certain northern colleagues come down to reproach us for everything, even spaghetti. And I tell them: first of all, you eat spaghetti too by now, even more than we do. And then: how very sweet your polenta is!"

Marcello said nothing. Actually, he wasn't sorry that Orlando was talking about things that had nothing to do with the mission; it was a way to avoid familiarity on a terrible subject, which he could not have borne.

Suddenly Orlando said forcefully, "Sicily: great, slandered Sicily. For example, the mafia: if you knew all the things they come up with to say about the mafia . . . according to them, there's not a Sicilian who's not mafioso . . . apart from the fact that they know absolutely nothing about the mafia, anyway."

Marcello said, "The mafia doesn't exist anymore."

"Of course, right, it doesn't exist anymore," said Orlando, with the air of someone who remains unconvinced, "but Dottore, even if it did still exist, believe me, it would still be better, infinitely better than similar phenomena in the north — the vandals and hoods in Milan, the criminals in Turin . . . scoundrels, cowards, bullies, exploiters of women, petty thieves, . . . The mafia, if nothing else, was a school of courage."

"Excuse me, Orlando," said Marcello coldly, "but would you care to explain to me just what the mafia's school of courage consists of?"

The question seemed to disconcert Orlando, not so much because of the almost bureaucratic chill in Marcello's tone of voice, as much because of the complexity of the subject, which could not begin to be covered by an immediate response.

"Eh, Dottore," he said with a sigh, "you're asking me a question it's not easy to answer. In Sicily courage is the primary quality of a man of honor, and the mafia calls itself 'Honored Society.' What do you want me to tell you? It's hard for anyone who hasn't seen it with their own eyes to understand it. Try to imagine, Dottore, some place — a bar, a café, an inn, a restaurant — where a group of armed men were gathered, and these men were acting hostile to the mafioso. So what did he do? He didn't run to the police and complain, he didn't leave town . . . Instead, he would walk out of his house every day dressed to the nines, freshly shaved, and go to that locale alone and unarmed. He would speak the two or three words sufficient for courtesy and that was all. Now do you believe me? Everyone there — I mean his group of enemies, his friends, the whole town — had their eyes on him. He knew it, and he knew that if he showed he was afraid in any way . . . if his glance wavered or his voice wasn't calm enough or if his face wasn't completely cheerful, he was done for. He had to devote himself completely to passing this test: firm glances, tranquil voice, measured gestures, normal coloring . . . to tell it it sounds easy . . . but you have to find yourself in that situation to understand how difficult it is . . . Dottore, this was, just to give you an example, the mafia's school of courage."

Orlando, who had been carried away as he talked, now launched a cold, curious glance at Marcello's face, as if to say, "But if I'm not mistaken, we two didn't come here to talk about the mafia, did we."

Marcello caught the look and looked ostentatiously at the watch he wore on his wrist.

"Now let's get down to our business, Orlando," he said with authority. "I'm meeting Professor Quadri today. According to the instructions, I need to point out the professor to you so that you can verify his identity . . . that's my role, isn't it?"

"Yes, Dottore."

"All right, I'll invite Professor Quadri to dinner or to a café this evening . . . I'm not sure where yet . . . but phone me at the hotel this evening around seven, I'll know the place by then. As far as Professor Quadri goes, let's establish how I'm going to point him out right now. For example, let's say that Professor Quadri will be the first person I shake hands with when I enter the café or restaurant . . . Is that all right with you?"

"Absolutely, Dottore."

"And now I have to go," said Marcello, glancing at his watch again. He put the money for their coffees on the table, rose, and walked out, followed at a distance by the agent.

On the sidewalk, Orlando took in the dense traffic in the street — two rows of cars moving at a snail's pace in opposite directions — and said in an emphatic tone: "Paris."

"This isn't the first time you've been here, is it, Orlando?" asked Marcello, his eyes roving over the cars in search of a free taxi.

"The first time?" said the agent with a kind of mindless pride. "Far from it . . . go ahead and try, Dottore, guess a number."

"Oh, I wouldn't know."

"Twelve," said the agent, "thirteen, this time."

A taxi driver intercepted Marcello's glance and came to a halt in front of him.

"Good-bye, Orlando," said Marcello, climbing in, "I'll expect your phone call this evening."

The agent gestured his assent. Marcello climbed in, giving the driver the hotel's address.

But as the taxi rolled through the streets, the agent's final words, that twelve and thirteen (twelve times in Paris and this makes thirteen) continued to ring in his ears and arouse ancient echoes in his memory. He was like someone who peers into a cave, shouting, and discovers that his voice is reverberating in unsuspected depths. Then, all at once, reminded by those numbers, he recalled that he would point Quadri out to the agent with a handshake, and he understood why, instead of simply informing Orlando that Quadri was recognizable by his humpback, he had suggested this device of the greeting. His distant, childhood memories of the sacred story were what had made him forget the professor's deformity, so much more convenient than a handshake as a means of certain recognition. The apostles were twelve; and it was he who was the thirteenth, the one who embraced the Christ to point him out to the guards gathered in the garden to arrest him. Now the traditional figures of the stations of the Passion of Christ, contemplated so many times in various churches, superimposed themselves on the modern scene of a French restaurant, with sumptuously laid-out tables, patrons seated to eat, he himself who rose and walked toward Quadri, offering him his hand, and the agent Orlando, who, sitting to one side, observed them both. Then the figure of Judas, the thirteenth apostle, merged with Marcello's, wedded itself to his contours, became his own.

He felt an almost amused desire to reflect on this discovery. "Probably Judas did what he did for the same reasons I'm doing it," he thought, "and he, too, had to do it even though he didn't like to, because it was necessary, after all, that *someone* do it . . . but why be scared about it? Let's admit right up front that I've chosen the part of Judas . . . so what?"

He realized that he wasn't at all frightened, in fact. At the most, he thought, he was pervaded by his usual cold melancholy, which he didn't really mind. Then he thought — not to justify himself but to deepen the comparison and recognize its limits — that yes, Judas was like him, but only up to a certain point. Up to the hand-shake; perhaps even (to stretch a point, though he wasn't one of Quadri's disciples), up to the betrayal, in a very generic sense. Then everything was different. Judas had hung himself, or at least had felt that he could do no other than hang himself, because those same men who had suggested and paid for the betrayal had not had the courage afterward to support and justify his action. But Marcello would not kill himself, would not even fall into de-spair, because behind him . . . he saw the crowds gathered in the squares, cheering on the man who gave him his orders and im-plicitly justifying him, Marcello, who obeyed them. And lastly, he thought that he received nothing, in a literal sense, for what he was doing. No thirty gold coins. Only "service," as agent Orlando said. The analogy faded and dissolved, leaving behind it no more than a trace of pride-tinged irony. If anything, he concluded, what mattered was that the comparison had come to mind, that he had explored it and had, for a moment, found it right.

4

*A*FTER BREAKFAST, GIULIA wanted to return to the hotel to change clothes before going to Quadri's. But when they had emerged from the elevator, she put an arm around Marcello's waist and murmured, "I didn't really want to change . . . I just wanted to be alone with you for a little while."

Walking down the long, deserted hallway between two rows of closed doors, his waist encircled by that loving arm, Marcello realized once again that, while for him this trip to Paris was also, and above all, the mission, for Giulia it was simply their honeymoon trip. Which meant, he thought, that he was not allowed to deviate from the role of new groom he had agreed to play when he climbed onto the train with her; even if sometimes, as was now the case, he was in the grip of an anguish very far from the excitement of love. But this was the normality he had so longed for: this arm around his waist, these looks, these caresses; and what he was about to do with Orlando was the blood-price he must pay for it. Meanwhile, they had reached their room and

Giulia, without letting go of his waist, opened the door with her other hand and walked in with him.

Once they were inside she let go of him, turned the key in the lock, and said, "Close the window, will you?"

Marcello went to the window and lowered the blinds. When he turned around he saw that Giulia was standing by the bed, already sliding her dress off over her head, and he thought he understood what she had had in mind when she said, "I just wanted to be alone with you for a little while." In silence he went to sit on the edge of the bed, on the side farthest from Giulia, who was now dressed only in a slip and stockings. She very carefully draped her dress over a chair near the head of the bed, took off her shoes, and finally, clumsily lifting up first one leg and then the other, stretched out on her back behind him, with one arm folded beneath her neck.

She was silent for a moment and then said, "Marcello."

"What's up?"

"Why don't you lie down here beside me?"

Obediently Marcello took off his shoes and stretched out on the bed beside his wife. Giulia immediately cuddled up to him, pressing her body against his and asking anxiously, "What's the matter with you?"

"With me? Nothing. Why?"

"I don't know, you seem so worried."

"That's an impression you must have a lot," he replied. "My usual mood, you know, is hardly carefree . . . but that doesn't mean I'm worried."

She hugged him silently. Then she said, "It wasn't true that I asked you to come up here so I could get ready . . . but it wasn't true, either, that I just wanted to be alone with you . . . the truth is something else."

This time Marcello was caught by surprise and almost felt remorse at having suspected her of simple erotic greed. Lowering his gaze, he saw her eyes looking up at him, full of tears.

Affectionately, although he felt somewhat annoyed, he said, "Now it's my turn to ask you what's the matter."

"You're right," she answered. And right away she began to cry, silent sobs that he could feel shaking her body against his own.

Marcello waited awhile, hoping that her incomprehensible weeping would cease. But instead it seemed to redouble in intensity. At last he asked, staring up at the ceiling, "Would you please tell me why you're crying?"

Giulia sobbed awhile more and then answered, "No reason . . . because I'm stupid." But there was already a hint of consolation in her sorrowful voice.

Marcello looked down at her and insisted, "Come on, why are you crying?"

He saw her gaze at him with those tearful eyes of hers, already shining with a faint hopeful light. She gave him a weak smile and rummaged around for a handkerchief. Then she dried her eyes, blew her nose, put down the handkerchief and murmured, hugging him again, "If I tell you why I was crying, you'll think I'm crazy."

"Come on," he said, caressing her. "Tell me why you were crying."

"Well," she said, "during lunch you seemed so distracted, so worried, actually, that I thought you'd already had enough of me and that you were regretting marrying me . . . maybe because of what I told you in the train, you know, about the lawyer, maybe just because you already knew you'd done something foolish, you, with the future you have in front of you, with your intelligence and your goodness, too, marrying a wretch like me . . . And so, after I thought about it, I thought I'd do it first . . . you know, go away without telling you so you wouldn't have the bother of saying good-bye . . . I decided that as soon as we came back to the hotel I'd pack my bag and leave . . . go back to Italy and leave you in Paris."

"You can't be serious!" exclaimed Marcello in surprise.

"But I was serious," she said with a smile, flattered by his astonishment. "Just think, while we were in the hotel lobby and you went off for a minute to buy cigarettes, I went to the porter and asked him to reserve me a place in the sleeping car for Rome, tonight . . . oh, as you can see, I was serious, all right."

"But you're crazy," said Marcello, raising his voice despite himself.

"I told you," she replied, "that you'd think I was crazy. But at that moment I was sure, absolutely sure that I'd be doing you a favor by leaving you and going away . . . yes, I was as sure of it as I'm sure now," she added, pulling herself up enough to brush his mouth with her lips, "that I'm giving you this kiss."

"Why were you so sure?" asked Marcello, troubled.

"I don't know . . . I just was . . . the way you're sure of things . . . without any reason."

"And so," he couldn't help exclaiming, with the very slightest hint of regret, "why did you change your mind?"

"Why? Who knows? Maybe because in the elevator you looked at me a certain way or at least I got the impression you were looking at me in a certain way . . . but then I remembered that I had decided to leave and had reserved a place on the sleeping car and then when I thought I couldn't go back on it, I started to cry."

Marcello said nothing.

Giulia interpreted this silence in her own way and asked, "Are you annoyed? Tell me, are you annoyed because of the sleeping car? But they'll cancel it, you know . . . and we'll only have to pay the twenty percent."

"How absurd," he answered slowly, as if reflecting.

"Or," she said, and stifled an incredulous laugh still trembling with a trace of fear, "are you annoyed because I didn't really go?"

"Absurd again," he answered. But this time he felt he was not being wholly sincere. And as if to suppress any last hesitation or remorse, he added, "If you had gone off, my whole life would have collapsed."

And this time he felt he was telling the truth, however ambiguously. Wouldn't it be better if his life — the life he had built up since the fact of Lino — collapsed completely instead of being overloaded with other burdens and duties, like some absurd palace to which an infatuated owner keeps adding terraces and turrets and balconies until its solidity is compromised?

He felt Giulia's arms wrap around him and her voice whispering, "Are you telling the truth?"

"Yes," he said, "I'm telling the truth."

"But what would you have done," she insisted with pleased, almost vain curiosity, "if I had really left you and gone away? Would you have run after me?"

He hesitated before responding, and once again he seemed to hear that far-off regret echoing in his voice. "No, I don't think so . . . haven't I just told you that my whole life would collapse?"

"Would you have stayed in France?"

"Yes, maybe."

"And your career? Would you have thrown up your career?"

"Without you it wouldn't have made sense anymore," he explained calmly. "I do what I do because you're here."

"But what would you have done, then?" She seemed to feel an almost cruel pleasure at imagining him alone, without her.

"Oh, I would have done what anyone does who abandons his own country and profession for this sort of reason . . . I would have adapted to a job of some kind: busboy, sailor, chauffeur . . . or I would have enlisted in the Foreign Legion . . . But why does it matter to you so much to know?"

"Just because . . . just talking . . . the Foreign Legion? Under another name?"

"Probably."

"Where is the Foreign Legion based?"

"In Morocco, I think. And in other places, too."

"In Morocco . . . and instead I stayed here," she murmured, wrapping herself around him with a kind of greedy, jealous strength.

A silence followed; Giulia stopped moving, and when Marcello looked at her, he saw that she had closed her eyes and appeared to be asleep. Then he, too, closed his eyes, hoping to drowse off. But he wasn't able to go to sleep, although he felt prostrated by a deathly weariness and torpor. He experienced a deep and sorrowful sensation, as if in complete rebellion against his own being; and a strange analogy came to his mind.

He was a wire, none other than a human wire, through which a terrible current of energy was flowing continuously, which was not up to him to refuse or accept. A wire like those high-tension wires attached to poles that say: DANGER OF DEATH. He was nothing but one of those conducting wires; and sometimes the current hummed through his body without bothering him, actually infusing him with greater energy instead. But at other times — like now, for instance — it felt too strong to him, too intense, and he wanted not to be a taut and vibrating wire but to be pulled down and abandoned to the rust on some trash heap, at the bottom of some office courtyard. And anyway, why was *he* the one who had to endure transmitting the current, while so many people were not even brushed by it? And again, why did the current never interrupt itself, why did it never cease, even for a single moment, to flow through him? The comparison split and divided, branching off into questions without answers; and meanwhile his willful, melancholy torpor kept growing, swirling into his mind like fog, obscuring the mirror of his consciousness. Finally he drowsed off, and it seemed to him that sleep had interrupted the current in some way, and that for once he was really a length of rusty wire, thrown into a corner with the rest of the trash. But at that same moment he felt a hand touching his arm; he jerked awake and sat up to see Giulia standing by the bed, completely dressed, with her hat in her hand. She said, in a low voice, "Are you sleeping? Don't we have to visit Quadri?"

Marcello pulled himself up with an effort and stared into the half-light of the room for a moment, mentally translating, "Don't we have to murder Quadri?"

Then he asked, almost as if he were joking, "What if we didn't go to Quadri's? What if we took a nice nap instead?"

It was an important question, he thought, looking up at Giulia from under his lashes; and maybe it wasn't too late to throw everything to the wind. He saw her consider it uncertainly, almost unhappy, it seemed, that he was proposing to stay in the hotel now that she had prepared to go out.

Then she said, "But you've already slept . . . almost an hour. Besides, didn't you tell me that this visit to Quadri was important for your career?"

Marcello was silent for a moment and then replied, "Yes, it's true, it's very important."

"Well, then," she said gaily, leaning down to give him a kiss on the forehead, "what are you doing thinking about it then? Get a move on, get up and get dressed, don't be a lazybones."

"But I'd rather not go there," said Marcello, pretending to yawn. "I'd like to just sleep," he added, and this time he felt he was sincere. "Sleep and sleep and sleep."

"You can sleep tonight," answered Giulia lightly, walking over to the mirror and looking at herself attentively. "You took on a responsibility, it's too late by now to change the plans."

She spoke with good-natured wisdom, as usual; and it was surprising, thought Marcello, and at the same time obscurely significant, that she always said the right things without knowing it. Right then the phone on the bedside table rang. Marcello, lifting himself up on one elbow, picked up the receiver and put it to his ear. It was the porter, informing him that he had reserved a sleeping car for tonight going to Rome.

"Cancel it," said Marcello without hesitation. "The lady's not going now."

Giulia threw him back a glance of timid gratitude from the mirror in which she had been examining herself.

Marcello hung up the phone and said, "That's it, then . . . They'll cancel it and that way you won't leave."

"Are you mad at me?"

"What gets into your head?"

He got out of bed, slipped on his shoes, and went into the bathroom. While he was washing and combing his hair, he wondered what Giulia would have said if he had revealed the truth about his profession and their honeymoon to her. He felt he could safely say that not only would she not have condemned him, but in the end she would actually have approved of him, although she would probably have been frightened and perhaps would even have asked him if it was really necessary that he do what he did. Giulia was good, that went without saying, but not outside the sacred limits of intimate affection; as far as she was concerned, beyond these limits lay a world that was obscure and confused, in which it could even happen that a bearded, hunchbacked professor might be murdered for political purposes. Agent Orlando's wife, he concluded inside himself as he emerged from the bathroom, must feel and reason the same way.

Giulia, who was waiting for him, sitting on the bed, got up and said, "Are you mad because I didn't let you sleep? Would you have preferred not to go to Quadri's?"

"Not at all, you did the right thing," answered Marcello, preceding her down the corridor. He felt refreshed now and it seemed to him that he no longer felt any sense of rebellion against his own fate. The current of energy was flowing through his body even now, but without pain or difficulty, as if through a natural channel. Outside the hotel, beside the Seine, he gazed at the gray profile of the immense city beyond the parapets, under the vast, cloudless sky. The booths of used books were lined up in front of him and the strolling passersby stopped to glance over them. He even seemed to see the badly dressed young man, with his book under his arm, walking up the sidewalk toward Notre Dame. Or maybe it was someone else, similar in his way of dressing, his attitude, even his destiny. But he felt he was looking at him without envy, even if it was with an ice-cold, motionless sense of impotence. He was himself and the young man was the young man, and there was nothing to be done about it. A taxi passed and he stopped it with a wave of his hand and climbed in after Giulia, giving Quadri's address.

5

WHEN MARCELLO ENTERED Quadri's house, he was immediately struck by how different it was from the apartment in which he had visited him for the first and last time in Rome. This apartment house, situated in a modern neighborhood at the end of a winding street, and which looked, with its many rectangular balconies protruding from a smooth facade, like a big bureau with all its drawers open, had already given him the sense of a retiring and anonymous lifestyle, devoted to a kind of social camouflage; as if Quadri, establishing himself in Paris, had wished to mingle with and become lost in the undifferentiated mass of the well-to-do French bourgeoisie. Then, once he had entered the building, the difference became even greater: the residence in Rome had been old, dark, cluttered with furniture, books, and papers, dusty and neglected; but this place was bright, new, and clean, with very little furniture and not a trace of the scholarly life. They waited for some minutes in the living room, a bare, spacious room with a single group of armchairs confined to a corner around a low table with a glass top. The only sign of taste beyond the common was a large painting hung on one of the walls, the work of a Cubist painter: a cold and decorative mixture of spheres, cubes, cylinders, and parallel lines in various colors. Of books — all those books that had struck Marcello in Rome — there was not a one. He seemed to be, he thought — looking at the wooden, well-waxed floor, the long light curtains, the empty walls — on a modern theater stage, in a brief and elegant production whose set was designed for a drama of few characters and only a single situation. What drama? Doubtlessly his and Quadri's; but, although the situation was known to him already, he felt inexplicably that not all the characters had revealed themselves yet. Someone was still missing, and who knows? That person's arrival might completely change the situation itself.

Almost as if to confirm this faint presentiment, the door at the end of the living room opened and instead of Quadri, a young woman came in, probably the same woman, thought Marcello, with whom he had spoken in French on the phone. She walked toward them across the mirrorlike floor. She was tall and singularly elastic and graceful in her way of walking, dressed in a white summer dress with a flared skirt. For a moment Marcello couldn't keep himself from staring, with a sort of furtive pleasure, at the shadowed outline of her body, whose contours were visible within the transparency of the dress; the shadow was opaque but its outlines were precise and elegant, as if she were a gymnast or a dancer. Then he raised his eyes to her face and felt sure that he had already seen her before, although he didn't know where or when. She approached Giulia, took both her hands in her own with an almost fond familiarity, and explained to her, in correct Italian flavored with a strong French accent, that the professor was busy and would be a few more minutes. She greeted Marcello much less cordially, he thought, almost obliquely, keeping her distance; then she invited them both to sit down. While she talked with Giulia, Marcello studied her attentively, trying to pinpoint the faint memory that led him to think he had seen her before. She was tall, with large hands and feet, broad shoulders, and an incredibly slender waist that emphasized her generous breasts and ample hips. Her long, slender neck supported a pale face innocent of rouge, young but weary, as if consumed by some worry, with a spirited, anxious, restless, intelligent expression. Where had he seen her? As if she felt observed, she suddenly turned toward him; and then he understood, from the contrast between her intense, troubled gaze and the luminous serenity of her high white forehead, where he had already met her, or rather, where he had met someone like her: in the brothel at S., when he had gone back in to retrieve his hat and had found Orlando in the company of the prostitute Luisa. To tell the truth, the similarity consisted completely in the particular shape, whiteness, and radiance of the forehead, which resembled a royal diadem in both of them; in all other respects the two women differed appreciably. The prostitute had had a wide, thin mouth, while this woman's mouth was small, full, and tightly closed, like a tiny rose, thought Marcello, with thick, slightly wilted petals. Another difference: the whore's hand had been womanly, smooth, and fleshy, while this one had almost a man's hand, hard, red, and nervous. Lastly, Luisa had possessed that horrible, hoarse voice so frequently heard in women of her profession, while this woman's voice was dry, clear, and abstract, pleasing as elegant, rational music is pleasing — a classy voice.

Marcello noticed these similarities and differences; and then, while the woman was talking with his wife, he also noticed the extreme coldness of her attitude toward him. Maybe, he thought, Quadri had informed her about his past political stance, and she would have preferred not to receive him. He wondered who she could be. Quadri, as far as he remembered, was not married; judging from her unofficial manner, she might be a secretary, or simply an admirer in the guise of a secretary. He thought back to the feeling he had experienced in the brothel at S., when he had watched the whore Luisa go upstairs followed by Orlando: an emotion of impotent rebellion, of harrowed pity. And all of a sudden he understood that that emotion had been, in reality, sensual desire masked by spiritual jealousy, which he was now feeling in its entirety, completely unmasked, for the woman sitting in front of him. She pleased him in a disturbing, even overwhelming way that was new to him, and he wanted to please her, too; and the hostility revealed by her every gesture pained him as if he were still an adolescent.

At last he said, almost despite himself, and thinking not of Quadri but of her, "I get the impression that our visit is not to the professor's liking . . . perhaps he's too busy."

The woman replied immediately, without looking at him, "On the contrary, my husband told me that he would be very pleased to see you. He remembers you very well . . . everyone who comes from Italy is welcome here. He *is* very busy, it's true . . . but he especially appreciates you coming to visit . . . wait a minute, I'll go see if he's ready."

These words were uttered with an unexpected solicitude that warmed Marcello's heart.

When she had left, Giulia asked without showing any real curiosity, "Why do you think Professor Quadri doesn't want to see us?"

Marcello answered calmly, "The hostile attitude of the signora made me think it."

"How strange," exclaimed Giulia. "She gave me the exact opposite impression. She seemed so happy to see us . . . as if we already knew each other. Had you already met her before?"

"No," he replied, feeling as if he were lying, "never before today. I don't even know who she is."

"Isn't she the professor's wife?"

"I don't know. As far as I know, Quadri's not married . . . maybe she's his secretary."

"But she said 'my husband,'" cried Giulia, surprised. "Where was your head? She said it just like that: 'my husband.' What were you thinking about?"

So, Marcello couldn't help thinking, the woman disturbed him to the point that he was rendered deaf by his distraction. This discovery pleased him and for a moment he felt a strange desire to talk to Giulia about it, as if it didn't concern her at all, as if she were some uninvolved person in whom he could confide freely.

But he said, "I was distracted . . . his wife? Then he must not have been married for long."

"Why?"

"Because when I knew him he was single."

"But didn't you and Quadri write to each other?"

"No, he was my professor, then he went to live in France, and today I'll be seeing him for the first time since then."

"Funny, I thought you were friends."

A long silence followed. Then the door Marcello had patiently been staring at opened, and someone appeared on the threshold whom he did not immediately recognize as Quadri. Then, shifting his eyes from the man's face to his shoulder, he recognized the hump that raised it almost to his ear, and understood that Quadri had simply shaved his beard. Now he rediscovered the bizarre, almost hexagonal shape of the face, its one-dimensional quality, as if it were a flat, painted mask topped with a black wig. He recognized the fixed and brilliant eyes, rimmed in red; the triangular nose shaped like a door knocker; the shapeless mouth, a kind of circle of living red flesh. The only new thing was his chin, formerly hidden by his beard. It was small and crooked, receding deeply beneath his lower lip; it was significantly ugly, perhaps denoting an aspect of the man's character.

Instead of the banker's suit Quadri had been wearing the first and last time Marcello had seen him, he was now wearing (with a hunchback's preference for light shades) a sporty outfit in dove-gray. Under his jacket he wore a red-and-green checked shirt, like an American cowboy, and a flashy tie.

Coming toward Marcello, he said in a tone at once cordial and completely indifferent, "Clerici, right? But of course, I remember you well . . . especially since you were the last student to come visit me before I left Italy. I'm delighted to see you again, Clerici."

Even his voice, thought Marcello, had stayed the same: at once deeply sweet and casual, affectionate and distracted. Meanwhile, he was introducing Giulia to Quadri, who, with a perhaps ostentatious gallantry, bent down to kiss the hand she was extending toward him.

When they had resumed their seats, Marcello said in embarrassment, "I'm on my honeymoon in Paris, and so I thought I'd come see you . . . you were my professor . . . but maybe I've disturbed you."

"No, no, dear boy," answered Quadri with his usual honeyed sweetness, "on the contrary, I'm very pleased. You did very well to remember me . . . and anyone from Italy, if only because they speak to me in the beautiful Italian language, is welcome here." He took up a box of cigarettes from the table, looked inside, and seeing that there was only one left, offered it to Giulia with a sigh. "Go ahead, Signora. I don't smoke and neither does my wife, so we always forget that other people love it . . . So, do you like Paris? I don't imagine it's the first time you've been here."

So, thought Marcello, Quadri wanted to make conventional conversation. He answered for Giulia, "No, it's the first time for both of us."

"In that case," said Quadri quickly, "I envy you. I always envy anyone coming to this beautiful city for the first time . . . and on your honeymoon, besides, and in this season when Paris is most lovely." He sighed again and asked Giulia politely, "And what impression has Paris made on you, Signora?"

"On me?" asked Giulia, looking not at Quadri but at her husband. "Actually, I haven't had time to see it yet . . . we only arrived yesterday."

"You'll see, Signora, it's a very beautiful city, truly truly beautiful," said Quadri in a generic tone, as if he were thinking of something else. "And the longer one lives here the more one is conquered by this beauty. But Signora, don't just look at the monuments, which are wonderful, of course, but not in any way superior to those in Italian cities . . . Walk around, have your husband accompany you through the different quarters of Paris . . . life in this city has a really surprising variety of aspects."

"We haven't seen much yet," said Giulia, who seemed unaware of the conventional and almost ironic character of Quadri's conversation. She turned to her husband, caressed his hand briefly with her own, and said, "But we will walk all around, won't we, Marcello?"

"Sure," said Marcello.

"You should, above all, get to know the French people," Quadri went on in the same tone. "They're a very likeable people . . . intelligent, liberated . . . and though it contradicts in part the usual image of the French, good, too. Their intelligence, so sensitive and subtle, becomes a form of goodness . . . Do you know anyone in Paris?"

"No, we don't know anyone," answered Marcello, "and I'm afraid, besides, that that won't be possible. We'll barely be here a week."

"That's a shame, a real shame. You can never appreciate the true worth of a country if you don't get to know the inhabitants . . ."

"Paris is the city of nightlife, isn't it?" asked Giulia, who seemed perfectly at ease in this conversation right out of a tourist manual. "We haven't seen any yet, but we'd like to go . . . There are a lot of dance halls and nightspots, aren't there?"

"Oh, yes, the *tabarins*, the *boites*, 'the boxes,' as they call them here," said the professor with a distracted air. "Montmartre, Montparnasse . . . to tell the truth, we've never frequented them much. Sometimes when an Italian friend passes this way, we take advantage of his ignorance of the subject to learn about it ourselves. They're always the same old things, though . . . although they're brought off with the grace and elegance native to this city. You see, Signora, the French people is a serious people, a very serious people . . . with strong family attachments. Maybe it will surprise you to know that the great majority of Parisians have never set foot in the *boites*. Family is important here, even more so than in Italy. And they're often good Catholics, more so than in Italy, with a less formal, more substantial faith . . . So it's not surprising that they leave the *boites* to us foreigners. Yet it's an excellent source of income for them . . . Paris owes a good part of its prosperity to the *boites* and to its nightlife in general."

"That's funny," said Giulia. "I always thought the French partied a lot at night." She blushed and added, "I was told that the *tabarins* stay open all night and are always packed . . . like us once, during Carnival."

"Yes," said the professor absently, "but it's mostly foreigners who go there."

"It doesn't matter," said Giulia. "I'd still really like to see at least one, if only to be able to say I was there."

The door opened and Quadri's wife came in, supporting in both hands a tray with coffeepot and cups.

"Excuse me," she said gaily, shutting the door with one foot, "but French maids aren't like Italian ones. This was my maid's day off, so she left right after breakfast . . . we'll have to do everything ourselves."

She was truly happy, thought Marcello, in a wholly unexpected way; and there was much grace in her gaiety and in the gestures of her large, light, confident body.

"Lina," said the professor, perplexed, "Signora Clerici would like to see a *boite*. Which one should we recommend to her?"

"Oh, there are so many to choose from," she said happily as she poured coffee into their cups, supporting her entire weight on one leg, the other extended behind her as if to show off her large foot in its flat shoe, "there's one for every taste and every purse." She handed Giulia her cup and added carelessly, "But we could take them to a *boite* ourselves, Edmondo . . . It would be a good opportunity for you, you could distract yourself for a while."

Her husband passed a hand over his chin as if he wished to stroke his beard and answered, "Sure, all right, why not?"

"You know what we'll do?" she continued, serving coffee to Marcello and her husband. "Since we have to eat out anyway, we can have supper together in a little restaurant on the right bank called Le Coq au Vin. It's inexpensive but the food is good . . . and then after dinner we can go see a really bizarre nightspot. But Signora Clerici musn't be scandalized."

Giulia laughed, cheered by Lina's gaiety. "I'm not that easily shocked."

"It's a *boite* called La Cravate Noire, The Black Tie," she explained, sitting down on the couch next to Giulia. "It's a place where the clientele is a little peculiar," she added, looking at Giulia and smiling.

"Meaning what?"

"Women with special tastes . . . you'll see. The owner and waitresses all dress in tuxedos with black ties . . . you'll see, they're so funny."

"Oh, now I understand," said Giulia, a little confused. "But can men go there, too?"

This question made the woman laugh. "Of course! It's a public place, a little dance hall. It's run by a woman with particular tastes, very intelligent actually, but anyone who wants to can go there. It's not a convent." She laughed in small bursts, looking at Giulia, and then added vivaciously, "But if you don't like it, we can go someplace else . . . less original, though."

"No," said Giulia, "let's go there. Now I'm curious about it."

"Wretched women," said the professor generically. He got up. "Dear Clerici, I want to tell you what a pleasure it's been to see you and how much I look forward to dining with you and your wife this evening . . . We'll talk . . . Do you still have the same ideas and feelings you had then?"

Marcello answered calmly, "I don't keep up with politics."

"All the better, all the better." The professor took Marcello's hand and, pressing it between both his own, added, "Then we can hope, perhaps, to win you over," in a sweet, yearning, heartfelt tone, like a priest speaking to an atheist. He brought the hand to his breast right over his heart, and Marcello could see, to his amazement, that his large, round, protuberant eyes were shining with tears that made them appear to be beseeching him. Then, as if to conceal his emotion, Quadri hurried away to say good-bye to Giulia and then left the room, saying, "My wife will work out the details for tonight with you."

The door closed and Marcello, somewhat embarrassed, sat down in an armchair facing the couch both women were sitting on. Now that Quadri had left, his wife's hostility seemed very evident to him. She pretended to ignore his presence, speaking only to Giulia.

"Have you already seen the fashion stores, the seamstresses, the milliners? Rue de la Paix, Faubourg Saint-Honoré, Avenue de Matignon?"

"Not really," said Giulia, with the air of someone hearing those names for the first time, "actually, no."

"Would you like to see those streets, go into some of the shops, visit some high-fashion houses? I assure you, it's very interesting," continued Signora Quadri with an insistent, insinuating, enveloping, protective cordiality.

"Ah, yes, certainly." Giulia looked at her husband and then added, "I'd like to buy something, too . . . a hat, maybe."

"Do you want me to take you?" proposed the woman, reaching the obligatory conclusion of all those questions. "I know some of the high-fashion places really well . . . and I could also give you some advice."

"That would be nice," said Giulia, grateful but insecure.

"Shall we go today, this afternoon, in an hour? You'll allow me, won't you, to carry off your wife for an hour or so?"

These last words were directed toward Marcello, but in a very different tone of voice than the one she had used with Giulia: brisk, almost contemptuous.

Marcello started and said, "Of course, if Giulia wants to."

He intuited that his wife would have preferred to escape Signora Quadri's protective guardianship, based on the interrogative glance she turned toward him; and he was aware of responding in his turn with a look that ordered her to accept it instead. But right afterward he wondered: Am I doing this because I like the woman and want to see her again, or am I doing it because I'm on a mission and it's not convenient to cross her? Suddenly it felt agonizing to him not to know if he was doing things because he wanted to do them or because they suited his plans.

Meanwhile, Giulia was objecting, "Really, I was thinking of going back to the hotel for a minute . . ."

But the other woman didn't let her finish. "Do you want to freshen up a little before you go out? Touch up your face? You don't have to go all the way back to the hotel . . . if you want, you can lie down and take a nap on my bed. I know how tiring it is when you travel, walking around all day without a moment's rest, especially for us women . . . Come on, come with me, dear."

Before Giulia even had time to breathe, she had already pulled her up from the couch; and now she was pushing her gently but firmly toward the door. When they were on the threshold she said in a bittersweet tone, almost as if to reassure her, "Your husband will wait here . . . don't worry, you won't lose him." Then, putting an arm around Giulia's waist, she drew her into the hallway and closed the door.

Left alone, Marcello rose to his feet swiftly and took a few steps around the room. It was clear to him that the woman nurtured some unshakable aversion for him and he wanted to know the reason for it. But at this point his emotions became confused: on the one hand, this hostility on the part of a person he wished would love him, instead, grieved him; on the other, the thought that she might know the truth about who he was worried him, since in that case the mission would be not only difficult but dangerous. But what made him suffer the most, perhaps, was feeling how these two different anxieties were mixed up in his mind, so that he was no longer capable of distinguishing one from the other — that of the lover who sees himself rejected from that of the secret agent who fears he will be discovered. And of course, as he understood with a revival of his old melancholy, even if he managed to disarm the woman's hostility, he would be constrained one more time to put the relationship that might follow at the disposal of the mission. Just as when he had proposed to the minister that he combine his honeymoon trip with his political duty. As always.

The door opened behind him and Signora Quadri came back in. Approaching the table, she said, "Your wife was very tired, I think she dozed off on my bed . . . Later we'll all go out together."

"This means," said Marcello calmly, "that you're sending me away."

"Oh, Lord, no," she replied in a cold and world-weary voice, "but I have a lot to do . . . so does the professor. You'd have to stay here alone in the living room . . . There are better things for you to do in Paris."

"Excuse me," said Marcello, putting both hands on the back of an armchair and staring at her, "but I'm getting the impression that you feel hostile toward me. Isn't that right?"

She answered immediately, recklessly, fearlessly, "And that surprises you?"

"Yes, actually," said Marcello. "We don't know each other at all, today is the first time we've seen each other . . ."

"I know you very well," she interrupted, "even if you don't know me."

"Here it comes," thought Marcello. He realized that the woman's hostility, indubitably confirmed by now, struck at his heart with a pain so sharp he almost cried out. He sighed in anguish and said softly, "Ah, so you know me?"

"Yes," she replied, her eyes sparkling aggressively, "I know that you're an agent of the police, a paid spy of your government. Does my hostility surprise you now? I don't know about anyone else, but I've never been able to stand *les mouchards* — spies," she added, translating from the French with insulting courtesy.

Marcello lowered his eyes in silence for a moment. His suffering was acute; the woman's contempt was like a thin knife probing pitilessly in an open wound. Finally he said, "Does your husband know?"

"Of course he does," she replied, with insulting amazement. "How could you think he wouldn't know? It was he who told me."

"Ah, they're well informed," Marcello couldn't help thinking. But he said, in a reasonable tone, "Then why did you receive us? Wouldn't it have been simpler to refuse to see us?"

"Actually, I didn't want to let you come by," she said, "but my husband is different . . . My husband is a kind of saint. He still believes that kindness is the best system."

"A very sly saint," Marcello would have liked to answer. But it came to him that that's just how it was: all the saints must have been very sly. And he remained silent. Then he said, "I'm sorry you dislike me so much, because . . . I like you very much."

"Thanks, your friendship horrifies me."

Later, Marcello had to wonder what had come over him that

moment: a dazzling light that seemed to emanate from the woman's luminous forehead and at the same time a profound, violent, powerful impulse, a mixture of excitement and desperate affection. Suddenly he realized that he was very close to Signora Quadri, that he was encircling her waist with his arm, pulling her to him, saying to her in a low voice, "And also because I find you very attractive."

Pressed against him so that Marcello could feel the swollen tenderness of her breasts throb against his own, she stared at him dumbfounded for a moment, then cried in a shrill and triumphant voice, "Oh, perfect! Perfect! On his honeymoon and already eager to betray his wife . . . perfect."

She made a furious gesture to free herself from Marcello's arm, saying, "Let me go or I'll call my husband."

Marcello let go of her immediately, but the woman, transported by her own hostile impulse, fell back against him as if he were still holding her and slapped him on the cheek. She seemed to regret her gesture immediately. She went to the window, looked outside for a moment, and then turned back around, saying, "Forgive me."

But it seemed to Marcello that she was not so much penitent as afraid of the effect the slap might have produced. There was, he thought, more will and calculation than remorse in the reluctant and still malevolent tone of her voice.

He said decisively, "Now there's really nothing left for me to do but go . . . please go tell my wife and have her come here. You'll make our excuses to your husband about this evening . . . You can tell him I had forgotten I had another appointment."

This time, he thought, it was really over; and the mission as well as his love for the woman was hopelessly compromised.

He stood back to let her pass and go to the door. But instead, he saw her stare at him fixedly for an instant, twist her mouth in an expression of sulky discontent, and then come toward him. Marcello saw that a dark, decisive flame had leapt up in her eyes.

When she was only a step away from him, she raised one arm slowly and, still keeping her distance, brought her hand to Marcello's cheek and said, "No, don't go . . . I like you a lot, too . . . if

I was so violent, it was just because of that, because I'm attracted to you . . . don't go. Forget what just happened."

Meanwhile, she was slowly caressing his entire cheek with an assured yet clumsy gesture full of imperious willfulness, almost as if to cool the burn of her slap.

Marcello looked at her, stared at her forehead; and under her own gaze, at the slightly rough touch of her masculine hand, he felt — to his amazement, since this was the first time in his life that he had felt it — a profound disturbance and excitement full of emotion, full of affection and hope, swell his breast and cut off his breath. She stood before him, her arm outstretched to caress him, and in a single glance he experienced her beauty as something that had been destined for him forever, as if it were his whole life's vocation. And he understood that he had loved her always, even before this day, even before he had felt her coming toward him, in the woman of S. Yes, he thought, this was the love he would have nurtured for Giulia if he had loved her, but which he felt instead for this woman he did not know. Then he moved toward her, his arms outstretched to embrace her. But the woman freed herself, though in a way that seemed to suggest affection and complicity, and putting a finger to her lips, murmured, "Now go away . . . we'll see each other tonight."

Before Marcello was even aware of it, she had pushed him out of the living room and into the hallway, she had opened the door. Then the door closed and Marcello found himself alone once more on the landing.

6

*L*INA AND GIULIA WERE going to rest and then go visit
the fashion shops. Then Giulia would return to the hotel,
and later the Quadris would come to pick them up and they
would all go out to supper together. It was about four o'clock,
four hours to go before supper, but only three till Orlando called
the hotel to find out the address of the restaurant. So Marcello
had three hours in which to be alone. What had happened at
Quadri's house made him want to be alone, if for no other
reason than to try to understand himself better. Because, he
thought as he went downstairs, while Lina's behavior — with a
husband so much older than herself who was completely absorbed in politics — was not surprising, his own, instead, since
he was on his honeymoon only a few days after his wedding, both
astonished and frightened, as well as vaguely pleased him. Up
until now he had believed that he knew himself fairly well,
and that he could control himself in any situation that came up
if he wanted to. But now he realized that he might have been

mistaken; and he wasn't sure whether this realization satisfied or alarmed him.

He walked from one alley to another for a while and finally emerged onto a broad street sloping slightly upward, the Avenue de la Grande Armée, as he read on the corner of a house. And in fact when he raised his eyes, the upright rectangle of the Arc du Triomphe appeared before him in profile at the end of the street. Massive yet almost mythical, it seemed suspended in the pale sky, perhaps because of the summer haze that tinted it with blue. As he was walking, his eyes fixed on that massive, triumphal shape, Marcello suddenly felt an intoxicating sensation of freedom and utter liberty that was entirely new to him, as if, without warning, some huge weight that had been oppressing him had been lifted from his back. His step became lighter; he almost felt that he was flying. He wondered, for a moment, whether he should attribute this enormous relief to the simple fact of finding himself in Paris, far away from his familiar, narrow streets, in front of this grandiloquent monument; sometimes you could mistake ephemeral sensations of physical well-being for deep spiritual responses. Then, thinking back over it, he realized that the sensation had arisen from Lina's embrace, instead: the tide of tumultuous, disturbing thoughts that rushed into his mind at the very thought of her touch made him aware of this. He passed his hand mechanically over his cheek, where she had laid hers, and couldn't help closing his eyes for the sweetness of it; it was as if he were reexperiencing the touch of that bold hand stroking his face, almost as if lovingly learning its contours.

What was love, he asked himself, walking up the broad sidewalk, his eyes turned toward the Arc du Triomphe, what was love — for which, he realized, he was now ready to unravel his entire life, abandon the wife he had barely married, betray his political faith, risk everything in an irreparable love affair? He recalled that many years ago this question, posed to him by a girl at the university who was stubbornly resisting his courtship, had led him to answer bitterly that for him, love was the cow standing still in the middle of the meadow in spring, and the bull rising up on his hind legs to mount her. That meadow, thought Marcello now, was the middle-class carpet in Quadri's living room, and Lina was the cow and he the bull. Naked — the difference of place and the fact that they did not have the limbs of beasts notwithstanding — they would be like the two animals in every way. And the fury of desire, expressed with awkward, urgent violence, would be the same, as well. But this was where the similarities, at once so obvious and so unimportant, stopped. Because, by a mysterious and spiritual alchemy, that fury soon turned into completely different kinds of thoughts and emotions, which received the seal of necessity from lust but could never, in any way, be attributed to lust alone. In reality, desire was no more than the urgent, powerful help of nature to something that had existed before it and without it. It was the hand of nature, pulling the wholly human and mortal infant of future things out of the womb of the time to come.

"To put it bluntly," he thought, seeking to cool and reduce the extraordinary exaltation that had taken hold of his spirit, "to put it bluntly, I want to abandon my wife during our honeymoon trip and desert my post during a mission, in order to become Lina's lover and live with her in Paris. To put it bluntly," he continued, "I will do these things for sure if I find out that Lina loves me as I love her, for the same reasons and with the same intensity."

If he was left with any doubts about the seriousness of his decision, they vanished completely when, reaching the end of the Avenue de la Grande Armée, he raised his eyes toward the Arc du Triomphe. Now in fact, recalled because it was an analogy to this monument built to celebrate the victories of a glorious tyranny, he seemed almost to feel regret for the other tyranny, the one he had served up to this point and was preparing to betray. Lightened, rendered almost innocent by his anticipatory sense of this betrayal, the part he had played until this morning now seemed more comprehensible, as well as more acceptable to him: no longer, as he had thought until this moment, the fruit of an external wish for normality and for redemption, but almost a vocation, or at least an inclination that was not altogether artificial. On the other hand,

this detached and already retrospective regret was a sure indication in itself of the irrevocable nature of his decision.

He waited a long time for the carousel of cars driving around
the monument to open up. Then he crossed the piazza and
walked directly to the Arc, taking off his hat to go in under the
vault, to the tombstone of the Unknown Soldier. There it was, on
the walls of the Arc du Triomphe: the lists of battles won, each of
which had signified for innumerable men a loyalty and devotion
of the kind that had linked him, until a few minutes ago, to his
own government. Here was the tomb, watched over by the peren-
nially burning flame, symbol of other, no less complete, sacrifices.
Reading the names of the Napoleonic battles, he couldn't help remembering something Orlando had said: "Anything for the family
and homeland"; and he suddenly understood that what distin-
guished him from the agent, so convinced, yet so powerless to justify rationally his conviction, was simply his capacity to choose;
and the sadness that had persecuted him for as long as he could remember gave him away. Yes, he thought, he had made choices in
the past and he would start to make choices again. And his melancholy was that kind of sorrow mixed with regret that sparks off
thoughts of how things might have been, things that his choice required him absolutely to renounce.

He emerged from under the Arc, waited once more for the
flow of moving cars to open up, and reached the sidewalk of the
Avenue des Champs Elysées. It seemed to him that the Arc extended like an invisible shadow over the rich and festive street that
descended from it; and that an indubitable connection linked that
warlike monument and the happy, peaceful prosperity of the
crowd moving along the sidewalks. This too, he thought, was an
aspect of what he was renouncing: the great, bloody acts of injustice, which later metamorphosed into a joy and wealth that were
ignorant of their origins — a cruel sacrifice that, with time, became power, liberty, and wealth for generations to come. Another
argument in favor of Judas, he thought with amusement.

But now the decision had been made, and he had only one
wish: he wanted to think about Lina and why and how he loved

her. With his heart full of this desire, he walked very slowly down the Avenue des Champs Elysées, stopping every once in a while to look at the shops, the newspapers displayed on the kiosks, the people sitting down to their coffees, the movie posters, the theater signs. The dense crowd on the sidewalks surrounded him on every side, with a swarming movement that seemed to him to be the movement of life itself. With his right eye he caught the four rows of cars, two for each direction, that climbed up and rolled down the broad street; with his left, the wealthy shops alternating with bright signs and packed cafés. As he kept on walking, he gradually stepped up his pace, almost hoping to leave the Arc du Triomphe behind. And in fact, as he realized at some point when he turned around to look, he had left it in the distance; faraway, wrapped in the summer haze it looked wholly immaterial. When he reached the bottom of the street, he searched out a bench in the shade of the trees in the garden and sat down with relief, happy to be able to think about Lina in peace.

He wanted to go back, in his memory, to the first time he had intuited her existence: to his visit to the brothel at S. Why had the woman he had glimpsed in the salon next to agent Orlando inspired in him such a new and violent emotion? He recalled that he had been struck by the luminosity of her forehead, and understood that what had first attracted him in that woman and later, more completely, in Lina, was the purity he seemed to perceive there — mortified and profaned in the prostitute, triumphant in Lina. He now understood that only the radiant light emanating from Lina's forehead could dissipate the disgust for decadence, corruption, and impurity that had burdened him all his life and which his marriage to Giulia had in no way mitigated. It seemed to him that the coincidence of the names — *Lino*, who had first inspired that disgust, and *Lina*, who would free him of it — was a good omen. So naturally, spontaneously, by the strength of love alone, he would find through Lina the normality he had dreamt of for so long. But not the almost bureaucratic normality he had pursued all those years, but another, almost angelic kind of normality. And before this luminous and ethereal normality, the heavy harness of his political duties, his marriage to Giulia, and his dull, reasonable, ordered life revealed itself to be nothing but a cumbersome image he had adopted while he was waiting, all unaware, for a worthier destiny. Now he was liberated from all of that and he could rediscover himself.

As he was sitting on the bench lost in these thoughts, his idle glance fell suddenly onto a large car descending in the direction of Place de la Concorde, which seemed to be slowing down gradually; and in fact, it pulled up to the sidewalk not far from him and came to a stop. Although it was a luxury car, it was old and black, so old-fashioned that the almost excessive elegance and polish of its body's nickel-plating and brasses seemed out of place. A Rolls Royce, he thought; and all of a sudden, he was seized by an anxious fear, mixed — he was not sure why — with a terrifying sense of familiarity. Where and when had he seen that car before? The driver, a thin, gray-haired man in a dark blue uniform, was quick to get out and run to open the passenger door as soon as the car stopped. His action triggered an image in Marcello's memory, the answer to his question: the same car, of the same color and make, parked at the streetcorner on the broad avenue near the school, and Lino leaning out to open the passenger door so that he could get in and sit next to him.

In the meantime, as the driver was standing by the door with his beret in his hand, a masculine leg in gray flannel trousers, terminating in a foot shod in a polished yellow shoe as shining as the brasses on the car, stuck itself out carefully; then the driver stretched out his hand, and Marcello watched the entire person emerge painfully onto the sidewalk. Marcello judged him to be an elderly man, thin and very tall, with a florid face and hair that may still have been blond. He walked unsteadily, leaning on a cane with a rubber tip; yet he appeared strangely youthful. Marcello observed him attentively as he slowly approached the bench, wondering what gave the old man such a youthful air. Then he understood: it was his hairstyle, parted on one side, and the green bowtie he wore around the collar of a vivid shirt striped in pink and white. The old man was walking with his eyes to the ground, but when he reached the bench he raised them, and Marcello saw that they were a limpid blue, with a young, ingenuously hard expression to them. At last the man sat down with an effort next to Marcello, and the driver, who had been following him step for step, handed him a small, white paper package. Then he bowed briefly, returned to the car and got in, sitting stock-still at his place behind the windshield.

Marcello, who had been following the old man's progress, now lowered his eyes in reflection. He wished with his whole heart that he had not felt such horror at the very sight of a car like Lino's; and this in itself was enough to disturb him. But what frightened him most was the vivid, bitter, sinister sense of submission, powerlessness, and servitude that accompanied his repugnance. It was as if all those years had never passed, or worse, had passed in vain; and he was still that little boy, and Lino was waiting for him in the car, and Marcello was about to get in, obeying the man's invitation. It seemed to him that he was submitting once more to the ancient blackmail; but this time it was not Lino hooking him with the bait of the gun, but his own mindful and troubled flesh. Terrified by this sudden, disturbing outbreak of a fire he had long thought extinguished, he heaved a sigh and rummaged mechanically through his pockets in search of a cigarette.

Instantly a voice said to him in French, "Cigarettes? Here."

He turned and saw that the old man was offering him an unopened pack of American cigarettes, holding it out in a red, somewhat tremulous hand. Meanwhile, he was looking at Marcello with a strange expression, both imperious and benevolent. Extremely embarrassed, Marcello took the pack without thanks, opened it hurriedly, shook out a cigarette, and gave it back to the old man.

But taking the pack, the man tucked it with an authoritative hand into Marcello's jacket pocket and said in a suggestive tone of voice, "They're for you . . . you can keep them."

Marcello felt himself blush and then pale with a mixture of anger and shame he could not explain. Luckily, he lowered his eyes toward his own shoes: they were white with dust and shapeless

from much walking. It dawned on him that the old man had probably taken him for someone poor or unemployed; and his anger
died. Simply, without ostentation, he drew the pack from his
pocket and placed it on the bench between them.

But the old man, no longer concerned with him, was unaware
of the restitution. Marcello watched him open the package the
driver had given him and take out a roll. He broke it slowly and la-
boriously with trembling hands and threw two or three crumbs to
the ground. Immediately a big, plump, friendly sparrow flew out
of one of the leafy trees shading the bench and landed on the
earth. It hopped up to one of the crumbs, cocked its head two or
three times to look around, and then grasped the bread in its beak
and began to devour it. The old man threw down a few more bits
of roll, and more sparrows flew down from the tree branches onto
the sidewalk. Marcello observed the scene, the lit cigarette between his lips and his eyes half-closed. The old man might be bent
in the back and his hands might shake, but he still conserved
something of the adolescent about him, or rather, it took no great
effort to imagine him as an adolescent. Seen in profile, his pouty
red mouth, strong straight nose, and blond hair falling in an almost boyish lock over his forehead made one think, in fact, that he
must have been a very lovely adolescent — one of those Nordic
athletes, perhaps, that unite girlish grace with virile strength.
Folded over himself with his head resting thoughtfully on his
breast, he crumbled up the rest of the roll for the sparrows.

Then, without moving or turning, he asked, still in French,
"What country are you from?"

"I'm Italian," answered Marcello briefly.

"Now why didn't I figure that out?" exclaimed the old man,
slapping his own forehead hard with a kind of lively, quick
temper. "I was just asking myself where I might have seen a face
like yours, so perfect . . . damn, how stupid of me, in Italy! What's
your name?"

"Marcello Clerici," replied Marcello after a moment's hesitation.

"Marcello," repeated the man, lifting his face and gazing into
the air in front of him.

A long silence followed. The old man appeared to be lost in reflection; or rather, thought Marcello, he seemed to be making an effort to remember something.

At last he turned toward Marcello and recited, with an air of triumph, "Heu miserande puer, si qua fata aspera rumpas, tu Marcellus eris."

Marcello knew the verses well; he had been required to translate them in school, and at the time they had made him the brunt of the other boys' jokes. But uttered at that moment, coming right after the offer of the cigarettes, those famous words gave him an unpleasant sense of awkward flattery.

This changed to irritation as the old man launched a long, summary look at him from head to toes and then said informatively, "Virgil."

"Yes, Virgil," replied Marcello dryly, "and what country are you from?"

"I'm British," said the man — suddenly, bizarrely speaking in a refined and perhaps ironic Italian. Then, even more bizarrely, he began mixing Neapolitan with the Italian: "Aggio vissuto a Napoli . . . I lived in Naples for many years . . . . Are you Neapolitan?"

"No," said Marcello, taken aback by the man's sudden switch from voi to the more intimate tu. By now the sparrows had devoured all the crumbs and flown away again; a few steps away, the Rolls Royce was parked by the sidewalk, waiting.

The old man grasped his cane and rose to his feet with an effort. He said to Marcello, this time in French, in a tone of command, "Will you accompany me to the car? Do you mind giving me your arm?"

Marcello rose mechanically and held out his arm. The pack of cigarettes was still on the bench where he had left it.

"You're forgetting your cigarettes," said the old man, pointing to the pack with the tip of his cane. Marcello pretended not to hear him and took the first step toward the car. This time the old man did not insist but went with him.

He walked slowly, much more slowly than when he had walked alone shortly before, supporting himself on Marcello's arm with one hand. But this hand didn't stay in one place; it moved up and down the young man's arm in an already possessive caress. Suddenly Marcello felt his heart stop, and when he lifted his eyes he understood why: the car was there, waiting for both of them, and he knew that he would be invited to get in, as he had so many years before. But what terrified him the most was knowing that he would not refuse the invitation. With Lino he had felt, aside from his desire for the gun, a kind of unconscious flirtatiousness; with this man — he realized in amazement — he felt a sensation of subjection steeped in memory, as of someone who, having been subjected once already in the past to a dark temptation, is caught by surprise many years later in the same trap and can find no reason to resist. As if Lino had taken his pleasure with him, he thought; as if in reality he had not resisted Lino and had not killed him. These thoughts passed through his mind extremely rapidly; they were almost more illuminations than thoughts. Then he raised his eyes and saw that they had reached the car. The driver had gotten back out and was waiting next to the open door, his beret in his hand.

Without letting go of Marcello's arm, the old man said, "So, do you want to get in?"

Marcello replied immediately, happy with his own resolution, "Thank you, but I have to get back to my hotel. My wife is waiting for me."

"Poor little thing," said the old man with mischievous familiarity, "let her wait awhile. It will do her good."

So he would have to explain himself, thought Marcello. He said, "We're not understanding each other." He hesitated, then glimpsed a young man of the streets, who had stopped beside the bench where they had left the cigarette pack, out of the corner of his eye and added, "I'm not what you think I am. Maybe he would be more to your liking." And he pointed to the vagabond who was, just that moment, furtively pocketing the cigarettes in one swift motion.

The old man looked over at him, too, smiled, and replied with playful impudence, "I have more than I need of those."

"I'm sorry," said Marcello coldly, feeling completely reassured; and he started to go. But the old man held him back.

"At least allow me to accompany you . . ."

Marcello hesitated and glanced at his watch. "All right, drive me there . . . since it gives you pleasure."

"It gives me great pleasure."

They climbed in, first Marcello and then the old man. The driver closed the door and sat down quickly behind the wheel.

"Where to?" asked the old man.

Marcello said the name of the hotel; the old man turned to the driver and said something in English. The car drove off.

It was a soft-riding, silent car, as Marcello noticed while it ran rapidly and quietly beneath the trees of the Tuileries in the direction of the Place de la Concorde. The inside was upholstered in gray felt; a crystal flower vase of old-fashioned design, affixed next to the door, held several gardenias.

After a moment of silence, the old man turned toward Marcello and said, "Forgive me for those cigarettes . . . I took you for a poor man."

"It doesn't matter," said Marcello.

The old man was quiet for a bit and then went on, "I'm so rarely mistaken. I could have sworn that you . . . I was so sure of it that I was almost ashamed to use the cigarettes as an excuse. I was convinced that a look would be enough."

He spoke with light, cynical, civil nonchalance; it was clear that he still considered Marcello to be a homosexual. In fact, his tone of complicity carried such authority that Marcello was almost tempted to please him by responding, "Yes, maybe you're right, and I am . . . without even knowing it, despite myself. And the proof is that I agreed to get in your car."

Instead he said dryly, "You were mistaken, that's all."

"Right."

The car was now circling the obelisk in the Place de la Concorde. Then it stopped abruptly before the bridge. The old man said, "You know what made me think it?"

"No, what?"

"Your eyes. They're so sweet, they're like a caress even as you're trying to frown . . . they speak for you despite yourself."

Marcello said nothing. After a brief halt, the car began to move again. It crossed the bridge and then, instead of taking the road beside the Seine, it turned into the streets behind the Chambre des Députées. Marcello started and turned toward the old man.

"But my hotel is on the Seine."

"We're going to my house," said the old man. "Wouldn't you like something to drink? You'll stay awhile and then go back to your wife."

All of a sudden Marcello felt that he was experiencing the same sense of humiliation and powerless fury that he had felt so many years ago, when his companions had tied the skirt around him and teased him by yelling, "Marcellina!" The old man did not believe in his virility any more than those boys, and like them he insisted on considering him a kind of woman.

Marcello said, between clenched teeth, "Please take me to my hotel."

"Oh, come on, what does it matter? Just for a moment."

"I only got in because I was running late and it was convenient for you to drive me there. So now drive me there."

"Funny, I thought you wanted to be kidnapped, instead. You're all like that, you want to be forced."

"I assure you that you're mistaken, adopting this tone of voice with me. I'm not what you think I am at all. I've already told you that and now I'm telling you again."

"How suspicious you are! I don't think anything . . . go on, don't look at me that way."

"You asked for it," said Marcello, thrusting his hand into the inside pocket of his jacket. When he had left Rome, he had brought a little pistol with him; and instead of leaving it in the suitcase where Giulia might find it, he always kept it on him. He drew the weapon out of his pocket and pointed it discreetly, in such a way so that the driver couldn't see it, at the old man, who had been regarding him with an air of affectionate irony. But then he lowered his eyes. Marcello saw him become suddenly serious and make a perplexed, almost uncomprehending face.

Marcello said, "You see? And now order your driver to take me to my hotel."

The man grabbed the microphone immediately and shouted out the name of Marcello's hotel. The car slowed down and turned off into a cross street. Marcello put the gun back in his pocket and said, "That's better."

The old man said nothing. He seemed to have recovered from his surprise now and was looking at Marcello attentively, studying his face. The car came out onto the river road and started running beside the parapets. Suddenly Marcello recognized the entrance to his hotel, with its revolving door under the glass roof. The car stopped.

"Allow me to offer you this flower," said the old man, taking a gardenia out of the vase and holding it out to him. Marcello hesitated, and the man added, "For your wife."

Marcello took the flower, thanked him, and leapt out of the car in front of the driver, who was waiting bareheaded beside the open door. He seemed to hear — or maybe it was a hallucination — the voice of the old man saying, in Italian, "Good-bye, Marcello!" But he did not turn around; squeezing the gardenia between two fingers, he walked swiftly into the hotel.

7

*H*E WENT TO THE CONCIERGE'S desk and asked for the key to the room.

"It's up there," said the concierge, after peering into the key cabinet. "Your wife took it. She went upstairs with a lady."

"A lady?"

"Yes."

Wildly disturbed and at the same time immensely happy, after his encounter with the old man, to be excited in this way just at the news that Lina was in the room with Giulia, Marcello headed for the elevator. Stepping into it, he glanced at his wristwatch and saw that it was not yet six. He had all the time in the world to carry Lina off on some pretext, sit down with her in some dark corner of the hotel lounge, and decide about the future. Right after that he would make a definitive break with agent Orlando, who was to call at seven. These coincidences felt like good omens. While the elevator was ascending, he glanced at the gardenia he was still squeezing between his fingers and was suddenly sure that the old man had given it to him, not for Giulia, but for his real wife, Lina. It was up to him now to give her some token of their love.

He rushed down the corridor to his room and entered without knocking. It was a large room with a double bed and a small entrance hall that also led to the bathroom. Marcello approached the door noiselessly and hesitated a moment in the darkness of the vestibule. Then he realized that the door to the bedroom was ajar and that light was seeping through it, and he was seized with a desire to spy on Lina without being seen himself, thinking of it, almost, as a way to make sure whether Lina really loved him. He put his eye to the crack and looked in.

A lamp shone on the bedside table; the rest of the room was wrapped in shadow. He saw Giulia sitting against the bolster, her back against the pillows, all wrapped up in a white cloth: the thick, soft towel from the bathroom. She was holding the towel to her breasts with both hands, but seemed unable or unwilling to keep it from opening widely at the bottom to reveal her belly and legs. Crouching on the floor at Giulia's feet, within the circle of the wide, white skirt, in the act of embracing her legs with both arms, her forehead pressed to Giulia's knees and her breasts against Giulia's shins, was Lina. Without reproof, on the contrary, with a kind of amused and indulgent curiosity, Giulia was stretching her neck to observe the woman who, because of her own somewhat supine position, she could see only imperfectly. Finally Lina said in a low voice, without moving, "You don't mind if I stay here like this for a little while?"

"No, but soon I'll have to get dressed."

Lina went on, after a moment of silence, as if picking up a previous conversation, "You're so stupid, though . . . what would it matter to you? When you yourself said that if you weren't married, you wouldn't have anything against it."

"Maybe I said that," replied Giulia flirtatiously, "so as not to offend you. And anyway, I am married."

Watching, Marcello saw that now, even as she was talking, Lina had withdrawn an arm from Giulia's legs and was sliding her hand slowly, tenaciously up her thigh, pushing back the edge of the towel in her progress. "Married," she said with intense sarcasm, without interrupting her slow advance, "but look at who you're married to."

"He's fine with me," said Giulia.

Now Lina's hand had crept from Giulia's hip to her naked groin, as hesitant and insinuating as the head of a snake. But Giulia took it by the wrist and pushed it back down, saying in an indulgent tone, rather like a nanny reproaching a restless child, "Don't think I don't see you."

Lina held Giulia's hand and began to kiss it slowly, reflectively, every once in a while nuzzling her whole face in its palm forcefully, like a dog. Then she said breathily and with intense tenderness, "Silly little thing."

A long silence followed. The concentrated passion that emanated from Lina's every gesture was in singular contrast to Giulia's distraction and indifference. She no longer seemed even curious and, while abandoning her hand to Lina's kisses and caresses, looked around like someone in search of a pretext. Finally, she reclaimed her hand and started to get up, saying, "Now I really have to get dressed, though."

Lina was quick to jump to her feet and exclaim: "Don't move! Just tell me where the stuff is, I'll dress you myself."

Standing up with her back to the door, she hid Giulia completely. Marcello heard his wife's voice say, with a laugh, "So you want to be my maid, as well . . ."

"Why not? It means nothing to you . . . and it gives me so much pleasure."

"No, I'll get dressed by myself." Giulia emerged, completely naked, from the clothed figure of Lina as if splitting off from her, passed on tiptoes in front of Marcello's eyes, and vanished at the bottom of the room. Then he heard her voice saying, "Please don't watch me. Actually, turn around. You make me embarrassed."

"Embarrassed in front of me? I'm a woman, too."

"You're a woman in a manner of speaking. You look at me the way men do."

"Then say straight out that you want me to go."

"No, stay here, just don't look at me."

"I'm not looking at you, silly, do you think it matters to me whether I look at you?"

"Don't get mad, try to understand me. If you hadn't talked to me that way at first, I wouldn't be embarrassed now and you could look at me as much as you like." This came out in a suffocated voice, as from inside a dress being pulled over her head.

"Don't you want me to help you?"

"Oh, God, if you really want to so much . . ."

Decisive yet unsure in her movements, at once hesitant and aggressive, aroused and humiliated, Lina moved, passed for a moment in profile in front of Marcello, and disappeared toward the part of the room from which Giulia's voice was coming. There was a moment of silence and then Giulia exclaimed, impatiently but not angrily, "*Auffa*, how tiresome you are!"

Lina said nothing.

Now the light from the lamp fell on the empty bed, illuminated the dip left by Giulia's hips in the damp towel. Marcello withdrew from the crack and went back down the hall.

After he had taken a few steps away from the door, he became aware that his surprise and distress had made him do something significant without realizing it: he had crushed the gardenia the old man had given him, and which he had intended to give to Lina, mechanically between his fingers. He let the flower drop onto the carpet and headed for the stairs.

He went down to the ground floor and out along the Seine, in the false, misty light of the dusk. Lights were already lit — the white lamps in clusters on the far bridges, the paired yellow head-lights of cars, the rectangular orange illuminations of windows; and the night was rising like dark smoke to the clear green sky be-hind the black profiles of the spires and roofs on the opposite shore. Marcello walked over to the parapet and leaned his elbows on it, looking down at the darkened waters of the Seine, which now seemed to bear streaks of jewels and circles of diamonds on the back of its black waves. What he was feeling was already more like the mortal quiet that follows the disaster than the tumult of the disaster itself. He understood that for a few hours that afternoon he had believed in love. Now instead he realized that he was wandering through a profoundly shaken, parched, and soured world, in which the gift of real love did not exist, only sensual relations, from the most natural and common to the most abnormal and bizarre. Certainly what Lina had felt for him had not been love; nor was love what Lina felt for Giulia; his own relationship with his wife could not be called love; and maybe even Giulia — so indulgent, almost tempted by Lina's advances — didn't love him in the true sense of the word. In this dark and flashing world, like some stormy twilight, these ambiguous figures of men-women and women-men who crossed paths at random, doubling and mingling their ambiguity, seemed to allude to an equally ambiguous significance connected, he felt, to his own destiny and to the proven impossibility of escaping it. Since love was not, and for this reason alone, he would carry out his mission and persist in his intention to create a family with the animal-like and unpredictable Giulia. This was normality: this makeshift solution, this empty form. Outside of it, all was confusion and anarchy.

He also felt pushed to act this way by the clarity that now illuminated Lina's behavior. She despised him and probably hated him, as well, as she had declared when she was still being honest; but in order not to cut short their relationship and so preclude the possibility of seeing Giulia, whom she wanted so badly, she had pretended to be attracted to him. But now Marcello understood that he could expect neither comprehension nor pity from her; and faced with this irremediable and definitive hostility, armored by sexual abnormality, political aversion, and moral contempt, he felt a sharp and powerless pain. So, that pure and intelligent light spilling from her eyes and forehead that had so fascinated him would never be bent over him, lovingly to calm and illumine him. Lina preferred to abase and humiliate it in sensual flattery, supplication, and hellish embraces. At this point he recalled that when he had seen her thrust her face against Giulia's knees, he had been struck by the same sense of profanation that he had felt in the brothel at S., watching the prostitute Luisa let Orlando embrace her. Giulia wasn't Orlando, he thought; but he had not wanted that forehead to abase itself before anyone, and he had been disappointed.

Night had fallen while he had been thinking. Marcello straightened up and turned toward the hotel. He was in time to glimpse the white figure of Lina coming out and moving hurriedly toward an automobile parked close by beside the sidewalk. He was struck by her happy and almost furtive air, like a marten or weasel escaping from a hen house with her prey in her mouth. It was not the attitude of someone who has been rejected, he thought; quite the opposite. Maybe Lina had managed to wring some promise out of Giulia; or maybe Giulia, from weariness or sensual passivity, had yielded to some caress that meant nothing to her, as indulgent as she was toward herself and others, but precious to Lina. Meanwhile the woman had opened the car door and gotten in, sitting down sideways and then drawing in her legs. Marcello watched her drive by, her beautiful face in profile both elegant and proud, her hands on the wheel. The car continued on into the distance, and Marcello went back into the hotel.

He walked upstairs and entered the room without knocking. Everything was in order. Giulia was completely dressed, sitting in front of the bureau mirror, combing her hair. She asked calmly, without turning around, "Is that you?"

"Yes, it's me," answered Marcello, sitting down on the bed. He waited a minute and then asked, "Did you have fun?"

Immediately his wife turned halfway around on her seat and said vivaciously, "Yes, a lot . . . we saw so many beautiful things! I left my heart in at least ten stores."

Marcello said nothing. Giulia finished combing her hair in silence and then got up and came over to sit beside him on the bed. She was wearing a black dress with a wide, low neckline from which the two dark, glowing, solid spheres of her breasts thrust up like two beautiful fruits from a basket. A scarlet cloth rose was pinned near one shoulder. Her sweet young face with its large, shining eyes and luxuriant mouth was wearing its usual expression of lazy sensuality. She smiled, perhaps unconsciously, and between her lips painted with vivid lipstick, he saw her regular, brilliantly white teeth.

She took his hand affectionately and said, "Guess what happened to me."

"What?"

"That lady, Professor Quadri's wife . . . just think, she's not a normal woman."

"Meaning?"

"She's one of those women who love women. And the thing is, if you can imagine it, she fell in love with me, just like that, at first sight . . . She told me so after you left. That's why she was so insistent that I stay at her house to rest. She made me a real, proper declaration of love . . . who would have thought it?"

"And you?"

"I really wasn't expecting it. I was about to fall asleep because I was so tired . . . I didn't understand her at first. Finally I got it, and then I wasn't sure *what* to do . . . It was a real, furious passion, you know, just like a man's. Tell me the truth, would you have expected that from a woman like her, so controlled, with such a good hold on herself?"

"No," replied Marcello gently, "I wouldn't have expected it . . . just as," he added, "I wouldn't expect you to reciprocate such effusions."

"What's this? Are you jealous by any chance?" she cried, bursting into joyful, flattered laughter. "Jealous of a woman? Even if, let's say, I had paid any attention to her, you still shouldn't be jealous . . . a woman's not a man. But don't worry, almost nothing happened between us."

"Almost?"

"I'm saying 'almost,'" she replied in a reticent tone, "because, seeing her so desperate, I let her hold my hand while she was driving me back to the hotel."

"Just hold your hand?"

"Well, well, you are jealous," she exclaimed again, very happy. "You're jealous for sure. I didn't know this aspect of you. All right then, if you really want to know," she added after a moment, "I let her give me a kiss, too . . . but like a sister kisses a sister. Then, since she was so demanding she was annoying me, I sent her away — that's all. Now tell me, are you still jealous?"

Marcello had insisted that Giulia talk about Lina chiefly to redis- cover yet one more time the basic difference between him and his wife: he, shaken to the core all his life by something that had never happened; his wife, instead, open to all experiences, indulgent, her flesh shedding its memories even before her mind forgot them.

He asked gently, "But you . . . have you ever had this kind of re- lationship in the past?"

"No, never," she answered decisively. This curt tone was so un- usual in her that Marcello knew she was lying right away.

He insisted, "Come on, why lie? A person who didn't know about these things wouldn't behave the way you did with Signora Quadri. Tell the truth!"

"But why does it matter to you?"

"It interests me to know about it."

Giulia lowered her eyes and was silent for a moment; then she said slowly, "You know the story about that man, that lawyer? Up until the day I met you he'd given me a real horror of men . . . so I had a friendship, but it didn't last long . . . with a girl my own age, a student. She really loved me and it was this affection, above all, at a time when I needed it so much, that convinced me. Then she became possessive, demanding, and jealous and so I broke it off . . . every once in a while I see her in Rome, here and there. Poor thing, she still loves me."

Now, after a moment's reticence and embarrassment, her face resumed its usual placid expression. Taking his hand, she added, "Don't worry, don't be jealous. You know I only love you."

"I know it," said Marcello. Now he recalled Giulia's tears in the train and her suicide attempt, and he understood that she had been sincere. While she had seen, in a conventional way, betrayal in her missing virginity, she actually attached no importance to these past mistakes of hers.

Meanwhile, Giulia was saying, "I tell you, that woman is really crazy . . . you know what she wants? She wants to take us all to

Savoy in a few days; they have a house there. Just think, she's already drawn up a schedule."

"What schedule?"

"Her husband's leaving tomorrow. She's going to stay a few more days in Paris, though . . . for her own business, she says, but I'm convinced she's staying because of me. She wants us to all leave together and go spend a week with them in the mountains. That we're on our honeymoon doesn't enter her head . . . for her, it's as if you didn't exist. She wrote me the address of their house in Savoy and made me swear I'd persuade you to accept the invitation."

"What's the address?"

"There it is," said Giulia, pointing to a piece of paper on the marble of the bedside table. "But why? You're not thinking of accepting?"

"No, but you, maybe."

"For God's sake, do you really think I attach any importance to that woman? When I told you I sent her away because she was annoying me with her demands . . ."

Meanwhile, she had risen from the bed and, still talking, left the room. "By the way," she yelled from the bathroom, "someone called for you a half an hour ago . . . a man's voice, an Italian . . . He didn't want to say who he was. But he left me a number and asked you to call as soon as you could . . . I wrote the number down on that same piece of paper."

Marcello picked up the paper, pulled a notebook out of his pocket, and carefully wrote down the address of the Quadri's house in Savoy, as well as Orlando's number. He felt, now, as if he had come back to his senses after the ephemeral exaltation of that afternoon; he knew it, above all, by the automatic quality of his actions and the melancholy resignation that accompanied them. So it was all over, he thought as he put the notebook back in his pocket, and that fleeting apparition of love in his life had been nothing more in the end than a shock in the process of settling down to that same life in its definitive form. He thought of Lina again for a moment and seemed to glimpse a manifest sign of destiny in her sudden passion for Giulia, since it had not only furnished him the address of the house in Savoy, but had also made sure that when Orlando and his men showed up, she would not yet be there. Quadri's solitary departure and Lina's decision to stay in Paris suited the mission's plan perfectly; if things had gone otherwise, he didn't see how Orlando and he could have carried it out.

He got up, shouted out to his wife that he would be waiting for her in the lobby, and left. There was a telephone booth at the end of the hall and he walked toward it slowly, almost automatically. Only when he heard the agent's voice asking him jocularly from the receiver, "So, Dottore, where are we having this little dinner?" did he emerge from the fog of his own thoughts. Calmly, speaking softly but clearly, he began to inform Orlando about Quadri's trip.

8

*W*HEN THEY GOT OUT OF the taxi on a little side
street in the Latin Quarter, Marcello looked up at the
sign. Le Coq au Vin was written in white letters on a brown background on the second-floor level of an old gray house. They went
into the restaurant. A red velvet sofa ran all around the sides of the
room; the tables were lined up in front of the sofa; old rectangular
mirrors in gilt frames reflected the central chandelier and the
heads of the few customers in a tranquil light. Marcello recognized Quadri right away, seated in a corner next to his wife,
smaller than her by a head, dressed in black, studying the wine list
over his glasses. Lina, on the other hand, who was sitting up
straight and immobile in a black velvet dress that emphasized the
whiteness of her arms and breasts and the pallor of her face,
seemed to be anxiously watching the door. Seeing Giulia, she
stood up suddenly and behind her, almost hidden by her, the professor stood up, too. The two women shook hands. Marcello
raised his eyes casually and saw, suspended in the unremarkable

yellow light of one of the mirrors, an incredible apparition: the head of Orlando, watching him. At the same moment, the restaurant's grandfather clock roused itself; its metallic bowels began to writhe and complain; at last it began to strike the hours.

"Eight o'clock," he heard Lina exclaim contentedly. "How punctual you are."

Marcello shivered and, as the clock continued to strike, each stroke lugubrious, solemn, and sonorous, he held out his hand to shake the hand that Quadri was offering him. The clock struck the last hour loudly and then he remembered, pressing his palm against Quadri's, that this handshake, according to the agreement, was to point out the victim to Orlando. Suddenly he was almost tempted to lean over and kiss Quadri on the left cheek, just as Judas — with whom he had jokingly compared himself that afternoon — had done. In fact, he seemed to feel the rough touch of that cheek beneath his lips and marveled at the power of the suggestion. Then he lifted his eyes to the mirror again: Orlando's head was still there, suspended in the void, his eyes fixed on them. Finally all four of them sat down, he and Quadri on the chairs and the two women opposite them on the divan.

The wine steward came with the list, and Quadri began to order the wines with minute attention to detail. He seemed completely absorbed in his task and held a lengthy discussion with the steward about the quality of the wines, which he evidently knew very well. At last he ordered a dry white wine to go with the fish, a red wine to accompany the roast, and some champagne on ice. The wine steward left, the waiter appeared, and the same scene was repeated: competent discussions concerning the foods, hesitations, reflections, questions, answers, and finally a decision to order three courses — antipasto, then fish, then meat. In the meantime Lina and Giulia were speaking to each other in low voices, and Marcello, his eyes fixed on Lina, had fallen into a kind of a trance. He still seemed to hear the frenzied striking of the pendulum clock at his back as he shook Quadri's hand; he still seemed to see Orlando's bodiless head looking at him in the mirror. And he understood that he had never before this moment found himself so concretely faced with his destiny, as if it were a stone standing in the middle of a crossroads with two roads diverging around it, each different from the other and equally definitive. He came to as he heard Quadri asking, in his usual indifferent tone, "Been around Paris?"

"Yes, a bit."

"Like it?"

"Very much."

"Yes, it's a lovable city," said Quadri, as if he were talking to himself and almost making a concession to Marcello, "but I wish you would direct your attention to the point I was making yesterday. This isn't the vice-ridden city full of corruption the Italian newspapers make it out to be . . . You surely subscribe to this idea, which actually has nothing to do with reality."

"I don't have that idea of Paris," said Marcello, a little surprised.

"It would astonish me if you didn't," said the professor without looking at him. "All the young people of your generation have ideas of this kind. They think that to be strong one must be austere, and in order to feel austere they fabricate scapegoats that don't really exist."

"I don't think I'm particularly austere," said Marcello dryly.

"I'm sure you are, and now I'll prove it to you," said the professor. He waited until the waiter had placed the antipasto plate on the table and then went on, "Let's see . . . I bet that while I was ordering the wines, you were secretly surprised that I could appreciate such things . . . isn't that right?"

How had he figured that out? Marcello admitted reluctantly, "You may be right, but I wasn't judging you. It just seemed strange because you seem so — to use your own word — austere."

"Nothing like you are, dear boy, nothing like you are," repeated the professor with pleasure. "And then, let's go on . . . tell the truth: you don't like wine and you don't understand it."

"No, to tell the truth, I hardly ever drink," said Marcello. "But how important is that?"

"Very important," said Quadri calmly. "Extremely important. And I'll make another bet — that you don't appreciate good food."

"I eat . . . ," began Marcello.

"To live," finished the professor triumphantly, "and that makes my point. And finally, I'm sure you have a prejudice against love. For example, if you're in a park and you see a couple kissing, your first impulse is condemnation and disgust, and you very probably infer that the city the park is in is shameless . . . isn't that how it is?"

Now Marcello got what Quadri was driving at. He said forcefully, "I don't infer anything. The truth is I was probably born without a taste for these things."

"Not only that, but people who *do* have a taste for them seem guilty and so despicable to you . . . confess the truth."

"No, that's wrong, they're just different from me, that's all."

"Who's not with us is against us," said the professor, making an abrupt sortie into politics. "That's one of the mottoes repeated so cheerfully in Italy and other places, too, these days, isn't it?

Meanwhile, he had begun to eat with such vigorous enjoyment that his glasses had fallen down on his nose.

"I really don't think," said Marcello dryly, "that politics enter into these things."

"Edmondo," said Lina.

"Dear."

"You promised me we wouldn't talk politics."

"But in fact we're not talking politics," said Quadri. "We're talking about Paris. And the conclusion — since Paris is a city in which people love to drink, eat, dance, kiss each other in the parks, in other words, have fun — is that I'm sure his judgment of Paris can't help but be unfavorable."

This time Marcello said nothing.

Giulia replied for him, smiling, "Well, I like the people in Paris a lot. They're so gay!"

"Well said," answered the professor in approval. "Signora, you should heal your husband."

"But he's not sick."

"Yes he is, he's sick with austerity," said the professor, his head bent over his plate. And he added, almost forcing the words through his teeth, "Or rather, his austerity is only a symptom."

Now it was apparent to Marcello that the professor, who, according to Lina, knew everything about him, was amusing himself, playing with him somewhat like a cat with a mouse. Still, he couldn't help thinking that this was a very innocent game compared to his own, so dark, begun that afternoon at Quadri's house and destined to end bloodily at the villa in Savoy.

He asked Lina, with a sort of melancholy flirtatiousness, "Do I really seem so austere, even to you?"

He saw her look at him with a cold and reluctant glance in which he could read, to his sorrow, the deep aversion she felt for him. Then, evidently, Lina decided to take back up the role of a woman in love that she had set out to play, because she answered, forcing herself to smile, "I don't know you well enough . . . but certainly you give the impression of being very serious."

"Oh, yes," said Giulia, gazing with affection at her husband. "Just think, I may have seen him smile a dozen times since I've known him . . . serious is the word, all right."

Lina was now staring at him fixedly, with malicious attention. "No," she said slowly, "no, I was mistaken. Serious is not the word . . . I'd say he was worried."

"Worried about what?"

Marcello saw her shrug her shoulders in indifference. "I really wouldn't know about that," she said.

But at the same time, to his profound astonishment, he felt her foot under the table slowly and intentionally brush his own and then press against it.

Quadri said good-naturedly, "Clerici, don't worry too much about seeming worried! This is all just small talk to pass the time. You're on your honeymoon, and that's all that should be on your mind . . . Isn't that right, Signora?"

He smiled at Giulia, with his particular smile that looked like a grimace caused by some mutilation; and Giulia smiled back at him, saying happily, "Maybe that's exactly what's on his mind, right, Marcello?"

Lina's foot continued to press against his own, and at this contact he almost felt he was splitting in two, as if the ambiguity of his love relationships had invaded his whole life, and instead of one scenario, there were two: the first, in which he pointed Quadri out to Orlando and returned to Italy with Giulia; and the second, in which he saved Quadri, abandoned Giulia, and stayed on in Paris with Lina. The two scenarios intersected and merged like two superimposed photographs, colored variously by his feelings of regret and horror, hope and sorrow, resignation and revolt. He knew beyond doubt that Lina was playing footsie only to deceive him and remain faithful to her role of a woman enamored; all the same, absurd as it was, he hoped that it wasn't true and that she really loved him. Meanwhile, he was wondering why in the world she had chosen, from the many gestures of sentimental complicity, exactly this one, so traditional and so coarse; and once again he seemed to read her contempt for him in the choice, as if he were someone who didn't require too much subtlety and invention to be deceived.

In the meantime Lina was saying — still pressing his foot and staring at him with willful intensity, "And speaking of your honeymoon . . . I already talked to Giulia about it, but since I know she won't have the courage to mention it to you, I'm taking it on myself to make the proposal. Why don't you come spend the rest of it in Savoy? At our place? We'll be there all summer . . . We have a lovely guest room. You can stay for a week, ten days, as long as you want . . . and then go directly from there back to Italy."

So, thought Marcello, almost disappointed, this was the reason for the foot game. He thought once more, but this time with spite, that the invitation to Savoy coincided all too well with Orlando's plans: by accepting the invitation, they would keep Lina in Paris, and meanwhile Orlando would have all the time he needed to deal with Quadri down in the mountains.

He said slowly, "As far as I'm concerned, I don't have anything against a trip to Savoy. But not for another week — not till we've seen Paris."

"Perfect," said Lina swiftly and triumphantly. "That way you can come down with me! My husband is going on ahead tomorrow, but I have to stay another week in Paris, too."

Marcello felt the woman's foot stop pressing his. Once the necessity that had inspired it had ceased, the flattering caress ceased as well; and Lina had not even deigned to thank him with a glance. His own gaze passed from Lina to his wife and he saw that she looked discontented.

Then she said, "I'm sorry I can't agree with my husband. And I'm also sorry to seem impolite toward you, Signora Quadri . . . but it's impossible for us to go to Savoy."

"Why?" Marcello couldn't help exclaiming. "After Paris . . ."

"After Paris, you know, we have to go to the Côte d'Azur to see those friends of ours."

It was a lie; they had no friends on the Côte d'Azur. Marcello understood that Giulia was lying to get rid of Lina and at the same time show him her own indifference toward the woman. But there was the danger that Lina, disgusted by Giulia's rejection, would leave with Quadri. He needed to remedy the situation, then, and make his recalcitrant wife accept the invitation definitively.

He said hurriedly, "Oh, we can give up seeing them . . . we'll have time to see them later."

"The Côte d'Azur . . . what a horror!" cried Lina, glad that Marcello had helped her, speaking gaily, impetuously, in a lilting voice. "Who goes to the Côte d'Azur? The *rastà*, the South Americans, the *cocottes*."

"Yes, but we made a promise," said Giulia obstinately. Marcello felt Lina's foot pressing against his own again.

With an effort, he asked, "Come on, Giulia, why shouldn't we accept?"

"If you really want to," she said, lowering her head. Marcello saw Lina turn an anxious, sad, irritated, surprised face toward Giulia.

"But why," she shouted with a kind of reflective dismay in her voice, "why just to see that horrible Côte d'Azur? That's so provincial . . . only provincials want to visit the Côte d'Azur! I'm telling you, no one else would hesitate in your place . . . Come on," she added suddenly with desperate vivacity, "there must be some reason you're not telling us. Maybe my husband and I just aren't to your liking."

Marcello could not help but admire this passionate violence, which allowed Lina to have what amounted to a lovers' quarrel with Giulia in his and Quadri's presence.

Somewhat surprised, Giulia protested, "For goodness' sake . . . what are you saying?"

Quadri, who was eating in silence, seemingly enjoying his food much more than following the conversation, now observed with his usual indifference, "Lina, you're embarrassing the lady. Even if it were true that she didn't like us, as you're saying, she would never tell us."

"Yes, you dislike us," continued the woman without paying the slightest attention to her husband, "or actually, maybe it's just me you dislike . . . isn't that right, dear? You do dislike me! You go around thinking," she added, turning to Marcello and still speaking with that desperate, worldly, and suggestive vivacity, "that people like you, and sometimes instead the exact people you most wish would like you can't stand you. Tell the truth, dear, you can't stand me . . . and while I'm talking and stupidly insisting that you come visit us in Savoy, you're thinking, 'What does this crazy woman want from me? How come she doesn't realize I can't stand her face, her voice, her manners, her whole being, in other words?' Tell me the truth, you're thinking things like that right this minute!"

By now, thought Marcello, she had abandoned all caution; and even if her husband failed, perhaps, to attribute any importance to her heartbroken insinuations, Marcello, on whom, according to the fiction, all this insistence was being lavished, could not help but realize to whom they were directed in truth.

Giulia protested mildly in astonishment, "But . . . what are you thinking? I'd really like to know why you're saying these things."

"So it's true!" cried Lina sorrowfully. "You dislike me." Then, turning to her husband with bitter, feverish satisfaction, she said, "You see, Edmondo, you said the signora wouldn't tell us . . . and instead she has: she doesn't like me."

"I didn't say that," said Giulia, smiling. "I wouldn't even dream of it . . ."

"You didn't say it but you let me know it."

Quadri said, without raising his eyes from his plate, "Lina, I don't understand this insistence of yours. Why should Signora Clerici dislike you? She's only known you for a few hours, she probably doesn't feel one way or another."

Marcello understood that he would have to interfere again; Lina's imperious, almost insulting eyes filled with scorn and anger were imposing it on him. Now she was no longer pressing his foot, but when he laid his hand on the table for a moment, she pretended to reach for the salt and squeezed his fingers in a gesture so rash it was hallucinatory.

He said, in a firm and conciliatory tone, "Giulia and I actually like you very much . . . and we accept your invitation with pleasure. We'll definitely come, won't we, Giulia?"

"Of course," said Giulia, suddenly yielding. "It was mostly because of our prior commitment . . . but we wanted to accept."

"Wonderful! Then it's all set . . . we'll leave together in a week." Radiant, Lina started immediately talking about the walks they would take in Savoy, the beauty of those places, the house they'd be living in. But Marcello noticed that her speech was confused; it seemed to be prompted more by an impulse to song, like a caged bird suddenly cheered by a ray of sun, than by any real need to say certain things or furnish certain information. And as the bird is made more lively by its own song, Lina seemed inebriated by the sound of her own voice, trembling with exaltation and a heedless and unsubdued joy.

Feeling himself excluded from the women's conversation, Marcello raised his eyes almost mechanically to the mirror hanging behind Quadri's back: Orlando's honest, good-natured face was still there, suspended in the void, beheaded but alive. But it was no longer alone; just as clear and no less absurd, the profile of another head could be seen, talking to Orlando's. It was the head of some sad and inferior kind of raptor, a bird of prey with nothing aquiline in it: small, dull, deeply sunken eyes under a low forehead; a great, hooked, melancholy nose; hollow cheeks filled with ascetic shadow; small mouth; stiff chin. Marcello observed this person at length, wondering if he had seen him before.

He started at the sound of Quadri's voice, asking him, "By the way, Clerici, if I asked you a favor, would you do it for me?"

It was an unexpected question; and Marcello noticed that Quadri had waited until his wife had fallen silent to ask it.

"Certainly, if it's at all possible," said Marcello.

It seemed to him that Quadri glanced at Lina before speaking, as if to receive the confirmation of an already discussed and established agreement.

"This is the thing," said Quadri, in a tone at once cynical and sweet. "I'm sure you're not unaware of my activities here in Paris and why I haven't returned to Italy. Well, we have friends in Italy with whom we correspond in whatever way we can. One way is to entrust letters to people who aren't involved in politics and who are therefore not under suspicion as political activists . . . I thought you might be able to take one of these letters to Italy and mail it at the first train station you happen to pass through . . . Turin, for example."

A silence followed. Marcello realized now that the only purpose of Quadri's request was to put him to the test, or at least to embarrass him; and he also understood that this request had been made with Lina's approval. Probably Quadri, faithful to his methods of persuasion, had convinced his wife that this would be an opportune maneuver, but not enough to lessen her hostility toward Marcello, which he seemed to read in her tense, cold, almost irritated face. For the moment, however, he couldn't guess what Quadri was really aiming at.

Playing for time, he said, "But if they discover me, I'll end up in jail."

Quadri smiled and said playfully, "That wouldn't be so bad . . . actually, for us it might even be good. Don't you know that political movements need martyrs and victims?"

Lina frowned but said nothing. Giulia looked at Marcello anxiously; clearly, she was hoping that her husband would refuse.

Marcello said slowly, "Actually, then, you almost want the letter to be discovered."

"Not really," said the professor, pouring himself more wine with an amiable nonchalance that suddenly, incomprehensibly inspired Marcello with something close to compassion. "The main thing we want is for the largest possible number of people to put themselves on the line, to struggle with us . . . going to jail for our cause is just one of many ways to fight the good fight . . . certainly not the only one." He drank slowly, then added seriously and unexpectedly, "But I only asked it of you pro forma, so to speak . . . I know you'll refuse."

"You were right," said Marcello, who had been weighing the pros and cons of the proposal in the meantime. "I'm sorry, but I don't feel I can do you this favor."

"My husband doesn't involve himself with politics," explained Giulia quickly, in a frightened tone. "He's an employee of the state."

"Of course," said Quadri with an indulgent, almost affectionate air, "of course: he's an employee of the state."

It seemed to Marcello that Quadri was strangely satisfied with his response. His wife, however, seemed annoyed. She asked Giulia in an aggressive tone, "Why are you so afraid for your husband to get into politics?"

"What good would it do him?" said Giulia unaffectedly. "He has to think about his future, not about politics."

"See how the women in Italy reason?" asked Lina, turning to her husband. "And then you're surprised at the way things go."

Giulia was annoyed. "Really, Italy has nothing to do with this. Under certain circumstances women from any country would feel the same way . . . if you lived in Italy, you'd think like I do."

"Come on, don't get mad," said Lina with a dark, sad, affectionate laugh, passing a hand over Giulia's frowning face in a rapid caress. "I was joking . . . You may be right. And anyway, you're so sweet when you get mad and defend your husband . . . Isn't that true, Edmondo? Isn't she sweet?"

Quadri nodded his head distractedly and a little irritably in assent, as if to say, "Woman talk," and then said seriously, "You're right, Signora. You should never put a man in the position of having to choose between truth and bread."

The subject, thought Marcello, was exhausted. Yet he was still curious to know the real reason for Quadri's proposal. The waiter changed the plates and placed a full basket of fruit on the table. The wine steward came and asked if he could uncork the bottle of champagne.

"Yes," said Quadri, "go ahead and open it."

The steward drew the bottle up out of the bucket, wrapped its neck in a napkin, pushed up on the cork, and then swiftly poured the foaming wine into their chalicelike glasses. Quadri stood up, his glass in his hand.

"Let us drink to the health of the cause," he said; and then, turning to Marcello, "You didn't want to take the letter, but at least you'll want to make a toast, won't you?"

He appeared to be moved, and his eyes were shining with tears; and yet, as Marcello observed, in both the gesture of the toast and the expression of his face, there was a certain slyness, almost a calculation. Marcello glanced at his wife and at Lina before responding to the toast. Giulia, who had already gotten to her feet, gave him a look as if to say, "It's all right to toast to it." Lina, her chalice in hand, her eyes lowered, had an annoyed, cold, almost bored air about her.

Marcello stood up and said, "Then here's to the health of the cause," and clinked his glass against Quadri's. A childish scruple made him want to add mentally, "of *my* cause," even though he no longer seemed to have any cause to defend, only a painful, incomprehensible duty to carry out. He noticed with displeasure that Lina avoided touching her glass to his. Giulia, on the other hand, exaggerating her cordiality, was making sure she got everyone's glass, pathetically calling out their names: "Lina, Signor Quadri, Marcello."

The sharp yet faint clinking of crystal made him shiver again, as the strokes of the grandfather clock had done earlier. He looked up at the mirror and saw Orlando's head suspended in midair, staring at him with gleaming, inexpressive eyes, like the eyes of a decapitated head.

Quadri held his glass out to the wine steward, who filled it once more. Then, putting a certain sentimental emphasis into the gesture, he turned toward Marcello, raised his glass, and said,

"And now to your own personal health, Clerici . . . and thank you." He underlined "thank you" in an allusive tone, emptied the glass in a breath, and sat down.

For some minutes they drank in silence. Giulia had emptied her glass twice and was now gazing at her husband with a tender, grateful, drunken expression.

Suddenly she exclaimed, "How good the champagne is! Say, Marcello, don't you think the champagne is good?"

"Yes, it's a very good wine," he admitted.

"You don't appreciate it enough," said Giulia. "It's really delicious . . . and I'm already drunk." She laughed, shaking her head, and then added suddenly, raising her glass, "Come on, Marcello, let's drink to our love."

She held out her glass, laughing drunkenly. The professor looked away; Lina looked cold and disgusted and made no effort to conceal her disapproval. Immediately, Giulia changed her mind.

"No," she shouted. "You're too austere, it's true . . . you're ashamed to toast to our love . . . so I'll toast, *alone*, to life! that I love so much, that's so beautiful . . . to life!" She drank down the champagne with a joyful, clumsy, impetuous gesture, so that some of it spilled on the table. Then she cried, "It's good luck!" and, wetting her fingers with wine, tried to touch them to Marcello's temples. He couldn't help making a gesture as if to shield himself. Giulia got to her feet, crying out, "You're ashamed! Well, I'm not ashamed!" And coming round the table, she hugged Marcello, almost falling on top of him and kissing him hard on the mouth. "We're on our honeymoon," she said in a challenging tone as she went back to her place, breathless and laughing. "We're here on our honeymoon and not to do politics and get letters to take to Italy."

Quadri, to whom these words seemed directed, said placidly, "You're right, Signora."

Marcello, caught between Quadri's conscious and his wife's unconscious and innocent allusions, preferred to say nothing, lowering his eyes.

Lina waited for a moment of silence to pass and then asked, as if it were a casual question, "What are you doing tomorrow?"

"We're going to Versailles," answered Marcello, wiping Giulia's lipstick off his mouth with his handkerchief.

"I'll come, too," said Lina quickly. "We can leave in the morning and have breakfast there. I'll help my husband pack his bags and then I'll come get you."

"Fine," said Marcello.

Lina added conscientiously, "I wish I could drive you there in the car, but my husband's taking it . . . We'll have to go by train. It's more fun, anyway."

Quadri seemed not to have heard her; he was paying the bill, extracting the banknotes folded in quarters from the pocket of his striped pants with a hunchback's particular gesture. Marcello tried to offer him some money, but Quadri waved him away, saying, "You can get it the next time . . . in Italy."

Giulia said suddenly, in a very loud and drunken voice, "In Savoy we can be together, but I want to go to Versailles alone with my husband."

"Thank you," said Lina ironically, getting up from the table. "I'd say you put that clearly enough."

"Don't be offended," began Marcello, embarrassed. "It's the champagne . . ."

"No, it's the love I feel for you, stupid," yelled Giulia. Laughing, she headed toward the door with the professor. Marcello heard her asking him, "Does it seem unfair to you that I should want to be alone with my husband during my honeymoon?"

"No, dear," answered Quadri gently, "you're absolutely right."

Meanwhile, Lina was commenting in a bitter tone, "I'm such a fool, I hadn't thought about that . . . of course, a trip to Versailles is *the* ritual for newlyweds."

At the door, Marcello stepped back so that Quadri could go through ahead of him. As he was leaving he heard the clock strike again: it was ten o'clock.

9

ONCE THEY WERE OUTSIDE, the professor sat down behind the wheel of the car, leaving the car door open.

"Your husband can go in front with mine," Lina said to Giulia, "and you can sit back here with me."

But Giulia answered in a tipsy, teasing voice, "Why? I prefer to sit in front, myself," and she climbed in and sat down firmly beside Quadri.

So Marcello and Lina found themselves next to each other in the back seat. Now Marcello wanted to take the woman at her word, acting as if he really believed that she loved him. There was, in this desire, not only a vindictive impulse, but also almost a last little bit of hope, as if, after all, he was still deluded about Lina's feelings for him in some contradictory and involuntary way. The car was moving and slowed down to turn into a cross street at a particularly dark spot. Taking advantage of the darkness, Marcello grabbed the hand Lina had placed on her knees and brought it down to the seat, between their two bodies. He saw her turn at the touch with an angry start, which she quickly transformed into a false, complicit gesture of pleading admonishment. The car rolled on, turning down one narrow street after another of the Latin Quarter, and Marcello squeezed Lina's hand. He felt it tense within his own, as if she were rejecting his caress not only with her muscles but even, he thought, with her skin; disgust, indignation, and anger were mixed in the powerless twitching of her fingers. The car skidded around a turn and they fell on top of each other. Marcello grabbed Lina by the neck, as if she were a cat that could twist and scratch him, and turning her face to one side, kissed her on the mouth. At first she tried to free herself, but Marcello held her shaved, slender, boyish neck even more firmly; with a low moan of pain, she stopped resisting altogether and submitted to the kiss. But Marcello clearly felt her lips twist in a grimace of disgust; and at the same time her hand, which he was still grasping in his own, stuck its sharp nails into his palm — an apparently voluptuous gesture that Marcello knew in reality was burning with repugnance and aversion. He made the kiss last as long as possible, looking now into her eyes, sparkling with hatred and repulsed impatience, now at the two black and motionless heads of Quadri and Giulia in the front. Then the headlights of an oncoming car cast a bright light onto the windshield; Marcello let Lina go and threw himself back on the seat.

Out of the corner of his eye he saw her fall back, too, and then slowly, raising a handkerchief to her mouth, wipe it off with a reflexive gesture filled with disgust. As he watched the care and repugnance with which she was wiping her lips — which, according to the pretence, should have still been throbbing and avid for the kiss — he felt a desperate, obscure, frightening sorrow and pain.

"Love me!" he wished he could shout. "Love me . . . for the love of God!" It suddenly seemed to him that not only his own life, now, but hers as well, depended on Lina's loving him, which he desired so much and which was so impossible. Now, in fact, as if Lina's irreducible aversion were contagious, he realized that he, too, was feeling a bloody, murderous hatred, mixed in with and inseparable from his love. He felt he could gladly have killed her at that moment, since he couldn't stand knowing she was at once alive and his enemy; and he also thought, though it frightened him to think it, that by now watching her die might even inspire more pleasure in him than being loved by her. Then, with an instant and generous motion of the heart, he reproached himself, thinking, "Thank God she won't be in Savoy when Orlando and the others get there . . . thank God." And he understood that he had truly wanted for a moment to make her die with her husband, in the same way and on the same occasion.

The car came to a halt and they got out. Marcello glimpsed a dark suburban street between a crooked row of little houses and a garden wall.

"You'll see," said Lina, taking Giulia by the arm, "it's not exactly a place for schoolgirls . . . but it's interesting."

They were walking toward an illuminated door. Above it on a small rectangle of red glass was written LA CRAVATE NOIRE in blue letters.

"The Black Tie," Lina explained to Giulia, "the tie men wear with their tuxedos and that all the women in here wear, from the waitresses to the owner."

They entered the vestibule; and right away a face with hard features and short hair, but beardless, with a woman's figure and pale complexion, appeared behind the counter of the coatroom, saying in a dry voice, "*Vestiaire.*" Amused, Giulia went up to the counter and turned around, letting her cape slide down her bare shoulders into the hands of this checkroom attendant in a black jacket, starched shirt, and bowtie. Then, in the air thick with smoke, deafened by music and the roar of voices, they passed into the dance hall.

A full-bodied woman of an uncertain age but surely past youth with a fat, pale, smooth face squeezed under the chin by the uniform black bowtie came to meet them between the crowded tables. She greeted Quadri's wife with affectionate familiarity and then, raising a monocle tied by a silken cord to the lapel of her masculine jacket to her imperious eye, she said, "Four people . . . I have just what you need, Signora Quadri. Please follow me."

Lina, whom the place seemed to have put into a good mood, leaned on the woman with the monocle's shoulder and said something gay and malicious to which the woman responded, exactly like a man, with a shrug and a wry face. Following her, they reached the other end of the room, where there was an empty table.

"*Voilà*," said the manager. It was her turn to lean over Lina, who was sitting down, and whisper something in her ear with a playful, even mischievous air; then she strutted off between the tables, her body and her small, shining head held ramrod straight.

A short, stocky, very dark waitress came up, dressed in the same style, and Lina, with the careless and happy security of someone who finally finds herself in a place that suits her, ordered the drinks. Then she turned toward Giulia and said gaily, "Do you see how they're dressed? It's a real convent . . . isn't it curious?"

Marcello thought Giulia was looking embarrassed by this time; she was wearing a set, completely conventional smile. In a small round space between the tables, under a kind of overturned cement mushroom vibrating with false neon light, many couples were pressed tightly together, some of them pairs of women. The orchestra, which was also composed of women dressed like men, was confined under the stairway that led to the balcony.

The professor said, somewhat distractedly, "I don't like this place . . . These women seem to me to deserve more compassion than curiosity."

Lina did not appear to have heard her husband's observation. She was looking at Giulia, her eyes filled with a voracious light. Finally she said to her with a nervous laugh, as if yielding to an irresistible desire, "Shall we dance together? That way they'll take us for two of them . . . it's fun . . . let's pretend to be like them. Come on, come on . . ." Laughing and excited, she had already gotten to her feet and was urging Giulia to get up, putting one hand on her shoulder. Giulia was looking at her and then at her husband irresolutely.

Marcello said dryly, "Why are you looking at me? There's nothing wrong with it." He understood that he must second Lina this time, too. Giulia sighed and stood up slowly and reluctantly.

Meanwhile, Lina, who had completely lost her head, was repeating, "If even your husband says there's nothing wrong with it . . . come on, come on."

Giulia seemed put out and said as she was going, "To tell the truth, I don't care to be taken for one of them."

But she continued walking in front of Lina and, when they had reached the space reserved for dancing, turned toward her with her arms outstretched, waiting to be embraced. Marcello watched Lina move close, put her arm around Giulia's waist with masculine certainty and authority, and then dance her onto the floor among the other couples. For a moment he watched, with obscure and painful amazement, the two embraced and dancing women. Giulia was smaller than Lina and they were dancing cheek to cheek; and at every step, Lina's arm seemed to squeeze Giulia's waist more tightly. It was a sad and incredible sight. This, he couldn't help thinking, was the love that in a different world, with a different life, would have been destined for him, the love that would have saved him, the love he would have enjoyed. But a hand was touching his arm. He turned and saw Quadri's shapeless red face bent toward his own.

"Clerici," said Quadri in an emotional voice, "don't think I didn't understand."

Marcello stared at him and said slowly, "Excuse me, but now *I* don't understand."

"Clerici," the professor replied quickly, "you know who I am. But I, too, know who you are." He had taken the lapels of Marcello's jacket in both hands and was looking at him with great intensity.

Marcello, disturbed, frozen with a kind of terror, stared back into his face: no, there was no hatred in Quadri's eyes, only a sentimental, tearful, yearning emotion that was still, thought Marcello, discreetly calculating and malicious.

Then Quadri went on, "I know who you are and I realize that by speaking in this way I may give you the impression that I'm living under an illusion, that I'm naive or just plain stupid . . . it doesn't matter. Clerici, despite everything, I want to speak sincerely, and I'm telling you: thank you."

Marcello looked at him and said nothing. His jacket lapels were still in Quadri's hands and he felt the jacket pull tightly around his neck, as it does when someone grabs you to fling you away.

"I say to you, thank you," continued Quadri, in a moved voice. "Don't think I haven't understood you. If you had done your duty, you would have taken the letter and showed it to your superiors . . . to decipher, to arrest the people it was addressed to. You didn't do that, Clerici, you didn't *want* to do it . . . out of loyalty, a sudden re-alization that you were mistaken, an instant of doubt, honesty . . . I don't know . . . I only know that you didn't do it, and once more I say to you, thank you."

Marcello made a move as if to respond, but Quadri, finally let-ting go of the jacket, stopped his mouth with his hand. "No," he said, "don't tell me you didn't want to accept the letter so I wouldn't get suspicious, so you could remain faithful to your obligatory role of a newlywed on his honeymoon . . . Don't say it because I know it isn't true. In reality, you've taken the first step to-ward redemption, and I thank you for having given me the oppor-tunity to help you take it. Keep on, Clerici, and you can be truly reborn to a new life." Quadri sat back in his chair and pretended to quench his thirst with a long swallow from his glass. "But here are the ladies," he said, standing back up. Marcello, who was dumbstruck, stood up with him.

He noticed that Lina seemed out of sorts. When she was seated, she opened her compact with a piqued and hurried air and powdered her nose and cheeks swiftly, with repeated, angry little stabs. In contrast, Giulia appeared to be placid and indifferent. She sat down next to her husband and took one of his hands under the table with an affectionate gesture, as if to confirm her repug-nance for Lina. The manager with the monocle came back and, curling her smooth and pallid face into a honeyed smile, asked in an affected voice if all was well.

Lina replied dryly that everything couldn't be better.

The manager bent down to Giulia and said to her, "This is the first time you've come here . . . May I offer you a flower?"

"Yes, thank you," said Giulia, surprised.

"Cristina," called out the manager. A girl — she, too, in a man's vest — very different than the plump, pretty flower girls usually found in dance halls, approached the table. She was pale and haggard, without makeup, and had an Oriental face with a large nose, big lips, and a bald and bony forehead under hair cut very short and very badly, as if some illness had thinned it. She held out a basket full of gardenias, and the manager chose one and pinned it to Giulia's breast, saying, "Compliments of the management."

"Thank you," said Giulia.

"Don't mention it," said the manager. "I'm guessing the signora is Spanish. Am I right?"

"Italian," said Giulia.

"Ah, Italian . . . I should have known . . . with those black eyes . . ." The words were lost in the din of the crowd, as the manager and the thin and melancholy Cristina walked away together.

The orchestra began to play again. Lina turned to Marcello and said to him, almost ironically, "Why don't you invite me to dance? I'd like to." Without saying a word, he rose and followed her toward the dance floor.

They began to dance. Lina held herself so far from him that Marcello couldn't help remembering, to his sorrow, the possessive affection with which only a short time before she had pressed herself against Giulia. They danced for a while in silence and then Lina said suddenly, with an anger in which her pretence of loving complicity was strangely tinged with aversion and rage, "Instead of kissing me in the car where there was the danger that my husband might see us, you could have pressed your wife to let me come along on the trip to Versailles."

Marcello was astonished at the natural way she was able to graft her real anger onto their false relationship of love, as well as at the ease with which she had suddenly slipped into calling him *tu*, the more intimate form of address, like a woman without scruples about betraying her husband; and for a moment he said nothing.

Lina, interpreting this silence in her own way, insisted, "Why don't you talk now? Is this your love? You're not even capable of making your silly wife obey you."

"My wife isn't silly," he answered mildly, more curious than of-fended by her strange rage.

She hurled herself immediately into the breach he had opened by his response. "What do you mean, she's not silly," she ex-claimed irritably, almost surprised. "My dear, even a blind man could see it . . . She's lovely, of course, but perfectly stupid, a beau-tiful beast. How can you not be aware of it?"

"I like her the way she is," he said.

"A goose . . . an idiot . . . the Côte d'Azur . . . a little provincial without a crumb of a brain. The Côte d'Azur, really . . . why not Montecarlo or Deauville? Why not just the Eiffel Tower?"

She seemed out of her mind with frustration, a sign, thought Marcello, that there had been some unpleasant discussion be-tween her and Giulia while they were dancing. He said gently, "Don't worry about my wife. Tomorrow morning come to the hotel . . . Giulia will have to accept your being there. And then the three of us will go to Versailles together."

He saw her look at him with a gleam of hope. Then her anger prevailed and she said, "What an absurd idea! Your wife has al-ready said very clearly that she doesn't want me there, and I'm not in the habit of going where I'm not wanted."

Marcello replied simply, "Well, I want you to come."

"Yes, but your wife doesn't."

"What does my wife matter to you? Isn't it enough that we love each other?"

Restless and diffident, she drew back her head to consider him, her soft, swelling breasts pressing against his. "Honestly . . . you talk about 'our love' as if we had been lovers forever. Do you really believe that we love each other?"

Marcello would have liked to say to her, "Why don't you love me? I'd love you so much." But the words died on his lips, like echoes silenced by an unbridgeable distance. It seemed to him that he had never loved her so much as now, when she was forcing pretence to the point of parody by asking him falsely whether he was sure he loved her.

Finally he said sadly, "You know I wish we would love each other."

"Me, too," she answered distractedly; and it was obvious that she was thinking of Giulia. Then she added, as if waking up to reality with a sudden resurgence of anger, "Anyway, please don't kiss me in the car or anyplace like that again . . . I've never been able to stand that kind of public display. I consider it a lack of respect and even of manners."

"But you," he got out between his clenched teeth, "still haven't told me whether you're coming to Versailles."

He saw her hesitate, and then she asked uneasily, "Do you really think your wife won't be annoyed when she sees me coming? She won't insult me the way she did today at the restaurant?"

"I'm sure she won't. She might be a little surprised, maybe, that's all . . . But before you come over I'll have managed to persuade her."

"You'll do that?"

"Yes."

"I have the feeling that your wife can't stand me," she said, in an interrogative tone, as if expecting him to reassure her.

"You're wrong," he answered, faced with her now blatant desire. "The truth is, she likes you a great deal."

"Really?"

"Yes, really. She was telling me so just today."

"What did she say?"

"Oh, God, nothing in particular . . . that you were pretty, that you seemed intelligent . . . the truth, in other words."

"Then I'll come," she decided. "I'll come right after my husband leaves, at about nine, so we can take the ten o'clock train . . . I'll come to your hotel."

Marcello resented her haste and relief as one more insult to his love. But burning with he knew not what desire for a love of any kind, even pretended and ambiguous, he said, "I'm very happy you decided to come."

"Yes."

"Yes, because I think you wouldn't have if you didn't love me."

"I could always have done it for some other reason," she replied maliciously.

"What reason?"

"We women are spiteful . . . I could be doing it just to spite your wife."

So, she was still, and always, and only thinking of Giulia. Marcello said nothing but, still dancing, he guided her toward the door. Two more turns and they found themselves in front of the coatroom, a step from the door.

"Where are you taking me?" she asked.

"Listen," pleaded Marcello, in a low voice so that the coatroom attendant standing behind her counter couldn't hear him, "let's go out into the street for a minute."

"Why?"

"There's no one there. I'd like you to give me a kiss . . . spontaneously . . . to show me you really do love me."

"I wouldn't dream of it," she said, becoming angry again.

"But why not? The street is dark, it's deserted."

"I already told you I can't stand these public displays of affection."

"I'm begging you."

"Let me go," she said in a hard, high voice; and she wrenched herself free, immediately walking back toward the dance hall. As if he had been shoved out by her furious gesture, Marcello reeled over the threshold and found himself in the street.

It was dark and deserted, as he had told Lina; no one passed him on the sidewalks, only faintly illuminated by infrequent lampposts. A few cars were parked in a row on the other side of the street under a garden wall. Marcello drew out his handkerchief and dried the sweat from his forehead, looking at the leafy trees overhanging the wall. He felt stunned, as if he had received a sharp, hard blow on the head. He did not remember ever having begged a woman so hard and he was almost ashamed of having done so. At the same time, he realized that all hope of making Lina love him or even understand him had vanished.

At that moment he heard the sound of a car engine behind him, and then the car slid up beside him and stopped. The light was on inside; and at the wheel Marcello saw the figure, like a man on a family outing, of the agent Orlando. His companion sat to one side, the man with the long, thin face of a bird of prey.

"Dottore," said Orlando in a low voice.

Marcello approached mechanically.

"Dottore . . . we're taking off. He's leaving tomorrow morning in his car and we'll follow him . . . We probably won't wait till we get to Savoy."

"Why not?" asked Marcello, without really being aware of what he was saying.

"It's a long road and Savoy's far away . . . Why wait for Savoy if we can do it sooner under better conditions? Good-bye, Dottore . . . see you in Italy."

Orlando gestured as if to salute him and his companion nodded his head. The car slipped away, reached the end of the street, turned the corner, and disappeared.

Marcello stepped back onto the sidewalk. He walked through the door and headed back into the dance hall. The music had started up again while he was gone, and he found no one but Quadri at the table. Lina and Giulia were dancing together again, he observed, half-lost in the thickening crowd on the dance floor. He sat down, lifted his glass, still full of iced lemonade, and emptied it slowly, staring at the piece of ice at the bottom.

Suddenly Quadri said, "Clerici, do you know you could be very useful?"

"I don't understand," said Marcello, putting his glass back down on the table.

Quadri explained without any embarrassment, "I might suggest simply staying here in Paris to someone else . . . there's enough to do here for everyone, I assure you, and we have great need of young men like yourself. But you could be even more useful to us by remaining where you are, in your position."

"By giving you information," finished Marcello, looking him in the eyes.

"Precisely."

At these words, Marcello couldn't help remembering Quadri's eyes — shining with emotion, almost tearful, sincerely affectionate — as they had been shortly before, when he was holding him by the lapels of his jacket. That emotion, thought Marcello, was the sentimental velvet in which the cold claws of political calculation were concealed. It was the same emotion, he thought, that he had noticed in the eyes of some of his superiors, although of a different kind, patriotic instead of humanitarian. But what did these justificatory feelings matter if, in both cases, in all cases, they gave rise to no consideration for him, for his essence as a human being — if he were nonchalantly understood to be no more than one means among many to achieve certain ends? He thought with almost bureaucratic indifference that Quadri, by his request, had countersigned his own death warrant.

Then he raised his eyes and said, "You speak as if I had the same ideas you do . . . or as if I were about to. If that were the case, I would have offered you my services myself. But things being what they are, that is, my not sharing and not wanting to share your ideas, what you're asking me to do is simply a betrayal."

"Betrayal, never," said Quadri readily. "Traitors don't exist for us . . . only people who realize the error of their ways and mend them. I was, and am still, convinced that you are one of those people."

"You're wrong."

"Let it be as if it had never been said, then, as if it had never been said . . . Young lady!"

Hastily, perhaps to hide his disappointment, Quadri called over one of the waitresses and paid the bill. Then they fell silent, Quadri looking around the room with the expression of a tranquil spectator, Marcello sitting with his back to it, his eyes lowered. Finally he felt a hand on his shoulder and heard Giulia's slow, calm voice saying, "So, shall we go now? I'm so tired . . ."

Marcello stood up immediately, saying, "I think we're all feeling sleepy."

He noticed that Lina's face looked haggard and intensely pale, but he attributed the first to exhaustion from the evening and the second to the livid neon light. They left and walked toward the car, parked at the end of the street. Marcello pretended not to hear his wife whispering to him, "Let's sit where we did before," and climbed in quickly beside Quadri. During the entire course of the trip not one of the four said a word.

Except that Marcello, halfway through it, asked casually, "How long will it take you to get to Savoy?"

And Quadri replied, without turning, "It's a fast car, and since I'll be alone and won't have to make any stops, I think I'll reach Annecy by nightfall . . . the next day I should be on the road by dawn."

They got out of the car in front of the hotel to say good-bye. Quadri, after shaking Marcello's and Giulia's hands in a hurry, sat back down in the car. Lina lingered a moment to say something to Giulia, and then Giulia said good-bye and went into the hotel. For an instant Lina and Marcello remained alone together on the sidewalk.

He said, in embarrassment, "Till tomorrow, then."

"Till tomorrow," echoed the woman, tilting her head with a worldly smile.

Then she turned her back to him; and he caught up with Giulia in the lobby.

10

WHEN MARCELLO WOKE UP and raised his eyes to the ceiling in the uncertain half-light of the shutters left ajar, he remembered immediately that at that hour Quadri was driving down the roads of France, followed at a short distance by Orlando and his men; and he understood that the trip to Paris was over. The trip was over, he repeated to himself, although it had barely begun. It was over because with Quadri's death, which he already took as a *fait accompli*, that period of his life during which he had sought by any means to free himself from the burden of loneliness and abnormality that Lino's death had left him with had come to an end. He had managed to do it, at the cost of a crime — or rather, of what would have been a crime if he had not known how to justify and make sense of it. As far as he was concerned personally, he felt sure that such justification would not be lacking: he would be a good husband, a good father, a good citizen, also thanks to Quadri's death, which definitively precluded any going back, and he would watch his life slowly but surely acquire the certainty and solidity that up until now it had lacked. In this way Lino's death, which had been the chief cause of his obscure tragedy, would be resolved and annulled by Quadri's, just as in the past the expiatory sacrifice of an innocent human being had served to resolve and annul the impiety of a previous crime. But he was not alone in this matter; and the justification of his life and of Quadri's murder did not depend on him alone.

"Now," he thought lucidly, "the others need to do their duties, too . . . Otherwise I'll be left alone with this dead man in my arms and in the end I will have achieved nothing, nothing at all."

"The others," as he knew, were the government he had understood he was serving with that murder; the society embodied by that government; and the very nation that accepted guidance by that same society. It would never be enough for him to say, "I've done my duty; I acted this way under orders." Such a justification might be enough for agent Orlando, but not for him. What he needed was the *complete* success of that government, that society, that nation; and not only an outer, but also an intimate and crucial success. Only in this way could what was normally considered a common crime become, instead, a positive step in a necessary direction. In other words, thanks to forces that did not depend on him, a complete transmutation of values must take place: injustice must become justice; betrayal, heroism; death, life. He felt the need at this point to express his situation to himself in coarse, sarcastic words, and he thought coldly, "In other words, if Fascism falls on its face, and if all the bastards, incompetents, and imbeciles in Rome drag the Italian nation down into ruin, then I'm nothing but a miserable assassin." But right away he corrected himself mentally: "But things being as they are, I couldn't have acted any differently."

Beside him Giulia, who was still asleep, began to move, and with a slow, strong, gradual motion wrapped first her arms, then her legs around him, laying her head on his breast. Marcello let her do so, and stretching out one arm, picked up the small phosphorescent alarm clock from the bedside table and looked at the time: it was quarter past nine. He couldn't help thinking that, if things had gone the way Orlando had assumed they would go, at this very moment Quadri's car was lying abandoned in a ditch somewhere in France with a corpse at the wheel.

Giulia asked in a low voice, "What time is it?"

"Quarter past nine."

"Uh, how late it is," she said without moving. "We slept almost nine hours."

"Obviously we were tired."

"Aren't we going to Versailles, then?"

"Certainly we are. Actually, we should get dressed now," he said with a sigh. "Signora Quadri will be here soon."

"I'd prefer her not to come . . . she never leaves me in peace with that love of hers."

Marcello said nothing.

After a moment, Giulia went on, "What's the plan for the next few days?"

Before he could hold himself back, Marcello answered, "We're leaving," in a voice that he knew sounded almost dismal, such was the strength of his sorrow.

This time Giulia roused herself; without detaching herself from him, she pulled her head and shoulders back a little and said in a surprised, already alarmed voice, "Leaving? So soon? We just got here and already we have to leave?"

"I didn't tell you last night," he lied, "so as not to ruin your evening. But yesterday afternoon I received a telegram calling me back to Rome."

"What a shame . . . really, what a shame," said Giulia in a good-natured, already resigned tone of voice. "Just as I was starting to enjoy myself in Paris. And we haven't even seen anything yet."

"Are you very disappointed?" he asked gently, stroking her head.

"No, but I would have preferred to stay here a day or so, at least . . . if only to get some idea of Paris."

"We'll come back."

A silence followed. Then Giulia threw her arms around him and pressed her whole body against his, saying, "Then at least tell me what we're going to do in the future . . . tell me what our life is going to be like."

"Why do you want to know?"

"Just because," she answered, hugging him even more tightly. "Because I love to talk about the future . . . in bed . . . in the dark."

"All right," began Marcello, in a calm and colorless voice. "First we'll go back to Rome and look for a house."

"How big?"

"Four or five rooms with a kitchen and bath. Once we've found it, we'll buy everything we need to furnish it."

"I'd like an apartment on the ground floor," she said in a dreamy voice, "with a garden. It wouldn't have to be big . . . but with flowers and trees, so we could sit out there when the weather's nice."

"Nothing could be easier," confirmed Marcello. "So, we'll set up house . . . I think I'll have enough money to outfit it completely. Not with expensive furniture, of course . . ."

"You'll make a nice study for yourself," she said.

"Why should I have a study, when I do my work at the office? Better to have a big living room."

"Yes, a living room, you're right . . . sitting room and dining room together. And we'll have a beautiful bedroom, won't we?"

"Certainly."

"But no couches that fold out, they're so squalid . . . I want a regular bedroom, with a big double bed. And tell me, will we have a nice kitchen, too?"

"A nice kitchen, why not?"

"I want a double-burner stove, with gas and electricity, and I want to have a big beautiful Frigidaire . . . If we don't have enough money, we could buy them on the installment plan."

"Of course, on the installment plan."

"Tell me some more. What will we do in this house?"

"We'll live there and be happy."

"I need to be happy so much," she said, curling herself even more tightly against him, "so much. If you only knew . . . it feels like I've wanted to be happy ever since I was born."

"All right, we'll be happy," said Marcello firmly, almost aggressively.

"Will we have children?"

"Certainly."

"I want a lot of them," she said in a lilting voice. "I want one for every year, at least for the first four years of our marriage. That way we'll have a family, and I want to have a family as soon as possible . . . It seems to me we shouldn't wait, otherwise it will be too late . . . and when you have a family, all the rest comes by itself, doesn't it?"

"Certainly, all the rest comes by itself."

She was quiet for a minute and then asked, "Do you think I'm already pregnant?"

"How would I know that?"

"If I was," she laughed, "it would mean that our child was conceived on a train."

"Would you like that?"

"Yes, it would be a good omen for him. Who knows, maybe he'd become a great traveler! I want the first one to be a son . . . for the second, I'd prefer a girl . . . I'm sure she would be really beautiful. You're so handsome and I'm not exactly ugly . . . . The two of us will surely give birth to really beautiful children."

Marcello said nothing and Giulia went on, "Why aren't you saying anything? Wouldn't you like to have children with me?"

"Certainly," he replied; and all of a sudden, to his astonishment, he felt two tears well up from his eyes and slide down his cheeks. And then two more — hot, burning, as if they had already formed in some remote, long-ago time and remained in his eyes to fill them with fiery pain. He understood that what had made him cry was Giulia's earlier discourse on happiness, although he wasn't sure why. Maybe because this happiness had been paid for in advance and at such great cost; maybe because he realized that he would never be happy, at least in the simple and affectionate way Giulia had described. With an effort, he finally stifled his desire to weep and, without letting Giulia see it, dried his eyes with the back of his hand.

In the meantime Giulia was hugging him ever more tightly, gluing her body seductively to his, trying to guide his inert and distracted hands to hold and caress her. Then he felt her raise her face to his and start to kiss him hard, all over his cheeks, on his mouth, on his forehead, on his chin, with frenetic and infantile greed. At last she whispered, almost wailing, "Why don't you come into me . . . take me," and in her imploring voice he seemed to hear some reproach for having thought more of his own happiness than of hers. Then, as he was embracing her and sweetly and smoothly penetrating her; as beneath him, her eyes closed and her head on the pillow, she was beginning to raise and lower her hips in a regular, passive, and obscurely reflexive movement, like the motion of a wave in the sea that swells and flattens according to the ebb and flow, there was a resounding knock at the door.

"Express!"

"What can that be," she murmured, panting, half-opening her eyes. "Don't move. What do you care?"

Marcello turned and glimpsed — down on the floor, in the faint light by the door — a letter being pushed through the crack. At the same moment, Giulia fell back and stiffened beneath him, throwing back her head, sighing deeply, and digging her nails into his arms. She tossed her head back and forth on the pillow, and murmured, "Kill me."

For no reason Marcello suddenly remembered Lino's cry, "Kill me like a dog," and felt a terrible anxiety invade his spirit. He waited a long moment for Giulia's hands to fall back on the bed; then he switched on the lamp, put his feet on the floor, went to pick up the letter, and returned to stretch out beside his wife. Giulia had turned her back to him now and was curled up on herself with her eyes shut. Marcello looked at the letter before putting it on the edge of the bed, near her open, still panting lips. On the envelope was written: "Madame Giulia Clerici," in a clearly feminine hand.

"A letter from Signora Quadri," he said.

Giulia murmured, without opening her eyes, "Give it to me."

A long silence followed. The letter, placed at the level of Giulia's mouth, was plainly illuminated by the lamp; Giulia, motionless and collapsed, seemed to be asleep. Then she sighed, opened her eyes, and, holding the letter by its corner in one hand, tore the envelope open with her teeth, pulled out the paper, and read.

Marcello saw her smile; then she murmured, "They say that in love, they win who flee . . . . . Since I treated her badly yesterday evening, she's informing me that she changed her mind and left this morning with her husband. She hopes that I'll join her . . . Have a good trip."

"She left?"

"Yes, she left this morning at seven o'clock with her husband to go to Savoy. And you know why she left? Do you remember last night when I danced with her the second time? I asked *her* to dance, and she was happy since she hoped that I was finally going to give in to her. Well, instead I told her very frankly that she must absolutely leave me alone, and that if she kept it up I'd stop seeing her altogether and that I only loved you and would she leave me in peace and wasn't she ashamed of herself . . . Well, I gave her such a talking-to that she almost cried. So today she left. You understand how calculated it was . . . I'm leaving so that you can run after me . . . She'll wait awhile."

"Yes, she'll wait awhile," repeated Marcello.

"But, I'm glad she's gone," continued Giulia. "She was so insistent and annoying. As far as running after her, let's not even talk about it. I don't ever want to see that woman again."

"You'll never see her again," said Marcello.

*T*HE ROOM MARCELLO worked in at the ministry looked out on a secondary courtyard. It was very small, asymmetrical in shape, and contained only a desk and a couple of bookshelves. It was located at the bottom of a dead-end hallway far away from the rooms in the front; to get there Marcello climbed up backstairs that came out behind the palazzo into a more or less deserted alleyway.

One morning, a week after his return from Paris, Marcello was sitting at his desk. Despite the intense heat, he had not taken off his suit jacket or unknotted his tie, as his colleagues generally did; it was his punctilious habit not to modify his street clothes in any way when he was in the office. Completely dressed, then, his neck squeezed into a high, tight, detachable collar, he began to examine the foreign and Italian newspapers before starting work. This morning, too, although six days had passed, he looked first for news of Quadri's murder. He noticed that the articles and headlines about it were much reduced, undoubtedly a sign that the investigation had not made much progress. A couple of left-wing French papers were going over the tale of the crime one more time, dwelling on their interpretations of some of its strangest or most significant details: Quadri knifed to death in the thick of the woods; his wife, instead, struck by three pistol bullets at the edge of the road and then dragged, already dead, to lie beside her husband; the car taken into the woods as well and hidden in the brush. This careful concealment of the car and the corpses among the trees, far from the road, had kept them from being discovered for two days. The left-wing newspapers were sure that the married couple had been murdered by hired assassins come up from Italy for the express purpose of killing them. A few of the foreign right-wing papers ventured to print, somewhat hesitantly, the official explanation of the Italian newspapers: that they had been assassinated by anti-Fascist companions over dissensions regarding the conduct of the war in Spain.

Marcello hurled away the papers and picked up an illustrated French magazine. He was struck immediately by a photograph, printed on the second page as part of the whole journalistic coverage of the crime. It bore the caption TRAGEDY OF GEVAUDAN FOREST and must have been taken at the moment of discovery or shortly after. You could see underbrush, with the straight trunks of the trees bristling with branches, lighter splashes of sun between one trunk and another, and, on the ground, sunk in the tall grass, almost invisible at first sight in that shifting confusion of light and woodland shadow, the two bodies. Quadri was stretched out on his back and all you could see of him were his shoulders and head, and of this only the chin and the throat, sliced across with the black line of a knife cut. You could see Lina's whole body, however, thrown partway across her husband's. Marcello placed his lit cigarette calmly on the edge of the ashtray, took up a magnifying glass, and scrutinized the photograph with care. Although it was gray and out of focus, as well as being further blurred by splashes of sun and shade from the underbrush, he recognized Lina's body, both slender and generous, pure and sensual, beautiful and strange: the broad shoulders under the delicate nape of the neck and slender throat, the exuberant breasts above the wasp-small waist, the fullness of the hips and the elegant length of the legs. She was covering her husband with part of her body and with her widespread dress and seemed to want to speak into his ear; she was turned to one side, her face immersed in the grass, her mouth against his cheek. Marcello gazed at the photograph through the lens for a long time, trying to study every shadow, every line, every detail. It seemed to him that that image, full of an immobility that went beyond the mechanical immobility of the instant to reach the definitive immobility of death, breathed forth an air of enviable peace. It was a photograph, he thought, full of the last, profound stillness that must have followed the sudden, terrible agony. A few instants before all had been confusion, violence, terror, hatred, hope, and desperation; a few instants afterward, all was over and peaceful. He recalled that the two bodies had remained in the underbrush a long time, almost two days; and he imagined that the sun, after having warmed them for many hours and attracted the buzzing insects to them, had gone down slowly, leaving them to the silent shadows of the sweet summer night. The night dew had wept on their cheeks, the light wind had murmured through the highest branches and the bushes of the undergrowth. With sunrise the lights and shadows of the day before had returned, as if for a meeting, to play over the two outstretched, motionless figures. Cheered by the freshness in the air and the pure splendor of the morning, a bird had perched on a limb and sung. A bee had flown around Lina's head, a flower had opened near Quadri's ruined forehead. It was for them, so silent and still, that the babbling waters of the brooks that snaked through the forest had spoken, their bodies the inhabitants of the woods had skirted around — the secretive squirrels, the leaping, wild rabbits. And meanwhile, beneath them, the burdened earth had slowly shifted the rigid shapes of their bodies on their soft bed of grasses and moss; she was prepared for them, and had accepted their mute request that she receive them into her womb.

He started at a knock on the door, threw away the magazine, and shouted out, "Come in."

The door opened slowly and for a moment Marcello saw no one. Then the broad, honest, peaceful face of agent Orlando peered warily in through the crack.

"May I, Dottore?" asked the agent.

"Please come in, Orlando," said Marcello in an official tone of voice. "Make yourself comfortable. Did you have something to tell me?"

Orlando came in, shut the door, and approached Marcello, staring at him intently. For the first time, Marcello noticed that everything was affable in that florid, heated face except for the small, deepset eyes, which sparkled weirdly beneath the bald forehead.

"Strange," thought Marcello, looking at him, "how I wasn't aware of that sooner." He nodded to the agent to sit, and Orlando obeyed without saying a word, still fixing him with those shining eyes.

"A cigarette?" offered Marcello, pushing the box toward Orlando.

"Thank you, Dottore," said the agent, taking one. A silence followed. Then Orlando blew some smoke from his mouth, looked for an instant at the lit end of the cigarette, and said, "Do you know, Dottore, what the most curious aspect of the Quadri affair is?"

"No, what?"

"It wasn't necessary."

"Meaning what?"

"Meaning that after I got back from the mission, right after I crossed the border, I went to find Gabrio at S. to check in. Do you know the first thing he says to me? 'Have you received the counterorder?' I ask: What counterorder? 'The counterorder,' he says, 'to suspend the mission.' And why is it suspended? 'It's suspended,' he answers, 'because all of a sudden in Rome they've discovered that right now it would be useful to have a rapprochement with France and they think the mission could compromise the negotiations.' So I say: I didn't receive any counterorder all the time I was in Paris, obviously it was sent too late . . . Anyway, the mission has been carried out, as you'll see in tomorrow morning's papers. When I say this, he begins to yell: 'You're all beasts, you've ruined me, this could blow French-Italian relations at a very delicate point of international politics, you're criminals, what will I tell Rome now?'

You'll tell them, I answer calmly, the truth: that the counterorder was sent too late. Get it, Dottore? All that effort, two people dead, and it wasn't necessary, in fact it was counterproductive."

Marcello said nothing. The agent breathed in another mouthful of smoke and then said, with the naive and satisfied emphasis of the uncultured man who loves to fill his mouth with solemn words: "Fate."

A new silence followed. The agent went on, "But this is the last time I accept a mission like this . . . someone else can do it next time. Gabrio yelled, 'You're beasts' . . . but that's not really true . . . we're human beings, not beasts."

Marcello ground out the cigarette he had smoked halfway down and lit another. The agent continued, "They can say what they want, but some things are really unpleasant . . . Cirrincione for one."

"Who's Cirrincione?"

"One of the men who was with me. Right after the hit, in all that confusion, I turn around for no special reason and what do I see? He's licking his knife. I yell at him, What are you doing? Are you crazy? And he says, 'Humpback's blood is good luck.' Understand? Barbarian . . . I almost shot him."

Marcello lowered his eyes and reshuffled the papers on his desk mechanically. The agent shook his head in deprecation and then continued, "But what got to me most was the wife, she had nothing to do with it, she shouldn't have died . . . but she threw herself onto her husband to protect him and took two slugs for him. He ran away into the woods where that barbarian Cirrincione reached him. She was still alive and I had to give her the coup de grace . . . that woman was braver than a lot of men."

Marcello raised his eyes toward the agent to signify that the visit was over. The agent understood and got to his feet. But he didn't leave immediately. He put his two hands on the desk, looked at Marcello for a long moment with his sparkling eyes, and then, with the same emphasis with which he had uttered, "Fate," shortly before, he said, "Anything for the family and homeland, Dottore."

Suddenly Marcello knew where he had seen those eyes before, so strange and sparkling. Those eyes held the same expression as his father's eyes — his father, who was even now locked up in an asylum for the mentally ill.

He said coldly, "Maybe the homeland didn't require quite that much."

"If it didn't require it," asked Orlando, leaning toward him a little and raising his voice, "then why did they make us do it?"

Marcello hesitated and then said dryly, "Orlando, you did your duty and that should satisfy you."

He watched the agent make a slight, deferential bow, half of mortification and half of approval. Then, after a moment of silence he added gently, not sure himself why he was doing it — maybe somehow to dissipate the agent's anguish, so similar to his own, "Do you have any children, Orlando?"

"Do I, Dottore . . . I have five." He pulled a large, worn wallet out of his pocket, extracted a photograph from it, and handed it to Marcello, who took it and looked at it. The picture was of five children lined up according to height and ranging in age from thirteen to six — three girls and two boys all dressed up for a party, the girls in white, the boys in sailors' outfits. Marcello noticed that all five had round, peaceful, wise faces very like their father's.

"They live in the village with their mother," said the agent, taking back the photograph Marcello held out to him. "The oldest is already working as a seamstress."

"They're beautiful and they look like you," said Marcello.

"Thank you, Dottore . . . once again, Dottore." The agent stepped to one side to let Giulia by, then disappeared.

Giulia came up to Marcello and said immediately, "I was passing by and I thought I'd drop in and visit. How are you?"

"I'm just fine," said Marcello.

Standing up in front of the desk, she looked at him uncertainly, doubtfully, apprehensively. Finally she said, "Don't you think you're working too hard?"

"No," answered Marcello, with a fleeting glance out the open window. "Why?"

"You seem tired." Giulia came around the desk and stood still for a moment, leaning against the armrest of the chair and looking at the newspapers scattered on the desk. Then she asked, "Is there anything new?"

"About what?"

"In the newspapers, about the thing with Quadri."

"No, nothing."

After another moment of silence she said, "I'm more convinced all the time that he was killed by men from his own party. What do you think?"

It was the official version of the crime, furnished to the newspapers by the propaganda offices the very morning the news arrived from Paris. Giulia, Marcello noticed, had grasped at it with a kind of willed positivity, almost as if hoping to convince herself.

He replied dryly, "I don't know . . . I suppose it's possible."

"I'm convinced of it," she repeated resolutely. After a moment's hesitation, she went on ingenuously, "Sometimes I think that if that evening, in that nightclub, I hadn't treated Quadri's wife so badly, she would have stayed on in Paris and she wouldn't have died . . . and I feel such remorse . . . but what could I do? It was her fault, since she wouldn't leave me in peace for a minute."

Marcello wondered if Giulia suspected anything about the part he had played in Quadri's murder and then, after a brief reflection, he excluded the possibility. No love, he thought, could have survived such a discovery, and Giulia was telling the truth: she felt remorse at Lina's death because she had been its indirect cause, though in a wholly innocent manner. He wanted to reassure her, but he could find nothing better than the word Orlando had already uttered with such emphasis.

"Don't reproach yourself," he said, putting an arm around her waist and drawing her close. "It was fate."

She answered, lightly stroking his hair, "I don't believe in fate. It was really because I loved you . . . if I hadn't loved you, who knows, maybe I wouldn't have treated her so badly, and she wouldn't have gone and she wouldn't be dead. What does fate have to do with it?"

Marcello recalled Lino, the primary cause of all the vicissi-
tudes of his life, and explained thoughtfully, "When you say 'fate'
you're saying all these things, as well, love and all the rest of it. You
couldn't have not acted the way you acted, just as she couldn't
have not gone with her husband."

"Then we can't do anything?" asked Giulia in a dreamy voice,
gazing down at the papers scattered across the desk.

Marcello hesitated and then answered, with profound bitterness, "Yes, we can know that we can't do anything."

"What good does that do?"

"For us, the next time . . . or for others who come after us."

She broke from him with a sigh and went to the door. "Remember not to be late today," she said from the threshold.
"Mamma's made a good dinner . . . and remember not to make
any appointments for the afternoon. We have to go look at apartments together." She waved good-bye and disappeared.

Left by himself, Marcello picked up a pair of scissors, carefully
cut the photograph out of the French magazine, put it into a
drawer next to some other papers, and closed the drawer with a
key. At that moment the piercing wail of the noonday siren
dropped into the courtyard out of the burning sky. Right afterward,
the close and distant bells of the churches began to chime.

EPILOGUE

I

$\mathcal{E}$VENING HAD FALLEN, and Marcello, who had spent the day lying in bed smoking and thinking, got up and went to the window. Black against the green-tinged light of the summer dusk, the houses that surrounded his own rose up around bare cement courtyards relieved by small green yards and clipped myrtle hedges. An occasional window shone red in the twilight, and in the servants' rooms he could see waiters in their striped working jackets and cooks in white aprons tending to the household chores, moving to and fro between the lacquered cabinets and the flameless stoves of their electric kitchens. Marcello raised his eyes to gaze beyond the balconies of the apartments; the last smoky, purple wisps of sunset were vanishing in the evening sky. He lowered his eyes again and saw a car come in and stop in the courtyard, and the driver get out with a big white dog that immediately started running through the little plots of grass, whining and barking for joy. It was a wealthy neighborhood, completely new, built in the past few years; and looking at those courtyards and those windows, no one would have guessed that the war had been going on for four years and that this very day, a government that had lasted for twenty had fallen. No one but him, thought Marcello, and all those who found themselves in his circumstances. For a moment an image flashed through his mind, of a divine rod suspended above the great city lying so peacefully under the clear sky, which struck at families here and there, hurling them into terror, consternation, and grief while their neighbors remained unscathed. His family was among those struck down, as he knew and as he had foreseen since the beginning of the war. It was a family like all others, with the same affections and the same intimacy, completely normal, with that normality he had sought so tenaciously for years and which now revealed itself to be purely exterior and entirely composed of abnormalities. He recalled saying to his wife, the day the war broke out in Europe, "If I were logical, I'd kill myself today," and he remembered, too, the terror those words had caused her. As if she had known what they concealed, above and beyond the simple presentiment that the conflict would have an unfavorable outcome. He asked himself yet again whether Giulia knew the truth about him and the part he had played in Quadri's death; and it seemed impossible to him, yet again, that she should know, although by certain signs she seemed to indicate she did.

By now he realized with perfect clarity that he had, as they say, bet on the losing horse; but why he had bet that way and why the horse hadn't won was not, apart from observation of the most obvious facts, really clear to him. But he would have liked to be sure that everything that happened had *had* to happen — that is, that he could not have bet any differently or with any different result — and he needed this certainty more than he needed to be freed from a remorse he did not feel. In fact, the only possible source of remorse, for him, was to have been mistaken, that is, to have done what he had done without an absolute and destined necessity. To have, in other words, deliberately or involuntarily ignored the possibility that he could have done things completely differently. But if he could be certain that this was not true, it seemed to him that he could live in peace with himself, even if it were only in his usual listless and depressed way. In other words, he thought, he needed to be sure that he had recognized his own destiny and accepted it as it was, useful to himself and others — perhaps only in a negative way, but useful nonetheless.

Meanwhile, he was consoled in his doubt by the idea that even if there had been a mistake — and he couldn't exclude this — he had bet more on it than anyone else, more than all the others who now found themselves in the same circumstances. It was a consolation to his pride, the only one that remained. By tomorrow other people could have changed ideas, parties, lives, even characters; but for him this was impossible, not only in relationship to others but also to himself. He had done what he had done for reasons that were his alone, that had nothing to do with communion with others; to change, even if it were allowed him, would have meant annihilating himself. And now, in the midst of so much destruction, this was exactly what he wished to avoid.

At this point he thought that, if there had been an error, the first and greatest one had been his desire to escape his own abnormality, to find whatever sort of normality he could through which to communicate with other people. This error had sprung from a powerful instinct; but unfortunately, the normality this instinct had collided with was nothing but an empty form, within which all was abnormal and gratuitous. At the first jolt of contact, the form had shattered into pieces; and the instinct, so justified and so human, had turned him, from the victim he had been, into an executioner. His mistake, in other words, was not so much that he had killed Quadri, but that he had tried to obliterate the original sin of his own life with inadequate means. But, he went back to wondering, would it have been at all possible for things to have gone otherwise than they had?

No, it would not have been possible, he thought, answering himself. Lino had had to compromise his innocence and he, to defend himself, had been compelled to kill him; and then, to free himself from the sense of abnormality that had sprung from this, he had had no choice but to seek normality in the way he had sought it; and to obtain this normality he'd been forced to pay a price that corresponded to the burden of abnormality he had meant to free himself from; and this price had been Quadri's death. So all had been destined, though freely accepted, as all was at once just and unjust.

He seemed to be feeling rather than thinking these things, with the sharp and painful perception of an anguish he rejected and rebelled against. He would have liked to feel calm and detached, faced with the disastrous ruin of his life, as if observing a dismal but distant event. But his anguish made him suspect himself of panicking at the turn of events, in spite of the clarity with which he was forcing himself to examine them. Besides, it wasn't easy just then to distinguish clarity from fear; and perhaps the best he could do was to maintain, as always, a decorous and impassive mode of behavior. After all, he thought a little ironically, as if summing up his modest ambitions, he had nothing to lose; at least, if his "loss" was understood as the renunciation of his mediocre position as a civil servant, this house he had to pay for in installments for the next twenty-five years, the car he must pay for in the next two, and the few other sundry expenses of a comfortable life that he had felt he must concede to Giulia. It was true, he had nothing to lose; and if they had come to arrest him right that minute, the meagerness of the material benefits he had acquired by virtue of his position would have amazed even his enemies.

He stepped away from the window and turned to look at the room. It was a married couple's bedroom, as Giulia had wanted, of dark, shining mahogany and handles and ornaments of bronze in an approximation of Empire style. It came to him that this room had been bought on installment, too, and that they had just finished paying for it the year before.

"Our whole life," he thought with sarcasm, picking his jacket up from the chair and putting it on, "is in installments, but these last are the biggest and we'll never manage to pay them." He smoothed out the rumpled rug by the bed with his foot and walked out of the room.

Going down to the end of the hall, he reached a door that had been left ajar, through which a little light was shining. It was his daughter's bedroom; and as he entered, he delayed a moment on the threshold, almost unable to believe the ordinary, familial scene unfolding before his eyes. The room was small and furnished in the pretty, colorful style appropriate to rooms where young children sleep and live. The furniture was painted pink, the curtains were light blue, the walls were papered with a design of little baskets of flowers. Dolls of various sizes and other toys were scattered haphazardly here and there on the pink carpet. His wife was sitting on the side of the bed and Lucilla, his daughter, was already in it. Giulia, who was conversing with the child, turned around as soon as he entered and gave him a long look without saying a word. Marcello took one of the little pink chairs and sat down next to the bed, too.

The little girl said, "Hello, Papà."

"Hello, Lucilla," said Marcello, looking at her.

She was a dark, delicate child, with a round face, huge expressive eyes, and features so fine that they seemed almost affected in their excessive delicacy. He himself was not sure why, but in that moment she actually seemed *too* lovely and, above all, too conscious of her loveliness in a way, he thought, that suggested the beginnings of an innocent flirtatiousness and that reminded him in an unpleasant manner of his mother, whom she resembled closely. This flirtatiousness could be seen in the way she rolled her large, velvety eyes when she was talking to him or her mother, which produced a strange effect in a child of six; above all, it showed in the almost incredible self-confidence with which she spoke. Dressed in a light blue nightgown, all puffs and lace, she was sitting up in bed with her hands joined for the evening prayer, which the arrival of her father had interrupted.

"Come on, Lucilla, don't daydream," said her mother good-naturedly. "Come on, now, say the prayer with me."

"I'm not daydreaming," said the child, raising her eyes to the ceiling with an expression of impatient condescension. "You're the one who stopped when Papà came in . . . so I stopped, too."

"You're right," said Giulia with composure, "but you know the prayer. You could have gone on by yourself. When you're bigger, I won't always be here to prompt you, but you'll still have to say it."

"Look how you're wasting my time . . . I'm tired," said Lucilla, shrugging her shoulders slightly with her hands still joined. "You're sitting around talking and we could have finished the prayer by now."

"All right," said Giulia, smiling this time despite herself, "let's start over: *Hail Mary, full of grace.*"

The little girl repeated in a drawling voice, "*Hail Mary, full of grace.*"

"*The Lord is with thee, blessed art thou among women.*"

"*The Lord is with thee, blessed art thou among women.*"

"*And blessed is the fruit of thy womb, Jesus.*"

"*And blessed is the fruit of thy womb, Jesus.*"

"Can I rest for a minute?" asked the child at this point.

"Why?" asked Giulia. "Are you already tired?"

"You've kept me here an hour like this, with my hands together," said Lucilla, separating her hands and looking at her father. "When Papà came in, we'd already said half of the prayer." She rubbed her arms with her hands, spitefully, flirtatiously, making a show of how tired she was. Then she raised and joined her hands again and said, "I'm ready."

"*Holy Mary, mother of God,*" Giulia continued calmly.

"*Holy Mary, mother of God,*" repeated the child.

"*Pray for us sinners.*"

"*Pray for us sinners.*"

"*Now and in the hour of our death.*"

"*Now and in the hour of our death.*"

"*Amen.*"

"*Amen.*"

"Papà, don't you ever say your prayers?" asked Lucilla without pausing.

"We say them at night before we go to bed," answered Giulia quickly. The child, however, was looking at Marcello with an interrogative and, as it seemed to him, incredulous air. He rushed to confirm it: "Of course, every night before we go to bed."

"Now lie down and go to sleep," said Giulia, getting up and trying to make Lucilla lie down. She managed, but not without effort, as the child did not seem at all disposed to sleep, and then she pulled the sheet, her only cover, up to her daughter's chin.

"I'm hot," said Lucilla, kicking at the sheet, "I'm so hot."

"Tomorrow we're going to Grandma's and you won't be hot anymore," answered Giulia.

"Where does Grandma live?"

"Up in the hills, where it's cool."

"But where?"

"I've already told you a million times — Tagliacozzo. It's a cool place and we'll be staying there all summer."

"Won't the airplanes come?"

"The airplanes won't come anymore."

"Why not?"

"Because the war is over."

"Why is the war over?"

"Because two doesn't make three," said Giulia brusquely, but without losing temper. "Now that's enough questions . . . go to sleep, because tomorrow we're leaving early in the morning. Now I'm going to go get your medicine."

She went out, leaving her husband alone with his daughter.

"Papà," the little girl asked right away, sitting back up in the bed, "remember the cat that belongs to the people downstairs?"

"Yes," answered Marcello, leaving the chair to sit on the edge of the bed.

"She had four kittens."

"So?"

"Those girls' governess said that if I want to, I can have one of those kittens . . . can I take one? That way I can bring him to Tagliacozzo with me."

"When were these kittens born?" asked Marcello.

"The day before yesterday."

"Then it's not possible," said Marcello, stroking his daughter's head. "The kittens have to stay with their mother as long as they're nursing . . . you can have one when we come back from Tagliacozzo."

"What if we don't come back from Tagliacozzo?"

"Why wouldn't we come back? We'll come back at the end of the summer," replied Marcello, curling his daughter's soft, dark hair around his fingers.

"Ow, you're hurting me," complained the child immediately, at the first gentle tug.

Marcello let go of her hair and said with a smile, "Why are you saying that? You know it's not true."

"Yes it is, you were hurting me," she answered emphatically. Then, bringing her hands up to her temples in a stubbornly feminine gesture, she added, "Now I'm going to get a big headache."

"Then I'll pull your ears instead," said Marcello playfully. Very, very gently, he lifted the hair away from her small, round, rosy ear and gave it the slightest of tugs, ringing it like a little bell.

"Ow, ow, ow," she yelled in a shrill voice, pretending she was in pain, her whole face suffused with a faint blush, "ow, ow, you're hurting me!"

"Look what a liar you are," Marcello reproached her, letting go of her ear. "You know you're not supposed to tell lies."

"This time," she said judiciously, "I swear you really hurt me."

"Do you want me to give you a doll for the night?" asked Marcello, turning to look at the carpet scattered with toys.

She launched a look of calm disdain at the dolls and replied condescendingly, "If you want to."

"What do you mean, if I want to?" asked Marcello, smiling. "You talk as if you're doing me a favor. Don't you like to sleep with a doll?"

"Yes, I like to," she conceded. "Give me that one in the pink dress."

Marcello stood up and looked down at the carpet. "They all have pink dresses."

"There's pink and pink," said the child, conceited and impatient. "That doll's pink is exactly the same as the pink of the pink roses on the balcony."

"This one here?" asked Marcello, picking up the biggest and most beautiful of the dolls from the carpet.

"See how you don't understand anything?" she said severely.

Suddenly she jumped out of bed, ran in her bare feet to the corner of the rug, and gathered up a very ugly cloth doll with a squashed and blackened face. Then she ran back to bed and said, "There!"

This time she settled down on her back under the sheet, her peaceful, rosy face pressed fondly against the dirty, astonished face of the doll. Giulia came back in with a bottle and a spoon in her hand.

"Come on," she said, coming over to the bed, "take your medicine."

This time the child didn't make her plead. She lifted herself halfway up in the bed and obediently offered up her face and opened her mouth, like a baby bird waiting to be fed. Giulia popped the spoon into her mouth and then tipped it up quickly, pouring out the liquid. Lucilla lay back down, saying, "It tastes awful!"

"Good-night, then," said Giulia, leaning over to kiss her daughter.

"Good-night, Mamma, good-night, Papà," trilled the child.

Marcello took his turn and kissed her on the cheek, then followed his wife out of the room. Giulia turned off the light and closed the door.

In the hallway she half turned toward her husband and said, "I think it's ready."

Then Marcello noticed for the first time, in that accusing shadow, that Giulia's eyes were swollen, as if she had been crying. His exchange with Lucilla had refreshed him; but looking at his wife's eyes, he was afraid again that he wouldn't be able to act as firmly and calmly as he wished. Meanwhile, Giulia had preceded him into their tiny dining room with its little round table and its sideboard. The table was set, the ceiling lamp lit, and from the open window they could hear the voice of the radio describing, in the breathless and triumphant style usually reserved for soccer matches, the fall of the Fascist government. The maid entered, served the soup, and went back out. They began to eat slowly, with composed gestures. All of a sudden the radio became frenetic. The announcer was now saying, in exalted terms and a fevered voice, that a huge crowd was collecting in the streets of the city to applaud the king.

"They make me sick," said Giulia, putting down her spoon and looking out the window.

"Why?"

"Up until yesterday they were clapping their hands for Mussolini. A few days ago they were applauding the pope because they hoped he would save them from bombing. Today they're cheering the king who kicked out Mussolini."

Marcello said nothing. Giulia's reactions and opinions about public affairs were so well known to him that he could anticipate them in his mind. They were the reactions and opinions of a very simple person, completely devoid of curiosity about the underlying motives that gave rise to events, guided more by personal and emotional reasons than by anything else. They finished eating their soup in silence as the radio continued its torrential shouting. Then, all of a sudden, after the maid had brought them the second course, the radio cut off and there was silence. And with the silence, the suffocating closeness of the still summer night seemed to come back to oppress them.

They looked at each other and then Giulia asked, "Now what will you do?"

Marcello replied briefly, "I'll do what everyone in my situation will do . . . there are a lot of us here in Italy who believed."

Giulia hesitated before speaking. Then she said slowly, "No, I mean what are you going to do about the business with Quadri?"

So she knew, maybe she had always known, after all. Marcello was aware that at those words his heart had skipped a beat, as it would have done ten years before if someone had asked him, "Now what are you going to do about the business with Lino?" Then, if he had possessed the gift of prophecy, he would have answered, "Kill Quadri." But now? He set his fork down by his plate and, as soon as he felt sure that his voice wouldn't waver, he said, "I don't understand what you're talking about."

He saw her lower her eyes, her face twisting as if she were about to cry again. Then she said in a slow, sad voice, "In Paris Lina, maybe because she wanted to get me away from you, told me that you were part of the political police."

"And what did you answer her?"

"That it didn't matter to me . . . that I was your wife and that I loved you no matter what you did . . . that if you were doing it, it meant that you thought it was right to do it."

Marcello said nothing, moved despite himself by her blind, inflexible loyalty.

Giulia continued in a hesitant voice, "But then when Quadri and Lina were murdered, I was so afraid that you had had a hand in it . . . and from that time on I've hardly thought about anything else. But I never talked to you about it because you'd never said anything about your work, so I thought that I in particular couldn't talk to you about this."

"And what do you think now?" asked Marcello, after a moment of silence.

"Me?" said Giulia, raising her eyes and looking at him. Marcello saw that her eyes were brimming and understood that her tears were already an answer. All the same, she went on with an effort, "In Paris you yourself told me that the visit to Quadri was crucial to your career . . . so I think it might be true."

He said immediately, "It is true."

In that instant he understood that Giulia had hoped till the last minute that she was wrong. Now, at his words, as if at a signal, she threw her head down on the table with her face in her arm and began to sob. Marcello stood up, went to the door, and turned the key in the lock. Then he walked up to her and without bending over, rested his hand on her hair and said, "If you want, we can separate after tomorrow . . . I'll drive you to Tagliacozzo with Lucilla and then I'll go away and won't show my face again . . . is that what you want us to do?"

Right away Giulia stopped sobbing, as if, he thought, she couldn't believe her own ears. Then, from the hollow of her arm where she was hiding her face, her sad, surprised voice reached him. "What are you talking about? Separate? That's not it . . . I'm just so afraid for you . . . what will they do to you now?"

So, he thought, Giulia felt no horror of him, no remorse for Quadri's and Lina's deaths; only fear for him, for his life, for his future. This insensitivity, strengthened by the force of her love, affected him strangely. He felt like someone who, climbing stairs in the dark, lifts up his foot thinking to find another step and encounters instead the emptiness of a landing. In truth, he had expected and even hoped for horror and severe judgment. And instead he had found only her usual blind and supportive love.

He said, a little impatiently, "They won't do anything to me, there's no proof. And besides, I was only following orders." He hesitated a moment, feeling a sort of shame mixed with repugnance for the cliche, then finished with an effort, "All I did was do my duty, like a soldier."

Immediately Giulia clutched at this worn-out phrase, which, in its time, had not sufficed to pacify even agent Orlando.

"Yes, I thought so, too," she said, raising her head, grabbing his hand and covering it with frantic kisses, "I've always told myself: Marcello is actually just a soldier . . . and soldiers kill because they're commanded to . . . it's not his fault if they make him do certain things . . . But don't you think they'll come after you? I'm sure the men who gave you the orders will escape . . . while you, who had nothing really to do with it and were only doing your duty will get caught in the middle . . ." Having covered the back of his hand with kisses, she turned it over and started kissing his palm with the same fury.

"Calm down," said Marcello, stroking her gently, "right now they have other things to do besides looking for me."

"But people are so awful . . . all it takes is one person who doesn't like you. They'll denounce you . . . That's the way it always goes. The big guys who give the orders and make millions save themselves, and the little guys like you who do their duty and can't save a cent suffer for it . . . Oh, Marcello, I'm so frightened!"

"Don't be frightened, it will all work out."

"Oh, it *won't* all work out, I know it, I feel it . . . and I'm so tired." Giulia was talking now with her face pressed against his hand, although she was not kissing it. "After I had Lucilla, even though I knew what you did for a living, I thought: now I'm set. I have a child, a husband I love, a house, a family . . . I'm happy, really happy . . . it was the first time in my life I was happy and it felt like it couldn't be true. I almost couldn't believe it . . . and I've always been so afraid that it would all come to an end and that happiness couldn't last. And in fact, it hasn't lasted, and now we have to escape . . . and you'll lose your job and who knows what they'll do to you . . . and that poor creature will be worse off than if she were an orphan . . . and we'll have to start all over again from the beginning . . . and maybe we won't even be able to start over and our family will be destroyed." She burst out crying again and threw herself back down with her face in her arm.

Marcello suddenly recalled the image that had flashed through his mind before: the divine rod, mercilessly striking down his whole family, not only himself, who was guilty, but his wife and his daughter, who were innocent; and he shivered at the thought.

Someone knocked at the door and he shouted to the maid that they had finished eating and had no more need of her. Then, leaning toward Giulia, he said gently, "I beg you to stop crying and calm down. Our family won't be destroyed. We'll go to America, Argentina . . . We'll start a new life . . . We'll have a home there, too, and I'll be there, Lucilla will be there . . . have a little faith, you'll see, it will all work out."

This time Giulia lifted her tear-streaked face toward him and said, full of sudden hope, "We'll go to Argentina . . . when?"

"As soon as possible. As soon as the war is really over."

"And in the meantime?"

"In the meantime we'll go away from Rome and stay in Tagliacozzo. No one will look for us there . . . you'll see, things will be fine."

Giulia appeared to cheer up at these words and, above all, at the firm tone in which they had been uttered, thought Marcello, watching her get up and blow her nose.

"Forgive me," she said. "I'm so stupid . . . I should be helping you and instead all I know how to do is cry, I'm such an idiot." She started clearing up the table, taking away the plates and stacking them on the sideboard.

Marcello went to the window and looked out, leaning on the sill. Through the opaque windows of the house in front of him the dull lights of the staircase shone, floor after floor, all the way up to the sky. In the deep cement courtyards the shadows were thickening, black as coal. The night was still and hot; even the most attentive ear could not have heard a sound except for the sizzling of a garden hose where someone, down in the courtyard, was watering the grass in the dark. Marcello said, turning, "Shall we go for a walk downtown?"

"Why?" she asked. "What for? Who knows what kind of crowd there'll be?"

"So you can see," he replied almost lightly, "how a dictatorship falls."

"And then there's Lucilla . . . I can't leave her alone. What if the airplanes come?"

"Don't worry, they won't come tonight."

"But why go downtown?" she protested suddenly, "I really don't understand you. It's like you want to suffer . . . what do you get out of it?"

"You stay," he said. "I'll go by myself."

"No, then I'll come, too," she said quickly. "If something happens to you, I want to be there, too. It means the maid will look after the child."

"But don't be afraid. Tonight the airplanes won't come."

"I'm going to change," she said, leaving the room.

Left alone, Marcello went back to the window. Someone was climbing the stairs in the house in front, a man. He could see the profile of his shadow moving steadily from one floor to the next behind the opaque glass. He was climbing carelessly; judging by the slenderness of the shadow, he must be a young man; maybe, thought Marcello enviously, he was whistling. Then the radio started up again. Marcello heard the same voice concluding, as if ending a conversation: ". . . and the war continues."

It was the message of the new government; he had heard it already, shortly before. Marcello drew his case from his pocket and lit a cigarette.

2

THE STREETS OF THE PERIPHERY were deserted, silent, and dark, almost dead, like the extremities of a big body whose blood has suddenly gathered in one place alone. But the closer the car got to the center of town, the more frequently Marcello and Giulia saw groups of people, gesturing and shouting. Marcello slowed down at an intersection and stopped to let by a line of trucks, crowded with young men and women waving flags and posters with writing on them. These beflagged and overloaded trucks, with people clinging to the fenders and footboards, were greeted with confused applause by the people crowding the sidewalks. Someone stuck his head in the car window to yell in Giulia's face, "*Viva la libertà!*" and then vanished immediately, as if sucked back into the multitude darkening the streets.

Giulia said, "Wouldn't it be better to go back home?"

"Why?" asked Marcello, keeping an eye on the street through the glass of the windshield. "They're so happy, they're surely not out to hurt anyone . . . we can park the car somewhere and then walk back to see what's going on."

"Won't they steal the car?"

"How ridiculous."

In his usual thoughtful, placid, patient way, Marcello drove the car through the packed streets of the center of town. In the faint penumbra of the antiaircraft blackout, they could distinctly see the movements of the crowd, its many ways of gathering, colliding, spreading, and running — all different, but all pervaded and united by a single, sincere exultation at the dictatorship's collapse. People who didn't know each other hugged in the middle of the street; a man who had watched the passage of a flag-waving truck in speechless attention for a long time suddenly took off his hat, shouting and cheering; people rushed around like couriers from one group to another, repeating phrases of incitement and joy; a few, as if overwhelmed by a sudden outburst of hatred, raised threatening fists toward the dark, closed palazzi that had been, until today, the seats of public officials. Marcello noticed that many women were out on the arms of their husbands, sometimes even with children in tow, something that hadn't happened for a long time in the forced demonstrations of the fallen regime. Columns of resolute men, seemingly united by some secret party tie, gathered in formation and marched briefly to cheers and applause, then melted back into the crowd. Large, approving groups surrounded spontaneous orators, while others gathered together to sing libertarian anthems at the top of their voices. Marcello drove the car slowly and patiently, respectful of every assembly, moving at a snail's pace.

"How happy they are," said Giulia in a good-natured, almost supportive tone, suddenly forgetting her fears and self-interest.

"In their place, I would be, too."

They drove much of the length of the Corso, which was packed with people all the way, behind a couple of other cars advancing just as slowly. Then Marcello turned at the entrance to an alleyway and, after waiting for a column of demonstrators to go by, managed to slip into it. He drove the car swiftly into another, completely deserted alley, stopped, turned off the motor, and said, turning to his wife, "Let's get out here."

Giulia got out without saying a word and Marcello, after carefully shutting the doors, joined her and headed toward the street they had come from. Now he felt completely calm, in control of himself and detached, as he had wished to be all during the day. But he was keeping watch on himself; and when he came out again into the crowded street, with the joy of the crowd exploding in his face, boisterous, tumultuous, earnest, and aggressive, he asked himself anxiously whether this joy did not spark off some less than serene emotion in his heart. No, he thought, after a moment of attentive self-examination; he felt neither regret nor spite nor fear. He was truly calm, apathetic, almost totally spent, and disposed to contemplate the joy of others — without participating, of course, but also without resenting it as a threat or an affront.

They began to walk aimlessly through the crowd, from one group to another, from one block to another. By this time Giulia was no longer afraid; she seemed as calm and self-controlled as he did. But for different reasons, he thought, for her good-natured ability to empathize with the feelings of others.

The crowd, far from diminishing, seemed to get bigger every minute; and it was, Marcello observed, almost entirely joyful, with a stunned, incredulous joy, awkward in its expression, not yet sure it could do so with impunity. Opening a path through the multitude with effort, they passed other trucks full of workers, men and women, some of them waving red flags and others the tricolor. They walked past a small German convertible, with two calm officials idling in the seats and a uniformed soldier perched on the edge of the door with a submachine gun in his fist, trying to ignore the whistles and catcalls aimed at him from the sidewalks. Marcello noticed that there were a lot of soldiers on the streets, disheveled and weaponless, many of them hugging each other, their stolid peasant faces lit up by an intoxicated hope. Watching two of these soldiers, who were walking with their arms around each other's waists like lovers, their bayonets bouncing against their unbuttoned tunics, Marcello was aware for the first time that night of feeling something very like contempt: they were in uniform and, invincibly for him, a uniform meant decorum and dignity, whatever the person wearing it was feeling.

Giulia, as if she were guessing his thought, pointed out the two sloppy, affectionate soldiers and asked, "But didn't they say that the war wasn't over?"

"Yes, that's what they said," Marcello replied, suddenly reversing his judgment in an almost painful effort to comprehend, "but it's not true. And those poor guys are right to be happy . . . for them the war is truly over."

In front of the door of the ministry to which Marcello had gone to receive his orders on the eve of his departure for Paris, a large crowd was protesting, shouting, waving their fists in the air. Those that were closest to the door beat on it with their fists to make it open. The name of the newly fallen minister was being chanted over and over by many voices, in an unmistakable tone of hatred and scorn. Marcello observed this gathering for a long time but failed to understand what the demonstrators wanted. Finally the door opened, just barely, and an usher, pale and pleading in his braided uniform, appeared in the crack. He said something to the closest people; someone went in through the door, which shut immediately; the crowd shouted awhile more and then dispersed. But not all of them — a few of the most stubborn demonstrators hung around to shout and knock at the closed door.

Marcello left the ministry and started walking toward the adjacent piazza. A cry of "Make way! Make way!" pushed back the crowd, Marcello among them. Craning his neck, he saw three or four rough teenage boys dragging a big bust of the dictator behind them with a rope. The bust, the color of bronze, was really only painted plaster, as you could see from the white chips caused by the bumping they were giving it as they dragged it over the cobblestones. A dark little man, his face devoured by an enormous pair of round, tortoiseshell glasses, turned toward Marcello after looking at the bust and said, chuckling sententiously, "We thought he was bronze, but in reality he was just common clay."

Marcello didn't answer him; still craning his neck, he watched the bust intently for a moment as it bounced heavily past him. It was one of hundreds of similar busts scattered throughout the ministries and public offices, grossly stylized: jutting jaw; round, deepset eyes; smooth, swollen skull. He couldn't help but think of the living mouth, so arrogant, so *alive*, represented by its fake bronze replica now dragging through the dust, accompanied by jeering whistles and catcalls from the same crowd that had once so heatedly cheered it on.

Once more Giulia seemed to intuit his thoughts, and murmured, "Just think, once all it took was a bust like this in the lobby to make people talk in a whisper."

He replied dryly, "If they get ahold of him in flesh and blood right now, they'll treat him just like they're treating this bust."

"Do you think they'll kill him?"

"Absoutely, if they can."

They walked on a little farther, in the midst of the crowd streaming and swirling in the darkness like the waters of an untamed, directionless flood. At a street corner a group of people had leaned a long ladder against the corner of a palazzo and one of them had climbed to the top and was wielding a hammer in great blows against a stone marker inscribed with the name of the regime. Someone turned to Marcello and said, laughing, "The Fascists are everywhere . . . it will take years just to chip them away."

"Too true," said Marcello.

They crossed the piazza and, pushing their way through the crowd, reached the arcade. In almost complete darkness, with only the dim, diffused light of their veiled flashlights, a group of people had made a circle around something Marcello and Giulia couldn't see, right at the point where the two branches of the arcade came together. Marcello approached them, leaned over, and saw that they were watching a boy dance. He was doing a funny parody of a mime executing the movements and contortions of a belly dancer; and he was wearing a portrait of the dictator, a colored holograph, which he had made a slit in and slipped over his shoulders like a collar. He looked like someone who had been put in the pillory and who was dancing with the instrument of torture still locked around his neck.

As they were walking back toward the piazza, a young official with a little black beard and spirited eyes, arm in arm with an excited girl, her dark hair blowing in the wind, leaned toward Marcello and shouted in a tone that was at once exalted and didactic, "Long live liberty, of course . . . but above all, long live the king!"

Giulia glanced at her husband.

"Long live the king," said Marcello, without batting an eye. They walked on and he said, "There are a lot of monarchists who are hoping to turn this to the monarchy's advantage . . . let's go see what's happening in the Piazza del Quirinale."

With an effort, they managed to get back to the alley where they had left the car. Giulia said to Marcello, as he was starting it up, "Do we really have to go? I'm so tired of all this shouting."

"Why not? It's not as if we have anything better to do."

Marcello drove the car swiftly up the side streets to the Piazza del Quirinale. When they reached it, they saw that it was not completely full. The crowd was thickest beneath the balcony where the royal family was accustomed to show itself, but thinned out toward the edges of the piazza, leaving a lot of empty space. Here, too, there was very little light; the great iron lampposts with their sad, yellow lamps shaped like clusters of grapes only faintly illuminated the dark multitude in the square. Half-hearted applause and calls to the royal family broke out, but infrequently; even less than anywhere else, it seemed, did the crowd in this piazza know what it wanted. It seemed more curious than enthusiastic; the same way people used to gather to see and hear the dictator, as if they were at a performance, they now gathered to see and hear the one who had thrown the dictator over.

Giulia asked softly, as the car was slowly circling the square, "Do you think the king will come out onto the balcony?"

Before answering, Marcello scrunched up his neck to look up at the balcony through the glass of the windshield. It was dimly illuminated by two reddish torches, between which he could see the closed shutters of the window. Then he said, "I don't think so. Why should he come out?"

"Then what are all these people waiting for?"

"Nothing . . . they're just in the habit of going into the piazza and calling for someone."

Marcello circled the square very, very slowly, almost bumping his fenders gently against groups who were reluctant to move.

Giulia said unexpectedly, "You know, I'm almost disappointed."

"Why?"

"I don't know what I thought they'd be doing . . . burning houses, killing people . . . when we came out I was afraid for you and that's why I came along. But they aren't doing anything, just shouting, cheering, saying 'up with,' 'down with,' singing, marching around . . ."

Before he could stop himself, Marcello answered, "The worst is yet to come."

"What do you mean?" she cried, in a suddenly frightened voice. "For us or for the others?"

"For us *and* the others."

Right away he regretted saying it, since he felt Giulia's hand grab his arm hard and heard her say in an anguished voice, "I knew all the time that what you were telling me wasn't true, when you said that everything would work out . . . and now you're saying it yourself."

"Don't be scared, I was just talking to hear my own voice."

This time Giulia said nothing, limiting herself to holding onto his arm with both hands and pressing herself against him. Hampered but unwilling to reject her, Marcello drove back along secondary streets toward the Corso. Once he had reached it, he went down the less crowded side streets and came out into the Piazza del Popolo. From there he headed up the steep side of the Pincian Hill toward the Villa Borghese. They crossed the darkened Pincio, populated by its marble busts, and circled through the park in the direction of Via Veneto. When they reached the gate of the Porta Pinciana, Giulia said suddenly in a low, sad voice, "I don't want to go home."

"Why not?" asked Marcello, slowing down.

"I don't know why," she answered, looking straight ahead, "but it wrings my heart just to think about it . . . it feels like a home we're about to leave forever. Nothing terrible, though," she added quickly, "just a house we have to move out of."

"So where do you want to go?"

"Wherever you want."

"Do you want to drive around Villa Borghese?"

"Yes, let's do that."

Marcello drove down a long, dark avenue, at the end of which they could see the Borghese museum, white against the night. When they reached the piazza in front of the building, he stopped the car, turned it off, and said, "Shall we take a little walk?"

"Yes, if you like."

They got out of the car and headed, arm in arm, for the gardens behind the museum. The park was deserted; political events had emptied it even of lovers. In the penumbra they could see the marble statues, white against the dark woodland background of the trees, gesturing heroically, delivering elegies. They walked as far as the fountain and relaxed for a moment in silence, gazing at the black and motionless water. Now Giulia squeezed her husband's hand, strongly insinuating her fingers between his own in a tiny embrace. They began to walk again, turned onto a very dark path that led through an oak grove. After a few steps, Giulia stopped suddenly and turned around, throwing one arm around Marcello's neck and kissing him on the mouth. They stood like that a long time, embracing each other, kissing each other, in the middle of the path.

Then they separated and Giulia whispered, taking her husband by the hand and pulling him toward the woods, "Come on, let's make love here . . . on the ground."

"No," Marcello couldn't help exclaiming, "here?"

"Yes, here," she said. "Why not? Come on, I need to do it to feel reassured."

"Reassured about what?"

"Everybody's thinking about the war, the politics, the planes . . . and instead we could be so happy . . . Come on . . . I'd even do it in the middle of one of their piazzas," she added, with sudden exasperation, "just to show them that I'm actually capable of thinking about something else . . . Come on!"

She seemed exalted now, and preceded him through the thick shadows among the tree trunks. "See, what a beautiful bedroom," he heard her murmur. "Soon we won't have a home anymore . . . but this is a bedroom they can't take away from us . . . we can sleep and make love here any time we want." Suddenly she disappeared from sight, as if she had entered the earth.

Marcello looked for her and then he caught sight of her in the darkness, stretched out on the ground at the foot of a tree, one arm beneath her, pillowing her head, the other raised toward him in silence, inviting him to stretch out by her side. He obeyed, and, as soon as he was lying down, Giulia wound her legs and arms around him tightly, kissing him with a blind, dazed force all over his face, as if in search of other mouths on his forehead and cheeks by which to penetrate him. But almost right away her embrace relaxed, and Marcello saw her raise herself slightly on top of him and stare out into the dark.

"Someone's coming," she said.

Marcello sat up as well and looked out. Between the trees, still in the distance, they could see the beam of a pocket-sized flashlight making a wavery advance, preceded on the ground by a faint circular light. Not a sound could be heard; the dead leaves covering the earth muffled the stranger's footsteps. The flashlight continued to advance in their direction and Giulia suddenly recomposed herself and sat up, hugging her knees between her arms. Sitting side by side against the tree, they watched the light approach.

"Maybe he's a guard," murmured Giulia.

Now the flashlight projected its beam onto the ground nearby, lifted, and struck them full in the face. Dazzled, they stared back at the masculine figure, no more than a shadow, from whose hand the white light was streaming — a light, thought Marcello, that would be lowered once the guard had looked them well in the face. But no, the light remained trained on them instead while the man looked on in a silence, thought Marcello, filled with reflection and wonder.

"Do you mind telling us what you want?" he asked, in a resentful voice.

"I don't want anything, Marcello," a gentle voice replied at once. At the same time the light was lowered and started to move away from them again.

"Who is he?" murmured Giulia. "He seems to know you."

Marcello sat motionless and breathless, profoundly disturbed. Then he said to his wife, "Excuse me a moment. I'll be back right away." He leapt to his feet and ran after the stranger.

He caught up with him at the edge of the woods, next to the pedestal of one of the pale statues. Nearby was a streetlamp; and when the man turned at the sound of footsteps, Marcello recognized him immediately, after all those years, by his smooth, ascetic face beneath the crew cut. Then, he had seen him dressed in his chauffeur's tunic; now, he was still wearing a uniform, black, buttoned up to the neck, with puffed-out pants and black leather leggings. He was holding his cap under his arm and the flashlight in his hand.

He smiled and said quickly, "*Chi non muore si rivede*, Anyone who doesn't die will meet again."

Marcello thought the idiom all too apt under the circumstances, although it had been said playfully and perhaps unconsciously. He said, panting from the run and his deep anxiety, "But I thought I . . . I thought I killed you."

"I was hoping you'd find out they saved me, Marcello," said Lino tranquilly. "It's true, a newspaper did announce that I was dead but that was because there was a mistake. Somone else died at that hospital, in the bed next to mine . . . And so you thought I was dead. So I did well to say *chi non muore si rivede*."

Marcello was horrified, not so much by the rediscovery of Lino as by the conversational, familiar, yet funereal tone that had been established between them at once.

He said sorrowfully, "But so many consequences came from thinking you were dead. And instead you weren't dead."

"There were a lot of consequences for me, too, Marcello," said Lino, looking at him with a kind of compassion. "I thought it was a warning and got married. Then my wife died," he added more slowly. "Everything started up again . . . Now I'm a night watchman. These gardens are full of beautiful boys like you."

He uttered these words with gentle, placid impudence, but without a shadow of flattery. Marcello noticed for the first time that his hair was almost gray and his face somewhat filled out.

"And you got married . . . That was your wife, wasn't it?"

Suddenly Marcello couldn't stand the submissive, squalid small talk anymore. He said, grabbing the man by his shoulders and shaking him, "You're talking to me as if nothing happened! Do you realize you destroyed my life?"

Lino replied, without attempting to free himself, "Why are you saying that to me, Marcello? You're married, you probably have children, you look like you're well-off, what are you complaining about? It would have been worse if you'd really killed me."

"But," Marcello couldn't help exclaiming, "when I met you I was innocent! And afterward I wasn't, not ever again."

He saw Lino look at him with surprise.

"But Marcello, we were all innocent. Don't you think I was innocent, too? And we all lose our innocence, one way or another. That's normality."

He freed himself with an effort from Marcello's already loosened grip and added in a tone of complicity, "Look, there's your wife . . . it would be better to go our separate ways."

"Marcello," Giulia's voice said from the shadows.

He turned and saw Giulia approaching uncertainly. At the same time, Lino, settling his cap on his head, waved good-bye and hurried off quickly in the direction of the museum.

"Who was that?" asked Giulia.

"One of my friends from school," answered Marcello, "who ended up as a night watchman."

"Let's go home," she said, taking his arm again.

"Don't you want to take a walk anymore?"

"No . . . I'd rather go home."

They reached the car, got in, and drove home without speaking. Even as he was driving, Marcello was thinking back on Lino's unconsciously meaningful words: we all lose our innocence in one way or another. That's normality. Within those words, thought Marcello, was condensed a judgment on his entire life. He had done what he had done to redeem himself from an imaginary crime. All the same, Lino's words had made him understand for the first time that even if he had not met him, had not shot him, had not been convinced he had killed him — in other words, if absolutely none of it had happened — since he would have had to lose his innocence anyway, and would consequently have wanted to get it back, he still would have done what he had done. *This* was what normality was — this breathless, futile desire to justify one's own life, already stained by original sin — not the deceptive mirage he had been following since the day of his meeting with Lino.

He heard Giulia ask him, "What time are we leaving tomorrow morning?" and flung away his thoughts as just so many troublesome, by now also useless, witnesses to his own error.

"As soon as possible," he said.

3

TOWARD DAWN, MARCELLO woke up and saw, or thought he saw, his wife standing in the corner near the window, looking out through the glass in the first gray light of the early hours. Entirely naked, she was holding back the curtain with one hand and covering her breasts with the other, whether from modesty or fear he didn't know. A long lock of her hair had come undone and was hanging down beside her cheek; and the face she was holding up to the window, colorless and pale, wore an expression of desolate reflection, of sorrowful contemplation. Even her body seemed to have lost overnight its robust and lusty exuberance: her breasts, which motherhood had somewhat flattened and slackened, revealed in profile a fold of flaccid weariness he had never noticed before; and her belly, not so much round as swollen, gave her an awkward, heavy vulnerability, emphasized by the way she was holding her trembling thighs, as if to conceal her sex. The cold light of the dawning day illumined her nakedness squalidly, like an indiscreet and apathetic glance. As he was watching her, Marcello couldn't help wondering what was going through her mind as she stood there, motionless in that sliver of first, faint light before the dawn, looking down at the empty court-yard. With a vivid sense of compassion, he told himself that he could imagine those thoughts all too well. "Here I am," she was surely thinking, "here I am, driven out of my home in almost the middle of my life, with a tender young child and a ruined hus-band who no longer has any hopes for the future; whose fate is un-certain; whose life may be in danger. So this is the result of all that effort, all that passion, all those hopes."

She was truly, he thought, Eve driven out of Eden; and Eden was that house with all the modest objects it contained: the stuff in the closets, the utensils in the kitchen, the living room she enter-tained her girlfriends in, the silver plate, the imitation Persian rugs, the china crockery her mother had given her, the icebox, the vase of flowers in the entrance hall, this bedroom in fake Imperial style bought on installments, and him, in the bed, looking at her. Eden was also, without a doubt, the pleasure of sitting down to the table twice a day with her family, of formulating plans for her fu-ture and the futures of her husband and child. Lastly, Eden was peace of mind, of soul, harmony with herself and her world, the serenity of the appeased and satisfied heart. Now a raging and merciless angel armed with a flaming sword was driving her out of this Eden forever, thrusting her, defenseless and naked, into the hostile outside world.

Marcello watched her for a while more as she stood motion-less, lost in her melancholy contemplation; then, through the sleep that had returned to weigh down his eyelids, he saw her turn from the window, tiptoe to the peg she had hung her robe on, put it on, and slip out of the room without a sound. He thought she was probably going off to sit beside the sleeping child's bedside and think more unhappy thoughts; or perhaps she was finishing up the packing for the trip. He thought for a moment of getting up and going to her to console her in some way. But he was still very sleepy and after a minute or two he fell back asleep.

Later, while he was driving the car toward Tagliacozzo in the pure light of the late summer morning, he thought back to that heartbreaking vision and wondered whether he had dreamed it or really seen it. His wife was sitting at his side, pressing her hip against him to make room for Lucilla, who was kneeling on the seat with her head out the window, enjoying the ride. Giulia was sitting very straight, her light jacket unbuttoned over a white blouse, her head erect, her face shadowed by a traveling hat. Marcello noticed that she was holding an oblong-shaped object on her knees, wrapped in brown paper and tied with strings.

"What do you have in that package?" he asked in surprise.

"It will make you laugh," she answered, "but I couldn't seem to leave behind that crystal vase that we kept in the entrance hall . . . I was fond of it first of all because it's lovely and then because you gave it to me . . . do you remember? A little after Lucilla was born . . . it's a weakness, I know, but it will help . . . I'll put flowers in it in Tagliacozzo."

So it was really true, he thought, he hadn't dreamed it; it was really her in flesh and blood and not an image from a dream he had seen that morning, standing by the window. After a moment he said, "If it gave you pleasure to bring it along, that's fine . . . but I swear to you, we'll go back home just as soon as the summer's over. There's absolutely no reason for you to be alarmed."

"I'm not alarmed."

"Everything will work out for the best," said Marcello, shifting gears as the car attacked a hill, "and then you'll be as happy as you've been the past few years and even happier."

Giulia didn't say anything but she didn't seem convinced. Although he was driving, he turned to observe her for a moment. With one hand she was holding the vase on her knees; her other arm encircled Lucilla's waist as the child hung out the window. All her loves and all her possessions were right here now, her gestures seemed to say, in this car: her husband on one side, her daughter on the other, and, as a symbol of their family life, the crystal vase on her knees. He recalled that just as they left she had said, casting one last look at the front of the house, "Who knows who will come to live in our apartment," and he understood that he could never convince her because she had no room in her for indirect conviction, only for the terrified presentiments of instinct.

Still, he asked calmly, "Will you tell me what you're thinking now?"

"Nothing," she replied, "I'm not thinking anything . . . I'm looking at the countryside."

"No, I mean, what do you think in general?"

"In general? I think things are going badly for us . . . but no one's to blame."

"Maybe they're my fault."

"Why should they be your fault? It's never anyone's fault . . . everyone's wrong and right at the same time. Things go wrong because they go wrong, that's all." She said this in a curt tone, as if to indicate that she didn't want to talk anymore. Marcello said nothing, and from that moment on there was silence between them for quite a while.

It was still early in the morning, but the day was already hot; and already in front of the car, between the dusty hedges dazzling with light, the air trembled and the reflection from the summer heat lifted mirrorlike mirages from the asphalt. The road was winding through rolling country between yellow hills bristling with dry stubble, an occasional brown or gray farmhouse lost at the bottom of desertlike, treeless valleys. Every once in a while they crossed paths with a horse-drawn wagon or an old provincial car; it was a seldom-frequented backroad and the military traffic was taking other routes. Everything was calm, normal, indifferent, thought Marcello as he drove; no one would ever have thought they were in the heart of a country torn by revolution and war. The faces of the few peasants they passed, leaning against the fences or in the middle of the fields, spade in hand, expressed only the time-honored feelings of solid, peaceful attention to the normal, obvious, everyday things in life. They were all people whose thoughts were of harvests, sun, rain, the price of food, or nothing at all. Giulia had been like those peasants for years, he thought, and now it hurt her to be ripped away from that peace.

He thought suddenly, almost irritably: it serves her right. For human beings life didn't mean letting go to the sluggish peace offered by indulgent nature, but to be restless, to be struggling continually, to be resolving at every moment a tiny problem within the confines of vaster problems, contained in their turn within the overall problem: the problem of life.

This thought gave him back faith in himself, as the car left the flat, desolate country behind and wound between the high red cliffs of a chain of hills. Maybe because, driving the car, it seemed to him that his body was merging with the motor, which was easily and inflexibly confronting and resolving the difficulties of the road, all climbing curves, he felt a kind of cocky, adventurous optimism, for the first time after so many years, finally clearing the stormy skies of his heart like a sudden gust of wind. He would now consider a whole period of his life closed and buried, he thought, and start over from the beginning, on another level and in other ways. His meeting with Lino had been very useful; not so much because it had freed him from remorse for a crime he hadn't committed, but because with the few words Lino had spoken at random on the inevitability and normality of the loss of innocence, he had made Marcello understand that he had stubbornly persisted for twenty years on a wrong path, which he must now abandon without looking back. This time there would be no need for justification and communication, he thought, and he was determined not to let the crime he had actually committed, his crime against Quadri, poison him with the torments of a futile search for purification and normality. What had been had been; Quadri was dead; and he would have liked to drop on top of that death, heavier than a tombstone, the definitive stone of complete and utter oblivion. Perhaps because the landscape had now changed from the suffocating desert it had been, and an abundance of invisible waters had given rise to grasses, flowers, and ferns at the sides of the road and, farther up, on top of the tuff, to the thick, luxurious green of woodland copses, it seemed to him that from now on he would know how to avoid forever the desolation of the deserts in which man follows his own shadow and feels

persecuted and guilty; and would instead, freely and adventur-
ously, seek out places like this one he was driving through now,
rocky and inaccessible places, fit only for brigands and wild beasts.
He had voluntarily, stubbornly, stupidly bound himself in unworthy chains and to even more unworthy duties; and all this for
the mirage of a normality that did not exist. But now those chains
were broken, those duties dissolved, and he was free again and
would know what to do with his freedom. At that moment the
landscape was showing itself at its most picturesque. On one side
of the road stretched the woods, covering the hillside; on the other
lay a grassy slope scattered with a handful of enormous oaks in full
leaf, and at its foot a ditch thick with bushes and the shining waters
of a foaming torrent. Beyond the ditch towered a rocky wall down
which the gleaming ribbon of a waterfall was streaming. Suddenly
Marcello stopped the car and said, "This is a very beautiful place
. . . let's stop for a minute."

His daughter turned from the window and asked, "Have we already arrived?"

"No, we haven't arrived, we're just stopping for a minute," said
Giulia, taking her in her arms and helping her get out of the car.

Once they were out, she said they might as well take advantage
of the stop to satisfy the child's natural needs, and Marcello stayed
next to the car while Giulia, holding Lucilla by the hand, walked
a little ways away. She was walking slowly without leaning toward
her daughter, who was wearing a short white dress and a big bow
in her hair, which flowed loosely down her back, and was chat-
tering away with her usual animation, lifting her face every so
often toward her mother as if asking her a question. Marcello
asked himself what place his daughter would have in the free, new
future his sudden exaltation had painted for him shortly before;
and he told himself with vivid affection that if nothing else, he
would know enough to steer her toward a life inspired by entirely
different values than the ones that had guided his own. Everything
in his daughter's life, he thought, should be spirited and inspired,
graceful, light, limpid, fresh, and adventurous; everything in it
should resemble a landscape that knows neither fog nor the close

oppression of heat, but only the swift, purifying storms that render the air clearer and colors brighter. Nothing should remain of the bloody pedantry that up until yesterday had been his own fate. Yes, he thought again, she must live in full freedom.

Lost in reflection, he left the roadside and strolled toward the woods that shaded the other side. The trees were tall and thick with leaves; beneath them blackberry brambles and other wild briars grew up in a tangle; and under these he could see grasses and flowers in the woodland shadow, and a bellflower of a blue that was almost purple. The bellflower was simple, its petals streaked with white; when he brought it to his nostrils, he smelled a bitter scent of grass. This flower had grown in the shaded tangle of the underbrush, thought Marcello, in the little bit of earth clinging to the barren tuff; it had not sought to limit the taller, stronger plants or to recognize its own destiny so that it could accept it or reject it. In full unconsciousness and freedom, it had grown where the seed had happened to fall, up until the day he had picked it. To be like that solitary flower on a strip of moss in the dark underbrush, he thought, was a truly humble, natural destiny. Whereas the voluntary humility of an impossible adaptation to a deceptive normality concealed only vanity, pride, self-love reversed.

He came to at the sound of his wife's voice, saying, "Let's go, then," and took back his place at the wheel. The car wound swiftly up the curving road, following the slope of the hill scattered with oak trees and then, after a thick tract of brush, emerged through a notch in the hill onto the vista of an immense plain. The close humidity of July blurred the distant horizons, ringed by blue mountains; in the golden, slightly foggy light Marcello made out a solitary, craggy hill in the midst of the plain, surmounted by a village of a few houses huddled together under the towers and walls of a castle as if by an acropolis. He could see the gray sides of the houses suspended vertically along the highway that wound around the hill in spirals; the castle was square, with a rough, cylindrical tower to one side; the village was a rosy color and the sun burning in the sky struck deadly sparks from the windows of the houses. The road ran straight on at the foot of the hill, an absolutely straight stretch toward the farthest boundaries of the plain; opposite the hill, on the other side of the road, lay the vast, razed, yellowing green of an airfield. In contrast to the ancient homes of the village, everything in the airfield looked new and modern: the three long hangars, camouflaged in green, blue, and brown; the antenna from the top of which a red and white flag was waving; the many shining pieces of equipment, placed as if at random around the edges of the camp.

Marcello observed this landscape at length while the car, turning around one bend after another of the steep road, descended swiftly toward the plain. The contrast between the ancient fortress and the very modern airfield felt full of meaning to him, although a sudden distraction kept him from being able to pinpoint its precise significance. At the same time he became aware of a strange sense of familiarity, as if he had already seen this landscape in the past. But he knew it was the first time he had ever driven down this road.

Once the car had reached the bottom of the hill, it turned onto a straight stretch that seemed interminable. Marcello speeded up and the speedometer's arrow climbed gradually to eighty, then ninety kilometers an hour. The road was now running between two stretches of metallic yellow harvested fields, without a tree or a house. Evidently, thought Marcello, the inhabitants all lived in the village and came down in the morning to go to work in the fields. Then in the evening, they returned to the village . . .

His wife's voice distracted him from his reflections. "Look," she said, pointing toward the airfield. "What's happening?"

Marcello looked and saw that a lot of people were running back and forth across the great razed field, waving their arms. At the same time, strange sight in the dazzling light of the summer sun, a sharp, red, almost smokeless tongue of flame licked up from one of the hangars. Then another flame burst upward from the second roof, yet another from the third. The three fires joined and merged into one, which moved violently in all directions while clouds of black smoke drifted to earth, hiding the hangars and billowing outward. Meanwhile, all signs of life had vanished and the airfield was deserted once more.

Marcello said calmly, "An air raid."

"Is it dangerous?"

"No, they will have passed over already."

He speeded up; the arrow of the tachometer climbed to a hundred, a hundred and twenty kilometers. Now they were beneath the town; you could see the spiraling road, the sides of the houses, the castle. At the same time, Marcello heard the angry iron roar of the attacking airplane behind him. He could distinguish, in all the noise, the thick hail of bullets from a machine gun and understood that the plane was behind them and would soon be on top of them; the noise of its engine was in line with the road, as direct and inflexible as the road itself. Then the metallic roar was above them, deafening, just for a moment before receding into the distance.

He felt a strong blow to the shoulder, like a punch, and then a deathly weariness. Desperate, he managed to gather his forces and stop and park the car on the edge of the road.

"Let's get out," he said in a spent voice, putting his hand on the door and opening it.

The door opened and Marcello fell out. Then, dragging himself forward with his face and hands in the grass, he pulled his legs out of the car and lay on the ground near the ditch. But nobody spoke and nobody, though the door remained open, got out of the car. Just then he heard the roar of the airplane banking and turning again. He thought once more, "God, let them not be hit . . . they're innocent."

And then, resigned, his mouth in the grass, he waited for the plane to return. The car with its open door was silent, and he had time to understand with a sharp sorrow that no one would get out. Finally the plane was on top of him, trailing after it, as it distanced itself in the burning sky, silence and the night.

A B O U T   T H E   B O O K

The text for this book was composed by Steerforth Press
using a digital version of Electra, a typeface designed in
1935 by William Addison Dwiggins. Electra has been a
standard book typeface since its release because of its
evenness of design and high legibility. All Steerforth
books are printed on acid-free papers and this book was
bound by BookCrafters of Chelsea, Michigan

ABOUT THE AUTHOR

ALBERTO MORAVIA was born in Rome in 1907 and
published his first novel at twenty-one. In the 1930s,
censored by Mussolini and the Vatican alike, he re-
sorted to writing under a pseudonym, and during the
war, he and his wife Elsa Morante lived in hiding in
the mountains south of Rome until the liberation.
His numerous other novels include *The Woman of
Rome*, *Two Women*, and *The Time of Indifference*. He
died in 1990.

Other Steerforth Italia Books